"Years ago I had the occasion to change ␣␣␣␣␣␣␣␣␣␣␣␣ time he finished college, I taught him h␣␣␣␣␣␣␣␣␣␣␣ writing talent comes from my side of the family, so maybe that's why he stuck me in his book."

My name is Asbury, and I live on Pawleys Island

"When Ray first asked if he could use my car in his novel, I declined, thinking everyone in the South would just be honking at me for the next fifty years until I was old and deaf. Well, not only did he use my car in the story, he had the audacity to use me!"

My name is Darcy, and I am tall and blonde

"I just had to be in this book, so I offered Ray powdered donuts and lots of dating advice. He's a pushover."

My name is Lydia, and I am a short redhead

"Had to wedge my way in, too. So I gave Ray a ride to the beach in my Jeep."

My name is Steve, and I kill bugs

"As a bribe to get me in his book, Ray offered me a root beer and a turkey sandwich. I just happened to have left my lunch at home that day, so I took a second swig and said, 'Yeah, okay Ray, go ahead, but only if I get to do something fun, something besides mop floors.' He shook my hand and agreed."

My name is Maurice, and I am a church janitor

"Ray-dude can still be found hanging out on my end of the beach. Like Steve Cole, he's sorta uncoordinated, but at least he wears cool shorts."

My name is Ransom, and I am a surfer

"Ray traveled more than four thousand miles to interview me. He even got stopped and interrogated at a small South American military outpost before finding my location. Then he spent two days begging for permission to use me as the female star of his novel. I bit into a mango and told him only if I got to drive Darcy's car. After all, she's my best friend."

My name is Allie, and I work for God

"Welcome, dear reader, to *Flabbergasted*."

My name is Jay, and I will be your narrator

Flabbergasted

A Novel

Ray Blackston

Revell
a division of Baker Publishing Group
Grand Rapids, Michigan

© 2003 by Ray Blackston

Published by Revell
a division of Baker Publishing Group
P.O. Box 6287, Grand Rapids, MI 49516-6287
www.revellbooks.com.

New paperback edition published 2010

ISBN 978-0-8007-3453-4

Printed in the United States of America

The Library of Congress has cataloged the original edition as follows:
Blackston, Ray.
    Flabbergasted : a novel / Ray Blackston.
        p.   cm.
    ISBN 0-8007-1837-2 (cloth)
    ISBN 0-8007-5909-5 (pbk.)
    1. Dating (Social customs)—Fiction. 2. Real estate agents—Fiction. 3. Church members—Fiction. I. Title
PS3602.L3255F58 2003
813′.6—dc21   2002155312

The epigraph on page 265 is taken from C. S. Lewis's *A Grief Observed* (London: Faber and Faber, 1961), 83.

The characters and events written about in this book are fictional.

10   11   12   13   14   15   16   7   6   5   4   3   2   1

For Mrs. Kretzer, my second grade teacher,
who liked my stories and poems
and was the first person to encourage me to write

In his heart a man plans his course,
but the Lord determines his steps.
—Proverbs 16:9

Prologue

This is not my story to tell. Even if I wanted to, I could not tell it. Two dozen orphans, a remote locale, and lack of paper allowed me to write only this brief introduction, and even it had to be scribbled hastily in pencil and sent via snail mail. My letters take two weeks to reach the United States.

If you guessed that I am a missionary, you are correct. If you guessed that I am in my mid-twenties and have brown hair, then you are clairvoyant. If you guessed that I am about to tell you why I'm bending your ear instead of the story's rightful owner, then you need to be patient and spend a moment pondering yesterday's lesson in the village.

Yesterday I tried to explain to the children that life is full of ups and downs, and that some of the downs are actually ups, and some of the ups, downs.

They only wanted to know how far is down.

I said it depends.

Depends on what? they asked.

I told them it depends on if you view the downs as a green valley or an endless abyss.

After I explained what an abyss was, they said that was way too far down and that they hoped our village would never play soccer or eat jungle muffins in an abyss.

What you need to know is, by North America's standard of logic, what happened to the narrator of this story also involved something of an abyss. Call it a deep plunge.

The strange thing is that during my last furlough—home to visit the South, the beach, the seafood—I witnessed his plunge. Well, at least the beginning of it.

At the last second he tried to reach out and grab my hand.

I refused.

But I did wave.

Now, whether the young man's down was really an up, I'll let you decide.

As for the orphans and the residue of yesterday's lesson, we settled on something shallower than an abyss, and with a red magic marker I wrote our lesson on a small section of plywood. It hangs on the wall of my hut:

There are potholes on the road less traveled. Some deep, some not so deep, some you dig yourself. Most are filled with mud. Many contain rocks. Once in a while, however, you'll be walking along and step in one a bit more accommodating . . . shabby, green, and pulsing with life.

It'll tickle your feet, like clover.

Act I

Ninety percent of life is just showing up.

—Woody Allen

1

At a quarter past midnight I set my paint roller in the pan, the pan in the tub, my bathroom the latest victim in a week of odd-hour renovations.

Hands scrubbed, teeth brushed, I walked down the hall, cut off the lights, and fell prostrate across a mattress in my spare bedroom. A whiff of khaki latex seeped into the darkness, drifted past my pillow, and reminded me to be up at 8:00 A.M.

In the fuzzy state between sleep and awake, I reached to set the alarm on my digital clock. But I held the button too long and had to wait for the eight to come around as I dozed and saw the numbers, saw the numbers then dozed, and around again went the numbers.

The rumbling of a car engine woke me. It was Sunday morning. I sniffed the air, and above the fresh paint I detected the scent of females four miles away at North Hills Presbyterian Church.

The wind strained to cool my Blazer when I ran the yellow lights, and I ran three. Greenville was an unfamiliar city, and it bloomed green across my new geography, the upstate of South Carolina.

Sprawled between two office buildings on the uppity side of downtown, North Hills appeared manicured and popular. A tiny steeple rose from the red brick sanctuary.

The lot was filling fast. I parked in the back row, pausing there to watch well-dressed couples with immaculate children hurry toward the building. I checked my hair in the mirror and wondered who might be inside.

Understand that I did not resort to such tactics without good cause—and the cause was not that unusual.

Modern communication was the cause.

Kimberly Hargrove had communicated to me, by e-mail, that she was now interested in a surgical resident at West Dallas Hospital and would no longer be requiring my attention. This humbling piece of news arrived just six days after I had moved halfway across the country. Her contribution to this story ends here. Just know that what had looked promising had totally unraveled with two Thursday afternoon e-mails.

Relational rope burn.

Maybe you can relate.

Now, I'm aware that being dumped was poor motivation for what I was about to do. But what I was about to do would not have happened had it not been for a second piece of communication.

From an older woman.

No, not a romantic interest.

The real-estate lady.

Having just been transferred, I knew not a soul in Greenville, S.C.—until she had agreed to meet me at a mistreated three-bedroom in the middle of a suburban cul-de-sac. I had signed the contract on the hood of her Saab as she stood beside me in her gold jacket and black heels, looking over my shoulder and drooling for commission. Seconds later she had tromped through the yard, proudly slapped a SOLD sticker across her FOR SALE sign, and nearly turned her ankle in the process.

"So where do the single people hang out in this town?" I inquired, noting that the sellers had even uprooted the mailbox.

"Well, Jay," she said, leaning over to brush grass clippings from her black heels, "there's the occasional outdoor concert, and in the fall there'll be plenty of football, but your best bet is in the same places where I find clients. I usually rotate between Baptist and Methodist."

"Churches?" I asked, not sure of her meaning.

She pulled off her left shoe and shook out the grassy contents. "You know . . . the networking thing. Although sometimes it looks good to tote along a Bible, just to fit in."

"You use churches to network for clients?"

"Almost exclusively."

"Is that, um, legal?" I had a finance degree, and this sounded like the spiritual equivalent of insider trading.

"Who knows. But half the city does it." She paused to empty her other shoe. "You don't have a girlfriend? You look like the type who would have a girlfriend."

"I used to. She sorta dumped me."

"Well, is it 'sorta,' or is it permanent?" She was quite aggressive, the real-estate lady.

I walked over to peer into the mailbox hole. "Feels permanent."

"And she did this recently?"

"By e-mail."

"Sounds like an airhead to me."

After this brief exchange, she leaned against her Saab to check over the contract. She thanked me, tore off my copy, and got into her car. I was inspecting a bent drain spout as she backed out of the driveway. She honked twice, then stopped and stuck her head out the window. "Ya know, Jay, if you really want to meet people, try the Pentecostals. They're very outgoing."

"How so?"

"Quite loud . . . and they stand up a lot."

"I'd prefer to sit."

"Then pick another one. Our churches outnumber the bars by a twenty-to-one margin. You'll figure it out."

So there I sat in my Chevy Blazer on a Sunday morning in May, in the last row of the parking lot of North Hills Presbyterian Church, trying to figure it out, trying to remember the last time I'd set foot inside a church. Four, five years, perhaps?

In retrospect, I suppose it was not the best-laid plan. And one much more common to men than mice.

I checked my hair again. Then my slacks, my jacket, and the buttons on my light blue oxford. *Just blend in, scope the field, and try not to volunteer for anything.*

I stepped out of my truck.

Did I mention I was not wearing a tie?

Bells rang out in two-second intervals as I crossed the parking lot and reached the front steps. Beyond the top step loomed a wooden double door, nine feet high and richly detailed. I pulled it open, and there was a middle-aged man in a midpriced suit standing in the middle of the foyer.

He gave the customary nod and handed me a bulletin.

Down the burgundy carpet sat pews of dark wood, detailed along the sides in the same pattern as the door. I searched for an empty slot. No one looked up. Just five hundred heads staring into bulletins, fascinated, as if Shakespeare himself had penned the announcements.

I took a seat in row twenty-something, next to an old man whose Bible lay open beside him, the pages psychedelic from his marks. Two children scribbled in the next pew, their hands stained by magic markers. Their mother shushed them as a hymn began. The choir sounded rich and reverent, and several sopranos made an impression, although the long green robes prevented me from checking for wedding bands.

Hymn over, the congregation stood to recite a creed, their voices a low monotone, my lips moving in mock conformity. We sat again. The old guy pulled out his checkbook.

Six men in suits worked the aisles, passing and receiving brass plates in the quiet manner of servants. A plate reached me containing a pile of envelopes and a twenty; it left with the contents unaffected.

The two kids turned and smiled. I made a face, and they whirred back around, giggling as their mother gave a firmer shush.

The pastor spoke of being in the world but not of the world, of having eternal thoughts in the midst of the temporary. His sermon was lengthy, definitely not monotone, but left me the same way I'd left the brass plate.

Blessed and dismissed, I shook strange hands, then looked around for a deacon to point me toward the singles class. Kids pulled parents through the pews, parents grabbed markers from the floor, and the elderly—the teeming mass of elderly—paused and dawdled on the burgundy carpet.

Leaving the twenty-fourth pew (I had counted the rows during the sermon), I heard the organist playing a lullaby and wondered if I should've tried the Pentecostals.

I caught the bulletin man midway up the aisle.

"The college class meets in the Sunday school wing," he directed, "just past the junior highs."

"What if I'm a bit older?" I asked. "College was five years ago."

"Ah, the singles," he said. "They meet in the little brick building across the parking lot."

The crowd forced me forward. "Thanks, I'll find it."

My first glance into the building revealed three rows of chairs arranged in semicircles. A thick wooden podium faced the center. A gray-suited man rested one arm on the podium, his back to the chairs, his attention in a book.

I strolled past the empty rows. Muted conversations made their way from around a corner. Morning sunlight angled in through sheer white curtains, and I turned to see a kitchen full of singles. They were having coffee, orange juice, and those white powdered donuts.

The first person to make eye contact with me was a heavyset girl with short red hair, her round face beaming hospitality. She wiped a crumb from her flower-print dress, smiled briefly, and extended a hand. "No ring? Then you're in the right place."

Disarmed by the humor, I returned the greeting. "Jay Jarvis. No hidden rings."

"I'm Lydia," she said, letting go of my hand. "Your first time?"

"Just moved to South Carolina last month."

She gave me a Styrofoam coffee cup and left to greet more visitors. I was filling the cup with decaf when someone tapped my shoulder. And I turned to meet one Stanley Rhone, complete with navy blue suit, sculpted black hair, and a handshake three degrees too firm.

"From where did you move?" he asked. He looked at me cautiously, warily, in the same way toddlers view asparagus. A white hankie sprouted from his coat pocket.

"Dallas," I replied. "My firm transferred me just this—"

The gray-suited podium leaner had called us to attention. Fifty singles began taking their seats in the familiar social pattern of women in front and middle, with males occupying the perimeter. I took a seat at the end of the second row, behind Stanley, and tried to look alert.

A latecomer hurried in and took her seat. "Mr. Rhone will open us," said Gray-suit.

In the act of bowing my head, I deduced that I was a half second behind. I glanced left to check my timing and, across the heads and the silence, our eyes met.

She was likewise in mid-drop, glancing to her right from the far end of the second semicircle. The glare through the curtain backlit the brunette hair resting at her shoulders, but that same glare prevented me from confirming the hint of a smile.

I went with my preferred answer and shut my eyes.

Audible grunts rose from the row behind me. The grunts seemed well coordinated with Stanley's voice inflection, a rising tone producing a louder grunt. I considered turning quietly for a one-eyed peek, but to the best of my knowledge, peekage wasn't allowed.

Stanley finished the prayer, the grunting stopped, and Gray-suit began our lesson from Galatians. Fortunately, there were hardcover Bibles under each chair, and I unstuck some pages to reveal Psalm 139. I figured Galatians was to the east of Psalms, and by the time he finished reading the five verses, I was there.

The word *idolatry* floated through the air, up and around behind the semicircles and past the donuts, bypassed everyone else and landed smartly in my conscience. It stirred around for a moment, clanged between my skull, then disappeared, like the sermon, to that place where all conversation fades.

I glanced again across the room, but she quickly looked away—out the window, at the empty chair in front of her, then down at her sandals, well worn below her yellow sundress. She was one shade darker than the fifty other reverent Caucasians. Definitely American, but without the American condiments. No makeup. No jewelry.

I figured that she, too, might be a visitor. But who knew. Regardless, I wanted to meet her.

More Galatian words hovered over me, dropping now, searching for sin. Gray-suit spoke of fruit, of faith, of goodness and self-control. Heads nodded their agreement, the grunter gave an affirmation, and strictly from peer pressure, I reached in my jacket for a pen.

"Fruit, not *fruits*," said our teacher. "We cannot pick and choose among the attributes of God like the dinner line at a Baptist buffet."

Everyone laughed, but she refused to look my direction. *Please look my direction.*

Closing announcements followed, mentioning a food drive, a visit to see a sick person, and something about a trip to the beach over the long Memorial Day weekend.

I had no plans for the long Memorial Day weekend; maybe she'd be going. Anxious for an introduction, I left my coffee cup on my chair and hurried toward the door.

Too late. The dark-haired girl was already in the parking lot. After a quick and insincere nice-to-meet-ya to Stanley, I peeled off my jacket, flung it over one shoulder, and strolled toward my Blazer.

One row over, her faded red Beetle puttered away.

Tuesday evening while grilling chicken on my deck, I was thinking of brass plates and women, of women and brass plates, and wondered if contributing to that plate would hurry God up as far as meeting the right one. I flipped the chicken over, sprinkled it with lemon pepper, and thought maybe dropping two twenties in the plate would help me meet her this year, or a hundred bucks and we'd meet within a month, or five hundred and the person would arrive in warp speed, like Spock to Captain Kirk.

Smoke was pouring from the grill, my dinner only two minutes from perfection, when the cordless phone rang. The voice on the other end thanked me for visiting North Hills and asked if I had any questions. I was

17

tempted to ask about the girl in the Beetle but stopped myself and muttered something about planning to visit again soon.

"You're in the singles class, then?" asked Mr. Kyle, who mentioned he was both an elder and the membership chairman.

I swatted at a fly with my spatula and said, "Yessir, but I haven't been in one for a while."

"Perhaps you met my daughter, Allie?"

"I don't think so, sir."

"She attends that class," he said. "Whenever she's in town, that is."

I was certain he had some homely daughter with whom he'd try to set me up. I was not interested. "Sir, I'm sure your daughter is a nice girl, but my dinner is on the grill and . . ."

"I understand, Jay. We'll talk more later. But when you do visit us again, please say hello to my Allie. She's easy to recognize—she has dark hair and a year-round tan."

I dropped the spatula on my picnic table. "You say she has dark hair and a nice tan?"

"Yes. She's been working near the equator."

My chicken began to blacken. "Elder Kyle, what kind of car does your daughter drive?"

"An old VW."

I was back at 9:30 sharp the following Sunday. After the church service, after another uninspiring sermon, and after I had dropped two twenties and a five in the brass plate, I made my way across the parking lot in a drizzle, using my just-found Good Book for an umbrella.

I suspect there are various reasons for sticking the singles class across the parking lot, in a building by itself: The married-adult classes may be discussing sex from a spiritual point of view and worry we might overhear them, or the elders may think our single minds are cluttered with sex and believe we should meet alone to repent, or the parents may worry that we're hung up on sex, and fear a bad influence on their children. Whatever the answer, it's got something to do with sex.

18

Entering the mecca of half circles, I wiped off my Bible and said hello to Lydia, and to Wade, who stood at the podium in the same gray suit. From the coffee crowd, mingled nods welcomed me back.

I'd nearly finished my orange juice when we were called to our seats, though I decided against a refill because I did not want to walk back in and have to sit by Stanley.

I sat at the opposite end of the row from my first visit and looked around for the elusive Allie Kyle.

She was not in the room.

I didn't know what had happened to Galatians either. For now Wade was speaking on inheritance and lineage and begating.

Obed begat Jesse. Jesse begat David. No notes were taken because all the lesson contained was three thousand years of begating, and I supposed if an Old Testament man did not begat he'd get banished to the singles class, which met by itself, in a tent, out across a wheat field from the temple courts.

"The trip to Myrtle Beach is scheduled for Memorial Weekend," announced Stanley, back in the role of emcee as our lesson ended. "Rooms are already reserved, but we need four volunteers to serve on the planning committee."

He tugged at a cuff link, ran two fingers through his perfect hair, and scanned the room.

Raising his hand was a stocky fellow named Steve, the only other guy in the class who forgot to wear a tie. Didn't shave much, either, and from the way he was leaning back in his chair, I could tell he was a singles-class veteran.

Lydia took the last bite of a donut, coughed, and said she could help.

"That gives us two," said Stanley. "No, make that three. Allie's not here but said she'd volunteer. There'll be a meeting Wednesday night . . . anyone else?"

The class was silent. I sensed opportunity.

Suddenly my hand pulled away from my side and rose into the air. "I can help."

Heads turned toward me. Polite smiles all around.

"Thanks, Jay."

I missed the meeting. No Wednesday night with tiny steeples, powdered donuts, or the Beetle-driving daughter of Elder Kyle.

A gray-haired client had insisted on talking with me. I was a stockbroker, firmly entrenched in the world's largest paper shuffle, turning cash into shares and shares back into cash, as many times per week as possible.

Buying low and selling high, but occasionally buying high and selling low, it was always with other people's accounts, so I got paid regardless. The pace was frantic, but a day passed quickly. The firm liked my tenacity; I liked the money.

Glenda, our secretary, liked to do her nails and say "Mr. Franklin Gruber on the phone, sir."

"Mr. Franklin Gruber on the phone, sir."

"Thank you, Glenda. . . . You can't sell now, Mr. Gruber, at a loss. Just buy some more and be patient. Yessir, that fund was up 40 percent last year, but that was last year. Ever go to a party after all the guests are walking out and the punch bowl has nothing but foam and crumbs floating around the bottom? That's what you're doing when you buy last year's winner. Be early to the next party, Mr. Gruber. You gotta buy into panics and sell euphoria, not buy euphoria and sell into panics."

"Another call for you, sir."

My headset slipped off. I held the mouthpiece to my lips. "Yes, ma'am, Microsoft is down eighteen points, but let's buy some more and be patient. No, ma'am, there are no do-overs in the stock market. It's sorta like dating—just look forward to a new day."

"Mr. Gruber on the phone again, sir."

"Buy Toys 'R' Us? You buy that before Christmas, Mr. Gruber, not in May. You heard they're coming out with a remote G. I. Joe? Buy a G. I. Joe for your grandson, Mr. Gruber; now let's you and me talk about Microsoft. It's down another three points from yesterday, a real bargain."

This was the most entertaining aspect of the brokerage business—the old people. I mean the really old people. Best of all was the widow Dean. Beatrice Dean.

I was given her account early on, after one of our older brokers retired. Like Mr. Gruber, she called me often, and sometimes just to chat.

That Wednesday night, her high-pitched voice crackled over the phone, and I was ready for anything.

"Hellooo, Mr. Jarvis?"

"Yes, Beatrice?" I said, propping my feet on the desk.

"I . . . I saw on the news that Atheon is way down. I don't like it when my stocks go down."

"You don't own Atheon, Beatrice. You own AT&T."

"Oh, well, good for me. What's the stock symbol for AT&T?"

"T."

"What?"

"The symbol is T."

"Sweeten my tea? No, dear, I can't drink tea anymore. Makes me have to go too often."

"I said the symbol for AT&T is T, Beatrice."

"Of course, it is, dear. . . . Now, how many shares do I own?"

"Same as last week. Nine thousand, four hundred shares."

"I've owned it a long time, haven't I?"

"According to the firm's records, you've held the stock since 1961."

"Oh, my. How much is it worth?"

I checked the quote screen for a price. "Multiplying the current price times the amount of shares gives you about 160,000 dollars. But that doesn't include your larger holdings of Wal-Mart, Ford, and Procter & Gamble stock."

She paused for a moment, then asked, "Do you think I should sell some, dear?"

"To be honest, Beatrice, if I was near eighty and in your good health, I would grab my three craziest friends, a wad of cash, and travel the world."

"Travel . . . hmmm, never thought about that."

"Isn't there something you'd like to spend money on?"

"Well, there are some new daylilies in fabulous colors at the nursery. I thought I had all the colors, but you should see these, just radiant! He wants a dollar too much, though, and when you buy a half dozen at a time, like me, well, that really adds up."

"Yes, ma'am, a half dozen daylilies would add up to two whole shares of AT&T."

"Okay, then sell two shares, Jay. You are so sweet to spend all this time with me."

"But Beatrice, the commission on selling two shares is more than the proceeds."

"Do you *have* to charge me a commission?"

"Well, ma'am, I'm supposed to. I mean, the firm would prefer—"

"I'll bring you some snapdragons."

"What are snapdragons?"

"I grow them in my garden, dear. Would you prefer the primrose yellow or the deep crimson?"

I glanced down the hallway and lowered my voice. "I'll go with the crimson."

"You'll have to water them daily."

"I will, I promise. Every day. Anything else, Beatrice?"

"Enjoy your tea, dear."

As I hung up with Beatrice, line two glowed red. The voice said he was from North Hills Presbyterian Church, that his name was Steve, did I want to share a ride to the beach, and could I please get Friday off.

I put him on hold as Glenda beeped in. *"Mr. Franklin Gruber on the phone again, sir."*

"No, sir, Mr. Gruber, I do not know what time Toys 'R' Us closes."

Two thoughts dominated my drive home that afternoon: Me and my sunblock are definitely taking Friday off, and I might've just found religion.

That first thought had me smiling; it was the second one that felt ominous.

2

Steve Cole didn't say much, just scratched the dark stubble on his chin and checked his rearview for the police. He had said a travel prayer in my driveway, so maybe that gave him license to speed. I scooted the passenger seat back one notch and tried to hear the music, but the music was muted from the wind rushing over the half doors of his Jeep. We merged onto I-385, the sun reflecting off the driver's side while I sat content in the shade.

Whipping into the fast lane, we were vehicle five in a nine-car convoy, the midsection of a metallic snake, weaving from fast lane to slow lane and back again. The breeze felt warm and humid, but it was welcome relief from stale air, fluorescent lights, and the twelve calls per day from Franklin Gruber.

Twenty miles passed in silence, and there was little to see from the highway. Pine trees begat pine trees begat kudzu vines. Kudzu, if edible, would do for South Carolina what oil did for Texas.

"Steve?"

He checked his speed. "Yeah?"

"How'd ya end up at North Hills Presbyterian?"

"Honest truth?"

"Honest truth."

He weaved back to the slow lane. "More females there than at Baptist or Lutheran."

"Sounds logical." I pulled a map from his glove box.

Back in the fast lane, he steered with one hand. "Down there is where the money's at," he said, pointing at the map.

I held it closer, scanning the Carolina coast. "Hilton Head?"

"Lotsa money there. Ahead of us is Columbia. That's the state furnace."

I asked about Myrtle Beach, but Steve only wrinkled the edge of his mouth and said to let Myrtle surprise me. The convoy split up, and we eased down to eighty.

I stuffed the map back in the glove box. "Concrete and neon?"

"Be there in three hours," he said, weaving again.

Blue lights snuck up behind us and reflected in the Jeep even before we heard the siren. Braking hard, Steve gave me an I-can't-believe-this look and pulled to the shoulder. Through my mirror I watched the officer approach, and there was no swinging nightstick or mirrored shades, just a side-to-side swagger, wrapped in navy, that suggested he did this forty times a day and drowned it all in barbeque.

"Slowly, son." He stood to the side, leaning over; I could only see his chin.

"Yessir, just gettin' my wallet," said Steve, bending forward in his seat.

"Just pull it out slowly."

"Here's my license, sir."

Thick fingers took the license. "You boys headin' for the beach?"

"Yessir."

"Did ya know, Mr. Cole, that you were doing eighty-six in a sixty-five zone?"

Steve sighed and said, "No sir, but I was probably going a bit fast."

The officer peered through the window. First at me, then back at Steve. "Can you explain your hurry, Mr. Cole?"

"To be honest, sir, thirty-two single women from our church are gonna be on the beach in about three hours."

"Aww, son," he said. "You drive like that and you attend church?"

"Yessir, sorry," said Steve, wincing through his words.

The officer frowned. "I gotta give you a ticket."

"Yessir."

For ten minutes Steve and I sat motionless, the cop returning to his car to write the ticket, his lights flashing out blue reminders of our sin. With traffic rushing past, I wondered what would be expected of me over the course of the weekend. Would I have to look up obscure verses of which I had no knowledge? Would there be, unbelievably, a curfew?

All I knew was that my new olive beach shorts with the palm-tree print were not much use as long as we were parked on the side of a sweltering interstate.

Hurry up, officer.

The officer returned and asked Steve to sign the ticket. Steve dropped the pen. As he recovered, a Mercedes passed and honked her horn. At first we thought she was flirting, but Mercedes rarely flirt with Jeeps. Steve was signing his name when a minivan rubbed it in with another honk. The cop looked over his shoulder and smirked.

"How many women gonna be at this beach?" he asked.

"Thirty-two at last count," I said.

"And how many guys?"

"Nineteen," Steve muttered.

The officer folded his copy of the ticket, his lips straining to hold back a smile. "You boys have a safe trip."

"Jesus is my copilot," said Steve, setting the ticket on the console.

The officer, with his back turned, hesitated then slowly turned around. "Don't believe Jesus would drive an orange Jeep with whitewalls."

"So what would he drive?" asked Steve.

"I'd figure on a big Lincoln."

I had no idea what the Almighty would tool around in but was willing to give it a shot. "You don't think he'd drive some old jalopy and pick up hitchhikers?"

"Nah, I don't think so," said Steve.

"Me either," said the officer, leaning one arm against the roof. "Lemme tell you something, boys. I been in church for most of my forty-eight years, and I think Jesus would either drive the Lincoln, or if pressed for time, maybe one of those muscle cars. You know, the *power* and the glory."

The mirrored shades were on now; he put two fingers to his cap and said, "Drive careful, boys."

The next thirty miles passed in silence, except for the music, now resembling a funeral dirge. The white dashes on the highway, formerly a continuous blur, had become dashes once again. I glanced at the speedometer; Steve was doing sixty-three on a seventy-mile-per-hour interstate and was getting passed by the elderly in gray Oldsmobiles and migrant workers in the backs of pickups.

I offered to drive. He shook his head.

I offered to pay half the ticket. He said that cop wouldn't know Jesus from Aunt Jemima.

"Now, Aunt Jemima," I said, "there's someone who'd need a big Lincoln."

"Stifle it, Jay," he said. "I just blew my vacation money on that ticket."

"Aww, get over it," I countered, opening a bag of pretzels. "Think of whatsername."

"Who?"

"The one you were talking to after church . . . the tall, willowy, blonde-haired whatsername."

He glanced in his rearview. "Oh. Darcy."

I decided to dig into both the pretzels and his personal life. "Anything up with her?"

"Smart girl. Looks good in that ol' Cadillac. You seen it?"

"Nope."

"A '75 Cadillac convertible. Parents gave it to her after she got her master's."

"But is anything between you two?"

"She painted that car lime green; everyone calls it Lime Sherbet. She's driving it down today."

"Was that a no?"

"Okay, we went out once."

"Cool."

We passed Columbia, the state furnace, inhaling hot garnet air as if straight from Aunt Bea's oven. I kept looking in my passenger mirror for some approaching lime sherbet, but only eighteen-wheelers, SUVs, and minivans dotted the highway.

I stuck a towel behind my head and reclined the seat. The pavement sent heat through the bottom of the Jeep, and I was back in the fuzzy place between sleep and awake, the breeze lulling me off, then bringing me back.

"Hey," said Steve.

"Yeah?"

"You daydreamin'?"

Not interested in talking, I flopped the towel over my head. "Sorta."

"Gotta question for ya."

"Not till after my daydream."

He jerked the wheel, jarring me from slumber. "I was gonna ask which of those single women have *you* been talking to?"

I spoke beneath blue terry cloth. "Tried to meet that one named Allie."

"So," he said, "you've been to our little church twice and already spied Allie, eh?"

"Yeah, during the prayer thing, between all the reverence and that glare through the curtains, I might've caught her eye."

"That's about all you're likely to catch, bro."

"Why you say that?"

He weaved right, cut his speed. "Independent, self-sufficient—she's always *gone*. Right before you came to church, she'd come back from South America. Some sorta mission thing. Just quit her job and went."

I jerked the towel from my head. "So what's she doing now?"

"Who knows? . . . Maybe working on her tan. Both she and Lydia are riding with Darcy, so I reckon you can ask her soon enough."

Below the steering wheel, his legs twitched. And I suppose, for two single males, we'd just had what amounts to deep conversation.

"Rest stop?" he asked.

"Sure."

Five minutes later Steve pulled into a rest stop and jumped from his Jeep. He took quick steps toward a rest room overflowing with the Memorial weekend crowd. The air smelled of Cheetos and warm cola. I lingered on the sidewalk until he came out, then decided that I, too, had better have a go.

"You're wasting beach time, Jarvis," said Steve, pointing at his watch.

"I'll hurry."

While waiting for an opening in a crowded men's room, I thought of the Atlantic Ocean and would it be warm, of the Carolina shore and would it be white, and why so many more girls had signed up than guys. This latter point was not an issue; in fact, it was quite a pleasant thought. I was still in line when behind me a southern drawl rung familiar.

"Lincoln or muscle car?" he asked.

I turned and got an eyeful of navy. "Officer, you following us?"

He frowned, tossed a candy wrapper in the trash. "Nah, middle of my route. Where is ol' Whitewall?"

"Out in the Jeep, stewing over the two hundred bucks you cost him."

"I gave him a break," he said. "Shoulda been three-twenty and four points."

Two stalls opened, we entered, and I could see the top of his cap over the metal wall. Awkward, going next to Officer Theologian.

"So how many tickets you given today?"

I heard him lift the lid. "'Bout twenty so far. Still early, though."

"I guess most of your customers are young males in Jeeps and sports cars, right?"

He paused a moment. "Nah, it's a mix. Just gave one to some babe in a Caddy."

"Wasn't green, was it?" I asked, curious now in my shiny cubicle. "Convertible?"

"Green? Son, it was the ugliest green, some awful bright lime color. She drove even faster than your buddy."

"Where?" I asked.

"Pulled 'em in front of this rest stop," he said. "Now don't go telling me they're also part of . . . no way, are you kiddin' me?"

"No sir, thanks."

"Son," he said over the top of the stall, "y'all drive worse than the pagans."

I dodged two cars in the parking lot, then jogged over and banged on the Jeep's hood.

With eyes shut, his head resting against the seat, Steve looked annoyed, mired in the reflective muck of the ticketed. Back in the passenger seat, I decided to cheer him up.

"Lime Sherbet is just ahead of us, bro."

"Howda you know that?" he asked, reaching for his sunglasses.

"Had a man-to-man inside with Officer Theologian. He gave Darcy a ticket, too."

"At least Darcy can afford it."

I gave my seat belt a yank. "He said you got off easy."

"Hardly." And we merged back onto the interstate.

Nearing Myrtle Beach, traffic slowed, tarried, then stopped abruptly. Exhaust fumes enveloped us and billboards hailed us, advertising everything from T-shirts to tanning oil. They were countless, colorful, and staggered in height, each straining for attention like pageant contestants with too much rouge.

We rolled forward for a mile. A congested bridge halted the flow.

"So this is Myrtle . . ."

"This is Myrtle," said Steve, tapping his fingers on the dash. The sun hovered just west of noon, sending white and gold lasers off our windshield. Steve tuned into a local radio station, and I heard unfamiliar music, the beat light, the lyrics lazy and beach-woven, making me want to sit under a palm tree and quit the brokerage business.

Horns blared, engines revved, and from the top of the bridge, over the billboards, I could see long rows of condos, hotels, and assorted high-rises. We arrived twenty minutes later at the Sand Towers on the oceanfront, where concrete had begat concrete, and bottle blondes had begat bottle blondes.

There was no grass, and the sound of boom boxes joined the roar of motorcycle gangs in echoing off Atlantic Avenue. As with downtown

Tokyo, the only direction Myrtle could expand was up. Guests in one condo could borrow toothpaste from the next by reaching an arm out a window. A giant could give one a shove, and twenty miles of high-rise would topple like dominoes.

In the parking lot, Steve checked his tire for glass. I opened the rear hatch, grabbed my duffel, and took a deep, balmy breath of the Carolina coast.

Inside the lobby, I stood on black marble flooring, hoping the girls had arrived. The air felt cold as I leaned against the wall, over a vent, flipping through a Myrtle Beach coupon book. The one with the picture of perfect people eating greasy shrimp.

Moments later Steve flung open the lobby door, faked a shiver as he felt the cold air, then wiped at his forehead with the bottom of his tank top.

"Seen anyone yet?" he asked.

"Just that desk clerk."

That desk clerk looked up our names. He reached for a folder on the corner of his desk and scanned two columns, one twice as long as the other. "It's now thirty-four females, nineteen males. Hmmm," he said, restraining a smile. "You guys had a change of residence."

"Different floor?" I asked.

"No, sir."

"Different hotel?" asked Steve, still sweaty and impatient.

"Not exactly. Seems we ran out of room for your group, so the girls who came in agreed to move everyone into five beach houses just south of here. We made an arrangement with the rental folks at Smith Realty," he explained, handing me a sheet of directions. "The place is called Litchfield, and your house should be unlocked."

It took us five minutes to turn left out of the Tower's parking lot, since Myrtle's main drag was awash in traffic. A huge yellowy figure squatted across the street, gazing out over a smattering of astroturf. He was twenty feet tall and the width of an elephant.

Buddha Golf beckoned to all.

Steve leaned down to glance through my window. "I didn't know Buddhists played golf."

"Me either."

Traffic thinned as we drove south along Highway 17. Billboards and Buddha faded from view, the terrain changing rapidly from tacky to understated. No more bottle blondes, just strawhatted women weaving baskets along the roadside; no more cement strips, just general stores tucked between moss-covered oaks; no more motorcycle gangs, just bicycles outfitted with wire baskets and bulging granny tires; and no more boom boxes agitating the air, just the blue Carolina sky filling slowly with pelicans, silent and flying single file.

We turned into the seaside community of North Litchfield, admiring weathered beach homes set high atop stilts. Elevated screen porches covered the fronts, filled with rocking chairs not rocking and sand dollars not earning interest, only stuck to the screens and bleached white from exposure.

At the next stop sign I looked skyward at tiny decks rising above the rooftops. "Feels calmer here, doesn't it?"

"Feels like nap time," said Steve.

"Those little roof decks are cool."

"It's called a crow's nest, Tex."

He made a left beside the oceanfront, and we paralleled the beach along a two-lane road, both lanes sandswept and sedate, nearly vacant at midday. To the ocean side, the dunes sprouted sea oats; wooden walkways curved between the dunes. The mounds appeared cloned, like an endless row of buried Volkswagens.

Steve slowed for a speed bump, watched three kids drag a pink float toward the beach, and turned onto Seaspray Drive, our weekend address. He parked his Jeep beneath house number four, then reclined in his seat. "Four hours, twenty-five minutes," he said, "and thank ya Lord for safe travel."

Standing in a driveway of crushed shells, I saw we had a house with a crow's nest, and I was up the front stairs, through the screened porch, and past a couple of whitewashed rocking chairs.

Inside the front door, inner stairs led to the roof, then two long flights of skinny stairs to the nest. Climbing the second flight, I felt my legs complain. Reaching the rooftop, I heard the wind strengthen. Salt air tickled my sniffer. The crow's nest was only six square feet, and it squeaked when I leaned on the wooden railing.

The Atlantic looked bluer than I'd figured.

I could see waves breaking against a rock jetty and the sand morphing from cream to beige to dark gray as the tide receded. A volleyball game was in progress on the beach, fishing boats speckled the sea, and, far to the north—where the dunes dissolved—concrete Myrtle jutted itself through an early afternoon haze.

Looking south, I watched a line of pelicans gliding just over the breakers, a flap of the wings and glide, now repeat. After a few minutes I turned away from the ocean and felt the breeze on the back of my neck. Three more rows of beach homes sat behind ours, and a dozen empty crow's nests stretched high their wooden necks.

Seagulls squawked overhead as my line of sight dropped from the rooflines down to the road. Two houses over, onto another driveway of crushed shells, a large, topless sedan pulled in.

Lime green, just like he said.

3

Palm trees whizzed by in the median, and a hot wind whistled through the convertible's backseat. Blown from its habitat, a light-colored hair wrapped around my chin. I wanted to hand it, across Lydia, over to Steve in exchange for a darker one. Darcy's mane was the blondest of blonde, with the slightest gold tinge in the sunlight, cut straight at the shoulders where it flayed back when she hit the accelerator. Which was often.

Impossible to talk given the speed, though in the front passenger seat, Allie raised her arms as if aboard a roller coaster. An embroidered toucan flapped on her shirt sleeve, its colorful beak all aflutter.

The girls had said only a brief hello as we jumped into the car; no formal introductions. I felt like the new guy, but at least we were at the beach. I wondered if the Pentecostals ever came to this beach.

Darcy parked Sherbet across two spaces, then turned in her seat. "So, Mr. Cole, how much did the officer charge you for your speeding frenzy?"

"Two hundred," said Steve, unhitching his seat belt. "And you, Miss Yeager?"

"Three hundred sixty."

Entering Piggly-Wiggly, I yanked five stubborn carts from a cluster and passed them around. Darcy pulled sunglasses atop her head, reached into her purse, and handed each of us an index card. "We are shopping for fifty-three people," she explained. "Just buy what's on the card. Quantities are noted on there, too."

"Tall, organized, and lead footed," muttered Steve as we split up.

Lydia and Allie stood on the back rail of their carts, pushing off with one foot, like they were on scooters. They were coasting toward fruits and vegetables when they disappeared.

Armed with the milk and cereal card, I made for the dairy section. Fifteen gallons, said the card, so I loaded five gallons of 2 percent, five of skim, and five of vitamin D fortified, wondering where I'd put twenty boxes of cereal. The cart felt heavy as I wheeled it around, rumbling past meat and seafood, tires clunking and milk sloshing but gaining momentum as the cereal aisle came into view. Flakes or puffs, puffs or flakes? Cutting the corner, almost on two wheels, I was a chrome locomotive.

Then a smashed locomotive. The jolt stopped us cold; my arms tingled.

On the floor lay five bags of grapes, uninjured, and two tomatoes in critical condition. Red guts stained the tiles just below the Fruit Loops, and Allie Kyle was in hysterics. She picked up an injured piece of tomato, said, "Poor guy, he's a goner," and without hesitation flung it at me.

Thick, red juice clung to my shirt. I grabbed a stray grape and, taking dead aim, bounced it off the side of her head. She was bent over, almost snorting, trying to slide another piece of tomato off the slick floor when a fleet-footed clerk entered the battle with a mop. "I'll get this for ya," he said, swiping tiles.

"Sorry," Allie said, glancing at my T-shirt. "I've been out of the country for a while and just lose it sometimes."

I reached past her for the Raisin Bran. "I won't tell you what we threw at girls while growing up in Texas."

She pushed onward, back toward the veggies, talking over her shoulder as she turned the corner. "Your vitamin D sprung a leak, Jay."

An odd introduction, for sure. But a decent start.

Five carts overflowed at the register, Steve Cole bringing up the rear, loaded with white bread and cheap bologna. Darcy's cart contained more t.p. than a man would use in a lifetime, plus gourmet coffee, premium jam, and ten bags of Pepperidge Farm Brussels Mint cookies.

"We forgot the chips," said Lydia, counting bags of bananas.

"Can you guys get another cart?" asked Darcy.

"Yeah, get another cart," said Allie, pulling in with fresher vegetables.

Our cashier girl with pierced tongue said that'll be $614.52. An eager grocery boy asked if he could help us unload. The girls said sure, and we made our way to the lot in a cart convoy; Allie pushing veggies, Steve pushing chips, and Darcy pushing a lifetime supply of t.p.

She unlocked Sherbet's trunk, and we peered into the large, empty space, then back at the even larger amount of food.

Lydia tossed in the first bag and said, "Shopping good, logistics bad."

The sixty-odd bags loaded into the trunk and the backseat and the front seat, but where would we all sit? There was only room for four, even if one sat on a lap. "Oh well, but here's a tip for ya," said Darcy to the grocery boy, and she handed him a ten.

"I'll go next door and look for flip-flops," said Allie, backpedaling. "Just come back for me in a bit." And off she went.

I wanted to stay behind also, but Lydia was on my lap now, Steve straddled the Raisin Bran, and Darcy floored it because she said the milk might go bad and she wanted it cold to wash down her Brussels Mint cookies.

Back in North Litchfield, we unloaded the bags into five weathered houses—three for girls, two for guys—and I was glad we guys didn't get house number two, the pastel pink one.

"No kidding," said Steve, setting down plastic bags. "No way would I stay in a pink beach house."

"Men are so self-conscious," said Lydia. "I love our pink house." She opened a package of Oreos on her counter, took two for herself, and passed them around.

I poured us all a tall glass of overpriced skim. "Natural wood, Lydia . . . a nice, manly exterior."

"Oh, brother."

In all of her considerable height and blondeness, Darcy paused on the porch stairs to gaze across the dunes. "I really wanna get out on the beach," she said, and an unspoken request hovered behind her words.

"So do we," Steve said, cleaning his shades but missing the message.

"Could one of you guys take my car and go get Allie?" she asked, clarifying herself.

"Sure," I said, already three steps below. And she tossed me two keys attached to a rabbit's foot, severed from the body of a helpless, lime green rabbit.

Getting into her shiny and abundant classic, I thought I looked too obvious, volunteering so quickly. But maybe this was directly from God. Maybe God was granting me opportunity, what with my willingness to help out, plus the fact that I'd been to church, on time, for two consecutive Sundays.

My just reward.

I was alone at the wheel of motorized ice cream. In Texas, old Cadillacs were white and had horns mounted to the hood. But then Texas didn't have Buddha Golf or music that made you want to sit under a palm tree and quit your job.

The Caddy felt awkward, like it didn't quite fit between the road stripes. The steering wheel, huge and knobby, appeared to have been borrowed off an eighteen-wheeler.

I mashed the gas, and the monster lunged onto Highway 17. Smaller vehicles gave way in the passing lane, and I felt like a teenager in a borrowed car, nervous as he picked up his first date.

At the storefront I pulled to the curb. Sunlight glinted off the hood. I fiddled with the radio dial, then reclined the seat as Mr. DJ spun yet another beach song.

With the passenger door already open for her, I listened to the lazy beat and rested my head against Sherbet's beige vinyl. Allie exited the beach store during the third verse, her dark brown hair bouncing as she walked.

"How's the shopping?" I asked.

"No flip-flops for women. Sold out."

"So, Allie," I said, noting her tan as she slid into the seat, "you always toss food at the new guys?"

She smiled and shot me a wry glance. "Not usually. But, hey, that was a pretty good shot with the grape."

36

"Ex–Little League pitcher," I said, pulling back onto the highway.

She adjusted her seat belt, then turned to face me. "Can I ask you something?"

"Sure."

"Do you know if Steve is seeing anyone?"

Sherbet veered onto the shoulder, then back between the stripes of Highway 17. Allie awaited my response, her face quizzical.

"Steve?" I stammered. "I think he went out once with Darcy."

"One date doesn't really mean much, Jay."

Neither does one piece of tomato.

4

Surfing looked so effortless at first glance, so at-one-with-nature. Looked macho, as if the universe of attentive women would expand thirtyfold by the mere fact that you held a board under your arm, never mind the farmer's tan.

His name was Ransom, and he had not been in the singles class the two Sundays I'd visited North Hills. I figured him for a local, so dark his skin, so confident his stride.

In bright orange shorts, Steve Cole joined him to swim through the breakers. Waves in South Carolina, from what they told me, were normally little more than ripples, but a few five-footers swelled and crashed through late afternoon as approaching thunderstorms loomed out over the Atlantic.

The absence of sun pulled the girls off the beach, and only two surf fishermen remained, besides the three of us. I peeled off my T-shirt, waded to waist deep, and dove into water that was warmer than expected. Drops of cold rain shocked my neck, so I dove again.

Ransom lay on the yellow-and-purple board, his mop of brown hair flopping down across dark surfer eyes. A wave swelled and began to roll over. With a quick burst of arms and legs, he popped to his feet, tilted left, then right, cutting with the breaker and gaining speed. Broad layers of spray shot up over the wave, the wave shrunk, and Ransom rode till the ripples ceased. Very cool, the way he rode those ripples.

"We can *do* this, Jarvis," said Steve, bobbing to his ears.

"We can drown and have our flesh eaten by crabs."

Big, sloppy drops pelted the ocean.

"Like ridin' a bike," said Steve, watching our new friend paddle back.

"Who's next?" asked Ransom, shoving his surfboard at us. I caught it by the nose and inspected the slick finish. In a loopy, tropical font, church words were inlaid on his board—a psalm among palms.

"You did this art yourself?" I asked, climbing on.

"Praise me later," he said. "Time to surf."

I sprawled across the board, and a wet reality rushed in: the slickness of wax against my stomach, the saltwater on my tongue, and the newness of seeing the ocean from surface level. In steady rhythms, beach homes and sand dunes disappeared then reappeared.

"Start paddling when I yell go," said Ransom, one hand gripping the board.

"Toward the beach?"

"Of course, toward the beach. Then push up with your hands, get your feet planted."

"No training wheels on this thing?"

I felt a push from behind and beneath. The swell lifted and powered me forward. I rose to my knees, wobbled twice, and heard only the roar of ocean as I placed my left foot on the board. For a split second, I felt like the big kahuna. But then the nose dipped, shot me forward, and there I went, head beneath knees, knees beneath feet.

I plunged beneath the board, my back skidding the ocean floor, my throat rejecting an alien liquid. Sand swirled about my head. I shot to the surface. Knee deep in the breakers, I tugged on my shorts and heaved quarts of seawater from both lungs.

"How was that?" I asked, half choking.

"Simply horrible!" yelled Steve. He mounted the board in roughly the same manner as a walrus would mount a balance beam. Ransom repeated his instructions, the sloppy drops continued, and something was nibbling my foot.

Steve paddled hard, pushed deep into the next wave but barely moved. He gave the impression of a stalk of corn cut at the base—falling right where it begins.

"Ya got no momentum, bro."

"I got no coordination," he said, climbing back aboard. "One more try?"

"Go for it," said Ransom.

But the waves had become moody, evasive. Gradually, the rain stopped, while to the west, above the rooftops and between two crow's nests, the sun peeked through again.

"Hold the board straight," said Ransom, pointing it at the shore. "Like this."

"Like this?" asked Steve, realizing his plight.

Thrust forward by the next wave, he suddenly was hidden by a wall of water. The wave shrunk. Steve wobbled. Then his right foot found its place, his left came up and around, but the yellow board tilted.

I had seen fraternity drunks fall into a bush more gracefully. Shoulder and head hit first, legs at an odd angle to the torso. Steve disappeared for a moment, a second wave washed over, and, riderless, the board slid nose-first into a crumbling sand castle, palms and psalms covered in mud.

I gave him a two for artistic presentation, zero for technical merit.

Ransom had the board under his arm as darkness approached, the beach empty, our stomachs growling, my toes shriveled. Steve hacked into his towel, and the soft sand gave way beneath our feet as we trudged between the dunes.

"So," said Ransom, without looking at either of us, "you guys golfers or what?"

Summer's steam rose through the asphalt of Seaspray Drive. Ahead, dozens of single folk gathered in front of house number two. They were cleaned up and polished; we were soaked through and shriveled.

From underneath the pink house, the lime Caddy backed heavily over crushed shells. Inside the car sat Darcy, Allie, and three guys we didn't recognize.

"I thought surfers got the girls . . ."

"Not a problem," said Ransom, as if he could care less.

We quickened our pace, and without breaking stride, Ransom reached over and pulled my hair into a blond spike. Three steps later I returned the favor, and after mild cajoling we convinced surfer Steve to spike his own, just for uniformity.

Darcy stopped in the street and waited till we arrived at Sherbet's hood. "Nice hair," she said. "We have reservations for fifty at Inlet Restaurant. We'll save you guys a seat if you'd like to join us."

"Might just do that," said Steve.

"How far is it?" I asked, admiring her passenger.

"Just depends," said Allie, who tightened her seat belt, then turned and winked at her driver. Darcy floored it, her rear tires flinging gravel at Ransom's surfboard.

"Never ask them that question," said Steve, scolding me amid the road steam.

"Unbelievable," mumbled Ransom. He leaned over to check his board for nicks.

Dripping into our beach house, I saw our gray-paneled living room now filled with various sleeping bags and shaving kits. We decided hot showers, clean shirts, and combed hair would serve us well. We were out the door in eight minutes.

Not a world record, but still faster than any three women.

Jutting out over salt marsh, the restaurant offered distant views of an inlet, breaking waves flashing streaks of orange, and firelight on the horizon. Across the rear of the restaurant stood an open-air porch, where four long tables had been pulled together to accommodate us.

The lights were soft, the mood jovial.

Hardy scents of seafood filled the air, and I squinted to see the far end of our group, the porch buzzing with conversation. Young waiters moved among the fray, refilling baskets of bread and reciting specials as if timed on a stopwatch.

Strangers nodded hello.

And hello to you, stranger.

Seats were saved for us—backs to the ocean—and I was heading for the buffet when Stanley said, "Let's bow our heads." Standing in the doorway with a bowed head would be uncomfortable, so I let the crew bless the shrimp and scallops without me.

The buffet stretched out across the middle of the restaurant, where an aquarium played host to a dozen lobsters, their pinchers clamped, their fate certain. Our line moved forward; I took a plate, then heard singing ahead at a table for ten. Bad singing, but singing nonetheless.

I recognized it—the same tune sung at sporting events when the home team is way ahead. A bearded man in a Harley T-shirt led the ensemble. "Nah-nah-naah-nah, hey-hey-hey, goood-bye." The chorus repeated and kept repeating. I stepped out of line for a better view and saw the cook, a large Greek-looking man in a floppy white hat, standing beside the aquarium. He directed the singing like a symphony conductor.

Voices reached a familiar key, the buffet line joined in, and as a tenor, I'll admit there's a Southern charm in singing eulogies to the seafood.

With our chorus growing louder, the cook rolled up a sleeve and reached in past his elbow. Twelve defenseless crustaceans fled to one side. He grabbed one at the waist, then hoisted the dripping creature overhead to our loud applause. The cook grinned, performed a perfect military about-face, and it was off to the boiling heat, lobster doom, where there is weeping and gnashing of claw.

I was reaching for more crab legs when the edge of her plate poked my rib.

"Jay," said Allie in her pale-yellow sundress and worn leather sandals, "I mighta given you a wrong impression earlier. I was asking about Steve for Jill, another girl who's staying with us. She's a bit shy."

Two scallops slid off my plate as I managed a weak, "Oh."

She had her hand in the shrimp now, and sadly for a guy who makes his living with his mouth, I could not think of anything to say. My plate

42

was full, and her scent was lingering above the crab legs, so I did as all men do in such predicaments: I began picking up shrimp one at a time from the buffet, stacking them slowly in a pyramid until the words came.

"Wanna throw fried ones or boiled ones?" she asked, placing hers carefully in a circle.

"Let's stick with the low-cholesterol stuff."

"Do you feel sorry for the lobster?"

I plated two more scallops. "No, I think he was predestined."

She scanned the buffet, a silly smile on her face. Not another morsel would fit on my plate. I turned to walk back to my seat, and a single fried shrimp bounced off the back of my head.

Seated next to me, Steve fumbled with his crab legs while most of the females, including Darcy the Leadfoot, dined twenty plates away. Conversation gave way to more eating, and I could not recall any seafood like this in Dallas.

In Dallas, seafood had a rubbery texture.

I borrowed the claw-crusher tool from Steve, demolished a crab, then looked the length of the table. Ransom had squatted down beside a petite, sandy blonde, his arm around the back of her chair. She laughed and looked up into his eyes. He rubbed her back.

I elbowed Brother Steve. "Doesn't take him long, does it? We really have to learn to surf."

"He's married," said Steve. "That's his wife."

"Honest?"

Steve tore open a sugar packet and dumped the contents in his tea. "He's married to her. She's staying with the women and he's staying with us."

Ransom returned with his own plate overflowing, looking very much the content surfer dude.

"You're married?" I asked, still not convinced.

He reached for the cocktail sauce. "Yeah. Six years. I know this sounds weird, but there weren't any extra bedrooms, so we decided we might appreciate each other even more if we just spent a weekend as singles again. Although we're secretly lusting for each other from the ends of the table."

By this time I was convinced that the entire religious community in South Carolina was wacko and that I should just eat my seafood. But then Ransom passed the sauce and promised to give me some relational advice once we got back to Greenville.

Across from us, gabbing away, Lydia looked miniscule seated next to a big Italian guy—military haircut, honker of a nose. He introduced himself as Joseph Caruzzi, the catcher for a minor league baseball team, but said we should call him Joe.

Big Joe's pyramid dwarfed mine.

"Need the sauce," he demanded, centering his bowl.

"In gumbo?" Steve asked.

"Gross," said Lydia. And she scrunched her nose.

Exhausted waiters refilled our glasses. Big Joe said he just had to hear everyone sing to the lobsters again, so he stuffed two bucks in a waiter's shirt pocket and asked him to bring out a huge one.

The chorus started over with the Harley guy, who seemed to have forgotten the words. The cook waved him off, took control, and our porch tables willingly joined in. But only for one verse—in midchorus Stanley jumped up, saying this was not a very spiritual way to behave.

Heads dropped. Women frowned. Stanley peeled his shrimp.

"He ruins my lobster song again, and I'll toss *him* in the tank," said Joe, visibly peeved.

I agreed with Joe's assessment of Stanley and told him that what with the ridiculous cost of lobsters today, a man should be entitled to a full chorus of the seafood eulogy, especially since some nature-loving songwriter went to all that trouble to compose the tune.

He said thanks Jay, and I said welcome Joe.

The waiter said too bad we stopped singing 'cause we sang much better than the sunburned Harley people, and would anyone care for pie.

"No sir," said Steve to the waiter. "No room for dessert."

"And will this be on one check or . . . ?"

"Separate."

The waiter scanned our group. "All separate?"

"Except for me," said Ransom. "Charge two buffets to my bill."

The waiter returned five minutes later and called us to attention. "The manager decided in the interest of time not to worry over who had an entree versus the buffet, so if everyone will just pay sixteen dollars at the register, we'll call it even. And thank you for dining with us."

"Does the sixteen bucks include my lobster?" asked Joe, reaching for his wallet.

"No sir, lobsters are twenty-five bucks extra."

"Tourist trap."

With the group departing, Steve and I commingled our tips and let Ransom Delaney drive the Jeep back home in exchange for more surfing lessons.

A full moon reflected silver and joined the phosphorous in the waves to light the beach. The dark clouds from our surfing hour had passed, the ocean had calmed, and the women leaned in toward the fire.

Steve bent and extended six hangers, and we passed them around. Embers crackled and spit while whiffs of burning wood merged with salt air. The heat came and went with the occasional breeze, but mostly it angled away from me as I tried to get my rear end comfortable on a log.

"Need another marshmallow," said Darcy, now donning a gray Carolina sweatshirt. She pulled her blonde mane over one shoulder, then readied her hands like an outfielder.

I reached in the bag, flipped one underhanded across the fire, and surprisingly for a rich girl, she caught it and threaded the thing onto her hanger.

"Toss me one, dude," said Ransom, and he threaded one on for his wife.

Her name was Jamie, and she rested her head against his shoulder as they sat on a smaller log, flicking sand with their toes. It was a log built for two, a love log. Ransom inspected a crispy mallow, allowed it to cool, offered her the first nibble. But soon her eyes began to shut and her hanger began to droop, stirring skyward a puff of orange-and-gray ash.

45

Ransom gently removed the hanger from her fingers and set it in the sand.

"She's a morning person," he said to no one in particular.

Two marshmallows occupied my own hanger as the flame shadows jumped across faces. A medium-brown edge was my goal. But as I watched a plane pass over the ocean, I, too, committed the ancient sin of droopage, then pulled the hanger back to see the blob on the end blackened, a drip of creamy innards seeping from the bottom. I held it aloft, allowing the morsel to cool against the night sky. A gooey planet. Sliding from the hanger, the stickiness eased and oozed between my fingers.

I looked back across the flames. Her arm was already cocked.

To be honest, I really didn't think she would do it—the incident with the tomato had been spontaneous; the shrimp-to-the-head a bit flirtatious. This, however, had no real basis other than plain ol' consistency.

But sitting there in her sundress, next to Darcy, she never hesitated.

In midflight, her white missile had that imminent look of fate, like when two grocery carts are about to clang together—no time for dodging. My return volley was launched from relative blindness, her most accurate glob already matted to my forehead and my blond bangs.

"You people have gone loony," said Darcy, as if such juvenile behavior were beneath her.

"Good fastball," said Steve, but he was not speaking to me.

Glancing again across the flames, I saw Allie Kyle wiping furiously at her hair, just above the left shoulder.

"See, honey," said Ransom to his wife, "we missed a lot by marrying so young."

"Hmm-umm," she said, snuggling into him again.

I walked over to the water. Knee deep in the breakers, I scooped handfuls of seawater to rinse away the globs, but the mess remained stubborn. One complete head dunk, though, and most of it rubbed out.

I was using the bottom of my shirt to dry off, wondering if Baptist women could throw like Presbyterians, when she walked up beside me.

"Truce?" she said, removing her sandals in the moonlight.

"Until breakfast, at least."

46

She stepped toward the water. "I'm making scrambled eggs."

With my dignity gone, sunken in a tidal pool, I figured there was not much left to lose. "Wanna take a walk?"

She hesitated, then pulled a hand through her wet hair. "Okay, but just a short one."

In a slow, get-to-know-ya stroll, we passed the last oceanfront house, North Litchfield Beach now dark and inviting. A steady, subdued crash of waves echoed from our right as the water licked the sand in front of us, then retreated.

She waited for me to speak first.

"Steve tells me you spent some time in South America."

"Yes," she said, looking straight ahead. "Almost a whole year. Was life-changing. Went down there to teach and to minister but ended up being ministered to."

"How do you mean?" I asked, glancing at the bottom of her sundress, the pale yellow now a deeper shade from the ripples splashing against it.

"In the U.S., I get caught up in the pace, the materialism, but down there in Ecuador we'd sit around and talk at night. No one had a car to drive, and even if someone did, nobody would care who drove what or how much they made. We'd even walk down the dirt road to visit neighbors, which I never do here. I got away from all my *stuff* and realized that people are more important."

I dragged a toe in wet sand. "I kinda like my stuff, but I could probably leave it for a couple weeks."

Moonlight caught her frown. "A couple weeks? I'm thinking about selling everything, maybe even my house. They want me to come back, maybe for good, maybe starting with summer semester, although down there the seasons all blend. . . . But I could end up somewhere else just as well."

We walked a good ways before I thought of what to say next. "Pardon the ignorance, Allie, but what exactly does a day consist of on the mission field?"

She didn't answer immediately, just stared up at the sky for a moment, lost in recollection. "Mostly different forms of the stereotype. Teaching kids, counseling women, sharing the gospel, and eating lots of weird food. Our little village was quite remote."

"How remote?"

"Rainforest remote. Think monkeys, lush vegetation, and no Internet access." She picked up a clump of seaweed, twirled it like a sling, and let fly into the breakers.

We walked farther, and our arms brushed. The balmy interview resumed. "Sounds prehistoric. You fluent in Spanish?"

"*Sí, señor.* I taught English to twenty children, most of them orphans. And I've learned just enough to help deliver an occasional baby. So, tell me about the stockbroker biz."

I answered without consulting the heavens, South America, or sea-weed. "It's hectic, no day is ever the same, and you have to console the crybabies. But it's financially rewarding . . . and you get weekends off."

"When you get rich, how about sending me some? I gotta start tallying my support pledges next week, and I'm way short."

"You have to raise it all yourself? There's no corporate—"

"It's nonprofit. Support-raising is a huge burden. Though I wish some-one would pledge a weekly cheeseburger."

I'd known her half a day, and already I wanted to hold her hand. But no way.

"Consider it pledged."

She swung a sandal on each thumb, her hair beginning to dry in the warm ocean breeze. "I also kept a journal while I was down there. Turned it into a collection of short stories. Sent it off to three publishers and just got back the rejections."

"Too bad. Haven't seen many food-chucking missionary memoirs at the bookstore."

She dropped back one step, like she was about to kick wet sand at my legs but had reconsidered. "They said I used some inappropriate language."

"Foul?"

"Not exactly. You do any writing?"

"Only e-mails," I replied, watching the lights of Myrtle Beach flicker in the distance.

"I love playing with words, making up poems from scratch . . . like literary biscuits."

Wedged between my toes, a shell fragment had me kneeling on a dark beach, Allie pausing at the shoreline, looking down amused as I tried to de-wedge the irritant.

Soon we were strolling again, and I was wanting to know more about her. "How can you own a house and continue, you know, going away like that?"

"I rented it to some girlfriends last time. Before that, I'd been doing minor restoration, painting, landscaping. My dad helped me fix the porch. I could sell it to help finance my next trip, wherever that may be."

Our pace slowed, and I thought her career path odd, though intriguing. "Let me guess the possibilities . . . Mongolia?"

"Nope."

"Uganda?"

She was staring at the sky again. "No, probably not."

I was scrambling for countries. "Jamaica? 'Cause you need to be near seafood to keep your throwing arm in shape?"

Her laughter was intoxicating. "I'm not sure where, yet. But the answer will come in its time. How about you? Any big plans?"

I tried to think of something impressive but had eaten way too many scallops. "Compared to you, Allie, my plans are pretty mundane."

"Then why don't you ask God to give direction?"

"Do you really think he does that?"

"I'm certain of it," she said. "We'd better turn around now."

Returning up the beach, I watched the footprints from our walk fade and melt beneath a rising tide. It was almost 1:00 A.M., there was an awkward silence, and as we neared the fire, the waves lapped up close behind the logs.

5

I tossed one last handful of sand over the embers as males lagged females, who were already between the dunes, shoulder to shoulder and chatting away. Across the oceanfront road, puddles of rainwater lay stagnant in a grassy ditch. The water puddles had given hatch to mosquitoes; the mosquitoes had gone forth and multiplied. They buzzed our ears, teased our faces, and hovered against the streetlight.

We stepped up the pace to catch the ladies, caught them, and said good night at their driveway. Jamie got a peck from her husband, I got a wave from Allie, and we walked down a blackened Seaspray Drive—Steve with his stubble, me with my salty marshmallow hair, and Ransom with his unfulfilled lust.

"Get her number?" asked Steve. He carried hangers in one hand, lighter fluid in the other.

"Where, in Central Africa?" I said, slapping at nothing in the dark.

"Now you see what I mean. You gotta have no job and a million frequent-flyer miles to keep up with her."

"So much for white picket fences," said Ransom.

"She thinks God directs her to do that mission stuff."

Ransom paused on the crushed shells. "I think she's right."

Up the stairs and into the screened porch, we peeled off our sandals and knocked off the sand. Steve held a finger to his lips. "Shh."

Five sleeping bags fanned out in perfect symmetry across our living-room floor. Three contained bodies, two were empty and unzipped.

We had claimed a bedroom upon arrival, a long room with a slanted ceiling, two single beds, and a dresser; we even had our own bathroom. Taped to the door, on a dangling sheet of official church letterhead, was a copy of the weekend agenda, including a suggested midnight curfew for all participants in church-sponsored retreats.

Steve and Ransom took the beds. Me, I wadded the agenda into a paper ball and agreed to take the floor on this, the first night of my very first churchy beach trip.

Sea green was our motif. The room was painted sea green, and the lone window at the far end had sea-green curtains pulled back to allow air through the screen. Seashells occupied the dresser and the bathroom wallpaper; obligatory beach art hung above the headboards.

I cut the lights and inserted myself in the sleeping bag. We enjoyed a full minute of silence, until Steve asked, "Do ya miss your wife?"

"Go to sleep, dude," said Ransom from his dark corner.

"This has got to be weird," I offered. "Staying with guys, two houses away."

"Not really. While you guys were unloading the groceries this after-noon, me and Jamie were upstairs in the hot tub over at that pink house. We heard the five of you eating Oreos in the kitchen, and when you all left, I snuck out the back door and took my surfboard to the beach."

"I hate your guts."

"Yeah," said Steve, "we hate your guts. And we ate more than just Oreos."

"G'night, boys," said Ransom.

"We had gourmet cookies."

I slapped my forehead during the night, near the same spot where the marshmallow had splattered. The faint buzz grew louder, and only a pale splotch of moonlight shone through the window. I backhanded the blackness but missed again.

Soon it brought friends, some still faint, others within inches of my head. I tried the forehand and the overhead smash, but the mosquitoes flew closer, teasing, lurking, suspending above me until I heard the sudden thud of a heel hitting the wall.

"Jarvis?"

"Hmmm?"

"They're everywhere," whispered Steve. "Got any bug spray?"

I hated whispering to a guy but did it anyway. "I think I saw a can under the kitchen sink. Those other guys are sleeping in the living room, so don't step on 'em."

Another thud, maybe his toe ramming the door. He said ouch under his breath. I heard skeeters circling my head and Ransom snoring in the corner. Convinced that surfers had immunity from insects, I swatted again, made contact, felt one brush my ear.

Groping in the dark for a shirt, a towel, anything, I heard the door open, then the sound of a can shaking. Steve was silhouetted against the window, spraying with abandon, the buzzes converging from all corners of the bedroom.

"I think there's a hole in the screen," he said.

"Just kill 'em."

"I'm tryin'." The whistling hiss of bug spray muted the snoring and the buzzing. I saw the outline of his arm waving back and forth and up and down around the window. My next swat also missed. The pale light in the window went dim.

Steve turned and said, "Here's a shot for ya."

The smell was overwhelming; my eyes burned and a stickiness lingered in the air. "What kinda bug killer is that?"

He flipped on the light to reveal long white streaks, still wet and shiny, arching across the window screen, the sea-green curtains, and the sea-green wall. A smattering of tiny white dots were drying on my sleeping bag.

Steve stood motionless, blinked twice. He looked down at the silver can and began reading to himself, wide-eyed.

"Whatsa light on for?" mumbled Ransom, finally waking.

"Steve just killed a platoon of mosquitoes with Krylon," I said. "White semigloss."

"I want my wife back." And he pulled a pillow over his head.

It was now 3:00 A.M., our beach trip off to a fine start. Steve and I dragged his mattress and two blankets onto the kitchen floor, slept there, and left Ransom in the corner of the bedroom, longing for his wife and domesticity.

Seaweed lounged in beds of foam to mark the high tide as my eyes adjusted to the sunrise, my nose to the salt air. Jogging along the hard sand near water's edge, I admired the unmarked beach, all footprints and sand castles washed smooth within nature's Etch A Sketch, shaken clean twice a day.

Down the shoreline, against a backdrop of pink sky smudged with orange, the two surf fishermen had returned, old guys side by side and staring out to sea. One pudgy, in cutoff jeans and a red baseball cap, the other short and thin, all whiskery-faced in his ragged gray shirt, sleeves lopped off at the elbows. He looked frail, fragile even. Both poles stood anchored in the sand, bending in rhythm with the push and pull of the waves.

I passed their empty bucket, then glanced over in midstride and met the gaze of the pudgy one. He nodded, a quick nod, but it seemed twice as sincere as the one from the bulletin guy back at North Hills.

Orange sky blended to yellow as I passed a woman and a toddler picking through shells among the sticks and foam, the Atlantic's lost and found. A rock jetty thwarted my run, the gnarly pile of boulders all surf-slathered and immense, the massive mediators of ebb and flow. Barnacles clung piggyback to the boulders, and tiny crabs scurried away with one oversized claw, snapping in disgust at my intrusion.

I turned south again, and now the woman held the toddler by her hand, leaning over and scrounging in the surf. The little girl looked no more than two, and she dropped one shell for every new one she picked up. I gave a two-fingered wave, but it went unnoticed. A narrow slice of sun threw my shadow long and thin. Ahead, the two anglers moved toward the ocean. I continued running and saw the frail fisherman in front of the pudgy one, bending seaward, arms extended. He leaned back, pulled his arms in, then bent toward the water again.

I jogged closer and saw Pudgy take the pole from the frail one. He braced himself in wet sand, standing rigid and determined, retaining his posture as I stopped, sweaty and curious, beside their bucket.

"Watcha got?"

"Don't know," he said over his shoulder. "Can't get any line in."

"Tried to slow the drag," said the frail one. And he held his thumb up to show me the burn mark, a narrow crevice, red and raw.

Tinted orange, their fishing line contrasted sharply against the ocean. It moved north for a minute, then reversed and headed south. Pudgy spread his feet for balance, and the line neither entered nor exited his reel, a standoff at sea. I was betting on the fish.

"Gotta be a shark," said Pudgy, lowering the brim of his cap.

"What kind?"

"Several kinds out there. Saw a couple fins yesterday while you guys were surfing, but nothin' bit."

The frail one elbowed Pudgy and asked if he could hold the pole again, since he was the one who had actually hooked the fish. Pudgy handed him the pole in slow motion, as if passing a barbell to a buddy. They inched out to ankle-deep water, where receding surf burrowed their feet farther in the sand.

I quickly took off my running shoes, edged closer, and asked what they used for bait.

"Cut mullet," said Pudgy. "Just thread 'em on a six-aught hook, then cast it deep."

"Whadda you do when you catch one?" I asked. More orange line spun out undisturbed.

He was distracted by the fish and took a moment to answer. "To be honest, son, I just pet 'em on the head and let 'em go."

A broadening slice of sun reflected off the waves. More line spun off, singing out in low then higher octaves. Minutes passed; no one spoke, and the fish moved in a spasmodic, north-south pattern.

"Wanna feel him pull?" asked the frail one, offering me the pole.

"Sure," I said, taking hold of his surf rod.

It felt as if I had hold of a car that had slipped out of gear and was rolling down a driveway. The next tug yanked my body forward. Sand swirled out rapidly beneath my feet, tickling as it departed, but my only thought was retaining balance. I leaned backward in imitation—to at least look proficient in the art of shark fighting—and watched even more line strip off the reel.

"Put your thumb on the spool to slow it," said Pudgy, an urgency in his voice.

The line sung out, and now I, too, had a red, raw crevice to match his friend, who'd actually hooked the fish. The pole grew heavy, the butt end stressing my ribs, the business end jerking with crazed bouts of quivering opposition.

"Lemme have it," said the frail one.

His arms were deeply tanned, his hands dry and weathered. He seemed mad at the fish now, his fish, and got back the four turns of line I'd lost, plus two more. After cranking the reel and finding it stubborn, he began taking slow steps away from the sea, as if to tow the creature from the depths.

Pudgy put one hand on his friend's back, then grabbed the bottom of the pole with the other. Together, they dragged backward for ten feet, stopping at the shoreline.

After two more cranks, the strategy resumed. They dragged and reeled, then reeled and towed. The line no longer moved north and south, but lay idle, resting on the waves.

"Need a break?" I asked. And suddenly I had the pole to myself again, trying to perfect the tow and reel procedure. My feet dug and slid in the wet sand, my arms tensed from the strain, and one step back took longer than finding Galatians to the east of Psalms.

"Don't point the pole straight out," cautioned Pudgy. "The line'll snap; keep it pointed up."

My next step backward was no quicker than the first, but I got three turns of line in, and the frail one gave me a nod of confirmation.

55

"Give the pole back to 'im," said Pudgy. "After all, it's his fish."

I handed the pole back. But I didn't want to.

"Let's get it in," said Pudgy, motioning for me to join him.

"Sir?"

"Follow me, son."

I had no idea what we were about to do, but I was back in the Atlantic, knee-deep beside Pudgy. Then behind Pudgy. In front of us, the gray figure of a shark swam beneath sea foam, the foam hiding him, then revealing.

Three-footer was my guesstimate. The stringy remains of a mullet hung from its snout. Its tail thrashed side to side, and Pudgy said for his buddy to drag a little more up the beach. The frail one stopped near a dune, his rod bent nearly in half, and we had to yell in order for him to hear us.

I stepped away from the shark and was immediately reprimanded.

"You gotta pet 'im on the head or it doesn't count as a catch," said Pudgy, hunched over in a stalking position, like a kid chasing grasshoppers.

"Say what?" My olive shorts were soaked, and I thought the old man was nuts.

He reached in his back pocket and produced a glove, thick and layered with tiny wire mesh, chainlike. Cool waves splashed over my knees. The shark thrashed again, then disappeared, camouflaged by sea foam. I shadowed Pudgy as he stalked the shark, and he stalked it right into the shallows. In one motion he gripped the tail with his bare right hand, pulled the shark into a foot of water, and thrust his gloved hand firmly on top of the head, forcing it down in the sand.

"Go on, rub it on the head," he demanded, as if this were a test.

I rubbed it on the head. Nicely. The head felt slick, warm even, and strained to rise beneath Pudgy's chain glove.

"Okay, let's switch," he said, moving left to allow me access.

"Oh, great."

Lethargic, the shark conceded defeat, its tail no longer thrashing but moving in a relaxed swoosh. Pudgy let go of the tail, stripped off the glove, and asked if I was right-handed.

"Hold tight," he yelled at his buddy, who had one foot up on the sand dune, his pole bent again to the snapping point.

I slid my newly gloved hand up behind the slick head, pressing down while Pudgy stroked the shark. He performed this act of affection gently, as one would with a poodle. Then he began talking to the shark in a soft voice. "You wouldn't eat surfers, now would ya, boy?"

With one hand on the head and the other gripping the tail, he pushed and pulled the shark through the water, saying he always revived them before he turned 'em loose.

"Are you two trying to catch sharks?" I asked, certain that there were laws against such behavior near public beaches.

He didn't look up from his work. "No, son, not exactly. It's just that they seem so . . . plentiful."

"You gonna remove the hook?"

"Patience, son."

The tail swooshed faster, resuscitation complete.

"Can I try that, too?"

"Just hold him here and push forward like this," he said. "But put the glove back on."

The shark's head spun around so fast I could not react. Front teeth grazed the glove and back teeth snapped the line. A flash of tail, a violent stirring of the sand, and the next wave wrapped limp orange line around my leg.

The frail one, now backward on his butt at the base of the sand dune, yelled, "Why'd you guys cut the line on me?"

Salt water stung the back of my left thumb. Pudgy said, "Let's have a look." The glove came off, and two drops of O-positive faded to pink in the backwash.

"Just a scrape," he said. "I been cut deeper'n that plenty of times."

Confident that shark fishermen never complain, I ignored the sting, my pride intact. "Is that the biggest you guys have caught?"

"Nah, not even close." He stepped back in the shallows and washed his face with a splash of seawater.

The frail one wound in the line. "Got a 120 pounder to our credit," he said, pausing to scratch his whiskers.

"Caught on the beach?" I asked.

"Sure. They're closer than you'd think. Most fun you can have with a chunk o' mullet." He extended his hand. "My name's Theo."

"Jay."

"I'm Asbury," said Pudgy. He said his name with a wink, as if to welcome me into some secret early-morning anglers club.

Content with the morning battle, they tossed their hooks and weights into a rusty tackle box and began passing a blue thermos back and forth, taking deep swigs and saying ahh the way only old guys can.

"Wanna swallow?" asked Asbury, wiping his chin on his sleeve.

Now the gash really stung. "What's in it?"

"A mixture," he said, admiring his thermos. "Gatorade, grapefruit juice, and grenadine."

"No thanks."

I was retying my running shoes and craving breakfast when Asbury slapped me on the back.

"Pleasure meetin' ya," he said. "You fish a lot better than you surf."

6

It was after 9:00 A.M when I arrived, panting, back at our beach house, my
story rehearsed twice, trickles of blood spread around my hand for proof.
Through the screened porch and into the living room, I saw five sleeping
bags rolled, tied, and stacked in a corner.

"Mornin'," I said to preoccupied strangers. There was no response.

Stanley and his four buddies sat against the far wall, reading verses
while scooping cereal from plastic bowls. Pastel beach art hung above
their heads, notepads rested at their feet, and I thought they all looked
clean-cut, cliquish, and just a bit pale.

I watched them for a moment. No one looked up. Stoked by the desire
to share my story with Steve and Ransom, I backpedaled to the bedroom,
turned, and opened the door. Long white streaks slashed across our walls
and window, like the beginning of some hurried, inner-city graffiti. My
roommates were gone, but a note dangled from inside the door.

I've gone to buy sea green paint.
  Steve

After applying a Band-Aid to my cut, I decided to make breakfast. Our
kitchen was separated from the living room by an L-shaped countertop
burdened with a peculiar shade of coral. Artsy types might've called it

some version of pink, but our entire house had agreed on coral. I leaned across it to issue an invitation.

"Wanna make pancakes with me when you're done, Stanley?"

"Shh," Stanley said from against the wall. He gave me one of those looks. Some looks infer you've done something you shouldn't have done; other looks infer you didn't do something you shoulda done. I had not done something. It took me a minute, but after sizing up the situation and the silence, I wiped off the counter with my good hand, put the milk away, and took the garbage to the street.

Across the driveway of crushed shells, then back up the stairs, I found Stanley waiting for me on the screened porch. With folded arms. A white rocker stood between us.

"Jay, we are all here as part of a church group. Mornings first thing, we have our quiet times."

I had not heard the term *quiet time* since twenty years ago, in first grade, when we'd take our multicolored mats out from under our desks to enjoy a post-lunch nap.

"You mean like reading verses?"

"That's a major part of it," he said, staring me down.

"And this must be done at 9:00 in the morning when the beach is sunny and the fish are biting?"

"It's a spiritual discipline."

I gave the rocker a jump start with my toe. "Have you seen my new friend Ransom? He's a surfer . . ."

Stanley stopped the rocker with his foot. "Walked down the street to have breakfast with his wife. But you can tell him we like to see the men have a daily course of spiritual food as well."

I was torn between responses, harsh or witty, witty or harsh, but could not summon either. I toed the rocker again. Stanley's stare was even more rigid than his Saturday-morning schedule. It put me off. Rather than stoke my curiosity, it drove me away, and I wanted nothing to do with his quiet times or anything else resembling his self-righteous karaoke.

So what I did was, I employed my fishing lesson and decided to wait him out.

60

He grabbed the rocker, held it firm. Suddenly he glanced down at my bandage. "What'd you do to your hand?"

"Me and an old guy named Asbury rubbed a shark on the head. He bit me."

"Asbury bit you?"

"No, Stanley, the shark."

Sunlight angled through the pines of Seaspray Drive, warming my feet, my neck, my salt-thickened hair. Gulls soared overhead, catching the wind and banking toward the sea. I wished human interaction could be that smooth.

With a purple beach towel flung over my shoulder and blue shades over my eyes, I strolled toward the beach by myself, pondering Stanley.

Oh, Stanley.

Someday one of his kids will hit three home runs in a Little League game, get voted most valuable player by ESPN, and Stanley will say fine for you but I don't wanna hear about it until you go sit against the wall and have a quiet time.

I crossed the wooden walkway between the dunes, trudged past a limp volleyball net, and spread my towel on hard sand, a prime location for scoping and hoping.

The rays were intense. And I'd forgotten my sunblock.

Little movement on the Carolina coast, only small clusters of kite flyers and squealing children dotting the shore. And a handsome shore it was, a serene Atlantic coaxing the day as scrawny waves rose and tumbled, rolling over in tight cylinders of blue and green, tiny shells eloping in the backwash.

I was wiping grains from my lenses when five women approached. They looked familiar, maybe from the seafood restaurant. They carried book bags, beach towels, and a rainbow assortment of folding chairs.

One said, "You must be Jay," and I met a blonde Nancy. Her one-piece was light blue. Her manner was right nice. Her four friends waved hello.

"Your first retreat with the singles?" she inquired, unfolding her chair.

I swiped a fly from my knee. "Yes, and you?"

"My third. Seems to be more people every year. You a lifelong Presbyterian?" she asked, wedging her chair in the sand.

"Hardly. My family was a strange hybrid, somewhere between not interested and workaholic. I went to church during junior high, then not again till college . . . and that was only because I took a devout Lutheran to homecoming." I disliked answering these types of questions, but at least I told the truth.

"That's interesting," she replied, adjusting the angle of her chair. She did this with one hand while holding a plastic cup in the other. Some of her drink sloshed out.

She seemed friendly enough, so I decided to ask her the question I was saving for my roommates. "Can you explain Stanley and his . . . entourage?"

She was very precise about her chair angle. "He invited those friends," she said, her voice slow and pure Southern. "They all take the same correspondence courses from some ultraconservative seminary. Nice guys, but they do seem full of rules. Rules for walking, rules for talking."

"You're kidding, right?" I asked, offering to hold her drink as she spread a red towel over her chair. The towel was stitched with smiling white bulldogs.

"A bit exaggerated. Take a sip if you want. You staying with them?"

"Yep. Me, Steve, and Ransom."

"Is he that surfer who's actually married?"

"That's him."

"Are they having problems?" she asked, reclaiming her cup.

"No, just single for the weekend. Although rumor has it they secretly lusted for each other at the restaurant last night."

She smiled, set her drink in the sand, and reached into her bag. "Where you from?"

"Texas. And you?"

"Athens, Georgia," she said with perfect nonchalance. She opened a book on dating and relating, but I deftly managed to keep the conversation alive.

"Are you staying in the same house with Allie and Darcy?"

"Yeah, but they left to go shopping." And she flipped to chapter one.

"Know when they'll be back?"

She did not look up. "Haven't a clue."

"What's that stuff you're drinking?"

"Sprite with lemonade."

The other four females arranged their chairs in a line, parallel to the waves. They removed their shorts, took their seats, passed sunblock down the line. Nancy rubbed the white stuff on her legs, then handed me the bottle. I wanted to ask her to rub some on my back, but she and her friends were all wearing conservative one-pieces, and this being only my first weekend with Presbyterians, I decided to do it myself.

After handing the bottle back, I watched them in all their glory, a glistening quintet aligning chairs perfectly with the sun. They were studiously reading when eight more women approached, plopped down their chairs and books, and now the line was thirteen females and me, a setting that compared quite favorably to having quiet times with Stanley.

Surveying the lineup, I saw several classics, but mostly books on dating and relating.

I knew I'd never be able to remember all their names, so I forewent introducing myself and began to number them, starting at the far end: number one, two, three, all the way down to Nancy, next to me, as number thirteen.

Nancy and the Numericals were a fascinating crew. Numbers Three and Six had great tans and matching paperbacks; Number Ten had freckles and Hemingway; Number Eight obviously pumped iron. And, stretching my neck a bit farther, I concluded that Number Two—with her raven hair, pierced eyebrow, and Tolstoy—was definitely the most dangerous.

No one seemed interested in talking or flirting, so I rolled over on my stomach.

Behind me, the breaking of waves was subdued but constant, a slow hiss of energy building toward the collapse of sea against land. From my prone position, I could see the walkway, its weathered boards angling over a dune and burying the bottom step in white sand. Beside the steps sat a trash barrel. A seagull hopped around the barrel, picking at scraps and rummaging for a meal. Suddenly it took two quick steps and went airborne, squawking as it passed over, its lunch delayed.

Back above the walkway, a reverent head rose above the dunes. Up came his perfect hair, then his torso, then he stood at the crest, surveying the beach as his four buddies piled up behind him. Stanley had donned plaid Bermuda shorts and a religious T-shirt, one size too small.

Surely he would go to the opposite end of our line, next to a girl. But I'd discovered there was no sure thing with this group, so the safest action, for me, was a nap.

I quickly folded my tank top into a pillow, buried my head in it, then wrapped my arms around my head, retreating like a fiddler crab to its sandy cave, far removed from perfect hair and plaid Bermuda shorts.

To the side and above me came the sound of a towel flapping, then another and another. Puffs of sand fell on my back; I heard male voices. "He must be asleep" and "That's the guy who—"

"Shh," whispered a third voice.

I wasn't sure how long I'd dozed, but my back was hot, my head was still buried, and I felt groggy from last night's aborted sleep. I smelled the wet sand. From my right came only the sound of pages flipping, so I figured the girls were deep into their books.

Intense debate burst forth from my left, male voices hanging strange words in the breeze, words I did not remember from Galatians: *Preeminence. Edification. Dispensational.* Big words. Coffee-table words. In stark contrast to the most common words of my profession: *buy, sell, hold,* and *oops.*

I tried not to listen, but the debate raged on, the stretch limousines of spiritual lingo now spewing from Stanley's larynx. His buddies attempted to contribute from their own stockpile of verbosity, but Stanley talked right over them. There was no escaping the wordy onslaught. I was Custer, with sunblock, lying on a sunny beach beside thirteen glistening women.

I considered my options: I could rise from the sand and say, "I'm going to help Steve with the sea-green paint," but Stanley would surely ask why we were painting. I could go back and eat breakfast with Ransom, but he'd just want to be alone with his wife. I could wade out in the ocean and battle the undertow, but Stanley would just follow me out there in his plaid Bermuda shorts, spewing the religious diatribe, and everyone knows that having to fight the undertow, the sunburn, and the religious diatribe in the same instant will ruin summer vacation in a heartbeat.

So with my head still buried and the spiritual debate growing ever deeper, I slowly raised a finger to stuff a corner of the tank top in my left ear.

"Pass the sunblock," said Nancy for the second time.

I turned over, scanned the beach, and saw short, redheaded Lydia and big Joe Caruzzi dragging Ransom's surfboard out to sea. Behind us, a volleyball game had broken out. From the language, I guessed the match was pagan versus Presbyterian. I almost dubbed it Budweiser versus Stanley, but Stanley and his four buddies rose to their feet, frowned at the interaction with beer drinkers, and walked proudly down the shore, dragging their jumbo words past the kite flyers, the squealing children, and a ruddy-cheeked man much too large for his choice of swimwear.

"It's time," said a female voice from the middle of the line.

Thirteen readers turned, all together, onto their stomachs, never looking up, still immersed in a diversity of windswept pages. But Number Eleven and Number Twelve must've forgotten I was only one towel away at the end of the line, napping, for surely they would not have knowingly discussed personal issues within earshot of a male.

"It's too far back to the house," said Number Eleven to Number Twelve. "Can't I just go in the ocean? You know the guys go out there all the time."

"Just go," said Number Twelve, flipping a page.

"What if the water's cold?" asked Eleven.

"Just go," said Twelve.

"What if a fish bites me while I'm—"

"Don't be silly, just go."

"Okay, but you'll come with me, won't you?"

"No," said Twelve. "Oh . . . all right, I gotta go, too." She marked her page with a broken sea oat and set the book in her chair.

It probably would've been my duty to warn Joe and Lydia of the impending taint of the lovely Atlantic, but they were sloshing through the breakers and dragging the surfboard to the beach when Eleven and Twelve, full bladders both, changed their minds and sprinted back toward a beach house.

"Scared 'em off, Jay?" asked Lydia, wrapping a towel around herself.

"Nah, but it's amazing what you overhear while lying on a beach towel."

Since our introduction at church, Lydia had been at the center of all things hospitable. This day was no different. "I brought sandwiches!" she announced, walking to her cooler and lifting the lid. There must have been thirty sandwiches in that cooler. She even fed the Numericals.

Turkey on wheat, heavy mustard, was my free lunch. The rummaging seagull returned, and I fed it the crust. I had just swallowed the last bite when Darcy and Allie, in a lime two-piece and peach two-piece respectively, strolled over the walkway. Down the wooden steps and between the dunes, they were a bright and welcome duet.

They carried three new floats—without the air—and Darcy asked if I wanted to blow one up.

"Here, marshmallow head," said Allie, tossing me a folded square of light-blue plastic.

A bit feminine, that light blue. "The orange one, please, Miss Kyle." And she agreed to swap. In midswap, her hand brushed mine, and a tingle went up my arm.

"Still couldn't find any flip-flops?" I asked, noticing their bare feet.

"Nothing to color coordinate with," said Darcy.

"She means they didn't have lime," said Allie, searching for a nozzle among the folds. "Myrtle's flip-flops are even gaudier than your orange float, Jay."

Halfway through blowing up the gaudy plastic floats, the three of us were ready to sprawl ourselves on the shore and beg for oxygen. I've never sniffed glue, but sitting there in my sandy olive shorts, I figured it couldn't be worse than blowing up floats.

And too bad for Steve having to paint, because Darcy had on an electric lime bikini, and surely a five-foot, eleven-inch blonde in a lime green bikini is a sight to behold, much preferable to white semiglossed mosquitoes stuck dead to a bedroom wall.

"Water's warmer than I thought," said Darcy. She had eased in to her waist.

"Told ya," said Allie, dunking herself.

Our flotilla launched in unison, and we drifted beyond the waves, lazy and aloof atop our orange, red, and blue plastic. The ocean was a waterbed, an aquatic massage passing slowly beneath, lifting us from head to toe in rolling repetition.

"Can you explain what Steve was doing with a gallon of paint?" asked Darcy. "We passed him on our way to the beach, and he was acting weird."

"You saw him with paint?" I countered, as if surprised.

"Yeah, why the paint?" demanded Allie, paddling around to face me.

I watched orange reflections tint my torso. "He had a little accident in our room. Nothing major."

"You're covering for him," said Her Limeness, contrasting with shiny red plastic.

"Yep, sounds like a cover-up to me," said Allie.

Scanning the shoreline, I watched a lemon yellow kite flutter and dive. Two kids looked up and pointed, waving plastic shovels as they gawked. The volleyball net did a weak imitation of a sail, and across the long line of beach chairs, the Numericals reclined at a fresh angle, each head hidden by a book.

"All I see are toes and books," said Darcy, backstroking. "What's the deal with all those books on dating? Maybe no one ever taught 'em how to flirt." She had a certain presence about her, a mix of Southern pride and rich-girl confidence. Much too independent for large group activities.

"Wonder where we'd end up if we just closed our eyes and drifted for an hour," said Allie, talking to the heavens. Her suggestion had a strange, ambiguous appeal, falling somewhere between adventuresome and perilous.

I dismissed perilous and agreed to do it. "Only one way to find out, Captain Kyle."

"Not me," said Darcy, her lengthy legs straddling her float. "I heard there were sharks out in the deep water."

"Chicken," said Allie, flicking water at her friend.

Darcy flinched. "I am not chicken."

"Are too."

"Am not."

Allie pleaded with her. "You risk your life driving like a maniac in your four-wheeled monstrosity but won't even go drifting for fear of sharks. How sad."

"Wise women choose their danger carefully," said Darcy.

"Doubt any sharks would come this close to shore," I offered as salt water stung the cut on the back of my thumb.

"I'm staying in shallow water, Jay," said Darcy. "No argument." And she kicked her float toward shore.

Whether she really feared a shark or was just allowing me an opportunity, I had to give Darcy high marks for her tact. And I had to be curious as to why they hadn't bought a fourth float.

Hooking my foot through a loop on the side of Allie's light-blue vessel, I heard her giggle, like she was in on some big secret. We agreed not to talk but to just close our eyes and drift.

And drift we did. A slow, rolling, Memorial Day weekend drift.

"No peeking," she said.

"Yeah, no peeking."

Time seemed to bob along behind us, loitering in the current. My first peek revealed our position—a long angle from where we'd started but only a bit farther out. My second peek revealed her right hand hanging limp across her forehead, her left autographing the sea.

Before moving to Carolina, I'd never even seen the Atlantic. Now I was floating in it beside a missionary girl, and somehow this made me smile.

Closing my eyes again, I licked a salty drop from my lip and felt the rolling massage beneath us, timid waves warm and buttery, pressing and caressing in the ceaseless cycle of tides.

7

Two miles north of our friends, we sat exhausted on a deserted beach, Allie saying the deserted beach was like Jesus, a refuge from death. I wasn't sure what she meant, but death had definitely raised its periscope.

Just two hours earlier, after my fourth peek, the image of her had stayed burned on the inside of my eyelids: peach-colored bikini against a glowing tan, and brunette hair spilling over a light blue float. The rays did not seem to tan her as much as exude from her. I thought that if there were any more sharks cruising down there, maybe they'd think her a mermaid and leave us be.

I began to hum.

"Shh," she said, gently kicking her feet. And we continued to drift.

Carried along with the current—my foot still hooked in the loop—I refused to peek, sing, or hum anymore. Instead, my mind wandered off great distances, to possible landfalls of nautical surprise—Caribbean isles with pristine beaches and waters of clear aqua, where natives with cool Jamaican accents would greet us with broad grins and tall glasses of coconut concoction; or Key West, where a weathered man with a weathered guitar would throw out a line, pull us to his dock, and serenade us with ballads of tropical leisure; or the breezy Copacabana, to be welcomed by Lola, that showgirl with yellow feathers in her hair and a dress cut down to there. Or if we caught the Gulf Stream tides just right, maybe we could pull a reverse Columbus and cross the great Atlantic till we reached the

Mediterranean, then over to Spain where Spaniards lounged graceful and cosmopolitan on the sun-drenched shores of Barcelona.

A splash in the face woke me from my dream.

"Look how far we've drifted!" she said, raising her head to stare. "There aren't any more houses on the beach."

"Sorry, but you said . . ."

"I know, but can we paddle that far?"

We stroked into a firm current but gained little. Bravery and panic duked it out inside my head, one whispering to impress the girl, the other hinting at watery graves. I dismissed them both when I spotted a sliver of sand, even farther out to sea but lying directly in our path. "We'll run into that sandbar if we keep floating east."

"Then let's keep floating east," she said, now on her stomach and kicking her feet.

Far to our left, the last oceanfront house bobbed up and down, up and down. Exhausted, we stopped fighting the current, but with its help drifted farther out, right into the shallows of the sandy sliver.

We canoed our flimsy floats on the bank. "Two handfuls of wet sand and maybe they won't blow away," she said, scooping down past her wrists.

And two handfuls it was, plus one extra scoop from me to her light blue feminine float, just to be gentlemanly.

"Tired?" I asked.

"I'll make it," she said, dunking her hands before wiping wet hair from her eyes.

We hiked across our private sandbar to admire the refuge: the soggy fragments of driftwood, the stringy clumps of kelp, all peppered with a random collection of shells left drying in the midday heat.

A lone blue crab looked surprised to see us, and it scurried to safety.

"Is this low tide?" she inquired, gazing back across the bar.

"Doubt it. But I'm from Dallas, so . . ."

"You wanna know why I love doing mission work in the jungles of Ecuador?" She seemed rejuvenated now, relishing her new status as castaway.

"I've been wondering."

She turned her back and started searching for something. "Because it feels like this sandbar, remote and unspoiled."

And in the center of our moist, remote sliver, Allie Kyle grabbed a splinter of driftwood and began carving words in the sand. She backed up as she wrote, bent over and oblivious to me, the ocean, and everything else.

"Is this a message for God?" I asked, backpedaling to follow along.

"Nope. I just enjoy writing poems in the sand."

"I bet he reads it anyway."

The letters were huge, and from the first verse to the last, her effort covered thirty feet. At one point she stopped and frowned, rubbed out a line with her foot, and revised it. Finally satisfied, she dropped her stick and proceeded to dot all the *i*'s with seashells. Then, with hands on hips and only a hint of pride, she asked me what I thought.

"What's the title of it?" I asked, impressed with the style of this missionary poet, this brown-eyed, food-chucking missionary poet.

"'Home on Furlough,'" she said, using her toe to initial her work. "I wrote it yesterday on the drive down. Lime convertibles inspire me . . . especially at ninety miles per hour."

I walked back to the far end of the sandbar to the first stanza and backpedaled again.

How shallow their roots
They chase only careers
These neighbors seem date-stamped
Like cartons of milk.

Comparative glances
Disingenuous smiles
Across my azaleas
Prosperity winks.

Blue pools of money
Gurgling with wealth

71

But men's souls are adrift
And so many lack roots.

Now furlough is over
My house is memoir
Latino air tickles
What is Spanish for tickle?

Ecuadorian children
South American streams
My roots grow like kudzu
Thru God's luscious jungle.

Wet sand clung to her hands and knees. Her smile was neither proud nor sexy but the smile of contentment. Out there on that sandbar, remote and unspoiled, she seemed half woman, half child. From ten feet away, I could do nothing but smile back.

"So, you like it?" she asked, wiping wet grains from her hands.

"Not bad, but America might roll your yard."

"My yard is a long ways away."

Standing on our sandy seclusion, a long ways from shore, I felt a load of insecurity welling up. "There's a nonmaterialistic bent to your words, Miss Kyle. Do you have, um, a general disregard for stockbrokers?"

She gazed out across the waves before answering. "Not in general; there's opportunity to bless others in any occupation. But I see lots of greed and selfishness back home. It's like a microcosm of the whole country."

"It's not that bad."

"Ha! It may be worse."

I walked between her third and fourth stanza. "So, can missionaries date nonmissionaries?"

"Will you stick to the subject?" she protested, grabbing one last shell to dot *luscious*.

72

"Okay, Allie, if the U.S. gave all its money to a poor country, don't you think they'd end up just like us—devout, free-spending consumers?"

She brushed sand from her knees. "I don't think so. The difference is that we're raised in it, we expect it, and we wallow in it. A people who have learned to value humanity over wealth would be much slower to change."

"You really believe that?"

"Jay, America is so jaded from prosperity that it boggles the mind . . . and my mind is not easily boggled."

I laughed at her turn of phrase. "Can I borrow your pen to write my own verse?"

"Can't wait to read this," she said, handing me her driftwood stick.

I peeled off a splinter to gain a sharper point. "First, a confession—my rhymes are usually limited to parodies of Dr. Seuss, though they only seem to pop up in pressure-packed situations."

"Your attempt to match my poetry isn't cause for pressure?"

"Nah, no problem."

At the far edge of the sandbar, with water lapping over my toes, I began to carve.

"What's this called?" she asked.

I had to pause to think of a title. She stood beside me with arms crossed, her head cocked to one side.

"'Immediacy,'" I replied.

> The tide is turning
> The current be strong
> Let's resume paddling
> Or we'll drown in God's luscious ocean.
> And P.S. Can missionaries date nonmissionaries?

"Don't quit your day job," she said, stepping on my first line. She used her toe to scrawl a big X through my feeble effort but made no attempt to answer the P.S. Such matters would have to wait, for the current really did be strong.

With her first verse melting, we launched from the sandbar, separated from the beach by waves both taller and grumpier than when we had arrived.

"I'm thirsty," she said. And we bobbed over the next crest.

Invisible sand scratched my stomach; tiny grains wedged between flesh and float.

"Useless," said Allie, slapping at the water in frustration. "We aren't gaining any ground . . . I mean water." Another slap. "Our dumb idea."

"Our idea? You suggested this blind flotilla."

"Okay, my dumb idea. But you agreed to it."

"You're just tired," I said. "Grab hold of the back of my float, and I'll get us in."

Getting us in took longer than I'd thought. After fifteen minutes of paddling, we were drifting farther north on flimsy floats. Then the waves got bigger, man was I thirsty, the sun scorching, arms aching, and it looked like a deserted beach shrunk there on the shore, and wow, we really *were* gonna visit Barcelona.

"Are you still paddling?" she asked from behind me, gripping my ankles like a lifeline.

"I need to rest a minute." The condos of a distant beach were visible again, and I remembered seeing a long pier somewhere. *Where are you, long pier?*

"You can't rest," she said, tugging my foot.

"Maybe the current will switch, and we'll get pushed in."

"I'll be a fried old maid by then." Her hands forced blood to my toes.

"Okay, I'm paddling."

"You paddle and I'll pray."

"Pray harder, Allie."

"Shh, you're messin' up my prayer."

"Sorry," I said, deciding to make any progress I could, toward any piece of accessible dry land, forgetting where we'd launched from and willing to

74

settle for a buoy, a marina, even the Outer Banks of North Carolina, which was now a distinct possibility considering the angle of our drift.

Far in the distance, a jet ski was heading in the opposite direction, bouncing over breakers, salt spray exploding with each descent. I doubted anyone could see us, and if we'd had a flare gun, I would not have been proud—I would have shot it and shot it high and sworn never but never to drift blind ever again.

"Jay," said Allie, her voice cracking, "I'm getting scared."

"Me too."

"You aren't supposed to say that."

But the current was steadfast, unyielding. My mouth was dry, and as far as I knew, three days and we'd wash up in Africa.

"Maybe someone will see us," she said.

"Yeah, maybe. Kick your feet." With energy depleting, I pictured us as salmon leaping against rapids.

We continued to drift and paddle, paddle and drift, past a stretch of undeveloped oceanfront, its high dunes staring back, long whiskers of sea oats waving in the wind.

"Aren't we getting closer?" she asked, her voice weakening.

"Maybe a little."

We were floating off to Barcelona, and like corks in a river, we toiled against a stronger will. And then she started praying again.

I stopped paddling and turned to face her. "Allie, I sure hope that does us some good."

She whispered a soft amen and said, "Surely someone saw us out here."

"Yeah, surely," I said, licking yet another salty drop.

A curious gull swept down, saw we had no food to offer, and banked toward land. For the first time in my life, I wished that I was just a dumb bird with the gift of flight. Or a dumb fish with the gift of swim.

"When's the last time *you* prayed, Jay?" she asked, still clutching my ankles.

"Three seconds ago."

"What if we really were to drown?"

"I wouldn't have to worry about my career anymore."

"I mean, are you prepared to die?"

"Not at twenty-seven, I'm not."

"That's not what I meant."

"I think the current is shifting."

"We need to talk."

I had a clue what she meant, knew that she was only being true to her vocation. Oddly, though, I was thinking about my own job—how some people lose their jobs to layoffs, or bad economies, or poor performance. But me, I'd lose mine to the cruel tides of the Gulf Stream. My career would be gurgles; gurgles, my career.

Corny as it sounds, I decided then and there to be a nicer person if we were allowed to live.

Five minutes later we were allowed to live.

I was making hard strokes through the ocean when she jerked my left foot.

"I hear a motor," she said.

"Yeah, I hear it, too."

A loud voice from a megaphone ricocheted across the waves. "BEACH PATROL. STOP PADDLING AND WE'LL PULL UP BESIDE YOU."

"Thank God," she said.

"Great praying."

She sat up on her float and grinned. "My pleasure."

The two men on the yellow jet ski had official-looking yellow shirts that read "Beach Patrol" in big black letters. The squatty one—the rider— motioned for us to grab hold of a towrope. He threw. We caught. The nylon rope had twin rubber handles split off at the end, and between two rolling waves, Allie grabbed the starboard handle with both hands. I settled for port.

"We'll go slow," said the driver. "You two gotta watch those currents a lot closer. A man disappeared off that sandbar last year."

"But we were gonna visit Key West," I countered, salt spray sloshing across my face.

"Sir, you would've been fish food by nightfall."

76

Bouncing along the waves, we made the request to be dropped off at the deserted beach, well out of sight of our friends.

"Yeah, sure," yelled the driver, turning sharp toward shore. "We get similar requests on a daily basis. Nobody wants the embarrassment of getting towed in by Beach Patrol."

After stopping in the shallow breakers, the two men cautioned us, then warned us. We stood waist deep, nodding and saying yessir and thank you gentlemen, no, we're staying two miles down the beach, and yes, we'll try to be more careful.

Allie waded over and hugged the driver's neck. He blushed.

I was not about to hug either of 'em but did offer to send a cash reward.

"Fuggetabout it," said the rider. "The Patrol is in control."

I thought him an even worse poet than me, but considering the fact that he saved us, I wouldn't have cared if the young man had performed a rescue rap song, right there in the Carolina surf. They motored away, bright yellow bouncing across breakers, and I sent up a silent but sincere, *Thanks, God.*

"We were really dumb to do that," said Allie, who sat down in the sand and began searching for the nozzle on her float. She paused and looked up at me. "Really dumb to just float off and drift blind and not peek at least once to see where we were."

"Total morons," I said, spitting out the last remnant of seawater. "But I, uh . . . did peek."

She pulled wet strands of hair from her lips, then raised her palms skyward. "Heavens, Lord, he peeked but stayed silent!"

"Sorry."

"But you did like my poem?"

"Yes. But use paper next time."

Sitting on the shore of a deserted beach, salty and private, I sensed rolling waves of woozy passing through me. I felt, well . . . wooziferous.

I lay back on hard sand, spread-eagled. "Allie?"

"Yes, Jay?"

"I feel wooziferous."

"Me too," she said, acting dizzy as she struggled with the nozzle. "I'm a lava lamp, without the lamp."

What remained now was just a long walk back on the shore, so we proceeded to squeeze and squash the air from our floats. Very stubborn, float air. It likes to stick around, like in-laws after a good dessert.

Allie tried a primitive, foot-stomping method; I preferred the bear hug. But as I leaned over to squeeze the life from my orange plastic, she threw a mud ball.

I did not see it. Only felt it.

"Jay?"

"Yes, Allie?"

"You'll never make it as a Presbyterian."

I looked up from the nozzle, brushed mud from my rear. "And you, Miss Kyle, will never make it as a boat captain, what with that closed-eye navigation technique."

"Ha!"

I squeezed my float even harder. "And if you really do go back to South America, you had better travel by plane, else no one will ever hear the gospel."

"Double ha!" And she stomped her float for emphasis.

On the walk back down the beach, I tried to hold her hand, but she said, "You can hold this," and handed me her deflated gob of gaudy blue plastic.

We were still a long way from home, wading through ankle-deep surf, when she asked if we could stop to look for shells. "You don't mind?" she asked.

"Guess not," I replied, dropping our shriveled floats on the shore.

Authentic manhood probably precludes shell hunting. But like the need to look joyful on Sunday morning, one can always fake it.

Allie examined two shells, then discarded them both, jabbering all the while. "That jet-ski driver was nice . . . and kinda cute, too."

"He was a yellow-clad know-it-all . . . and his buddy stinks at poetry."

She turned to wash a shell in the surf. "I bet those two have to work on Sundays and rarely make it to church, and did you see that barracuda tattoo on his back, that was the ugliest thing ever, and, oh yeah, you shouldn't have offered to send reward money."

I tossed my ugly shells away. "And why not?"

"Because you never have to pay for grace."

I wasn't sure what she meant by that. And I was too proud to ask.

We continued combing the shore. Allie found a perfect sand dollar, plus two small starfish dried burnt-orange, left to perish by a previous tide. I found some cool-looking seaweed and a disposable lighter.

"Trade you my seaweed for your sand dollar."

She dunked her starfish and inspected the legs. "Jay, do you like the little Hershey's dark chocolates, the ones with the gold wrappers?"

"Yes," I said, now on my knees and sifting fragments. "They're my favorite."

She backed into the water and continued her search. "We could never get those down in Ecuador. That's the only thing that really stunk about being a missionary."

"That's it?"

"Well, that and dancing. I haven't been dancing in two years."

"You like the oldies? Disco stuff?"

"During high school I had a mirror ball in my room. My brother broke it."

"Too bad."

She continued to gather only perfect shells, discarding the flawed. "Yeah, too bad. Say, if I do go back down to Ecuador, could you pledge to send dark chocolates, too?"

"Sure. But for now, I'll trade you this lighter for one of your starfish."

She considered my offer, then considered her starfish, then turned and flung them, like pointed Frisbees, back into the sea.

8

Draped in the scent of sunblock and seawater, neither Nancy nor the Numericals had anything cold to drink. Warm Coke in a can was all that was left, and muscular Number Eight said we could finish hers if we really were that thirsty.

We really were that thirsty.

Warm Coke in a can, however, is the very definition of gross.

Allie wiped sand from the opening, spit out the first sip, and said, "Let's go over to the volleyball court and visit the Bud guys."

I followed close behind her, curious. "You're not gonna ask for—"

"Just follow me," she said, sand squeaking beneath her feet.

We walked over to those sunburned strangers, who seemed in high spirits. The flat-topped one—the one with the volleyball, a pair of binoculars, and four empty beer cans strewn around his cooler—said to go ahead and help ourselves. I was about to help myself when Allie grabbed my arm. "We just wanted some ice," she said to Bud Guy, sounding slightly apologetic.

"You sure?" he asked. He seemed quite generous.

"No," I said. "We're not sure."

"Yes, we are," said Allie, and she held out her hand.

"Suit yourself," he said, pulling the top from his cooler.

We settled for ice, and she thanked Bud Guy. But he only burped and said it must be quite embarrassing getting towed in by Beach Patrol on flimsy plastic floats.

We sucked on cubes and nodded our agreement.

Sitting atop a light-green beach blanket, Darcy waved us over, like she'd missed us.

"And just where have you two been?" she asked. She sat up, squeezed drops of sunblock on her feet, and waited for a response.

I said nothing. Allie turned to watch the seagulls.

"Oh, c'mon," pleaded Darcy, rubbing her left foot. "Where did y'all go?"

"On a slow, relaxing drift," I replied.

I could tell she didn't believe me.

Just then, Jamie Delaney walked over, redoubling her hair band as she approached. Jamie was so small that she barely dented the sand. She turned to wave at her husband—who was out taming the breakers—then said, "Okay, where have you two been?"

"On a long shell hunt," said Allie. Miss Missionary plopped down on the blanket with them and began explaining our adventure, complete with flailing arm gestures and a wide-eyed exaggeration of how far we'd drifted. I tried to toss in a few yeahs and a you-shoulda-been-there, but soon they were off on some poetic tangent, so I slipped away, content to stand at the shoreline and watch Ransom surf the big ones.

Except at Litchfield Beach, there are no big ones.

So I spent the next little while by myself, dawdling on the shore, absently tossing shells in the sea but actively thinking of fate. Or was it providence? And were those jet-ski guys sent by God and how could her prayers be answered in such a timely manner?

I could not decide. But she'd looked so calm out there. How does anyone stay calm in the midst of oceanic doom?

By late afternoon I was toweling off after another failed attempt at surfing. Ransom was the patient sort, but the lesson had ended badly. After my ninth fall, he had paddled out alone, looked back over his shoulder, and told me to stick to fishing.

Whether it was out of pity, or whether they wanted some manly detail about the closed-eye drift, the girls decided to invite me back to their beach blanket. But soon after I sat down, Allie stood and walked off—without even saying where she was going.

Ten minutes later she returned with more ice cubes and was immediately confronted by Jamie, asking what was going on with her and that generous Bud guy.

"Going on?" asked Allie, as if she'd been accused. "How is it that married women get to carry a license to probe?"

"Oh, just tell us the good parts," said Darcy, brushing a horsefly from her knee.

"Okay, then, I tried to tell him about Jesus," said Allie. "But he wasn't much interested. Kept saying he couldn't believe *some* church people would join him for a beer, but that others might object. Then he asked me if Jesus would drink a brew on the beach."

"Oh . . . well, what did you say?" asked Jamie.

"Told him I didn't know. Missionary school covered everything but that."

When house shadows reached the shoreline, Darcy rose to walk home. Allie helped her shake off the blanket and said that she, too, had endured enough beach for one afternoon.

Before leaving, however, she leaned over to whisper in my ear. "Enjoyed our blind drifting, Jay."

"Me too, Captain."

They trudged between the dunes and modestly wrapped towels around their waists, never breaking stride or conversation.

They had not been gone a minute when up the beach came Stanley and his plaid Bermuda shorts, followed closely by his entourage, the five of them sloshing through backwash, still debating, still arguing over their jumbo words.

Stanley strolled over behind the Numericals, removed his religious T-shirt, and posed a question. "Which of you ladies would like to rub sunblock on my back?"

Not a one of the thirteen looked up.

A strange silence ensued, broken only by the rapid turning of pages, until finally Number Two with the raven hair peered over the top of Tolstoy and said, "Just do it yourself, please."

Dangerous looking, that Number Two.

Whiffs of fresh paint met me on the porch, and I entered our beach house to the sound of a roller swishing up and down a bedroom wall.

Steve appeared intent on painting the entire room. Tiny sea green droplets covered his arms, his feet, his stubble. Sea green apparently comes in many shades—none of which matched the original color—and the bedroom was only half finished when I stepped across the newspaper. "That's no way to get a tan."

He did not seem amused. "Grab a brush and do some trim, will ya?"

I started with the baseboards, the fumes growing stronger with each stroke of the brush. A warm wind blew through the window as Steve stood on his toes, rolling the far wall and whistling "Heartbreak Hotel." He turned to watch my progress. "Takes two coats to cover those white streaks," he warned.

I dipped my brush and said, "You really blasted those mosquitoes."

He shook his head and dunked his roller in the pan. "Any female interaction on the beach today?"

"Shoulda been there."

"Details, Jarvis."

"Maybe later. I need a shower . . . these fumes are killer."

Steve said I couldn't use our shower because his paint supplies were in there and he was using the tub to wash out the brushes.

"Use the shower underneath the house," he said, dipping his roller again.

So I grabbed a towel and headed for the stairs.

Beneath our beach house, white concrete felt cool against my bare feet. Wooden planks surrounded the shower; a balmy silence encircled the planks. As I took off my T-shirt, I was startled by an unexpected whoosh. Water heaved from the showerhead.

"Who's in there?" I asked.

"It's me," came a female voice rising above the spray. "My name's Rona."

I walked around the shower and saw a beach-soiled weightlifting magazine on the concrete. With that limited evidence, I deduced that she was,
in all likelihood, Number Eight. "Why, Rona, are you in a shower beneath
the men's house?"

"We have twelve girls in our own house . . . with only two bathrooms."

"Then you're impatient?"

"Those other girls take an hour to get ready. Just to go sit on the beach!"

"So I've heard."

"That's the only thing that really stinks about these beach trips. But
don't worry, I'm still wearing my swimsuit."

I put my T-shirt back on, leaned against the planks, and dug a fingernail
into a bar of Dial. "Were you one of the thirteen readers?"

"Yeah, I was in the middle, reading a relational book and that magazine
over there."

"Any sunburn?"

"A little. And you?"

"On my shoulders. I sorta got lost at sea."

Her shampoo bottle thudded on the floor. Her voice faded. "I heard
about that."

With my initials carved in soap, I pleaded with her. "Aren't you almost
done?"

"No, I just got here. Wanna go to dinner sometime?"

Oh, mercy. Why me. "Do you always take such initiative in asking men
for dates?"

"Sometimes. It's a strategy from the book."

"Does it work?"

"Occasionally. Gives me a sense of independence."

I sat on the concrete, my back still against the planks. "Independence
is a good thing."

"Most of the time. You think I'm crazy?"

"Maybe a little, but you're not alone."

"I'm not?"

"No. Darcy Yeager said she feels free and independent when she speeds."

Rona turned down the shower spray. "Is she the tall blonde with the lime Cadillac?"

"That would be her."

"She's snooty. Never speaks to me."

"She's not snooty."

"Yes, she is. She's so snooty the guys are afraid of her. You don't ever see her with any guys, do you?"

"Maybe she's secretive."

"I doubt it. I think she's snooty."

"Well, don't use all the hot water, Rona." I rose to my feet again.

"What about going to dinner?" she asked, her voice rising. "We could even go Dutch."

Shower spray pattered off the boards. I quickly pondered my options. Now *this* was pressure. Standing on cool concrete beneath a beach house, I tried to envision this future Dutch date. A date consisting of me, muscular Number Eight, and . . . the good doctor?

Disguised as a young waiter, Seuss approaches our table:

> Will this be one check or two?
> Will there be a sky of blue?
> Tell me, sir, one check or two?
> And are your friends as cheap as you?
>
> Would you Dutch it with a mouse?
> Would you Dutch it in your house?
> Would you Dutch an ounce of Spam?
> I am Dutch. Dutch Jay I am!

Oh, man, Jarvis, too long in the sun.

After sidestepping Rona's proposition, I postponed my shower, walked slowly up the porch stairs, and went back inside to lay down on our coral-print living-room sofa.

From the bedroom came the steady swish of a paint roller. I could've been more help to Brother Steve, but the afternoon had drained me.

I was nearly asleep when Stanley opened the front door, kicked off his sandals, and headed for the kitchen. He began rummaging through the fridge.

"Wanna Coke, Jay?"

I buried my head in a pillow and mumbled, "No thanks, Stanley."

"We were glad Beach Patrol found you two."

I sat up to peer over the sofa. "And just how did you know about that?"

He popped the tab of his drink and leaned against the wall. "I was the one who called 'em. On my cell phone. It was looking a bit dicey out there."

"Oh . . ."

Humbled, I allowed faint whiffs of sea green latex to lull me off, lull me further, and further still, as he left me there alone, alone on a beach house sofa beneath the swirling breeze of a rusty ceiling fan.

9

After showering with the paint brushes, Ransom leaned over the sink and tried not to drool on his obnoxious, yellow Hawaiian shirt. "I got a hot date with my wife," he said, rinsing his toothbrush. "We could only stay single for one night."

"Now we really hate your guts," said Steve. He was struggling to snap the top button of his shorts. I felt sorry for those shorts.

"Finish cleaning the shower, dude," Ransom said. "Soles of my feet are green."

He raised a foot for proof; I raised mine to give witness. We matched.

"You're right . . . sea green."

Steve pulled a fresh shirt over his head, grabbed his wallet off the dresser. "Stop the complaining and wear socks."

I threaded my leather belt through khaki cutoffs. I had little energy but lots of appetite. "Another dinner reservation for fifty?" I asked.

"Maybe not," said Steve. "Just need to gather a few more rebels."

Rebels gathered, we watched Stanley lead the convoy out of Litchfield Beach. We'd be the caboose. Squeezed into the backseat of the Jeep, Lydia, Allie, and Joe bobbed their heads to the sounds of coastal radio.

The first nine cars turned north, but we turned south and headed for the shrimp docks of Georgetown, ten miles away.

Antebellum homes girded the waterfront of the port city, their wraparound porches hinting at life slow and gracious. The locals actually waved.

Past the gracious and the antebellum, we approached the waterfront on a graveled driveway announcing our arrival with snaps and pops. Through the windshield, we watched a dockhand washing down the deck of a shrimp boat.

"How many pounds do we want?" asked Steve, unhitching his seat belt.

"Two," said Lydia.

"Three," countered Allie.

"Five," said Joe.

The weathered shack had hand-painted signs reading FRESH SEAFOOD, though the smell drifting past our noses was anything but fresh.

"That's the local paper mill," said Lydia as she and Allie hurried inside.

"Oh, what fragrant aroma," mumbled Steve, holding the door and sniffing the air.

The shack's bare wooden walls had a damp, crusty look to them. A small chalkboard hung crooked behind the counter, proclaiming the day's specials in stilted blue handwriting.

"I'll have you know these shrimp were swimming just two hours ago," said the old man behind the counter. "And that'll be just five bucks a pound for you young people."

"What a bargain. We'll take four pounds," said Joe, handing him our cash. "And you keep the change, sir."

The old guy stuffed the cash in his pocket, sat down in a wicker chair, and propped his feet on a cooler. On the way out, we paused to check his inventory. Atop icy mounds, various sea creatures lay frozen and priced.

"Oh, wow," said Allie, leaning in for a closer look. "Look at the eyes on that dead flounder. Poor thing needs plastic surgery."

On the short ride back to Litchfield—with the wind whipping through our crowded Jeep and the girls trying to car-dance to the beach music—I was sifting through Bud Guy's question, the one about Jesus and a brew on the beach. I pondered this question for a couple miles, then turned and faced the backseat to solicit group opinion.

Steve weaved into the fast lane and said, "I think he would."

"Gotta disagree," said Lydia. "Not his style."

"Sure he would," Joe protested, holding our plastic sack of shrimp, his big head wedged against the Jeep's roll bar. "He just wouldn't make a fuss over it."

"Just depends," said Allie, her dark bangs all windblown and happy. "If there were an alcoholic around, he'd decline. But if he'd been adrift on a gaudy plastic float for hours without a sip of water, then certainly." And her foot jolted my seat.

Seaspray Drive felt warm and serene as Steve parked the Jeep on our crushed-shell driveway. I got out and leaned the seat down for the girls.

"*Gracias*," they said, stepping carefully across the shells.

Following them up the stairs to a beach house kitchen, I paused to replay this first full day of my very first churchy beach trip, wondering if today was the highlight, or merely the prologue.

Through the kitchen window, I watched summer's sun melting toward the Pacific. I boiled our four pounds of shrimp, Joe covered them with ice, and Lydia suggested we go eat on the beach.

"But there's a baseball game on," Steve protested, spreading real butter across fake Italian bread.

"There's always a baseball game on," said Lydia, digging through the fridge. "In fact, I think they play baseball twelve months out of the year now. Game after game after game, then fly somewhere else for even more games, then back home to play the same team they just visited, only with different uniforms, which means they sweat too much, so no wonder those batters are always fidgety."

"I resent that synopsis," said Joe, sampling the dinner. "And besides, we're only arranging everything in its proper place before swinging."

"Women don't have that problem," said Lydia.

Steve stared blankly at the bread for a moment, then said, "Duh."

"Where do baseball players learn words like *synopsis*?" asked Allie. She grabbed an armful of canned drinks and backpedaled toward the front door.

"In a dictionary," said Joe. "We have dictionaries on the team bus to improve our vocabulary. In case we get interviewed."

"Any Bibles on that bus?" she asked.

"Driver always brings two Bibles, six dictionaries."

I grabbed the tartar sauce off the counter, the fake Italian bread from the stove. Allie held the door with her foot. "You coming, Mr. Cole?"

"Just to eat," said Steve. "Then Joe and I are watching the rest of this game on TV . . . to hear all the great vocabulary."

We strolled toward the beach, dinner in tow, and Lydia said what a shame it was for a baseball team to have the dictionaries outnumber the Bibles, especially after the batters embarrass themselves on national TV. Then Joe said he'd heard enough of this ignorance and maybe we could finish our seafood song since Stanley wasn't around to rudely interrupt.

"Yeah," said Lydia. "Why did Stanley rudely interrupt?"

"Maybe he prefers hymns," I offered in slight defense of Stanley, which felt a bit weird. But the guy *did* call Beach Patrol.

Allie said the canned drinks were freezing her arms and that the lobster song was just for lobsters, though maybe there was a shorter tune dedicated solely to shrimp, but who cared since it was no fun without a cook in a floppy white hat, and besides, Lydia couldn't hold a note anyway.

"Can too," said Lydia, elbowing her friend.

"You screech," said Allie.

"I do not screech."

"Then you bellow."

"I do not bellow."

"The lobster was glad to be put out of his misery."

"Jay told me the lobster went to hell."

As we crossed the oceanfront road, Steve shuffled up beside me and whispered that he thought there was a special purgatory just for crustaceans.

Yet another issue I'd never stopped to ponder.

At the base of a darkened sand dune, we sat cross-legged on beach towels, watching a rising tide lag the previous night by an hour, the waves pounding out slow and steady rhythms against the shore. Nature's percussion.

Warm scents of seafood trailed the breeze, and our smallish gathering seemed wearied, lazy even.

"No one asked a blessing," said Lydia, dunking her shrimp in cocktail sauce.

"Yea God, boo devil," said Steve, quickly peeling his shrimp to keep up with Joe.

"How eloquent," said Allie. She shut her eyes, in no hurry to finish her own return of thanks.

Briefly, I tried to imitate her. But I had only the form, not the substance. Her head was bowed so low that her hair brushed her towel. The terry cloth was a deep yellow, with loopy, red Spanish words flowing end to end.

I thought it a verse—and would've asked about the words—but figured I should learn a proper English blessing before delving into Spanish Scriptures.

"What happened to Darcy?" asked Steve, refilling his plate.

"Got herself a tummy ache," said Allie, not looking up from her meal. "After we came in from the beach today, Darcy ate a whole bag of Brussels Mint cookies. She's sitting up in our crow's nest, silent and pale."

"Poor thing," said Lydia. "Those cookies are addictive."

In a moment, Joe inhaled the balance of his shrimp, then rose to his feet. Over his shoulder he waved bye, saying he was leaving to watch his beloved Cubs.

"Baseball over coastal sunsets," said Allie, watching Joe depart. "How pitiful."

Minutes later, Steve followed suit. "I may go meet the crew in Myrtle Beach," he said, brushing sand from his legs. He seemed bored with us. "Anybody else wanna go?"

"No thanks," I said.

"I try to avoid concrete jungles," Allie added, her missionary fingers expertly prying shell from meat. Oddly, she peeled five at a time before eating.

I had no such patience.

With only the three of us left on the shore, she and Lydia lay back on their beach towels and, with hands behind their heads, suggested a nap.

"Can't believe I ate that much," said Lydia, turning to dump the peels in a shallow hole. "I'm gonna pop." She covered the peels with sand and kicked off her sandals.

Needing a subtle way to get her to leave me and Allie alone, I came up with an indirect approach. "There's some Pepto-Bismol back at our beach house."

She took a moment to consider my offer, then said, "No thanks, Jay. Might be a can of Krylon in disguise. I'm dozing off."

"Me too," said Allie, folding an arm across her forehead.

And no one spoke another word. Only the lazy tumbling of waves and sporadic squawking of gulls to coax our slumber. *Here, slumber.*

A dune blocked the breeze, a jet flashed the sky, and I thought perhaps someday I'd retire here; buy a boat, catch my lunch, stay tan in winter.

I lapsed off to recurring thoughts of nautical surprise and sandbar poetry, slowly reliving the wavy leftovers from our afternoon drift, my entire body now back in rolling repetition even though I lay motionless on dry sand.

I'm a Slinky, with skin.

With the tide drawing ever closer, my eyes opened to a brilliant silver moon, stars more numerous than Myrtle's billboards, and females in the midst of another talk.

"Do you think the universe really never stops expanding?" asked Lydia, wide awake and sitting cross-legged again.

"If God has no reason to conserve, then why not?" said Allie, tracing the Big Dipper with her finger.

"Never thought of it like that," I mumbled, only half conscious.

"Welcome back."

Low, lumbering waves hissed and sparkled. "What'd I miss about the universe?"

"Well, I think we'll only be able to *see* new galaxies from heaven," said Lydia, staring up at the stars. "But Allie thinks we'll be able to play there."

I sat up, unfamiliar with such deep, celestial thought. "Really, Miss Kyle?"

"Yep," she said, now propped on her elbows. "I think we'll be able to float around in the Milky Way and hide behind Neptune or Pluto or Mercury. And sometimes Jesus will join us, and he'll grab Saturn and spin it on the tip of his finger like a basketball."

"That's, um, interesting. Any more drinks?" I asked.

She thumped her empty can and shook her head. "Steve took the last one when he left."

I needed something cold. "Can I get you girls a refill?"

"Please," said Lydia.

"Fillerup," said Allie.

I walked barefoot between the dunes, feeling the warm sand sink between my toes, then cooler grains firm below the surface. A timid wind rattled a palm tree as I neared the walkway, where dozens of empty Bud cans overflowed from a trash receptacle.

At our street, I put on my sandals before checking my watch: 12:23 A.M. Seaspray Drive was now calm and composed, only the crickets to dub over a balmy backbeat of crashing surf. On our driveway, the shells crunched beneath my sandals, so I detoured around the Jeep and through the yard. The house was dark. And not a sound now other than the crickets.

I was nearly to the porch stairs when the first flash appeared. It couldn't be lightning, not on a night that clear. One more flash, two more, and a fourth, each one lacking thunder. Another flash. Then another. Still no thunder.

Confused, I backpedaled into the yard and looked skyward. Only stars. Then another flash. I heard a squeak and glanced over to the roof. A male figure, looking very much like Steve Cole, stood in our crow's nest with a flashlight. He was leaning against the rail, signaling.

Two houses over, up in the female crow's nest, she flashed return signals. It was too dark to tell who it was, so I took a few steps toward the road for a better view, peeked around a palm tree, and there she was, forty feet in the air, tall and blonde.

I knew it, or at least *suspected*.

No time to snicker, because here he came down the skinny stairs, taking slow, purposeful steps, like a burglar. I ducked behind his Jeep.

The screen door closed, and I could hear him crossing the crushed shells of our driveway. I fought the snorts, a fresh snort trying to burst through my nose, great pressure on the roof of my mouth.

I felt like a spy, but this was too good.

They met at the road, two houses over.

I was back behind the tree.

A quick peck from him to her, then a second one, longer, from her to him. Silhouetted against a streetlight, they walked off down the road, fingers interlocked and swinging their arms.

Quietly, I tiptoed up the stairs and across our screened porch. In the living room, five men were asleep on the floor. I stepped gingerly between Stanley and his verbiage, opened the fridge real slow so the seal on the door wouldn't make that reverse sucking sound, and found three canned drinks behind the lettuce. Two colas and a grape.

The front door closed without a creak, and I was through the yard again and down our street. No breeze, no lights, just the crickets as I made the turn toward the beach.

Ahead of me, a gold sedan pulled alongside the oceanfront road. I was a half block away and could barely make out the white lettering across the rear window: "Just Married."

That really stunk. Romance was busting out all over Litchfield Beach, and I was serving refreshments.

Both the bride and groom exited the car through the passenger door. They were middle-aged and still in formal clothes, laughing and giddy and barefooted. He tossed his jacket in the car, she pulled a clip from her hair, and they strolled arm in arm across the wooden walkway. I slowed my pace to give privacy. When I stepped up on the boards, they were already slow dancing in the surf. I figured he was humming in her ear. Suddenly grabbing hands, they ran north past the last oceanfront house—wedded bliss racing toward a deserted beach.

Watching them run made me feel like an intruder, so I turned the opposite way and did not look back.

To the south, Allie and Lydia had pulled all three beach towels back between the dunes as the tide continued its ascent. They sat face-to-face, animated and expressive, absorbed in the giggly chatter of young women.

I felt like sitting there on the wooden steps for a minute, to clear my head of all the love breaking loose that night.

That night for rooftop rendezvous.

For incognito Presbyterian romance.

For barefoot brides and grooms to slow dance in the surf.

And me toting two colas and a grape.

"Come over here and join us, Jay," said Lydia. "We're having 'the talk.'"

The moon was hiding behind a cloud, further dimming the girls, the shoreline, and our three cans of carbonation. Seawater inched up the sand as I plopped down on my towel, each wave less fatigued than its predecessor. I asked what drinks they preferred, and Allie said she'd take the grape. I wanted the grape.

"What talk?" I asked.

"You know," said Allie. "What guys look for, what girls look for."

Our dune-girdled niche of beach was now dark and serene enough to host such discussion, so I offered the first opinion. "I thought maybe we counted on there being only one person, and they've just been well hid."

"Don't believe that," said Lydia, opening her cola. "If I stay in South Carolina, I could meet somebody. Or if I were to move to Idaho, I could meet somebody else. But if I married either one, that one would be the right one."

"Well said," Allie offered, taking a swig of grape. "But the right one has to prove he's the right one."

"And just how does a dashing bachelor go about this proof?" I inquired.

A brief pause. They glanced at each other as if the talk had turned serious. In the silence, we reclined on our towels, hands behind our heads, looking skyward before any of us spoke. I saw the Little Dipper and the flashing lights of another jet.

"He has to treat you like a precious gem," said Allie, leaning into a cushion of sand. "But he needs to be in a real relationship with God first."

95

"A little more on the precious gem thing, please."

"All that opening of doors and bringing of flowers is a given," said Lydia, talking to the heavens. "A guy's momma shoulda taught 'im that."

"At least that," said Allie.

"Birthdays and anniversaries seared into his brain," said Lydia.

"That too," said Allie.

Lydia never took a breath. "Without even asking, he should know if I'm happy or sad or somewhere in between."

"Yeah," said Allie. "Also that."

"And none of those yes-men who agree with everything, like if a girl says she loves moldy cheese and the guy says he loves moldy cheese, too. We don't need that."

"Definitely don't need that," said Allie.

"And no calling us at 11:00 P.M. on Thursday, requesting a date for Friday."

"That wouldn't be courteous," said Allie.

"And if you want to skimp on something, skimp on the price of your lawnmower or your golf clubs, or sit in the cheap seats at the ball games. But don't skimp on us."

"That's a fact," said Allie.

"And after a nice evening, call us the next day and tell us we're special."

"That'd be nice," said Allie.

"And if we go to the same church and then break up, don't sit next to us during the Sunday morning service and ask to share a hymnal."

"Been there, done that," said Allie. "Yuck."

"But if we get back together, make it clear that we girls can order whatever meal we want, since the price of steak versus meatloaf pales in comparison to a lifetime of love and devotion."

"Sums that up," said Allie.

"And another thing," Lydia added. "He should never, on a date or any other social occasion, let us get into situations that might be even slightly perceived as compromising."

Allie nodded. "That's good stuff, Lydia," she said. "You should write a book . . . and I agree, not even a hint of compromise."

96

I needed help, but my two roommates were scattered. Ransom, the one-night pseudo-single, was out on a hot date with his wife, while unshaven Steve was exchanging romantic Morse code from a crow's nest with a five-foot, eleven-inch blonde.

Not fair. Not the way to treat the new guy.

I felt like the victim of some convoluted practical joke—one that left me defenseless at the base of a sand dune, defenseless against a short redhead who would surely publish books on dating etiquette, and a missionary who threw food at strangers.

I wanted to defend the brotherhood against that female ambush, but I could not do it alone. Could not defend the forgetting of flowers and the slightest hint of compromise.

However, for the sake of the gender, I would give it a shot. "Can I speak up for the men?"

"No!" said Lydia. "Just take good notes and inform the entire male populace."

Talk over. I knew when to quit.

Time lingered in the darkness, and we remained with hands behind heads, staring up at night sky as the tide, only steps away, exhausted itself.

The Atlantic now stretched, like my psyche, for all its worth.

10

I woke to a kick on my shin. It was Sunday, and my hair felt as though someone had covered it with sand.

"Ouch!" I said. Someone stood over me, kicking again.

"Wake up!" she said. "This is gonna look bad."

"Huh?" My eyes wouldn't focus.

"Jay, it's 6:05," she said. She sounded flustered.

It took me a moment to gather my thoughts, to realize that waves were lapping lazily against the shore.

Still drowsy, I propped myself on my elbows. "What happened to Lydia?"

Allie stood between me and the lazily lapping waves. "Who cares about Lydia! She probably walked home in the wee hours and left us out here alone. I can't believe we stayed on this beach all night. This is gonna look so bad."

"You said that already."

Shrimp peels had blown against my leg; sand had filled my pockets. Over the ocean, morning seemed to muddle between dark and light. Pink and orange hues melded together, the first slice of sun still below the horizon, preparing to beam across the Carolina coast and highlight our hint of compromise.

Allie tried to smile, but the smile quickly faded as her brown eyes turned serious, as though she wanted to say something but couldn't summon the sentence. She flapped her towel, raining more sand in my hair.

Awake now, I stood and gave a retaliatory flap. She started to laugh, but then stifled it. Instead, she looped her yellow towel around her neck and began trudging between the dunes, quickening her pace as if getting in at 6:15 would look better than 6:20. Her hair was tangled and matted, lightened just a touch by a weekend of sun and salt air. The native look.

I walked beside her—my own towel around my neck as we crossed the oceanfront road—and felt like apologizing, though I could not figure out why. We had merely fallen asleep.

She glanced over her shoulder at the sunrise, which was now a rich red, as if it were trying to blush right along with her.

"I know nothing happened," she said, gesturing spastically with her right arm. "You know nothing happened. And most importantly, God knows nothing happened."

"But our friends might be up and—"

"And it might be tolerated if it were just me and Lydia or all three of us or seven of us or if it was just girls. But you, you're just a visitor who . . . aww, this is gonna look bad."

I stopped in the road to brush sand from my legs. She kept going.

"So what are you saying, Allie . . . that rumors will fly?"

"They'll have a chat room dedicated to us by this afternoon."

I could hardly keep up with her stride. "That bad, eh?"

"Worse. I'm the daughter of an elder. I need to pray."

"Ouch."

"Shh. You're messing up my prayer."

"I got a sandspur."

"Shh."

With our sandy, matted hair and a strong sense of embarrassment, we made the turn onto Seaspray Drive. No lights on in the houses, no one in the crow's nests, just three gulls gliding quietly above the treetops.

Allie stopped in the road, a calculating look on her face. "Can't take the chance," she said, yanking the towel from around her neck. She wadded it in a ball to make a pillow, strode underneath her beach house, and climbed into the backseat of Lime Sherbet.

En route to my own house, I stopped in the road, shook the remaining sand from my purple towel, then reversed course. With a corner of the towel in each hand, I walked back beside the Caddy.

Her eyes were shut.

I spread my towel across her.

"G'night," she whispered.

"Good night, Allie."

I wanted to kiss her.

But I didn't, and she made that phony snoring sound as I walked quietly toward house number four.

I'll sneak into my beach house—that was my mind-set as I made my way around to the back deck, where I could peer into the lone window at the end of our freshly painted, sea green room. There was just enough daylight to see Ransom on the floor, still in his clothes, and Steve over on the corner bed, also sound asleep, his mouth wide open.

I checked the window. Locked.

Sliding glass door—also locked.

I'd have to try the front.

Imitating Steve's burglar steps, I crept up the stairs to the porch, peered through panes in the door, and saw clean-cut church men sleeping all about the living room. My hand felt for the doorknob, the knob turned, then I saw movement across the room.

Stanley was sitting against the wall, reading verses again. He did not see me.

I retreated down the steps, wincing with each squeak. A navy towel was draped over the stair rail, and someone had left a big black inner tube beneath the porch.

It would have to do. The heft of Stanley's jumbo words would surely burst the thing, but for me it would do.

100

Atop cool concrete beneath a beach house, I spread the towel over the tube. Then I plopped down and shut my eyes, my bottom submerged as if wedged into a black rubber commode.

Lydia's relational spiel clanged between my skull as I tried to process thought, gain perspective, but perspective would have to wait because I was headed for la-la land, right there inside an inner tube. And my snoring would not be phony.

Half an hour passed in my rubber bed. Could've been longer. But I would never recommend tube snoozing because it's very bouncy and weightless—and being single and sleeping alone is bad enough without funky, lopsided dreams of trampolines and golf on the moon.

With eyes still shut, I heard footsteps on the crushed shells. Birds chirped, and a female voice heralded morning.

"Jay?"

"Sleep well, Allie?"

"Nice bed," she said, taking a seat on the stairs.

"Thanks. How was the backseat?"

She'd brushed her hair, though sand still clung to her neck, her legs, her lovely thin ankles. Her khaki shorts were wrinkled, as was her yellow T-shirt. She frowned, rested her chin in her hands. "Beige vinyl is a bit warm. But I can't get up the nerve to go inside my house. The looks I'll get will be just awful."

"How awful?"

"Bad awful. I did speak to Darcy, though, and she understood the situation."

I struggled to rise from the tube. "I'd imagine Darcy to be very understanding. But what's she doing up so early?"

Allie looked confused. "She came outside to put a flashlight in her trunk. I can't figure out what she was doing with it."

"Maybe looking for shells in the dark last night?"

"Guess so." And she shrugged her shoulders as if to dismiss the topic.

I draped the navy towel back over the stair rail. "You hungry?"

101

"Sorta. They're having a Sunday morning service at our house in an hour," she said, standing now, trying to smooth a wrinkle from her shorts. "But I think . . . well, I'm not sure, but Darcy gave me her car keys."

"Then let's go get some breakfast."

She glanced down the street at her beach house, then up at our porch. "Okay, but you need to know that I always go to church on Sunday. Wherever I am, if there's a church nearby, I go. It's an unbreakable rule."

I slipped my sandals back on. "Just hope it's casual dress."

She dangled Darcy's keys from her finger. "I'll drive," she said.

And at 6:55 A.M. on the last Sunday in May, a missionary girl who woke embarrassed but innocent on Litchfield Beach drove me to breakfast in a lime green Cadillac convertible.

11

A diner on Highway 17 served us coffee in pastel cups and toasted English muffins on seashell plates. We covered the muffins with honey poured from little square packets. It was all we could afford, since our money sat in our rooms back at our houses. Allie had found eighty-seven cents and a five-dollar bill in Sherbet's glove compartment, compliments of Darcy, the rich girl who knew Morse code.

"Have you ever been to Australia, Jay?" asked Allie, yawning as she spoke.

"No . . . you?"

"No."

"But you want to go?"

"Yeah," she said, cutting her muffin in half. "There's a mission opportunity there, but I feel that if God sends me anywhere, it'll be back to Ecuador."

"Then go visit Australia."

"Not on my income. Not unless I get a windfall from Jehovah."

I signaled the waitress for a coffee refill, then dipped my finger in the honey. "You didn't like Ecuador?"

Allie had both hands around her coffee mug. She sipped it slowly and said, "I loved it. It's just that most missionaries tend to stay in one place for years and years, and I may not get to see all the places I want to see."

"You have time. You're what, twenty-five?"

"Twenty-six."

"Plenty of time left to see Australia."

"I hope so, because me and Darcy talked about going two years ago but her driving scares me so much that I'm afraid if we were in the Outback she'd wreck and no one would come by and we'd have to kill a kangaroo for food but since I just love the way they go hop hop hop if I went to the Outback I'd have to become a vegetarian first."

I licked honey from my finger. "They don't teach punctuation at missionary school, do they?"

"No. How about at stockbroker school?"

"Not there, either."

I went over to a newsstand in the diner and bought a local paper with our last two quarters so we could scan for churches. She looked over my shoulder to examine the list; I sniffed her hair and thought, *Please, anything but Pentecostal.* Because after Friday night with the white semiglossed mosquitoes, then last night tube-snoozing on black rubber, I was in no mood to whoop, holler, or dance before Jehovah.

"Do we have any change left for a tip?" she asked, watching our busy waitress rush to serve a neighboring table.

"Only twelve cents."

"That'll never do." She motioned for me to pick up my plate and cup. We walked our dirty dishes back to the kitchen and handed them to the dishwasher, a high school boy all sleepy looking, his arms covered in soap. With his hands in the bubbles, he looked at us with a curious smile.

"We're poor today," said Allie. "It's the least we could do."

"This is a first," said Soapy Dishwasher Boy.

"Have *you* ever been to Australia?" she asked, wiping her hands on her shorts.

"On dishwasher's pay? I can barely go to Wal-Mart."

A few miles down the highway, past the general stores selling hammocks and rockers, two cars turned left into the driveway of a whitewashed church building.

Baptist. Service began in ten minutes. I was still sleepy, and my spiritual interest was low as I pulled into the turn lane.

"It'll do?"

"It'll do," said Allie.

I parked Sherbet in a grass lot that contained, at most, twenty other cars. Morning dew glinted off the grass; seagulls circled the church. Down a path of flat stones, we walked between pink and red azaleas, then paused to brush the remaining sand from our legs and ankles.

"I feel grody," said Allie, tucking her hair behind her ears.

"Yeah, and my hair's all sticky."

The church was small and of a simple A-frame construction. As we approached the front steps, I saw a stack of bulletins atop a chair. Just help yourself.

An elderly couple stood in front of us. They lifted each other by the elbows, then reached the top step, breathing hard. "Like Methuselah after StairMaster," Allie whispered.

I motioned for her to go ahead of me. We picked up our bulletins and walked down worn hardwood floors, past eight rows of unpadded pews, and took a seat in the front.

I preferred the middle or the back, but Allie said the front pew had less distractions.

To our left, a bifocaled lady began playing the piano. The instrument was an old stand-up model, with chips and dents in the legs. She played the melody with a mechanized coordination, her whole body dipping into the chords as if recollecting details with a long-lost friend.

When she finished the song, the room went quiet and she sat at the end of our pew.

A side door opened. The preacher walked out to the podium, his wing tips clunking across the wood floor. His pale forehead contrasted against a tanned face and neck. He placed his Bible on the podium, looked out at the congregation of forty, and said, "Today's Scripture reading is—"

We made eye contact. I raised my left thumb in front of my chest. He cleared his throat, tried to restrain a grin, but could not do it and reached under the podium for a glass of water. Allie looked confused again.

"Today's Scripture reading is from the Book of Jonah," said the preacher. "Turn there with me."

I found Jonah in the pew Bible, to the west of Galatians, and checked my bulletin. Across the bottom it read:

Asbury Smoak, Pastor

He began his sermon immediately—no more hymns or memorized creeds, no offerings taken by men in dark suits. In fact, he was the only one in the room wearing a suit.

After reading through the first chapter of Jonah, Asbury explained how people too often have their own agendas, attempt to manipulate their circumstances, and wake up in their very own Tarshish. This keeps God extremely busy undoing things, like when your fishing line gets tangled in your buddy's and neither can fish until all is untangled, rewound, and recast into the proper spot.

"Amen, Brother Smoak," echoed someone from the back row.

I closed my eyes tight, just to clear my head again. People might've thought I was praying, but how could anyone pray after a night of being surrounded by wedded bliss and incognito Presbyterian romance while sleeping on a beach beside a missionary girl whom you never touched, then waking up in your very own Tarshish with a preacher who pets sharks on the head?

This never happened in Dallas. In Dallas, life was normal.

Asbury began telling us of the good that came to Jonah after being redirected, and that twelve years earlier he'd been redirected himself, at age fifty-six. Said he was older than the seminary professors, but that was okay because he knew God had him preaching for a purpose, and there was a purpose for each person seated there today.

I was glad that purpose was seated there today, because up till then the weekend had seemed very random.

After praying a long, worthy-of-Sunday prayer, the preacher dismissed us. I thought about what he'd said, then turned to Allie to explain my brief history with Pastor Asbury Smoak.

"Hello, Miss," said Asbury, stepping down from his tiny pulpit.

"Enjoyed your sermon," she said, extending her hand.

"Thank you. And how's the thumb, Jay?"

"Just a scratch. Been cut deeper'n that plenty of times."

Pastor Smoak said to excuse him for one second. He handed cash money to the piano lady, then shook hands with all the departing beach-goers, polishing off each shake with the patented preacher nod.

The seminaries must teach that—the official nod.

After the shaking and the nodding, Asbury said he had fish fillets thawing and wondered what were we doing for lunch.

As long as we didn't have to sing to it, I was game. "No plans, Preacher."

Allie shrugged and said, "Okay, but only if we *cook* the fish, because after eating so much weird food in Ecuador, raw fish on a church retreat would only conjure vile remembrances, memories inappropriate to share while lunching with clergy."

Asbury smiled and closed the door to his church. He asked us to meet him around back at his grill beneath the oak tree. Allie yawned when we walked outside the church and into sunlight. Then I yawned, twice, just to make her feel better.

"So, you actually rubbed the shark on the head?" she asked, standing in the shade of the massive oak.

"Yeah, but he was only a three-footer. Strong little guy, though."

"I caught a catfish once, when I was eight."

I leaned against the tree. "Did he bite you?"

"No. My dad put it in a bucket. He wanted to eat it, but I wanted it to be happy. So when Dad turned his back, I dumped the catfish back in the lake."

"Nature lover."

"You need a shave."

We sat down on a picnic bench, and she shut her eyes. Said she was taking a three-minute nap.

So I sat there in a coastal daze, trying to piece together exactly how I had arrived at this place in time. Images flashed quickly before me: a job transfer; the real-estate lady; my two Sunday visits; a ride to the beach from sneaky Steve Cole. One blink and there I was—on a picnic bench behind a tiny Baptist church on the Carolina coast, about to grill lunch with a fisherman preacher and an unpredictable missionary poet.

A vague connectivity weaved through it all. But it remained only that—vague.

Asbury returned in cutoffs, a marlin T-shirt, and his red baseball cap. He carried a jug of iced tea in one hand, a platter of fillets in the other. I offered to help, but he said, "No, son, I got it. And besides, you look a little beat. Didn't sleep too well?"

"Sand in my bed."

He spread the fillets across tinfoil, then lit his grill. Allie and I joined him to admire the assortment: three fillets thick and pinkish, two of a darker texture, and one nearly colorless.

Allie asked if she could have the white piece on the end. But Preacher Smoak said, "No, ma'am, that's my pompano, and I've been saving it for myself."

She frowned, stuck out her bottom lip, and launched into a story about what had happened to her once after eating mushrooms and ripe bananas deep in the Amazon jungle.

I had never thought about that angle of missionary life. Nor did I care to.

"And no one had brought any tissue or t.p. or anything," said Allie. She finished her story in a barrage of nonstop sentences, then held her stomach and laughed at the memory.

"Okay, okay," said Asbury, sweaty from the heat. "You can have the pompano."

"Works every time," she whispered to me. And my preconceived notions of religious folk in South Carolina—uptight, petty, and dull—were now completely shattered. I simply wished to survive the weekend, to return safely to my desk in the much saner world of stocks and bonds.

Preacher Smoak adjusted the gas, then grabbed his spatula to begin grilling. Allie picked up the platter of fillets, holding it steady as he spaced the fish.

"How long were you out of the country, Allie?" he asked.

"Eleven months," she replied. "I'd always wanted to try the mission field. I loved it."

He wiped off his spatula with a paper towel. "You had to raise support?"

"Most of it," she said, sniffing the raw fish. "Might sell my house if I go back."

The preacher nudged the fillets carefully into two lines and said, "I have a good mission idea myself."

She looked surprised. "You, Preacher Smoak, are going overseas?"

"Nope," he said. "I own a house, too. A very old house; some would call it historic. It's a good hour south of here, deep in the lowcountry, sittin' empty. Been in the family for decades. Can you pour us some tea, Jay?"

Once again, I was serving refreshments. "Okey-dokey," I said, setting his plastic cups out on the picnic table. "Ever lived down there, Preach?"

I only asked the question to be social, for I didn't really feel a part of their missions conversation. My two main missions had always fluctuated between making money and dating. Money being the easy part.

"For a few years when I was a kid," he said. "The place needs lots of work. Floors are falling in on one side, the porch sags, the whole thing needs a good scrape and paint. I'd like to turn it into something useful . . . shame to let it go to waste."

A hot wind blew the cups off the table. Allie rushed over and held them vertical. I poured.

As I dripped iced tea on the table, she turned to face Asbury. "You done any work to your house yet?"

He flipped the fillets and said, "No money to get it going. And my congregation is too old to help out. So maybe one day I'll sell the place and buy myself something nice. Or maybe Jay here can come back down and hammer nails with me."

I let his request go as delicious scents of fish seeped from the grill.

The preacher pinched a corner off the pompano, savoring the bite before sliding the fillet onto Allie's paper plate. She rolled her eyes, but he just winked and kept on grilling.

Beneath the shade, Asbury served lunch, and we ate the fish and washed it down with very sweet tea. It suddenly occurred to me that I had no idea what I'd just eaten.

"What was this, Preacher Smoak?"

"Grilled wahoo," he said, wiping his chin. "Bought it fresh at the docks."

At least he was honest; I'd figured he'd caught it himself.

Allie said she had to go to the ladies room. Asbury gave her directions, then sat beside me on the bench. He put one arm around my shoulder and allowed his male curiosity to surface.

"So, Jay, you and her spending a lotta time together?"

"A little, just hanging out . . . drifting around on floats."

He gulped a last ounce of tea. "Did she let you hook your foot through the loop?"

"Yeah, she did."

"That's always a good sign." And he began clearing the table.

I helped him out, gathering paper plates and plastic forks and tossing them in his trash barrel. "You married, Preacher Smoak?"

"I was. My wife has gone to be with the Lord."

I felt bad for asking, and for a moment, neither of us spoke. Then I changed the subject. "That old house you spoke of sounds like quite a project."

"Yep. Been a delayed project for over a decade now."

"I've been renovating my own house up in Greenville."

He leaned down to disconnect the propane from the grill. "Well, then, since you're so experienced, would you mind freeing up a weekend to lend me a hand?"

I didn't want to commit myself, although the preacher *had* let me help catch the shark on Saturday and grilled us lunch on Sunday. Besides, I was sympathetic toward him, living alone like he did.

So I said maybe.

Allie returned, and so did Asbury's curiosity. He wiped his hands on his shorts, then pointed over at the grass lot. "Noticed that car you two arrived in," he said. "Can I have a look?"

"Sure," said Allie. "It belongs to a girlfriend."

Sherbet sat heavy and alone on the grass. When he arrived at the hood, Asbury ran a tanned finger across lime paint. Preacher envy.

He smiled, raised an eyebrow. "Can we go for a short drive?"

"Certainly," Allie said. Asbury opened the passenger door for her, and after she was in, he slid in himself and put his arm across the back of the seat.

"I had a '63 once," he said. "Back when I didn't need to appear so . . . conservative."

"To the ocean, Jeeves," said Allie. And I was back at the wheel, cranking the engine, with no idea where to go.

"Which way, Preach?"

Asbury turned his cap around backwards and said, "Hang a left."

A two-lane road led us over a bridge of crabbers and fishermen, then to a marsh rising lush and green with the arrival of summer. Old beach homes stood tall and weathered across the marsh, and there were no stores or gas stations or restaurants, only white sand and old houses.

The first few homes rose crackly and white, flanked by cousins in drab shades of beige, all anchored deep on creosote posts. The few cars in motion appeared sluggish and drowsy, the islanders idle and content. Only an egret, with its quick stab at a passive fish, showed any sign of adrenaline. A sense of leisure permeated the place, as if vast reserves of time had been sealed in mason jars, stored away for the sake of repose.

"These house names are hilarious," said Allie. Slivers of ocean showed themselves between fat wooden stilts. The speed limit was twenty-five; I slowed to fifteen.

"My friends own those two tall ones," said Asbury. "Ted's Turf and The Shuler Shack."

I turned Sherbet between a row of beach homes on the ocean side and another row on the marsh side. Skinny and aged, the island's south end sported only these two rows separated by a paved road. Then it narrowed even farther to where only the road and the oceanfront homes remained, the inlet to our right affirming yet another rising tide.

"Welcome to Pawleys Island," Asbury said, proud of his geography.

"I've heard about this place," Allie piped up. "They call it the shabby island?"

"Something like that. We don't tell too many people about it." He reached for the bill of his red cap and spun it back around.

The road ended at a sandswept cul-de-sac. I parked there, scattering gulls with one honk of the horn. They fled toward the ocean.

We walked out across acres of white sand that had collected on the southern tip, apparently washed down and deposited over the years until a mini-desert had formed, cut off from the mainland by an inlet that wound behind the island and back into the marsh.

"When it's nice out, I'll bring a beach chair and write my sermons," said Asbury, tromping along with the look of a man admiring his own backyard.

"Nice office," said Allie, stepping over sprigs of sea oat.

Hot, squishy sand soon firmed, then cooled as we neared the glassy water of the inlet. I watched a chunk of driftwood float past, then glanced above the dunes at a long line of pelicans, swooping low in a quiet glide of unity.

Asbury stopped and squinted south. "Goodness gracious," he said. "There's two of my members fishing in the bend. Skipped my sermon last week, too. Can y'all excuse me for a second?"

"Sure," said Allie.

"You have good vision, Preach," I offered.

"I'd recognize Theo and his wife a mile away," said Asbury over his shoulder. He removed his sneakers and walked barefoot up the shore. Allie whispered that maybe he kept mental records of attendance, what with his church being so small.

On the back side of the island, the inlet curved itself into a long, reverse C. White sand dropped off quickly from the eroding effect of rushing water, the swift current carving a cliff at the edge, dry at the top but crumbling wet at the base.

We kicked off our sandals. I yawned again. Allie sat beside me at water's edge, and we dipped our feet in the current.

"Think he'll convict them a bit?" she asked.

"Nah, he'll probably bait their hooks."

Her toenails, painted red, sparkled as she bobbed her feet in and out of the water. "So, ol' Stanley was responsible for our rescue, huh?"

The current pulled our legs to the right. "Sounds that way."

"I know why Stanley might be a little tough on you," she said.

I scooted closer to her. "Because we bought jam instead of jelly?"

"No, because I went out with him a year ago."

Surprising, this news. But I kept my composure. "Oh . . . just once?"

"Yeah. Just once."

"One date doesn't really mean much, Allie."

"Very funny." She lightly punched me on the shoulder. "He took me to dinner just before I left for Ecuador. I thought he was just being nice, but then he started writing me every week for two months, so I just pretended I was deep in the jungle and stopped writing back. That wasn't a very nice thing for me to do, but he talks and writes in these big words and I just . . ."

"I'm vaguely familiar with those words," I said, snagging a string of seaweed with my foot.

She stole it with her toe. "When we were at dinner that night, I had said one of my long sentences, you know, without the commas, but he never acknowledged it. Just got off on some antidispensational thing, and after I got home, it hit me."

"What hit you?" I asked, watching her fling the seaweed back in the inlet.

"Well, I've never really liked math very much, but Stanley had said a nine-word sentence at dinner and I counted the number of letters in it, and it was the same amount of letters as in my forty-one word run-on sentence. Isn't that weird?"

"Yes, very weird."

Two jellyfish cruised toward us, bobbing at the mercy of the current. She raised her feet, I raised mine, and the pearlescent duo drifted beneath her sparkling red toenails.

"Should we?"

"We should."

We tossed shells at the jellyfish. They did not retaliate.

Watching them drift helped me to avoid admitting what I did not want to admit. But only for another ten seconds.

"You look a bit puzzled," she said, studying my unshaven face.

"I have a small confession too, Allie."

She folded her arms, turned, and gave me a look. "Okay, let's hear it."

"I actually woke up once last night on the beach, around 3:30 or so. Saw you sleeping, thought about waking you. Even considered the possibility it could be embarrassing—with you being a missionary and all. But I shut my eyes and went back to sleep."

She gazed across the inlet for a moment. "That's okay."

"How can you say it's okay? I could've spared you from embarrassment in front of all your church friends."

"Well, I suppose it comes down to grace. You do know about grace, don't you, Jay?"

"I've heard the term . . . two thousand years ago and all that?"

"Not just that," she said, now on her elbows. "Grace isn't date-stamped like that carton of milk in my poem. Even if it were, the stamp would say 'eternal' . . . and the gracer needs to be sure and pour a glass, so that when needed, the gracee can have a swallow."

I had no idea what to say, except, "You should get up and preach one Sunday."

"They don't allow women to preach in our church. And I'd much rather be a missionary. Besides, you just heard my one-and-only sermon, and after a couple of times with the same sermon, the congregation would surely go to sleep . . . and I'd have to start throwing stuff to wake 'em up."

Sitting there beside her with our feet in the current, I was startled by her candor and attracted to her straightforward manner, her uncorrupted realness in a world I only knew as harsh and competitive.

"Speaking of throwing, can you explain the arm?"

"The arm?" she asked, sitting up again and swishing her feet in the water.

"The throwing arm. How did you—"

114

"I have four brothers, all older. They were a complete infield, missing only a second baseman, so when I turned five I got drafted to play second base. We used to ride our bikes over to other neighborhoods to play for a trophy we called 'The Gargoyle,' which really wasn't a gargoyle, just some ol' wooden head with crazy eyes and a pointed chin."

"And I suppose the Kyle team retained the gargoyle year after year."

"Yep. It's in the back of my closet in Greenville. I used to carry it to the games in the basket of my bike, right next to Barbie."

I flipped another shell in the current. "What about Ken?"

"Didn't you think Ken was dorky?"

"I don't remember."

The breeze whipped her hair across her eyes. She pulled it away as a gull landed clumsily to her left. It hopped closer, begging for a handout. Allie showed it her empty palms, a silent apology for our lack of food. The bird squawked its displeasure, then flew off in search of a more tangible charity.

"Well, that's my childhood. What about yours?" she asked, splashing her feet again.

"You want the whole thing?"

"If you like. Or you can sum it up in one long sentence."

"I ate the paste."

"Me too," she said, her hair continuing to misbehave.

"Ever sprinkle cinnamon on it?"

"Ketchup."

"You're sick."

"Hey, did you ever try drugs?" she asked, crinkling her nose like she'd just sniffed vinegar.

I disliked answering this question, but like the salt air swirling about Pawleys Island, confession seemed to bring about a certain cleansing. "Pot, twice. Didn't like it. You?"

"Helium. I sucked it from balloons."

"A helium addict . . . just say no to birthday parties."

"You're insane."

115

"Maybe so, but you're the one who just used bathroom humor to cajole a fish fillet from a poor Baptist preacher."

"That darker fish grossed me out. I couldn't help myself," she said.

I plucked two more shells from the sand before changing the subject. "You were lucky, Allie, to have all those brothers. I never had any brothers or sisters."

"It was never boring, that's for sure."

"I wouldn't mind having a houseful of kids myself one day."

She gave no response. She just let her head drop and watched the water flow under her feet. She seemed different somehow, distracted.

Her chin quivered. Then a tear.

"I said something wrong?"

"No," she said, her head still down.

"I brought up a bad memory?"

"No."

"Can you tell me what it is? You all of a sudden became sad."

She raised her feet from the water, wrapped her arms around her knees, and placed her head in between. Her face was hidden; her voice muffled. "I might not can *have* children."

"I'm sorry." It was all I could think to say, and I felt bad for having said the wrong thing to both a preacher and a missionary, all in the span of one hour.

"It's not your fault," she said, lifting her head and wiping her arm across her face. "It's called amenorrhea, and it has to do with the stress of living in foreign countries. It sometimes makes a woman's body not . . . well, it could reverse if I moved back to the States permanently, but I feel a calling to—"

"You needn't say more."

She slid her toes back in the current and continued all the way to her calves. Under the water, our feet touched, and after a few minutes she breathed deeply, snorted once on her sleeve, and seemed herself again.

I marveled at her recovery. "Are you okay now?"

"Yeah. But it's hard for a single girl, I mean, woman, to be back in the center of the Bible Belt, with nearly all the women having kids, and being surrounded by families every Sunday at church. The orphans I work with in South America help me escape, help me to experience motherhood in another way." She sighed. "Please don't tell anyone I told you this, so many people will think the wrong thing and . . ."

She stopped talking. Just clammed up and stared across the inlet. A quick glance at me, then back across the water. I thought of all the Southern girls I'd met in my twenty-seven years, and how nearly every one of them yearned to be a mother someday. Sympathy was in order here, but I was a broker, and my learned brand of sympathy was subtle and indirect.

"I won't tell. Won't repeat it ever, if that's your wish. But why did you share this with me?"

Her voice was just above a whisper. "I don't know. Maybe I feel you're trustworthy. Or maybe because you aren't a part of the gossipy church people I grew up around."

Her saying that made me feel good, though neither of us had further comment.

A hundred yards to the south, where the water curved back toward the ocean, Preacher Smoak stood beside his wayward members, hands on hips. A long pole bent from Theo's outstretched arms. We watched them for a moment and, once again, the pudgy one took the pole from the frail one.

Funny how rising tides sneak up on you—the water level of the inlet had risen to our knees, and the force of the current kept pulling my feet into hers. After a while we gently splashed each other. Once, then twice.

"So tell me about college," she said. "And I want the long version."

"This could take a while."

"Just hit the revealing parts, then."

We leaned back on our elbows, and I began to rehash a few chapters from the book of Jarvis. "I was pushed hard to be successful from my family, though I really didn't need their pushes. I'm pretty much self-motivated. Made the dean's list. Graduated in three-and-a-half years but probably cut short a great time in my life."

"What was so great about it?" she asked, admiring her periscoping toes.

"The freedom, the lack of responsibility other than for grades, which seemed to come easy for me. And, of course, the social life—meeting the opposite sex was a lot easier in college."

"Agreed. But that's an area requiring faith for God's supply—at God's appointed time."

"But if a man waits on God, then he must never allow the girl to eat meatloaf instead of steak, and he must always sit in the cheap seats, and he must always refuse to share hymnals if they break up, and he must never but never allow her to get into compromising situations."

Allie laughed again, and I allowed her laughter to intoxicate me. I even tried to imagine what it would be like to have a daily dose of her giggles.

"Maybe Lydia will give us credit on the book jacket," she said.

"You don't worry about that?"

"What? Finding my mate?"

"Yeah."

She raised her feet from the water and flicked sand with her toe. "Not as much as I used to. I'm certain that God will put the right one in my path when it's time."

"You never try to make things happen?"

"Well, in college . . ." She stopped in midsentence. She seemed embarrassed as she once again fixed her gaze across the inlet. The far shore was overgrown with marsh grass, and thick clusters of palm trees swayed grudgingly in the breeze.

"Where was college?" I asked, feeling the sun warm my neck.

"Appalachian State. Once, I signed up for a class because this guy I liked was in it."

"Didn't work out?"

"For a little while. But he lives in Kenya now with his wife and two kids. What about you?"

"Never signed up for a class to meet a specific person, but I, uh, did go to a church once to see who was there."

She turned to look me in the eye. "Wouldn't happen to be North Hills Presbyterian Church, now would it?"

More confession, more cleansing. Good grief. "Okay. I admit it. Am I that obvious?"

"Well, when you came to get me by yourself at the grocery store on Friday, I was a bit suspicious. That's why I asked about Steve . . . and made up that bit about Jill."

"You mean there *is* no Jill?"

She smiled and said, "I'm sure there is, somewhere. But I just invented her to slow you down."

"It worked."

"I know." She tilted her head back in mock pride, shut her eyes, and asked, "Do you think I'm attractive?"

I couldn't believe she had to ask. "You're joking, right?"

"No, I'm not. After spending a year in a foreign country and having no dates and not having anyone to say you look nice, well, it makes a girl wonder."

"Allie, you look incredibly nice, especially in that peach two-piece."

A slight blush. "Thanks. I didn't know guys realized peach was a color."

"A few of us do, but probably not Steve."

She giggled again. "Yeah, probably not."

We sat in silence for a moment. I didn't know how to request what I felt like requesting, so I just blurted it out.

"I may want what you have."

"You want my peach bikini?"

"No. I'm being serious. I want to know about that contentment, that whatever it is that makes you happier than everyone else."

"We'll talk about that later. Here comes your fishing buddy."

"And he seems to have what you have, too."

"Well, he'd better," she said, rising to her feet.

With his feet and ankles covered in sand, Asbury Smoak took two swigs from a canned drink. He was strolling beside the inlet and whistling a tune.

"Well, Preacher Smoak, did ya convict 'em?" I asked, rising to greet him.

119

"Started to," he said. "But they got four nice ones floppin' on the stringer. Then Theo gave me a root beer . . . so I thought why ruin their day? Say, I need to get back to my church now, if you two are done chatting."

We wiped moist sand from our legs and derrieres, then hiked back across the hot mini-desert, a Sunday threesome leaning into the breeze.

When we got to the car, I touched Sherbet's hood, and the lime paint nearly scalded my hand. Allie squeezed into the middle again, and while Preacher Smoak was reopening the passenger door to knock more sand from his sneakers, she leaned over to whisper to me. I felt her lips brush against my earlobe.

"You wanna go drifting again this afternoon?"

"Sure, Captain."

"I like drifting."

"Me too."

Leaving the shabby island, we approached the bridge beneath blue skies and one solitary poof of a cloud. Steamy scents of salt marsh engulfed us, a sliver of sandbar awaited us, and I felt the beige vinyl warm against my leg as the sun eased west of noon.

"Thanks for the tour, Asbury," said Allie.

He adjusted his red cap and said, "My pleasure."

I slowed for one more look across the marsh, though the marsh only served as an excuse for my right hand to slide from the steering wheel and reach for Allie's left. But suddenly her left foot jammed my right foot down on the accelerator, and we were flying across the bridge.

"Put your arms in the air like this," she said to Asbury.

They both reached high, and the preacher laughed as the wind whistled through Sherbet's front seat.

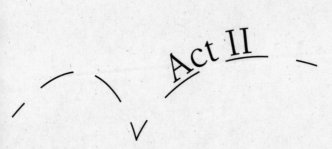

Act II

My strongest trait is curiosity.

—Bono

12

Inside my second-floor office and some 250 miles from its home off the Carolina coast, that lone sand dollar Allie had found in the surf lay flat on my desk, just behind a Rolodex and my burnt-orange University of Texas coffee mug. She'd given me the shell in front of the pink beach house at North Litchfield as 51 singles and a married couple were packing to leave on a cloudy Memorial Day morning. She said it was a reminder of grace, seeing as how we could've drowned, or at the very least washed up somewhere in Morocco with dry mouths and leathered skin.

"Mr. Franklin Gruber on the phone, sir."

"Thank you, Glenda. . . . You can afford six hundred shares, Mr. Gruber. We'll just have to sell one of your other stocks."

Try as I did to keep up with the incessant calls from Franklin Gruber, I would often pause from all the buying and the selling to reflect on the latter half of May—and how I ever ended up in a Presbyterian church.

Reflection, though, is an understatement; I'd often catch myself in random daydreams, oblivious to markets in motion.

Sometimes I'd wonder if events were fate, if the real-estate lady was a secret agent or if my picking that church was happenstance. No, surely not happenstance; nothing Presbyterian was ever happenstance, according to Asbury. But Asbury was Baptist, friendly to sharks but stingy with pompano, wrote sermons on the beach, slurped root beer from a can . . . and when would I ever be driven to breakfast again by a missionary in a classic Cadillac convertible?

Yes, I often wondered how I'd picked that church.

But she left the church; she left her family; she left her friends and her faded red Beetle. She left her house, her stuff, the three semicircles, and those white powdered donuts.

She left on a Tuesday.

I missed her, and I still wasn't sure what made her happier than everyone else.

Mail moved slowly from Ecuador. Her reply to my letter took two weeks to reach South Carolina. I kept it on my dresser and read it often, mostly on weekends, if only to bring balance and perspective to my life.

Jay,

It's been nearly a month since I left Greenville. What a change. My Ecuadorian home is less than ideal, though I've learned to cope. My two-room wooden hut sits on stilts, little skinny stilts, not like the fat ones under the beach houses in Litchfield. I might move into the long hut with the kids next week. We'll see. Stringy vines wrap around the stilts and have now reached the roof. It must be a cousin of kudzu, which by the way was the only plant that really listened when God said to go forth and multiply.

There's no hot water here, but being near the equator, I can leave buckets out to warm during the day and use them for baths in the evening.

We have no phone, although there is a pay phone forty miles away in Coca. On Fridays I go into town in a pickup truck with the women. The roads are very bad. The women go to buy groceries and medicine, and the store owner keeps a computer in the back of his store and I think he has e-mail but he doesn't trust Americans and only grunted and waved me away when I asked him if I could use it.

Look at a map sometime. I'm on the eastern edge of the country, at the outskirts of the Amazon Basin. It's very hot, and November starts our dry season.

The children love my being here and are slowly learning some English. They are so different from American kids—I had one Lifesaver left in a roll, and three little kids shared it with each other, passing it from mouth to mouth until the candy melted and vanished. The adults are hospitable, if somewhat suspicious of me.

We are taking the kids (or rather, they are taking me) on a canoe trip tomorrow, down a branch tributary thing from the big river. We also have a shabby ol' soccer field cut into the jungle. I feel so comfortable here (my corporate ladder is very short; scenic but short, and who needs a corporate ladder anyway when God is in control?).

I was disappointed we didn't get to go drifting again—God will get those Bud guys for stealing our floats that night. Tell Ransom and Jamie congratulations on their pregnancy. I think it's hysterical that she got pregnant on a church singles retreat. And, yes, Darcy and Steve are just friends. She told me that months ago.

Write me again.

And read your Bible. Start with Romans (end of chapter 8 hangs over my bed).

Blessings to you, Jay. I am so happy you are asking questions about God.

Allie

P.S. Could you send some of the little Hershey's dark chocolates in the gold wrappers? Most of it is for me, but I will share with the children and might even bribe that store owner for some computer time. His name is Miguel.

Pray for him, because he is mean.

The last time we'd talked was during a July Fourth picnic. A parade had begun that afternoon on Greenville's Main Street, the horns and drums and the confetti and the children all combining into one blaring celebration of freedom. She, Lydia, and myself joined in at the back of the parade, wearing Uncle Sam hats and marching like soldiers to the strains of "Anchors Aweigh."

She left for South America the next morning.

13

After the beach trip, Allie spent most of her time on the road, speaking at churches all over the Carolinas and Georgia while trying to raise support for a multi-year assignment. I spent my time in the office, trying to raise the price of the Nasdaq.

Her efforts were somewhat more successful than my own.

During the steamy month of July, I had used the evenings to complete the renovations to my home on the cul-de-sac. Installing hardwood floors, replacing bathroom fixtures, and painting the hideous hot-pink room of the former owner's young daughter gave me new appreciation for the intricacies of home repair. The spare bedroom had taken longer than I'd planned—it requires three coats of opal basil to cover hideous hot pink.

As for opal basil, I'm certain that such names are brought to market by the same people who call their BMWs a "motorcar" and their homes an "estate."

Opal basil is actually a soft green, although in the Deep South, descriptions of color are relative. I was at the paint counter on a Saturday morning, waiting for my gallon to be fully shook, when the Home Depot man reached in his orange apron and clarified opal basil for me. "Now remember," he said, handing me a free stir stick, "this here is a lighter green than John Deere tractors."

No excuses; it's just a Southern thing.

July slid indifferently into August, and I began sliding myself every other Sunday into pew number twenty-three—because twenty-four creaked too much and twenty-two was way too close to the front. Church had become my social circle; my new friends were at church, and the donuts were free.

But mostly I was right there in my office, trying to enrich and pacify a roster of elderly clients—one particular client requiring extra doses of pacification.

"Mr. Franklin Gruber on the phone again, sir."

"Thank you, Glenda. . . . Yes, Mr. Gruber, the stock is up two whole cents from where you bought it thirty minutes ago. Let's just give it some time. No, sir, Mr. Gruber, I do not bowl."

Mr. Gruber's account had dwindled, due mainly to his knack for letting emotions take control, the time-proven method for buying high and selling low.

Twelve brokers bought and sold between the dark olive walls of E. B. Cowen Investments. We ranged in age from twenty-five to sixty. Four Jaguars and several other exotics occupied our private parking lot. Compared to them, my old Blazer looked pitiful. But in July, however, Mr. Brophy gave me the broker-of-the-month award, and my name shined across the engraved plaque, a symbol of status.

Not as impressive as a Jaguar, but a status symbol just the same.

Tate Brophy was our fifty-year-old broker-in-charge, the Big Dog. He'd made a suggestion to the younger brokers, saying that growing a beard would help us because it would show our maturity to the gray-haired clients, who owned the bulk of the money. Mr. Brophy drove a silver Porsche Carrera and lived in a five-bedroom stucco on a golf course with his thirty-three-year-old wife, so all four of the young guys in our office had stopped shaving.

I wasn't growing a full beard—as if I could. Just the scruffy look, trimmed but scruffy. I wished it was darker, but the light brown scruff would just have to do.

"Jay?" Mr. Brophy said, sticking his gray head and black Gucci shoes in my doorway.

"Yessir?" I snuck another glance at my quote screen.

"Good call on the oil stocks. They're soaring."

"Learned it all from you, Mr. B."

"You bought some for yourself?"

"Three hundred shares."

He rubbed his chin and said, "Six hundred bucks in one day. Not bad for a Texan."

"It's a start," I replied, but then I was yet to own a pair of Gucci shoes.

Mr. Brophy perused my wall, past the UT diploma and my colossal picture of the 17th at St. Andrews.

"Bought any toys lately, Jay?" he asked, his back still to me. He was forever asking us about our toys, our latest spending sprees.

"Might get me a surfboard, sir."

"A surfboard? We're four hours from the beach, son."

"Yeah, but I want one anyway. I wanna prop one against my living-room wall, just to look cool."

The markets were wacky that day, and I was glad he'd stopped by. But then my stylish bossman moved closer, gripping my desk and leaning down over my monitor to look me in the eye. "Okay, 'fess up, Jarvis. Just who did you meet on that beach trip?"

I leaned back in my chair, reclaiming my personal space. "Some strange people, sir. But I did meet this one girl who—"

He raised up, hands on hips, then cocked his head in the posture of the all-knowing. "Oh, lemme guess . . . she's a lawyer who surfs?"

"Nope."

"A physical therapist?"

"Negatory."

"A CPA who hangs ten?"

"Actually, sir, this is where it gets strange. The person who surfs is named Ransom, and he's married. But sometimes he hangs out with the singles, although he lusted for his wife from across the seafood restaurant, so now they're pregnant. And the girl I met doesn't have a real job; she lives in the rainforest. In rural Ecuador. She works for God, I think."

Mr. Brophy backed away from my desk and shouldered up to my door. "Aww, son. Didn't everyone tell you to visit a Pentecostal church? Those Presbyterians will mess ya up every time."

"They both start with a *P,* sir. And besides, don't the Pentecostals whoop, holler, and—"

He reached for the doorknob. "I don't know what they do, son."

Everyone thought Bossman Tate Brophy was some hotshot broker whose trading prowess and wealthy clients paid for his lifestyle. But I knew the truth. He was no better a trader than the rest of us. He just got lucky. He bought Microsoft the day of its initial public offering. Same with AOL. Then he sold 'em both—at the high.

His wife told me this at a party while eating snails off a crystal plate.

Winning broker-of-the-month meant I had to treat my fellow brokers, so the next day I ordered a catered lunch—croissants and lunch meats, plus a platter of baby carrots and celery, since Mr. Brophy was on a diet. Between all their buying and selling, the other brokers stopped by to say congrats, pass the mustard, and had I seen the new Audi coupe with the six-speed transmission.

Trader Jay, they called me, the one who bought the panics and sold the euphoria.

After shutting down my computer that Friday afternoon, I was craving a workout and a good meal when Line One glowed red. I flinched, figuring it was Gruber again, but then relaxed as Glenda told me differently. I plopped back down in my desk chair and slid the headset on.

"Hello, Beatrice."

"Well, hello, young man! I've been in the garden. And how was your day?"

"Crazy day in the market, Beatrice. Way down, then way up."

A brief pause. "Way up? Hmmm, sounds like my sprig of zebra grass— it grew way up over my head. So high I had to get Trevor to cut it back for me. Do you know Trevor, dear?"

"No, ma'am."

"He's sixty-six. A bit young for me, I suppose. But a good handyman."

"What can I do for you, Beatrice?"

"Well, I thought I'd pay him in stock. Can we sell three shares of the ABC?"

"You mean the AT&T?"

"Of course, dear. Eight thousand shares, right?"

"It's over nine thousand, Beatrice."

"Glory be. That's nearly a bushel. You still think I should travel the world?"

"Sure, Beatrice. Take some friends. Meet Italians, tour Greece."

"The Italians pour grease? On who, dear?"

"I meant to say that if you go, you should visit all of Europe."

"You'll rush the money to me if I sell?"

"Yes, ma'am. Would be happy to."

"No, no, I changed my mind. You stay right there, Mr. Jarvis. I'm coming to get it."

"The market's closed, Beatrice. We'll have to sell Monday."

"Nonsense, dear. You tell them to open it back up for me. I'm calling Francine tonight to see if she'd like to go see the greasy Italians. She's eighty-three, you know. Might not can wait. And Trevor would like to go, too."

"I'm sure a handyman would enjoy traveling with you and Francine."

"Oh my, two old women and a younger man! What do folks call that . . . a triangle?"

"I think so, but you and Francine should probably talk that over."

"Enough about me and Francine, dear. What about you? Any young thing in your life?"

"Not at the moment. But I have a new friend down in Ecuador."

"Well, then you just go down and knock on that aqua door. Pay her a visit."

"It's a long walk. So will I see you Monday?"

"Of course, Monday. No, no, I host gardening club that day . . . but, dear?"

"Yes, Beatrice?"

"Aqua is a horrible color for a door. Tell her to go with Williamsburg red."

When I arrived home that evening, the message light on my answering machine flashed red—bright red, not Williamsburg. I pressed the button, waited for the beep, and listened to yet another church-related invitation.

I did not know it at the time, but God had me by the shirt collar and was about to take me on a tour of the Bible Belt's shiniest buckle.

14

Steve Cole—Mr. Sneaky himself—actually hosted a weekly men's group.

I found this disturbing, unsettling, like if Jack Nicholson were hosting Tupperware parties.

Most of the guys from our beach house were in the group, including Stanley and two of his clean-cut theological buddies. As for Steve, he still had not confessed anything relational—and I had not pressed him, either.

But I would.

Steve lived in the fixer-upper section of Greenville's North Main area. He had a modest home—a brick one-story with a carport and four sickly azaleas. A bent basketball hoop leaned over his driveway. Inside, hardwood floors and a picture window anchored his decor, along with two potted plants begging for nourishment.

A new rug, oval and brightly colored, graced the center of his living room. I had arrived early, and I asked Steve about the rug, since bold patterns of lime green seemed to dominate.

"Yeah, Darcy helped pick it out," he admitted, barefooted as he blipped the evening news. Soft drinks and potato chip bags filled his coffee table. I poured myself a drink and began interrogating Brother Steve.

"Oh, did she? And have you thought about asking her out again? Because didn't you mention, on the drive to the beach, that you two had been out once?"

He looked at me as if he were doing calculus in his head. "Yeah, I might take her out again, just as a friend. Her birthday's coming up. Maybe then."

I gave him a plastic cup. "You're quite the gentleman."

One by one the crew arrived, and soon eight single men plus Ransom—in a surfer T-shirt and sandals—had pulled chairs into a circle around Steve's new rug.

Ransom had not cut his hair, Steve had not shaved, and the rest of them I had rarely seen since the beach. And I had no clue as to our topic.

"Dudes," said Ransom, "we are the Circle of Nine. We were supposed to be a circle of ten, but Joe Caruzzi just got promoted to Triple A baseball in Richmond."

"I bet Lydia hates that news," Steve mumbled.

"Long-distance relationships never work," Stanley said, his Bible balanced on his knee.

"Tell the truth," Steve said, speaking through a mouthful of chips and to no one in particular. "How many of you guys got dates from that beach trip?"

"That wasn't our purpose," Stanley protested.

"Of course, it was the purpose," said Ransom. "It's always the purpose. Tell 'em, Jaybird."

I sipped my Coke and tried to remain calm. "Me? I got no dates from that trip."

"Oh, c'mon," said Stanley. "You spent the entire weekend with her."

I glanced around the circle. Five strange men were staring at me. The pressure was intense, but there was no time for Seuss, so I just blurted it out. "Honest, guys. She said to close my eyes and drift and so I closed my eyes and drifted and then we washed up on some sandbar, her carving anticapitalistic poems in the sand and telling me I had no talent for verse. Then the current washed us halfway to Spain, she prayed on her plastic float, and whammo, there was Beach Patrol. All thanks to you, of course, Brother Stanley."

I could tell he didn't like me calling him Brother Stanley. He frowned and said, "Someone never came home to his assigned house that night, did he, Jay?"

133

His buddies glared at me, dumbfounded.

With open palms, I pleaded my case. "Nothing sinful happened, guys. Honest. After eating a pound of shrimp, I dozed off between the dunes, then woke to talk of Jesus spinning Saturn on his finger like a basketball, which was right before the giddy newlyweds slow danced in the surf. Next thing I knew, Allie was kicking my shin while the sun rose over the Atlantic. We ended up in the front row of a little Baptist church, listening to a sermon on Jonah from a preacher who pets sharks on the head. His name is Asbury. That's all that happened. Honest. We sat in the *front* row."

Now the entire group was staring at me, mouths open, eyebrows raised. Even Steve, who owed me big time for my discretion.

Ransom pounded on the coffee table, diverting attention to himself. I praised God for diverted attention. "Men," he said, "regardless of Jay's adventures, we are supposed to at least try, for a few minutes, to discuss more serious issues."

"Yes," said Stanley, interrupting my surfer friend, "we're here for mutual edification, to seek wisdom from our omnipotent God."

Ransom rolled his eyes and addressed the group again. "Okay, dudes, who had impure thoughts this week?"

Steve dropped the chips. No one else moved.

Then one hand went up, and another and another, in half-second intervals, like pelicans taking flight. Our circle made a right-hand revolution as I grudgingly raised mine. Eight for eight. Then Ransom raised his own hand. Nine for nine. Even the married guy.

But we were only hands. No talk.

"Any discussion? C'mon guys," Ransom pleaded. "Gimme some comments."

"I can't help it," said Stanley.

"It's habitual, bro," said Steve.

"Very habitual," I offered.

"It lures us in . . . every billboard, every commercial."

"So what can we do about it?" asked Ransom.

"Pray?" Stanley answered.

"That'll help," said Ransom. "But we also need to realize that all dudes are in the same struggle, and we need to be consistent in encouraging one another, keeping each other out of tempting situations."

One of Stanley's buddies raised his hand. "But what about five-foot, eleven-inch blondes who wear lime green bikinis?"

"Can we move on to another subject?" asked Steve, tracing the rim of the rug with his toe.

"Okay. Next subject is materialism," said Ransom, checking his notes. "How many of you guys, over this past week, compared your stuff with another guy's stuff?"

I thought of the Jaguars in my office lot. My hand, now two, three, four, five, and . . . harmony. Honest little pelicans. Nine for nine again.

A young guy named Barry looked especially convicted. He tugged his navy blue Nike cap low over his eyes, then cleared his throat. "Okay, what about if you're in college and you come to church and see everyone getting out of new cars and you know they go to the nicest steak houses right after church but you have to go home and eat ravioli out of a can? What about that?"

"Chef Boyardee?" asked Steve. "I used to eat that."

"I lived off of bologna casseroles for weeks at a time," said Stanley. "Still have the recipe."

"I ate peanut butter 'n honey sandwiches every day for a year," Ransom added.

My turn. "I used to dump whatever I had into a blender and *drink* my poverty."

"Thanks, guys," said Barry. "Splendid advice for the poor and needy."

Impure thoughts and materialism—two topics with which I was familiar. Although I'd never been held accountable for it. Such vulnerability made me uncomfortable. I wasn't sure about that men's group—if I wanted to keep attending—but at least they didn't make me look up obscure verses to the east or west of Psalms.

To everyone's surprise, Ransom asked young Barry to remove his navy blue Nike cap. Barry took it off and bowed his head.

"That wasn't what I had in mind," said Ransom. "Just hand me your lid."

Barry grabbed the hat by the bill and handed it over. Ransom dropped two one-dollar bills in the cap, then passed it on to the next guy.

"What's that for?" asked Barry, his curly hair all matted.

"Dude, we're sending you to the nicest steak house in town. Aren't we, men?"

Impromptu charity—it too took us by surprise. But everyone reached quickly for their wallets.

Steve dropped three ones in the cap, and so did the next guy and the next. By the time the cap reached Stanley, it was spilling over with dollar bills. But Stanley let the cap rest in his lap a moment, right atop his Bible. He stared into his wallet, paused once more, then slowly dropped in a ten.

I did not pause at all. I dropped in a twenty and was quite content to have outgiven Stanley, who moments earlier had tried to embarrass me over my Litchfield Beach adventures.

His cap safely returned, Barry sat speechless. He just stared into it for a moment, then stuffed the cash into his wallet and shook his head.

"Okay," said Ransom, reaching across the coffee table to refill his drink, "that covers this week's agenda. Next week we'll cover a new topic. Now who else among you single guys met a cool female at the beach? We wanna hear all about it."

Again, no one moved, until Stanley picked up the bag of chips, ate one, and slowly raised his hand. Ransom sipped his drink and leaned forward in his chair, only a few feet from Stanley. "Well, tell us her name."

"No."

"C'mon," urged Ransom.

"No!"

"Where'd ya meet her?"

Stanley looked at the floor, shuffled his feet, and mumbled, "Under our beach house."

"What was she doing under there?"

"Showering off sand."

"Under the guys' house?"

Stanley nodded in the affirmative.

Ransom leaned back in his chair, cocked his head. "So tell us, dude, who is she?"

"Her name is Rona. And she asked *me* out."

Stanley and Number Eight—whodathunkit?

Yep, God had me by the shirt collar, and the tour had just begun.

15

There are only two things you need to know about the stock market: It's either gonna go up before it goes back down, or it's gonna go down before it goes back up.

Just pick one.

Right before the market opened, Lydia Hutto strolled into my office and chose "up." Short, hospitable, redheaded Lydia thought the market would definitely go up. Wearing a navy pantsuit burdened with a heavy dose of black pinstripes, she sat herself in my guest chair and offered a bite of her raspberry scone.

"I want to buy some Ann Taylor stock," she said proudly.

I began a frantic search of my database. "Does Ann have a stock?" I asked.

She nibbled her scone and said, "Well, you should know, Jay. You're the broker here."

In all honesty, I was not sure Miss Ann had a stock. I knew Miss Martha had a stock, but not Ann. I'd never traded it. But, yes, there it was—at $23 a share.

"You're right, Lydia," I said, turning the monitor for her benefit. "Now how much would you like to buy?"

"All I can with this." And she stood and pulled a wad of twenties from her pocket, arranging them in a neat green pile next to my keyboard.

Lydia had walked over from the downtown branch of Carolina First Bank, where she held the position of chief window teller. I thought the job a nice fit for her hospitable nature, with all the smiling and handing out packets of money.

"There's at least four hundred bucks here," I said, counting the bills into my palm.

"Four hundred forty," said Lydia. She crossed her short navy legs and waited for me to confirm her total.

Total confirmed, I marked the dough for deposit. "You wanna bet it all on Ann?"

"I trust Ann," said Lydia. "Much more so than men."

Until that comment, I was going to keep our visit strictly business. But she just had to bring up that topic again. "Does that mean things aren't going so well with you and Slugger Joe?"

She tossed the balance of her scone in my trash basket and recrossed her short navy legs. "I'm still deciding . . . but he may have potential."

"Does Joe open doors?"

"Mostly."

"Joes buys you front-row seats to his games?"

"Joe gets free tickets."

"And you can order steak instead of meatloaf?"

"We had meatloaf once. I cooked."

"Burned it?"

"Yep."

"Ordered takeout?"

"Twice in one hour."

"Chinese?"

"Joe ate six egg rolls."

Lydia squirmed in her seat, which I took as girl-speak for "Let's change the subject." I turned the monitor back toward me, then called up her account. "Okay, Lydia, you never did say why you left me and Allie asleep on the beach that night at Litchfield."

"I had to go potty."

"And you never came back?"

She paused for the memory. "It was a long walk back to the beach. Plus, you two looked so peaceful there on the sand—your backs to each other, one facing north, one south. Y'all looked like kids at a slumber party who'd had a disagreement and were trying to sleep it off. Say, are you going to buy me my stock or not?"

I entered the order and said, "Consider it bought. So why are you so bullish on Ann Taylor stock?"

She sat up straight and played with her hair. "Because last Saturday me and Darcy bought three dresses each in a whirlwind of shopping. And no, Jay, you do not even have to ask. Two of Darcy's dresses matched her car."

Lydia and Darcy—they were bullish on America.

An hour after Lydia left with her nineteen shares of fashionable stock, Mr. Brophy summoned me to his office. Smiling over red suspenders, he even held the mahogany door for me.

My guess was that he had either a request or an opportunity.

"I have an opportunity for you, Jay," he said, closing the door behind us.

A chrome-shafted putter and four orange golf balls sat next to his desk, a Slim Fast next to his monitor. Outside his window, spidery streams of water arched from a fountain, morning sunlight reflecting yellow-gold through the droplets.

I didn't know if Mr. Brophy had good news or if he simply was reminding himself that he was married to a thirty-three-year-old woman. But either way, his smile relaxed me. Maybe he'd compliment my scruff.

"Jay, we've had another good quarter."

"Yessir, we have," I said, gripping the back of his guest chair.

"We've had our clients, and ourselves, on the right side of the market."

"Yessir, we have."

"And twice now you've led the young guys in contributing to our fine performance."

"Just following your lead, Mr. B."

He held his silver-rimmed glasses by the frame and gestured with them as he spoke, just like the financial guys on television. That killed me.

"What's so funny?" he asked, inspecting a lens.

"Nothing, sir."

Mr. Brophy cleared his throat. "I realize, Jay, that you moved here only five months ago . . . but you have six solid years of experience and seem to have a real knack for spotting winners. Although you'll have stiff competition, I'd like to recommend you for a position on our institutional trading desk."

"Sir?" The one syllable was all I could utter. A shot at the institutional trading desk was rare; the money outstanding.

After resting his silver rims on the Journal, Mr. Brophy stood, sipped the Slim Fast, then took his putter and stroked one against the base of a potted plant.

For a fifty-year-old broker bossman in Greenville, S.C., this was the epitome of cool, this Slim-Fasting-see-I-gotta-corner-window-and-can-hit-the-potted-plant-with-a-golf-ball routine. He looked up from his putting position. "It'll require an interview in New York, and of course, if selected, you'd have to relocate there."

"New York City, sir?" I could still only manage the briefest of sound bites.

"That's right," he said, reloading. "Can you interview next week, say . . . Thursday?"

"Yessir, sure thing." I was shell-shocked, unaware of what I was saying.

He checked his golf grip. "Great. Ask Glenda to arrange the flight. And pay no attention to the street bums. And lemme know how it goes. Now, if you'll excuse me, I need to call the little wife."

I rubbed the leather backing of his guest chair before backpedaling toward the exit. "Appreciate your confidence in me, boss."

As I turned to leave, an orange golf ball rolled past my feet and thudded against his mahogany door.

"Nice scruff," he said.

"Nice putt, sir."

Moonlight flickered off my chrome spatula as I fired up the grill, adjusted the flame, and tried to contemplate New York City. My salmon fillet sat patiently on tinfoil.

141

I'd always planned on getting there—Manhattan. The City is, after all, the Holy Grail for everyone in the financial industry. It's just that the news had come so soon, so unexpectedly. I felt the same way I had back in third grade when Mrs. Wormby had given me an A in geography, even though, in my head, I was sure Lake Erie bordered Utah.

I was thinking of all that concrete, of all those people, not to mention all that cost of living, when my cordless phone rang. The voice on the other end was following up about church membership. Beneath the dull yellow glow of a deck light, I backhanded a fly into never-never land, then propped one foot on my picnic bench.

Elder Kyle seemed like a nice man, soft-spoken and pleasant; I wondered if he knew his missionary daughter threw food. "Yessir," I continued, "I've been a regular visitor."

He said there'd be a question-and-answer session coming up for potential members. I hoped I got to ask all the questions, because none of my answers seemed to impress anyone around Greenville.

That night, however, the questions were all Elder Kyle's. "Jay, your background is . . . ?"

"You mean as to denomination?"

"Yes."

I reached out with the spatula and flipped the salmon. "As I told someone at the beach, sir, my parents raised me to be a devout workaholic. And while I've tried to live a more balanced life than they did, church has never been a factor."

"So . . . you're not anything?"

"I'm a stockbroker, sir."

"I see. Well, perhaps we can get together to talk. . . . You say you're a stockbroker?"

"Yes. My sixth year."

A brief pause. "You wouldn't be the one my daughter met on that beach trip?"

"Yessir, I am. We sorta hung out for the weekend."

"Jay, I don't mean to pry, but did you really sleep in a black inner tube?"

"Just myself, sir. Circumstances were a bit complicated. And your daughter was safe in her own bed."

"You mean safe in the backseat of Darcy's Cadillac?"

"Allie told you that?"

"She tells me everything."

"Oh."

Another pause. "And you're the one who let her talk you into drifting blind in the ocean?"

"Yessir, I did . . . but never again."

He chuckled into the phone. "She's been doing that for years. Tries to get me to do it every family vacation."

I thought this odd, especially for a Bible Belt family. "Did you know, Elder Kyle, that your daughter likes to take splinters of driftwood and carve long verses in—"

"You mean her antimaterialistic poetry?"

"Yessir, that."

"I have all ten stanzas on my refrigerator."

"I thought it was only five stanzas."

"She said the sandbar was too small."

"Oh."

His voice became serious and settled. "Jay, she also asked me to recruit you to join our church. If you have any interest, that is."

"But, sir, she said I'd never make it as a Presbyterian."

"First we'll need to make sure you're gonna make it to heaven."

What, were they going to keep score? A record of attendance? Besides, I was being held accountable by a men's group and had read one Proverb per night for three straight weeks, so I was in good with the Almighty. "Got that covered, sir."

"Good. Say, I spoke with Allie two nights ago. She called me from a pay phone in Coca. Said if I ever saw you to tell you hello."

"Her letter sounded like she'll be away a long time."

"A very long time," he said. "Her little house across town just sold. I'm wiring the money to her mission agency after the closing, although it's not very much."

143

"You must be proud of your daughter."

"I am. She does seem at peace with life. Doesn't mind the conditions, either. Well, except for her foot. She cut it pulling a canoe to the bank of a river. Only five stitches, though. She'll be fine. Her only issue seems to be figuring out what to do about Thomas."

"Thomas, sir?"

"He's the missionary to Peru she met last month. She didn't mention him to you?"

I watched my salmon char, then scorch, then burn into inconsequence. "No."

"Well, anyway, our class for potential members meets next Sunday. We'd love to talk with you."

Enthusiasm gone, I could barely mutter, "Thank you, Elder Kyle."

"Grace and peace to you, Jay."

Dinner was now black, ruined. And my appetite had retreated to wherever it is lost appetites tend to congregate.

I leaned against the picnic table, deep into a bowl of cereal, and watched smoke seep from my grill, then rise in tiny gray puffs against the mid-August moon.

When flustered, my go-to food is cereal. There may not be wisdom in those flakes, but there is certainly comfort. Each crunch brings new angles and fresh perspective, although perspective, once again, was interrupted by a ring of the phone.

"Yeah?" I said, watching my flakes go soggy.

"Duuude!" was the reply.

I sat down on the bench again, spoon in one hand, phone in the other. "Ransom, I thought you married folk went to bed early."

"Nah. Jamie left for a teacher's retreat till Friday. But guess who I ran into today?"

"Jacques Cousteau?"

"Wrong, Jaybird. The one with the pierced eyebrow. You know, from the beach . . . the raven-haired one."

Raven hair, pierced eyebrow. "Oh, yeah, Number Two."

144

"Someone's parents named them Number Two? Dude, that is so slack. A second child should be given a proper name."

"I meant she was the second member of the Numericals."

"What're you talking about?"

"Never mind. What'd she say?"

"She walked into our store and started browsing around my section, checking out the kayaks and all the water-sport stuff. We talked about the beach trip, and then she asked about you, man. Her name is Alexis, she's twenty-five, and she just broke up with some motorcycle repair guy."

I dropped my spoon in the bowl. "C'mon Ransom, another Presbyterian girl whose name starts with *A*?"

"Don't know if she's a member or not, but they broke up last week. He wanted her to help him keep the nursery at his church. . . . He's Lutheran, I think. She doesn't like keeping nursery, so she broke up with him."

"So now I'm supposed to—"

"You know my policy, dude."

"What policy? That you're not hanging up until I agree to call her?"

"And I want all the details."

Something was amiss. I did not believe that matchmaking efforts from surfer dudes, especially married ones, meshed with my long-term agenda. But Number Two had looked quite intriguing at the beach, with her raven hair and Tolstoy novel—and I didn't mind a little brow piercing. As long as it was little.

Inside my head, possibilities clashed and clanged. Mostly clashed. Was this opportunity seeking me out, or mere distraction? Would there be chemistry? This felt like Plan B, but at least she didn't live in some remote foreign country.

Maybe I'll call her. Maybe I won't.

Okay, I'll call her.

But not till after I throw out my burnt fish.

Shoo fly, don't bother me.

16

On Wednesday morning, Mr. Gruber decided to buy more stock in Toys 'R' Us. It was my only sale of the day. I loved Mr. Gruber. My other big chance came when I took a call from the church secretary.

She did not want to buy stock.

Apparently an umbrella had left itself in the hall rack, and she'd found my name on the handle. I'm good at labeling my things, very bad at maintaining possession.

After the market closed, I drove to the church, my tie draped across the passenger seat, my thoughts still on Manhattan. The church property sat empty except for the elderly janitor, to whom the church had given the title of *sexton,* which does not roll off the tongue quite like *janitor* and even sounds a bit risqué. But I supposed he merely filled the position; someone else had named it.

In a baggy beige jumpsuit, he was sweeping the walk and did not see me approach—I take pride in quiet approaches.

"Afternoon, sir. I left my umbrella."

He kept on sweeping and said, "Oh my, that never happens 'round here."

"It's blue and white."

He still didn't look up. "Green 'n red, brown 'n tan, I seen 'em all. And most folk wait till the next Sunday to reclaim 'em."

"But I'm going to New York. Might need it."

"Letcha in in a sec," he said. He was about an inch taller than me, brown skinned and lanky and seemingly used to interruptions. He propped his push broom against the brick sanctuary and introduced himself, telling me his name was Maurice, that he'd worked there for twenty-four years and had found many an umbrella left in the hall rack. "Son, we get so many umbrellas left here that five years ago our benevolent pastor began giving me the unclaimed ones . . . so now all my relatives tell me they sick of getting these fancy Presbyterian umbrellas for birthday presents."

I jiggled the chrome doorknob and moved aside. "Called a job perk, I reckon."

Sweat beads covered his forehead as he reached in his pocket and produced a heavy ring of keys. "Yep, that's what it is, a perk. Now, tell me again what color?"

"Blue and white."

Maurice unlocked the side door and pointed down a dimly lit hallway, past various classrooms and offices, telling me my umbrella was probably still there on the rack. I told Maurice there sure were lots of eccentric people in his church and that after twenty-four years I imagined he had met them all.

"Probably have," he said. "Which ones you met?"

The names Darcy and Stanley and Ransom were met with shrugs, but when I got to the name of Allie, his eyes lit up.

"Allie Kyle?" he asked. "Been knowin' that girl since she was a two-year-old. She's an original."

"Yes, she sure is."

"A bit rambunctious as a child, though." And he turned to go back outside.

I quickly tapped his shoulder, wanting him to stay and chat a minute. "How so?"

"How so what?"

"How was Allie rambunctious?"

Maurice stuffed the keys in his pocket and held the door with his foot. "Smart child, don't get me wrong. And, well, she might not want this to get out, but when she was in kindergarten—my third year as sexton—she threw Fig Newtons at me. Every week."

"You don't say . . ."

"After a while I started throwing 'em back. You know, kinda easylike, but the assistant pastor said sextons shouldn't throw food at the children. We still had the occasional battle, though, usually in the church kitchen, up until she went off to college. I think she live in Brazil now . . . or some such place."

Maurice said he had to hurry outside to take care of an air-vent problem and that it was good meeting me. Same here, Maurice. Then I was down the hall with the dim lights and past three offices. First the small office labeled MUSIC MINISTER, then the slightly larger office labeled ASSISTANT PASTOR, then the largest office labeled SENIOR PASTOR.

I had often wondered if pecking orders were a sin, but I reckoned not.

Curious, I peeked inside the pastor's office. Walls of commentaries filled the room—at least twelve commentaries for each of the four Gospels and five commentaries for all the other books, except twenty, maybe thirty, for Revelation, a book on which I had no comment.

Satisfied as to the contents of a pastor's office, I walked farther down the hall, pausing to visit the men's room. A minute later I exited back into the hallway and saw glaring back from the far wall a corkboard labeled "New Members."

I felt guilty for thinking what I was thinking—that there could be new single females joining the church—but guilt faded quickly as I stopped for a closer look. The corkboard contained no photos of single women, however, just three families and a single man about my age.

"No young ladies, huh?" said a voice from down the hallway.

I turned to see Maurice striding toward me, clutching a toolbox that swung green and heavy at his side.

Embarrassed, I turned my back to the board. "I was just taking a quick look, Maurice."

He set his toolbox on the tile floor and stood beside me. "Single folk always checkin' out the New Members board. Like God gonna send 'em somebody Federal Express."

"Okay, I'm guilty. But no prospects this week, just another *guy*."

What Maurice did next is forever etched in my memory. He turned, looked the length of the hallway, and then looked back at me. "Wanna have some fun?" he asked.

"Secular or Presbyterian?"

He raised a finger to my chest. "Wait right there."

He ducked into the pastor's office. I heard a drawer open and shut. Out he came with a Post-it note on his finger. He walked back to the New Members board and stuck the yellow Post-it across the bottom of the single guy's picture.

I edged closer to read it: *Only here to meet girls.*

"How embarrassing for that guy," I said. "Is this how you church janitors have fun?"

With a slight smile (or a smirk, I couldn't quite tell), he shoved his toolbox into a storage closet. "The pastor hates it when I do stuff like that, but I gotta keep 'im stirred up. Helps energize his sermons, if ya know what I mean."

I read the note again, shook my head, and said, "Gets lonely here in the church hallways, don't it, Maurice?"

He paused to consider the question. "Occasionally, but everybody got their quirks, son." He pulled a mint from the pocket of his jumpsuit.

"Can I have—"

"Help yourself."

We walked together toward the exit, unwrapping mints as we made our way down the hall. "I'll never let my picture get on the New Members board, Maurice."

"I'll go easy on ya," he replied.

"You gonna leave that note up?"

He fumbled with his pound of keys and said, "Now, don't you worry 'bout that. The senior pastor, he'll yank it off when he comes in tomorrow morning. Then around lunchtime, he'll call me to his office . . . and we'll have ourselves a little chat."

"I bet you get chatted with frequently."

"'Bout twice a week."

I shook hands with Maurice and asked if he would like to come along on the next singles retreat. He said yeah but the wife would never approve.

On the drive home, I remembered that my umbrella was still in the hall rack.

I didn't go directly home. Nope, I stopped at the Publix grocery store to buy a bag of dark chocolates. The ones with the little gold wrappers.

I don't know exactly why I did that, what with her being all content and at peace in the rainforest and spending time with that Thomas fellow in Peru. But since she was a missionary and had asked nicely for 'em, I went ahead and bought 'em.

Finally home, I sat out on my deck at sunset, pen in hand, surrounded by deep crimson snapdragons while addressing a box to Allie Kyle, in Ecuador, South America.

I even wrote her a little note, telling her all about Beatrice Dean and the flowers, about my upcoming trip to New York, and about the fact that I'd actually read six Proverbs last night—a world record for three generations of the Jarvis family.

I concluded my note with two observances.

First of all, Allie, a Proverb from Mr. Solomon in the eighteenth chapter states clearly that if a man finds a wife, he finds what is good and will receive favor from the Lord. Favor. Not calamity, but favor. This is in direct contrast to Stanley, who quotes from Corinthians (which is only somewhat easier to find than Galatians) that a single man should not seek a wife. How all this squares up with the oft-quoted "seek and you shall find" is beyond my powers of reason. And if Stanley knows he should not seek a wife, why is he now dating muscular Number Eight? Hmmm?

So does Corinthians trump Proverbs? Or vice versa? (I have already concluded that they both trump Stanley.)

Also, after four months of visitation, I've come to believe that the singles at North Hills Prez are looked upon, by church leadership, as something of an oddity, the licorice at a potluck dinner.

This too is troublesome.

Your sand dollar continues to hibernate.

Jay

After thirteen of my self-adhesive stamps self-adheeded to the box, I stared at the strange address, at the odd mix of numbers and letters that made for an Ecuadorian zip code. I might as well have been sending the box to the planet Neptune.

In my note, I decided against including a vague question about her social life. None of my business to ask, but I *did* buy the jumbo bag of dark chocolates for her and even sealed the interior of the box with extra bubble-wrap stuff so they wouldn't get crushed, and I hoped she wouldn't share them with Thomas the Peruvian evangelist.

Plan B

After getting over the initial shock of Alexis saying yes to my dinner offer, I decided on a French place in the foothills of North Carolina. Inlaid with gray stone, the restaurant appeared to be nestled into a bank of dogwood trees. Summer's sun descended behind the Blue Ridge mountains as we entered; the lights dim, my cologne subtle, our chemistry undecided.

For I had been on time; Alexis had been on the phone.

I'd tuned in to a jazz station; she'd changed it twice.

With her loose charcoal skirt, black top, and only the slightest hint of makeup, Alexis could've passed for French. Her silver necklace and silver bracelet complemented her brow piercing. "Like it?" she asked, catching my gaze.

"Very cool," I replied with first-date exaggeration.

As I looked around for the maitre d', she leaned close to whisper, "This looks like a place where nobody talks loud."

"The whispering French . . ."

"Sounds like a movie title."

Watching the well-heeled patrons, I suddenly became Jarvis the Restaurant Critic: *Here in the hushed pageantry of fine dining, men in suits and women in pearls are both status and quo. They sip gracefully, eat reverently, and select their cutlery from table settings grand and meticulous. Burgundy napkins match the waiter jackets; soft music begs formality.*

"Look, Jay," Alexis whispered again. "Three forks per setting . . . three spoons, too!"

"Wow . . . a Brady Bunch of utensils."

A pleasant little man named Jean sat us at a window, smiled, and said he'd return with menus. A shallow stream curved just below the awning, and the gurgling of water over rock set a mood more suited to a fourth date than a first.

"Hungry?" I asked.

"Yes, very," she said, playing with her smallest fork.

On the drive up the mountain, I had chosen literature for an appropriate first-date conversational topic. I eased in slowly. "So, Alexis, is Tolstoy your favorite writer?"

She inspected her middle spoon and said, "Who?"

"Tolstoy . . . you were reading him at the beach."

"Oh, I just borrowed that book from someone to try and conform. Actually, I hate reading. On the beach I'd much rather scope out a cute guy's bod. And who *was* Tolstoy, anyway? Wasn't he that Russian who controlled all the nuclear weapons, the one Reagan was always arguing with?"

"I think that was someone else."

She clinked her water glass with the spoon and said, "History. Pffft."

Startled, I managed to recover as we accepted our menus from the smiling waiter named Jean.

"Sir," she said, pointing at page three, "what is this word?"

"Cordon bleu," said Jean, with emphasis on bleu.

"Let us think on it a minute."

"Very well. Would you like to try a red wine, perhaps a merlot?" asked Jean.

"Yeah, whatever," said Alexis. "Wine, tea, beer, just something to wash down the food."

Perhaps mademoiselle would prefer warm Coke in a can. Flustered by our lack of chemistry, I was tempted to order cereal. But I didn't.

Instead, from memory, I flipped through the dating handbook, landing dubiously in the *H* column. "Hobbies, Alexis. What sort of hobbies do you enjoy?"

Now brandishing the mama spoon, she said, "I've been helping T.J.— he's my ex—rebuild a carburetor for his bike."

Jean brought ice water, then two small glasses of merlot.

"And how long were you two together?" I asked, sipping with extended pinkie.

She slurped, wiped her lip, and said, "Off and on since tenth grade. We're currently off. But he'll come roaring up to my apartment any day now, I'm sure."

Since she asked no questions of me, I just continued on. "Ya know, Alexis, I had a completely different picture of you—after seeing you on your beach towel, pretty, looking so artsy and cultured with your seven-hundred-page novel."

She rearranged the spoons, small one in the middle. "You think I'm pretty? Really?"

"Absolutely."

"No one ever tells me that."

Perhaps you distract them with your table manners. "Not even T.J.?"

"Nope." And she took a second slurp.

I set down my glass. "And you've been seeing him since tenth grade?"

"We met in geometry."

"And you feel the two of you will get back together?"

"Highly probable. Then we'll split up again."

153

By the time we finished the main course and agreed to split a crème brûlée, I was out of questions but sure of one thing: If Solomon himself had walked into that very restaurant at that very moment and sat down at our table, he would've been unable to explain women to me.

I wiped a bread crumb from my shirt. "At the beach, Alexis, I was part of a late-night discussion about how guys should treat women."

"You mean how guys must treat women."

"Yeah, okay, how they *must* treat them."

She licked the baby fork as Jean delivered dessert. "That stuff should be baked in early, Jay."

"Flowers?" I asked.

"Constantly."

"Anniversaries?"

"Lavish her from dawn to dusk."

I took a second bite of our very sweet dessert. "What about restaurants?"

She slurped again and said, "Easy . . . if you have to buy cheap tires for your car in order to afford her the best dining, then buy the cheap tires. Same for football tickets. But for heaven's sake, if she orders a grilled cheese with four pickles, don't say that four-pickled grilled cheeses are your all-time favorite."

"You're good friends with Lydia, aren't you?"

"I don't know anyone named Lydia."

"Honest?"

"Honest."

Jean removed the empty dessert plate, eyed his tip, smiled broadly, and said to please come again soon. Outside, Alexis and I watched the stream from a footbridge, the mountain air crisp, the dating air awkward.

"Chilly up here after the sun goes down," said Alexis, clutching her arms.

"Yes. Yes it is."

"Mind if we talk in your car?"

"Sure."

"I hate being cold."

154

After unlocking her door, I was walking around the back bumper when she leaned across the seat to return the favor. Men love it when women return the favor. For if they do not return the favor, we get annoyed and start diluting our compliments, telling them they look nice (instead of beautiful) and are funny (instead of hysterical). It is surely a game, and according to the Circle of Nine, the game has been in extra innings ever since Eve bit into her Red Delicious. I had always pictured the fruit as green and sour, but Ransom and Steve insisted it was a Red Delicious. Even Stanley concurred.

In darkness, my ignition key found its slot. "Alexis?"

"Yes?" She was playing with the radio dial.

"Don't mean to probe into all your personal stuff, but I have a question that—"

"Ask it, Jay. Aren't first dates a time for discovery?"

"Sure, but . . ."

"So whadda you wanna know?"

"What I wanna know is, if you're so sure of getting back with T.J., who's Lutheran, then why do you hang out with the singles at North Hills Prez?"

"A girl has to have a Plan B."

Mountain highway twisted before us like tar-covered ribbon as I began comparing her strategy with my own. But Plan B? After gurgling rivers and French cuisine, I was a Plan B? "At least you're honest."

"Can you change the station?" she asked.

"Sure."

Deranged static escorted us down the mountain. Then that beach music again. Two hundred miles from the Carolina coast and they still tried to cajole everyone to sit in sand and watch golden tans.

"Turn it up," she said.

I turned it up.

Ten seconds later, she turned it back down. "Jay?"

"Yes?"

"Tonight, I was *your* Plan B, wasn't I?"

How did she know that? "How did you know that?"

"I'm a woman."

155

"Okay, you were Plan B." *But what you don't know, oh piercy woman, is that Plan A is simply not geographically available. She's somewhere in South America . . . and hopefully not with Thomas.*

After another five minutes, the mountain shrunk behind us. "You can turn the music up now," she said. "But can we listen to something else?"

"Sure." I found the golden oldies station. Chuck Berry was singing "Maybelline."

Again she reached over, muted the sound. "Jay?"

"Yes?"

"You forgot to ask a blessing before the meal."

"Sorry. Is that important to you?"

"Somewhat . . . helps to be genuine as we carry out our dating agendas."

How did she know I had an agenda? "How did you know I had an agenda?"

She looked out her window and summoned perfect female nonchalance. "Because I'm a woman."

We were back inside Greenville city limits, the tree-lined highway hiding suburbia, the mountain fully shrunk. She was now in charge of tunes, and she'd tuned into an alternative music station, yet another song of angst.

The second verse was dreadful, so this time I turned the volume down.

"Alexis?"

She pulled her raven hair over one shoulder. "Yes?"

"You slurp."

"I know. I didn't want you to like me."

"I don't. I mean, I do, but maybe not in that way."

"I just didn't have anything to do tonight," she said.

"Me either."

"So . . . maybe we can do this again if we're both bored?"

"Maybe. But you have to promise not to slurp."

"I promise."

On an empty Howell Road, a stoplight tinted us red, then lunar green. The third verse of angst faded to static, and she thanked me for dinner. I told her she was welcome but that I just had to know more about female strategy.

156

"Alexis," I said, turning onto her street, "have you ever rotated through various churches in order to meet guys?"

"Sure," she replied. "Do it all the time. But sometimes I wonder if the right guy is also out there rotating churches each Sunday, and we just pass like ships in the rain."

"You mean the night?"

"Whatever."

I pulled into her driveway and shut off the engine. "T.J. isn't the right guy?"

"Nah, but we'll probably get back together anyway."

"Which denominations are on your rotation?" I asked, cutting the headlights.

She looked startled. "My what?"

"On your church rotation . . . to meet guys."

"Oh, besides North Hills, lemme see . . . three Lutheran churches, a few months as a Methodist, and two Baptist. And you?"

"Not that many, but I'm sorta new in town and—"

"Keep practicing. You seem to fit in well."

I said thanks, but something didn't feel right, and now I was wondering if such strategies were viral. "How many girls in the singles class do you think are doing this?"

"Rotating through churches to meet guys?"

"Yeah."

"At least half of them," she said, checking herself in the mirror. "Maybe more. I have girlfriends who actually rate churches as to the quality of guys. They enter the data on a spreadsheet, update it each Monday, and e-mail it out around Greenville."

Though stunned by this disclosure, I pressed on. "Alexis, even I, a virtual church rookie, can figure out that God is gonna frown on that sort of behavior."

"We don't think so."

"Who is we?"

She rolled her eyes. "The girls on the e-mail list, Jay. We want husbands, and we intend to find them."

157

There was simply no fitting response. But I could not say good night yet, either—the desire to know more overwhelmed me. "So how does North Hills Presbyterian rank?"

"Consistently in the top ten."

"Out of how many?"

"Last week's update had sixty-five churches on it."

I fiddled with my keys for a moment. "Do your parents care that you do this?"

She reached for the door handle. "Well, Jay, I talked it over with my mom, and she actually encourages me. It's the same method she uses to network for clients."

I was afraid to ask. "Alexis, I'm afraid to ask, but what does your mom do?"

"She sells real estate."

At her door she asked if we could talk more sometime about God, but just talk, because she was sure she'd be getting back with T.J.

I said maybe and kissed her on the cheek, right below her little silver piercing.

Not sure why. Just seemed like the thing to do.

17

Sunday morning, I slipped into pew twenty-three during the opening prayer. A guest preacher took the stage, a black man named Tyrus Williams. He had a receding hairline but plenty of volume. Beside me was the old guy with his psychedelic Bible pages, though I was staring at the groovy blue panes in the stained glass.

Very seventies, those blue panes.

Tyrus asked us, then commanded us, to jot down the following terms: *Eternal Being, Divine Presence, Universal Force*. Not being a jotter, I was content to watch him pound the podium.

"We have taken 'Holy, Holy, Holy' and turned it into 'vague, vague, and very vague' . . . all this vaguery and the need to be inoffensive has saturated our country, saturated us to the point where an Eggo waffle might become known as a circular grid of battered substance."

All eyes were riveted on Tyrus as he grabbed the podium with both hands. "The word *waffle* might offend those who prefer pancakes, so let's all go have breakfast at the Circular Grid of Battered Substance House."

Two pews in front of me, Lydia, Nancy, and five Numericals giggled into bulletins.

Tyrus continued, wiping sweat from his forehead as he gained momentum. "Too many folks are scared of the word *Jesus*. They treat the name Jesus like a lemon meringue pie. Will stick their pinkie finger in for a taste but avoid a full slice because they think, over the long term . . . it might do something bad to 'em."

Maybe it was the interracial atmosphere, or maybe it was because I was hungry and found his pie-and-waffle talk alluring, but the man had my attention now; the groovy blue panes no longer a distraction, faded away like the last beacons of disco.

"But we know that isn't true," said Tyrus, pounding again. "It *cannot* be true. For the Scriptures tell us to come and taste that our Lord is *good* . . . He is *good*. . . . He is *good!* . . . He was good *yesterday*, he is good *today*, he will be good *tomorrow*. . . . Is there a witness in the house?"

Silence.

"I know y'all are mostly white Presbyterians, but can't a man get a witness?"

"Amen and amen," came meekly from behind me. I turned for a peek and saw it was Jamie Delaney, wife with child. Seated beside her, Ransom gave me the thumbs-up.

"Our Lord compared to fat grams," boomed the voice of Tyrus. "That's how far we've fallen."

Blessed and dismissed, I glanced down to reread my first attempt at a scribbled sermon note: *Jesus and the lemon meringue pie.* But I didn't get this Presbyterian fascination with food—food in the sermons, food hurled from missionaries, fruits of the spirit, and powdered donuts. Good grief.

Up the burgundy carpet, the congregation moved slow and sluggish, moping along with the idle apathy of molasses. I was shuffling toward sunlight when someone tapped my shoulder.

"Hi, Jay. Thanks again for the French dinner."

"My pleasure, Alexis." After I pushed open one side of North Hills's intricately detailed double door, she walked past, smiled, and stopped to chat. Her dress was deep red, her raven hair was pulled to one side, and she wore the same silver bracelet from our date.

"You going to singles class?" she asked.

"Yes. Yes I am. And you?"

"Nope. With good timing, I can hit two churches in one Sunday. So I'm scooting across town to check out the Pentecostals."

As I left the building, I got the departure nod from Bulletin Guy. I nodded back, then turned to Alexis, who was hurrying down the front steps. "Hey, you do know they're a bit more, um, proactive. In their style of worship, I mean."

Down the sidewalk now, she spoke over her shoulder. "I can be proactive."

I paused on the stairs and leaned into a wrought-iron railing. "I'll bet you can. So how do the Pentecostals rank?"

She stopped and turned to face me. "A Pentecostal church was number one last week."

"Ya think North Hills Prez can stay in the top ten?"

"Maybe . . . if you and Steve Cole start wearing ties."

After watching her get in her car and drive away, I loped across the parking lot to the singles class. But a note on the door said our teacher was sick and had no substitute.

As I drove home, a random thought hit me, actually *hit* me, right in the nose. What if *I* were to continue rotating through churches to meet the right girl, and the right girl was also out there rotating, and we picked different denominations every week? We'd simply crisscross in the same city without ever meeting—while decades passed and my blond went to gray and her eggs died.

I'd be sixty-eight, off to Litchfield Beach on yet another singles retreat, hobbling up to a seafood buffet, humming pop songs, and watching lobsters go to hell.

18

Luggage spilled from the closet as I began preparing for my New York interview. Navy pinstripe suit, white button-down, red tie. Be at the airport by 7:00 A.M.

The flight left Greenville at 7:40, and by 8:15 I was inside Charlotte International, munching on a waffle and waiting to change planes.

I always asked for a window seat, and on most flights, with the jet high above the clouds, I would even use the high altitude to try and make up for experiences that my generation had missed.

Like the draft.

I would pretend to be in an Allied bomber over Europe in 1944 and make high-pitched noises through my nose. Probably not normal for a guy in a pinstripe suit to do such things, but in four hours I'd be sitting across from some Ivy League blue blood grilling me about my market savvy, and this helped me relax.

And deep down, I knew that my vocation of staring at little numbers flashing across a computer screen—prosperity masquerading as video game—was only possible because others went before me, staring not at computer screens but at mortars, missiles, and machine-gun bullets.

We throw money at stocks; they threw themselves over grenades.

Mercy.

The ones who made it back home, the survivors, they should have the five-bedroom on the golf course. We should *give* it to 'em. Car of their choice, too.

In five seconds we'd be over Normandy, and I could sense the incoming artillery. But my concentration got interrupted as the pilot said we could unbuckle our seat belts, and that below us, it was sunny in Virginia.

"My son makes those noises, too," said the pantsuited lady seated next to me. "Usually in the back of the minivan after I pick him up from pre-school."

She could've just asked me to stop; no need to be sarcastic. I gave no response, just sat there picturing her leaving a restaurant with her husband, him unlocking her door, her not returning the favor.

Cloud cover wrapped our jet in swirling wisps of gray as beams of sunlight pierced the cumulus, the atmosphere on fast-forward. The pilot said we were approaching the city.

We descended over the Hudson River, and all my right-side window mates joined me to gaze out at the sunlit financial district, seconds later at the Empire State Building, then at the giant green rectangle of Central Park. The city looked intimidating with its row after row of concrete towers—a more polished and refined concrete than Myrtle Beach, however, and containing, most certainly, fewer bottle blondes.

Thirty minutes later, a cab dropped me off at Broad and Wall. The first thing I noticed was how much black they wear in New York City: Europeans in black, minorities in black, upscale women in black, old men in black, and college girls in the black garments of youth.

And me in a navy pinstripe and red tie.

Not a happy color, black, but the Yanks wore it well. And they all looked straight ahead as they trekked the sidewalks. Survival mode.

In South Carolina, I'd been getting used to casual waves, various shades of beige, and the fact that, in the health-conscious Palmetto State, barbecue was considered a vegetable.

After one more perusal of the skyscrapers and the fashions, I concluded that none of those things ever happened here.

When I entered our corporate office at the corner of Rector Street, I was greeted by a young Hispanic woman seated behind the front desk. She wore a black silk top and, for a New Yorker, a friendly smile. I felt relaxed, confident.

"I'll tell Mr. Galbraith you're here," she said, reaching for the phone.

On the tenth floor, she led me down a marble hallway, the floor all swirly and glossy-gray, so shiny I could see my reflection.

"You coming?" she asked, five paces ahead.

"Yes, ma'am."

We stepped into a trading room filled with quote screens, Reuters news feeds, and spastic traders in light-blue button-downs, large sweat spots expanding at their armpits.

"Which one is he?" I asked, scanning the room.

"The mean-looking one," she said, pointing toward the window.

"Thank you, Miss Martinez."

"Good luck, Mr. Jarvis."

And I thought only Southern women had big hair.

I waded through a hundred quote screens. Traders shouted buys and sells. Stocks moving up flashed green; those moving down flashed red— tens of millions of dollars moving in and out of the market as a hundred Wall Street firms just like this one watched every tick, at the same instant, with the same goal: to maximize profit. We'd become the consummate capitalists, creating wealth for clients, and ourselves, without any tangible benefit to the rest of society.

Four flat-panel monitors sat atop Vince Galbraith's oval cherry-wood desk, the desk where he barked orders to his assistant, a tall, twenty-something guy with gold suspenders worn tight over his obligatory light-blue button-down. Vince was total concentration, his eyes darting back and forth between screens with a rapidity rivaled only by air-traffic controllers. I would've bet that his parents bought him Ivy League pajamas as a kid. But he was the Big Dog in this upper-class yard, so me and my navy pinstripes stood silent, watching a nation's wealth rise and fall over his left shoulder.

"Take ten thousand G.E." he yelled, still not aware that I was standing behind him.

"The offer just dropped to five, sir," said the assistant, his eyes locked on the bid and ask.

"Then take the five and bid up an eighth for another five," barked Vince.

"I wouldn't get too heavy with G.E.," I said, interrupting. "They're half financial conglomerate now, and if the Fed raises rates . . . could be dicey."

Vince turned and looked at me as if I'd just told a Ph.D. in math how to convert fractions to decimals. "Duh," he said. "The Fed news is already priced in the stock."

I knew that.

He eyed my navy suit. "You're Jarvis, eh? I've heard about you. No deep accents allowed here, though. Confuses the clerks at the stock exchange."

"Slightly Texan," I said. "Nothing offensive."

"That's good," he said, "real good, because no one here would understand 'I'd lyke to buy fo-thousand shayuhs of Mayburry R.F.D., puhleez.'"

I gave no response to that.

He looked me over again, sizing me up before turning his attention back to the markets. "Did Brophy tell you to grow that scruff so you'd look older?"

"He told our whole office to grow it."

"Doesn't help. I tried it myself," he said, scanning his screens. "So, whaddaya like right now? I mean *right* now."

I did not hesitate. "OPEC sticking to their quotas means more pressure to drill for oil in the Gulf of Mexico. I like Transocean."

"What's that symbol? R what?" he shouted, looking left and right for a response. "Will someone please tell me the bleepin' symbol?"

"RIG."

"RIG is up three-eighths, heavy volume," said the assistant.

"Stick a bid in for ten thousand at the last trade," yelled Vince.

I couldn't believe he was buying my idea. "I didn't know you were going to—"

"What?" he asked. "This is the interview. If Jay *make* money, Jay might get job in New York; but if Jay *lose* money, Jay go back South and watch *Hee Haw*. Okay? Say, you wanna Diet Coke?"

"A regular Coke." The cocky, Ivy League blue blood.

165

"We got the ten thousand RIG, sir," said the assistant. "But it's down a quarter now from our price."

Vince pierced me with his stare. I didn't budge. Wasn't breathing, but I also didn't budge.

"I'd buy another ten thou," I said, swinging for the fences. "The pullbacks have been short lately with the underlying strength in crude-oil prices."

He shook his head, wiped his brow. "Take five thousand more RIG," he said to the assistant, but there was doubt in his voice. We had just bought fifteen thousand shares of a fifty-dollar stock, spent three-quarters of a million bucks from the house account and I wished Mr. Gruber could see this and where was that cola?

"A couple of fifty-thousand share blocks of RIG just crossed the tape, sir. It's up a half," said the assistant. He handed me a Diet Coke, took a swig from his own, and for several minutes we sat transfixed, united in the continual darting of three pair of eyes.

"Now it's up a full point!" he said.

Two more traders scurried over from neighboring desks to view the action. I watched pigeons flutter at the window, then took a casual glance at my watch, as if my Pop-Tarts should be coming up soon.

"What time do the Yankees play tonight?" I inquired.

All business, their eyes shifted from the monitors to me, anxiously looking for a decision. I waited ten more seconds, then gave one. "Okay, Vince, I'd sell a chunk."

"How much?" he demanded.

"Ten thousand shares, but scale out of it. Sell five thou, then three, then two. Feed the shares to the market like it's a duck waddling up a bank."

"Oh, gimme a break, Jarvis."

We sold ten thousand shares at the end of the day for a point-and-a-half profit, or fifteen thousand dollars. Took all of an hour and forty-five minutes.

He and his assistant lost three thousand bucks on their G.E.

Vince Galbraith took me to dinner at Sardi's, where we enjoyed filet mignon and fudge cheesecake below the red frames of celebrity. While I would describe no one in the place as dressed to the nines, the majority of patrons and all the waiters were at least to the eights, and I would even give the beggar we passed on the sidewalk, in his black trousers and dirty fedora, a solid five.

Impressive place, Sardi's. On every wall, the red frames held comic sketches of famous people, though I couldn't tell if the one over Vince's shoulder was Archie Bunker or Sergeant Schultz. I went with Archie and ate my dessert.

"I almost hate to admit it, Jarvis," said Vince, sipping an espresso, "but you're at the top of my list for the position."

"Sounds good. How many more interviews you giving?"

He took a last bite of cheesecake, savored it for a moment, and made eye contact. "Three more. Then I'll make my decision within a couple weeks."

I gently wiped my mouth and said, "You may not wanna wait that long."

He looked perturbed. "And just what, pray tell, is your reasoning?"

"The South, Vince . . . we might rise again."

Vince rolled his eyes, dropped a forty-dollar tip on the red tablecloth, and said he needed to get going, that he lived in Connecticut and it took him a subway, a cab, and a train to get there.

On the walk to my hotel room, I remembered to stare straight ahead while traversing below the bright lights, trying my best not to appear friendly. *Just act the part and stay stone-faced.*

My hotel was only three blocks away, on 45th, but a small crowd piled up at the intersection with 6th. They all stood silent and disengaged, waiting on the sign to say "walk." Across the street, another crowd waited to move toward us, their stares paralleling our own. Must've been a city ordinance against sight lines crossing.

The sign seemed stuck on "don't walk." Behind me, a warbled attempt at speech leaked from a bricked alley—and I did what I was told not to do.

I looked.

The sign finally changed, and the crowd stepped from the curb in synchronized detachment. Except for me. Planted on the sidewalk, I peered into the alley again while dodging a well-dressed horde of impatient Yanks.

He was sprawled against a damp brick wall. A sliver of light angled across his midsection. The bum's jacket appeared to have been tan or olive in its original state, the dirt and stains now giving it the appearance of an oily rag with thin lapels.

But maybe he wasn't a bum; maybe he was just homeless.

He lifted one arm and attempted a wave, though gravity pulled it down. Perplexed, he looked down at the arm as if to ask, "Why'd you do that?"

"Ya gots fifty cent?" he mumbled. "Quarter? . . . . Jes' anything, mistuh."

What struck me was not his appearance, nor even his language, but his method of collection. An office-sized water jug, complete with bluish tint and thin plastic circles molded into the middle, sat at his feet. It was half full with water, and a smattering of coins lay across the bottom.

He saw me staring at the jug and reached over and thumped it with his forefinger. "My bank," he said slowly. "My quiet little bank."

"Just a second," I said, digging in my pocket for change.

He glanced at my shoes, thumped the jug again. "Thems fine shoos, suh. Thems really fine shoos."

I counted my coinage. "All right, I have five quarters here. But you have to answer one question."

"I saids them was fine shoos." He pointed at my feet, but his eyes locked on my hand.

"I know the shoes are of good quality, but I need you to answer a question."

"About da shoos?"

"No, not about the shoos. . . . Why the water jug? You fish out the coins every night?"

His face went blank, his unkempt head moving up and down, bobbing in the sluggish rhythm of the listless. "Why? 'Cause I'm special. Verrry special."

"You're what?"

"All my competition, them guys use cups. Makes a coin rattle. But I let 'em fall soft in the water . . . float down in my jug. That way nobody know 'bout it but me and the giver. That why."

He looked exhausted from that bit of conversation and let his head drop. My first quarter fluttered quietly to the bottom. I reached to drop in the next one and felt his hand jerk my leg.

"Hold it," he said. "You gotta grin when you do that."

Startled, I stepped back, pulling away from his grip. "You want me to smile?"

"Nah, I wants to see you grin. Nobody in this town ever grin no more."

I grinned so big I had to shut my eyes. But when I opened them again, he was already asleep, his breathing shallow and indifferent.

After dropping my remaining four quarters in rapid succession, I watched the last one flutter left and lean against the side, as if hesitant to complete the journey.

I returned to an empty intersection and that same stubborn sign, the little square goblin stuck once again in a white light of opposition. So I figured it was time for a bit of New York nepotism. I Jaywalked.

Across the intersection, I made my way down New York's generous and well-lit sidewalks, wondering all the while how that bum works his jug technique in winter.

For $240 a night, I was expecting something more than a bed, one window, and a TV. Perhaps a crow's nest and an ocean view. The long, emerald green curtains were a nice touch, though, parted slightly where I could see a sliver of Times Square from my perch on the sixteenth floor.

While staring out across the city, I considered life's momentum—from midnight walks on a beach to wacko dates with Plan B; from Dallas to Carolina, from Carolina to Manhattan; from Bossman Tate Brophy to Yankee blue blood Vince Galbraith.

On the corporate ladder, there is no rung labeled "bliss."

Sleepy now, I closed the curtains and returned to thoughts of the bum and how a man arrived at such station, his meager 401k at the bottom of a water jug. With only a bedside lamp for illumination, I sprawled across the bed, on my back, still in my T-shirt and pinstriped slacks.

Me and New York.

New York and me.

Me, New York, and a fat, year-end bonus.

New York, me, a fat, year-end bonus, and becoming the boss of Vince Galbraith.

Full of myself, I decided a bit of counterbalance was called for—a brief consultation with the Gideons, sitting there unused and all shiny atop the dresser.

As had become my habit, I turned to the quick-and-easy Proverbs, stopping this time in row fourteen, seat twelve.

"There is a way which seems right unto a man, but its end is the way of death."

This did not seem applicable, so I set it back on the dresser and walked to the window for another gander at the bright lights.

I woke to the blaring of cab horns. Friday morning in the Big Apple. There was nothing on my agenda except travel, and the plane didn't leave until noon.

Aboard the subway, lost in Manhattan, I wore jeans and a black golf shirt, another feeble attempt at conformity. The quickening pace of wheel-on-rail slowed abruptly, and I grabbed hold of a pole, trying to gain some semblance of bearing. But they'd marked each stop with a new color, and I couldn't remember if my color was orange or yellow and Mr. Brophy said don't talk to the bums and don't look at anyone on the subway, so now thorough confusion set in because yesterday I was *above* ground in a taxi.

A multitude departed the subway, and I was up the crowded stairs toward daylight, asking myself what a person tries to see in New York City when they only have an hour.

The answer, I reckoned, was that you try to see it all.

Some eighty floors later, the elevator door slid open. People gasped; there was too much to take in. And I still didn't believe King Kong ever climbed this thing, this monstrosity, this Empire State Building. Curious and excited, the patrons wanted to go up higher, but the usher said no and cautioned everyone to stay behind glass.

I walked a hurried circumference, absorbing it all, each rectangular pane revealing a new aristocracy: first Brooklyn, then Soho, now Greenwich and Midtown, Harlem and Jersey and Queens. There's Liberty with her torch, and an empty Ellis Island where various spices of the melting pot first pledged allegiance.

Twenty minutes and I had already seen it all.

Tourist ferries circled the harbor, while tiny yellow ants—formerly taxi cabs—eased through the streets below. Such loftiness made for a good place to think, and I was thinking Vince Galbraith would offer me the job. My take-home pay would double, but housing costs would triple.

I wanted the job. Would tolerate Vince.

Beside me, two elderly ladies were placing coins in a viewing scope. One pointed it to the west and said in a slow, Irish accent, "I believe I can see the entire fruited plain, dear."

"Let me look," said the other, crowding in. "You can!"

They spun their scope to the east. "And there's me brother Paddy in Dublin. If you squint you can see him hoisting his pint. Wave at him, dear."

Shoulder to shoulder, they giggled and waved at Ireland.

Briefly, my thoughts turned inward, and I considered that maybe—like Allie said during our walk on the shore—God really does give direction.

I watched the yellow ants cross the Brooklyn Bridge, watched them blend with tiny trucks and shrunken buses. After a few minutes, I turned my back to uptown Manhattan, and from behind the glass, I imagined a breeze in my face. Another tourist boat circled Liberty, then my line of sight raised up and out over the hazy southwest.

I took a wild guess at longitude, stood on my toes, and waved at Ecuador.

19

The Circle of Nine gathered again in Steve's living room, the room with the lime-tinged rug chosen by the tall blonde to whom all things lime-ish merited great value, but who preferred her romance in no other color than invisible.

Chips and colas were scattered about, Stanley and his plaid Bermuda shorts sat across the circle, and Tuesday's stock quotes were embedded in my eyelids.

In his Laguna Beach T-shirt, Ransom brought our meeting to order. "I thought we might try for a deeper level of manly accountability," he said. "So in a few minutes, we'll break off into pairs."

And I figured the married guy would be the odd man out, since nine isn't divisible by two . . . except maybe in South Carolina, because I heard in some South Carolina public schools they'll let a kid spell *Louisiana* without vowels, then send him along to the next grade as if he were God's gift to linguistics.

"But first I wanna talk about our not becoming sponges," said Ransom. "We're all gonna become overweight sponges if we just soak up spiritual data and never get out into the world to be squeezed."

Steve rubbed his hairy leg and tried to look sophisticated. "So then a community full of spiritual data-soakers would be called, what . . . spongedom?"

"That's a good word, dude. Write that one down."

Steve clicked his pen.

"Hold it," said Stanley. "Are you calling the great city of Greenville *spongedom?*"

"I am," said Ransom. "Well, parts of it."

"I don't think so," said Stanley. "My knowledge and understanding of God's omnipotence is directly attributable to the antidispensational theological stance of our church leadership."

"Huh?" Steve said through a mouthful of chips.

My turn. "Yeah, me and Steve agree with Ransom."

"You're just a rookie," said Stanley, his cheeks puffed out.

"And you," countered Ransom, pointing his pen at Stanley, "you are the captain commander of all sponge forces."

We were postponing the inevitable, so I began the process. "When do we do the I lust/you lust confessional?"

Ransom rolled his eyes. "Wait till you pair off. While you were in New York, Jay, we discussed how we might try to make ourselves useful in the community. Maybe take on a project, a weekend of service to someone in need. This could be our opportunity to be squeezed." He scanned the circle. "Do we acknowledge the plan?"

We nodded our heads, acknowledged the plan.

"Okay," said Ransom, "you dudes break off into pairs now and try to be tough on each other, be accountable. We'll discuss the work project when I finish my tacos."

I did not want to be held accountable; I wanted to be the leader who is married and gets to eat tacos.

With a hopeful expression on his young, collegiate face, Barry asked if we could once again monetize his navy blue Nike cap. He removed his lid, holding it out to solicit our cash. But Stanley said donations were a one time deal and that Barry needed to learn humility. I silently pleaded with God not to pair me off with Stanley.

Steve and I manipulated the pairing-off, however, and ended up partners.

"Go in there," he said, pointing toward his kitchen. He swiped a chip from his Cubs jersey and motioned for me to sit at the breakfast table.

Mismatched dishes overflowed from his sink; matching baseballs adorned the windowsill. Alone now with Mr. Sneaky, I figured it was better to be the asker than the askee.

"So, how many denominations for you, Steve-O?" I asked as casually as possible.

He folded his arms and said, "What are you talking about, Jarvis?"

"You know . . . to meet women. How many churches have you rotated through during your seven years in Greenville?"

Steve fidgeted with a pencil, then glanced at the pretzels and soft drinks on his kitchen counter. "I don't remember. Is that what we're supposed to discuss?"

"In a roundabout way. So, how many?"

"I just wouldn't . . ."

This was fun, being the asker. "C'mon, how many?"

"I'm not tellin' unless you do."

"Okay, so how many?"

The Cubs logo deflated across his chest as he sighed and gave in. "Only three," he said. "Pentecostal, Methodist, and of course, North Hills Presbyterian. Now how about you, Jay Jarvis? This is two-sided accountability, ya know."

"Yeah, I know. Sorry . . . only Presbyterian for me."

Steve looked disappointed. He got up from the table, walked to the counter, and opened the pretzels. "Jay, have you heard that rumor about a group of girls in this town who've developed a spreadsheet that ranks churches by the quality of men?"

I took two pretzels and ate them one at a time. "Did hear some rumblings about that. The audacity of those girls."

Steve reached for the Pepsi, unscrewed the top. "It's crazy out there."

"Whose autograph you got?" I asked, nodding at the baseballs in his window.

Ice cubes rattled his glass. "Sosa and McGriff."

"Cool."

He paused to let the fizz diminish. "Your dad play sports, Jay?"

"Taught me the curveball. Yours?"

"Good knuckleball, decent curve. Wanna refill?"

I nodded my head. "Thanks," I said, taking back my glass. But the fizz went up my nose, smiting me for my impatience.

Steve sat again and slurped his drink. "So tell me . . . would Jesus do it?"

"Would he do what?"

"You know, would he drink a brew on the beach."

I set my glass on the table and leaned back in my chair. "Is this what we're supposed to talk about?" My question, however, was only an attempt to avoid the subject; so little data existed in my Jesus file.

"We can talk about anything we want," said Steve. "It's just the two of us. And man, am I ever glad I didn't get paired off with Stanley."

"Me too."

"So, would he drink the brew?"

"Stanley?"

"No, Jesus."

"I dunno. Maybe. He might be inconspicuous about it."

"So what are you saying . . . that God's own Son would wrap it in a brown paper bag?"

"What I'm saying is that I do not know. I do not know if he'd drive fast, eat slow, wear a Stetson, or hitchhike. So as to the matter of whether he'd partake or not, if I say yes, it makes him look like a wino. But if I say no, it makes him look legalistic. So the only reasonable answer is, it depends."

"So your answer is the same as Allie's?"

I paused, thought it over. "Seems the most reasonable."

He gulped the last of his Pepsi. "You miss her, don't ya?"

He was right, although more than missing her, I mostly thought her refreshing, one of the very few unjaded people currently inhabiting the planet. "Never met anyone like her."

Steve stood and dumped his ice in the sink. "Let's not talk about women."

"Okay. Let's not."

"So how was New York?" he asked.

"Big and eccentric," I replied. "And the interview went great, considering the interviewer was a jerk."

"You're not moving there, are ya? I mean, you just got here."

"Corporate America, my friend. They own us. And the money is *very* good." I thought, for a brief moment, that Steve looked downcast at the possibility of me moving.

But then he just shrugged and began loading the dishwasher, talking as he racked. "I do have one serious question, Jay. I haven't been paying much attention in church lately and feel like . . ."

"What's the question?"

"About why it says fruit instead of fruits. I don't get it."

Pausing for effect, I framed my answer the Presbyterian way. With food. "Near as I can tell, it seems to be saying that each bite contains the whole . . . like soup instead of LifeSavers."

Steve poured liquid detergent in the slot, then turned and raised an eyebrow. "Not bad for a rookie."

I held out my glass. "More Pepsi, bro."

Tacos gone, Ransom beckoned the rest of us to recircle our chairs around Steve's lime-tinged rug. "Okay," he said, wiping his chin. "We gotta decide about the volunteer project, our weekend of service. Any ideas yet?"

Steve walked in, twirling a dishrag. "I checked with Habitat for Humanity," he said, "but the Baptists have all the volunteer time filled through November."

"That's over two months away," said Ransom. "Too long a wait."

"I called the lady who leads Women of the Church," offered Stanley, sprawled in Steve's blue corduroy recliner. "They could use some gardening help."

"Gardening?" asked Ransom. "Did you say gardening? No way. This work must include the use of power tools."

"I'm no good with power tools," muttered Stanley.

"But you're pretty good with the women," Barry said. "Tell us about Rona."

"No," said Stanley.

"Oh, c'mon," said Ransom.

"No!"

"How many dates?"

Stanley looked at the floor, crossed his feet. "Seven."

Ransom grinned and said, "Nice going, Stanley, you surprised us all. But now we gotta take care of business." He said how pitiful that nine men couldn't come up with one good suggestion to make themselves useful in the community. "Guys, do we not know anyone outside of our yuppie circles?"

Silence.

"C'mon, dudes," pleaded Ransom. "Surely we can come up with at least one name."

Our second long silence grew unbearable, so I raised my hand. "I may know of something. It's a long drive, but this old preacher has a house that needs work down near—"

"Back down at the coast?" asked Steve, interrupting.

"Yeah, somewhere north of Charleston. Sounded like a dump. It's in a place he called the lowcountry, whatever that means."

"I'm not driving all the way to the lowcountry," said Stanley.

Ransom rubbed his chin as he considered my offer. "Jay, you're not talking about that guy who . . . the shark guy?"

"That would be him."

When Ransom asked me to call Asbury, I was a tad reluctant, for there was no telling what would happen if I hooked up with him again.

During my drive home from Steve's, a Lexus cut me off from the turn lane. I flashed my brights, the beam reflecting off a chrome-plated fish glued to the back of the trunk.

He made the light. I did not.

But I stifled road rage and used the extra time to contemplate the fruit, small samples from each basket, the good and the bad.

Debauchery and Idolatry . . . I had those two figured out—evil twin brothers who lurked deep inside the Internet and Porsche dealerships.

Self-control and Patience . . . probably related, like stepsisters. I had a bit of the first, hardly any of the second. Possible arch enemies of Idolatry and Debauchery.

Gentleness . . . surely reserved for women and children; had little to do with men.

Drunkenness . . . self-explanatory.

Faithfulness . . . I was working on that one, and assumed it had something to do with the old guy and his psychedelic pages.

Envy . . . see Idolatry.

Peace . . . that was the one that got me. Did anyone ever really achieve peace?

Married people could have their bliss, the elderly their contentment, and the wealthy their security, but peace I could not define. Maybe Faulkner had been right: Maybe peace was a past-tense quality. Maybe after we'd waded through our personal muck and the scrabble of daily routine, we could look back at an event, at a time, at a snippet from a perfect day under perfect skies and say ahh, then, right there, I had me some peace.

Maybe peace wasn't a present-tense phenomenon.

Maybe, like casual waves on Manhattan sidewalks, it just didn't happen in real time.

20

Monday morning I woke to big and little dogs howling at a distant siren. They were all off-key, and to make matters worse, half the dogs began barking when they should've been howling, then commenced to howling when they should've been barking.

This, too, never happened in Dallas. Monday mornings in Dallas, the dogs would harmonize.

Honest.

I drove to work in a drizzle. A warm drizzle, since it was still mid-September. At each of the six stoplights between my house and the office—having nothing better to do—I looked around to count the chrome-plated fish. Less than half the cars had one, but it seemed more were stuck to the rears of expensive cars than beat-up cars.

Maybe the poor could not afford them. Or maybe the rich figured such decor might help their chances, what with the odds stacked against them over that eye-of-the-needle thing.

I could not decide. But I didn't care to own one; a Dallas Cowboys sticker graced the rear of my Blazer, and that was enough ID.

On the other hand, if I got the New York job, I would soon be a camel myself. So as I pulled into reserved parking, I was neutral on the subject.

I sloshed into our office lobby, and as usual, the TV in the corner was fixed on the financial channel. It was also raining in Manhattan, and the young reporter lady on the screen said all premarket indicators looked down. Very down.

It would be a most volatile day.

"Mr. Franklin Gruber on the phone, sir."

I grabbed my headset. "Thank you, Glenda. . . . Yessir, Mr. Gruber, they have had to recall every remote-control G. I. Joe from the shelves due to heads and feet falling off and the fear that a young child could swallow one. The stock is getting hammered. Sorry, this is the downside of capitalism. We could buy more—"

Words not usually associated with the Bible Belt rattled in my headset.

"I know, I know, Mr. Gruber, we've already bought more on three separate occasions. We've chased it all the way down, but you still have all the shares you've ever purchased. All 1,260 shares of Toys 'R' Us are still in the account. They're just worth 40 percent less, at the current price, than what you paid for them."

In the world of Wall Street, September is one nutty month. With extra pecans. The market had plummeted from the opening bell, and our office was flooded with calls from panicky clients bailing out, cursing us for leading them astray.

By midmorning the clients were selling without regard to price. "Just get me a bid!" they screamed. Every stock on my screen flashed red as longtime owners of Cisco and Microsoft, Boeing and Merck, all lost their minds in a unity of foolishness, retreating to the safety of cash. This felt like a capitulation, the point at which no one wants to own anything and swears off investing forever.

The market dropped 200, 250, 300 points. Dialing number after number, I urged my clients to buy. They would not listen. "Just get me out!" they hollered.

Mr. Gruber was not spared from the fear. He called me back and sold all of his Toys 'R' Us stock—at a huge loss. I said, "Don't do it, Franklin." But he just could not take the pain anymore and insisted we sell. So we sold.

As if on cue, the market reversed in a whoosh as thousands realized they had acted herdlike—they had sold low, sold into the panic.

Very bad for your financial health, that selling into panic.

Even worse, a mere two hours after Gruber had sold, the Toys 'R' Us company announced that the problem wasn't as bad as they had originally thought.

By 4:00, the stock was up 30 percent.

After holding her stocks for over forty years, the prescient one—eighty-year-old Beatrice Dean—waited two days for the market to fully rebound, then came in before noon to sell it all. She shuffled into my office wearing a Gardening Club T-shirt, a yellow watch with a daisy face, and a straw hat encircled with two lavender bands. A single blue-jay feather stuck out from behind the lavender. Her soft eyes twinkled beneath the brim, and I thought her a wrinkled teenager.

"Mr. Jarvis, that's a fake, isn't it?" she asked, pointing toward my window.

"What's fake, Beatrice?"

"That plant in the corner; it's a fake."

"Yes, ma'am. It is."

"Shame on you, dear."

I offered her a seat, but she ignored my chivalry and instead huddled around my quote screen to watch her transactions process.

I punched in the first order: Sell 6,800 shares of Ford.

In an instant, the shares were gone. Swallowed up.

"My, my," she said, staring at the screen. "Stock goes from owned to sold much quicker than roses go from bud to bloom."

"Yes. Now for the PG," I said, reading the totals off her account statement.

"Yes," said Beatrice, smiling now. "Today I finally sell Piedmont Gas."

"No, Beatrice, PG is the symbol for Proctor & Gamble."

She blinked rapidly, then raised the brim of her hat. "Well, I declare. And all these years I thought I owned Piedmont Gas."

"No, ma'am, you own Proctor & Gamble. It's currently at eighty-seven per share."

For a long moment, she just sat there in a trance. "Just curious, dear, but what is the price for Piedmont Gas?"

I called up the quote. "It's at thirty-three and a half."

181

"Well, then, lucky me."

I punched in the order: Sell 4,600 shares of Proctor & Gamble.

She scooted in closer. "You know, dear, I've been using their soaps since I was in grade school."

The order was confirmed. "That's a lot of soap, Beatrice."

"Yes, Jay," she said, her nose inches from my quote screen. "Now for the ABC."

"You mean AT&T."

"Of course, dear. Sell all but one share."

"But you sold two shares back in May. Now you want to keep just one share?"

"Yes, so I can vote at shareholder meetings. They should reduce their rates."

I punched in 9,397 shares of AT&T. Ten seconds later, the trading desk in Manhattan called me back and asked if I was sure.

I said, "Yes, Manhattan, we are sure."

Then without warning, Beatrice leaned in to where she could speak into my headset and said, "Yes, Manhattan, some old Carolina ladies are going to Europe, and we are sure!"

While waiting for her cash balance to print, Beatrice excused herself and hurried from my office. Curious, I looked out my window and watched her cross the parking lot. She opened the door to a gray Oldsmobile and, while holding her hat in place, stooped over and pulled out a Saran-wrapped package. She returned to my office with a basket of homemade gingerbread cookies. Shaped like elves. Raisins for eyeballs.

"I was hoping you wouldn't charge me a commission, dear," she said, pulling back the Saran wrap. Fresh scents of ginger filled my office.

"Mmm, delicious, Beatrice," I said, biting the head off one. Crumbs fell onto my keyboard, but I didn't care.

She smiled and asked for 5 percent of her account for travel money.

Three minutes later, her check was cut. She held it up to a fluorescent light, inspecting the paper as if it were some undiscovered foliage. The check was for just over forty thousand bucks.

"Lovely, Jay." And she folded her check in two.

"Can I walk you out?" I asked, motioning toward the door.

She reached across the desk and patted my hand. "I know my way out, dear."

"Oh . . . okay. So, are Francine and Trevor still planning to travel with you?"

She didn't answer immediately but walked back over to inspect my fake potted plant. "We haven't worked it all out yet, dear. There are now eleven women wanting to go. But before we leave, you simply must fill me in on the aqua-door girl."

"She's still behind that door, ma'am."

Beatrice Dean didn't say anything else. She just flicked a plastic leaf with her finger, shook her head, and strolled out of my office.

21

Seated alone at the end of pew twenty-three, I heard the same hymns from my initial visit. Over a dozen visits now, and a recognizable pattern had emerged from the North Hills Presbyterian choir: Every fourth week the hymns repeated, starting with the longest.

Sorta like the moon phases, but less romantic.

I had become a note taker, and today I ended up with a half page of Israel wandering in the desert with a limited menu. A good Sunday morning for me, since I even remembered to bring a check for when they passed the brass.

Blessed and dismissed, I shuffled up the burgundy carpet, trapped behind the elderly. Though something didn't feel right: a page of notes, a check dropped in brass—both good, but how good? And what was the standard? Did something just accrue to me, like in a monthly savings account?

I could not decide.

Across the parking lot, Steve bid me sit next to him at the end of the second semicircle. He polished off a donut and straightened his tie.

Three weeks had elapsed since I'd last been a powdered Presbyterian. One bite, however, and flourlike powder sprinkled my khaki pants.

"You borrowed that tie, didn't you?" I asked, pestering Steve by running his silk accessory between my thumb and forefinger.

"Ransom took pity on me," Steve said. His shirt was white; his tie, bright yellow. Little green waves seemed to glide horizontally across the silk.

Progressive, those surfer ties.

I restrained a yawn and watched a horde of singles file in, suits and dresses color coordinated with Sunday smiles. On the far side of the room, Nancy and six Numericals took their seats—together. Tall, lime-lovin' Darcy sat behind them. Alone.

Seemed to me that a singles class would at least try to sit boy-girl-boy-girl, if only to hurry things up a bit.

In the front row, black-suited Stanley sat beside red-clad Rona, though crazy Alexis was nowhere to be seen. Maybe she was Methodist this week. Or Quaker.

"Heard from your interview yet?" asked Steve, wiping his chin.

I shook my head no. "Those Yanks take their time. So how's the world of civil engineering?"

"Makes my Jeep payment," he said. "Not much else."

Wade Dornan, our punctual, gray-suited teacher, adjusted his podium and called us to attention. "Be absolutely truthful, answer completely, and do not put your name on these sheets. This survey is only to find out where we are as a class and to provide feedback for church leadership, who feel somewhat disconnected from the singles."

"No kidding," said a voice from the back. "They stick us 'cross the lot in a building by ourselves."

"Take your time," said Wade, ignoring the comment. "Your answers can be as long or as short as they need to be. Do *not* put your name on the paper. I would like to read these back to the class for our mutual benefit, before turning the answers over to the pastor."

The stack had by then reached the end of our semicircle. I clicked my pen.

One simple question occupied the page. After ten minutes, the rustling of paper and the stirring of feet signaled to Wade that our quiz was complete. We turned the sheets upside down and passed them to the end of the row.

Wade rearranged the stack and cleared his throat. "The question is: Why do you attend this singles class? I've picked out twenty or so to read back to you. Maybe a consensus will emerge."

Oh, what consensus would emerge.

Coughs and cringes followed the pronouncement. Steve covered his face with a church bulletin.

Wade, calm and expressionless, peered up from the stack. "Here, class, are your answers." His voice had taken on a deep, monotonal quality.

"To get to know Jesus."

"To learn to pray."

"To go on the beach trips."

"Because Alexis said there were lots of cute guys here."

"Because I live next door to the church."

"Because Alexis said there were lots of cute guys here."

"Because there are no good TV shows on Sunday morning."

"Because my dad is a deacon."

"Because Leviticus says if I skip church I will turn into a block of salt like Isaiah's wife."

"Because I was blackballed from the Episcopal denomination. Don't ask."

"To be an obedient follower of Christ and prepare for seminary."

"To meet my soul mate."

"To meet a guy."

"To meet a girl."

"To meet Jesus and a girl."

"To meet the babe in the lime green Cadillac."

"Because Alexis said there were lots of cute guys here."

"Because my neighbor Maurice said it was cool to go to church."

"Because a girl named Allie invited me five months ago when she came thru my checkout line at the grocery store."

Wade looked up from the stack and held aloft one last sheet of paper. "Class, this last answer is a bit long and a bit, well . . . actually, I hesitate to read it out loud. But it's quite entertaining."

"Go ahead and read it," came the voice from the back.

"Go for it, Teach."

"Yeah, Wade," said Steve, "go ahead and read it."

Wade smiled, cleared his throat again.

"To visit purgatory. One does not recognize purgatory at first glance—they serve meatloaf and black-eyed peas. One would expect to gaze out at the distant edges of purgatory and see heaven beckoning from one end, Satan taunting from the other. But that is not so. What you see are Blue Ridge Mountains on one end, and rows of antebellum homes on the other. One more thing they never tell you about purgatory: You do not float there in a body of light or ascend invisibly with your soul intact. You drive. I drive to this class every Sunday. I come for the entertainment, to observe firsthand the tragicomedy of being single in the heart of the Bible Belt. This class is twice as funny as any sitcom on network television.
The End."

Wade attempted a closing prayer but cracked up and dismissed the class instead.

In the parking lot, leaning against his orange Jeep, Steve and I were curious to match answers with faces. I loosened my tie. Steve removed his wave-afflicted loaner and tossed it in his front seat.

We were against the front bumper when I elbowed my friend.

"Don't even ask me, Jarvis," he said, reading my mind. "I will not tell you my answer."

"C'mon. Wanna do mutual confession?"

"Not a chance."

As the class filed past, we pressed them all for answers, though no one would admit to that final, long-winded response. In fact, the only person from whom we could get an answer was red-clad Rona, formerly known as Number Eight, who admitted it was she whom Allie had invited five months ago at the grocery store. Rona waited beside her Toyota and finally left with black-suited Stanley. After we climbed into the Jeep to go grab some lunch, I made a third attempt to pressure Brother Steve. "C'mon, which answer was yours? I gotta know."

He put on his shades and stuck his key in the ignition. "Leviticus and the block of salt."

22

I'd spilled coffee on my client list, the market was melting, and Mr. Gruber would not return my calls. I got his answering machine instead.

"C'mon, Mr. Gruber . . . it's not my fault. We'll find another stock suited just for you. I'm certain of it. Pick up the phone, Mr. Gruber. Pleeeease."

I should not have been surprised. Nature of the business. When the market had been soaring, he'd said it was *we* who had teamed together to produce all those great profits. Now, with things going badly, it was *I* who was at fault—Jay, the lone gunman, plotting my client's demise from behind a grassy knoll.

I was about to try Gruber for a fifth time when Bossman Tate Brophy summoned me to his office. I hurried down the hall, and again he held open his mahogany door for me, although this time his suspenders were turquoise. After sitting down at his desk, he held his glasses carefully between thumb and forefinger, gesturing with them as he forwarded the news concerning my interview.

"First the bad news," he said, wasting no time. "Someone else made a bigger impression—a young Korean girl just out of Stanford. Vince Galbraith really likes her. She made twice the amount of profits as you did during her stint on the trading desk. Then she took *him* to Sardi's and left a hundred-dollar tip."

His face was blank; his tone condescending.

189

"So, no job offer for me, eh?" I was disappointed. And a little bit mad, since I had not thought of the take-Vince-to-dinner strategy.

Suddenly Mr. Brophy grinned and slapped his knee. "There's good news too, Jay."

"What, I get to keep my old job?"

He put his elbows on his desk, interlocked his fingers, and rested his chin there. "They now want you and the girl to comanage a new mutual fund, an aggressive fund concentrating on natural resources like oil, gas, metals, et cetera."

"You're kidding."

"I'm not kidding."

I stood again, hands on hips. "You're really, really not kidding?"

"They want you in New York by November 10," he said, reaching for his vanilla Slim Fast. "That gives you a little over six weeks to distribute your accounts here to the other brokers. But be careful who you give that Gruber guy to. He called me yesterday to complain about some wacked-out problem with plastic feet and G.I. Joes."

"I'll take care of Mr. Gruber, sir."

"Great. And one other thing—who decorated our lobby with all those flowers?"

"They're dahlias, sir. From Beatrice. She cashed out on Wednesday. Sold everything. Over three quarters of a million bucks. Wanted to say thanks. Said she's baking you a pie, too."

"A pie?"

"Peach, I think."

"And you say they're called dahlias?"

"Primrose yellow."

Mr. Brophy set his glasses on the desk and rubbed his eyes. "How do we *get* these people as clients?"

"This is South Carolina, boss."

"Yes . . . yes, it is," he said, extending his hand. "Congratulations, Jay. Proud of you."

"Thank you, sir." I pulled open the mahogany door.

"And Jay?"

"Yessir?"

"Who's that friend of yours who gives the surfing lessons?"

"His name is Ransom, sir."

"Could you get me his number?"

"Will e-mail it at lunch."

"Great. And one more thing . . ."

"Sir?"

"Just remember, that's a big city you'll be moving into. Don't talk to the bums."

"Appreciate the tip, sir."

Back in my office, I high-fived myself six times. Make that seven.

I stayed late that night, reassuring clients that the market would come back, but mostly I sat at my desk and thought, pondering once again life's mercurial momentum. Dallas to Carolina, Carolina to Manhattan. Where would it stop, and when? When did a person accumulate enough to just stop and bake cookies for their stockbroker?

But then reality hit. My drive home evaporated into the countless thoughts and anxieties that accompany promotion. Stoplights came and went, the traffic seemed liquid, and I did not remember turning onto my street.

After a celebratory pizza, I collapsed on my sofa, thinking of sprawling Manhattan and how I'd fit in, of blaring cab horns and if I'd learn to whistle, of Broadway plays and how many I'd get to see, and of the Amazon rainforest, wooden huts on skinny stilts, and a girl at peace with God and her bag of dark chocolates.

Sympathizing with a client who'd just lost thousands is easy, but doing the same with a girl who's been dumped—that's another matter.

Seated in the corner of a red plastic booth, alone with two females at lunch hour, I watched the crowd file into the deli, past our intensity and the warm scent of sourdough bread.

"He just said it without any emotion," complained Lydia, sobbing into a napkin. Her navy blouse hid the tear stains, and a Carolina First Bank name tag hung crooked at the third button.

191

"Surely Joe gave a reason, Lydia," I offered, the words halfhearted as I inspected my sandwich. My lunch plan had been to share my big news, but as soon as I'd walked in, it was evident that the relational would trump the vocational. Big news would have to wait.

Darcy adjusted a clip in her hair before helping to comfort her jilted friend. Oddly, the clip was white, though her dress was indeed an Ann Taylor, and it did indeed match her car. "Guys don't give reasons," said Darcy, talking directly to Lydia. "Ending a relationship to them is like ending a visit to the men's room. . . . They just expect a pull of the handle to clean everything up and leave nary a mess."

I swallowed a second bite of turkey on wheat. "That was so very eloquent, Darcy."

Lydia blew her nose, hid the tissue, and slurped her cola. "Joe said he was leaving to play winter baseball in the Dominican Republic and needed to be free to concentrate . . . as if some pro scout is more important than me."

"How long had you two been seeing each other?" I asked.

She picked at her salad, flicking tomatoes, gathering croutons. "Not long—about the same as Stanley and Rona. . . . We actually double-dated with them once."

"Whoa!" said Darcy. "How did *that* go?"

She blew her nose again and said, "Not so good. Joe said Stanley uses too many big words, and Joe was frustrated 'cause he didn't have his dictionary with him. He just kept nodding his head while Stanley preached a sermon over dessert. Me and Rona ended up drinking coffee and talking about the fall fashions."

"How many dates with Joe?" asked Darcy, adding cream to her gourmet coffee.

"Nine and a half," said Lydia. "Eight and then he went on a road trip for ten days and then he picked me up last week after I got off work at the bank. We went for pizza and the batting cages again, and I thought I *loved* him. Now I gotta explain everything to fifty nosy singles at church, which is even worse than getting dumped."

The tea was too sweet, and I was out of advice. Handing her fresh napkins was my final attempt at compassion.

"Men, they just do not . . ." said Darcy. She looked angry.

"We're not all that way."

"Yes, you are," said Lydia. "And the athletic guys are the worst. No wonder they're always cocky and always self-absorbed and always embarrassing themselves on national TV."

I tried again. "Isn't there a verse somewhere about all things working out for good . . ."

"That doesn't apply to baseball players," said Lydia.

"Jocks have their own verses," said Darcy. "Like, I am the center of the universe and I am immortal and I can dump whoever I want whenever I want."

"But I thought y'all said baseball players can't read."

"Audio cassettes," said Lydia.

"Yeah, audio cassettes," said Darcy, rising from the booth. "And it's one more piece of evidence to back up my theory."

"What theory?" I inquired.

She dropped her tip on the table. "The one I wrote about last Sunday. That the closest thing to purgatory is our church singles group."

"That was you?"

Darcy pulled her blonde mane over one shoulder and handed me the lunch tab.

Another talk was over, another tide crested.

I felt bad for Lydia and her relational rope burn. She wiped her eyes, stood, and dropped her napkin on the table. "Thanks for trying, Jay."

In line to pay the bill, I looked out the deli window to watch Lime Sherbet ramble away: a blonde mane, a red mane, one tall, one short. Like mismatched socks on a clothesline, just a-blowin' in the wind.

23

Blue lights flashed from the northbound lanes of I-385, but through the darkness and across the median it was impossible to tell if the patrolman was Officer Theologian.

I honked anyway—we were southbound.

There were few volunteers to join our work project—only four of us willing to spend the weekend pounding nails with Preacher Asbury Smoak. We were en route to McClellanville, a coastal town over two hundred miles away, somewhere north of Charleston and, according to our map, a mere dot on the road, a lone dot bordered by salt marsh on one side, national forest on the other. The preacher said he'd meet us Friday at midnight. We'd sleep at his house and begin work at daybreak.

At low volume I tuned in to the golden oldies, though rampant snoring, emanating from three of four corners, muted the lyrics. Ransom Delaney in the passenger seat with his head against the window, Steve Cole behind me, and Maurice Evans—sixty-three-year-old janitor extraordinaire—breathing light rhythms into corner number four. Like dogs who can't harmonize, they seemed content to snore and snort over each other in sporadic gulps of pure Southern air.

Forty miles passed. Ransom woke. Said he was hungry and could we stop at the next exit. But the next exit contained only a cheap motel and a convenience store.

He was already back asleep when I parked amid the neon.

My offer to buy snacks was met with a mumble for beef jerky and orange soda, which sounded good, so I doubled the order. Steve said a MoonPie and a chocolate drink would do for him, but Maurice said he didn't care for anything now, thank ya kindly.

"What's the matter, Maurice?"

"Nothin' the matter. I stopped eating junk food."

But an all-night grocer summoned his appetite. After ten minutes of browsing, Maurice walked out with raw carrots, blueberry bagels, and Perrier water.

"Everybody happy now?" I asked, cranking the engine.

"Yeah, uh-huh, mmmyeah."

Bypassing Charleston, we traveled north on the coastal route, a lonely stretch of highway lacking any feature except for a blackened stillness and the heavy scent of salt marsh. McClellanville lay somber. No streetlights to illuminate a sign; no landmark worthy of direction. Asbury said to turn left six miles north from the center of town, but if this qualified as a town, then I was qualified to teach Revelation.

At a quarter to twelve, my comrades were back asleep. Even worse, beef jerky had wedged between my teeth, and my drink was lukewarm.

Off the highway and onto a narrow dirt road, I felt claustrophobic from the tall grass lining the shoulders. Slasher grass, I called it. Like limber green razors, bending forth to slash the unwary.

"Anybody awake?"

There was no response. The odometer showed two miles since we had turned off the highway, though it felt like twenty. In my rearview mirror, trails of dust rose and collapsed into the glow of red taillights. Two lefts, then right again. The road dipped and curved, dust rose and fell, and the slasher grass scraped our doors in dry, bristly taunts.

The Blazer hit a root, jolting tires from ruts and friends from slumber.

"Where have you gotten us now?" asked Ransom, grumbly and half awake. He turned on the dome light. Drops of orange soda stained his shorts.

"He said the house was on this road."

"Who would live here?" he asked, pointing at the blackness.

"No one. It's his inheritance."

Steve tapped my shoulder. "Can we go back and garden with Stanley and the daylily club?"

I glanced in the mirror to see Maurice crossing his index fingers as if to fight off evil spirits, which was just fine, because if you're gonna get lost at night in the barren lowcountry, then what you need is an elderly janitor who thinks he's the exorcist.

Steve gripped and shook my headrest. "We should just turn around and go home."

I stopped in the road and cut off the dome light. "No way."

"You don't understand," said Steve. "All sorts of evil lurks in the low-country."

"Not sayin' you afraid, are ya?" asked Maurice between sips of Perrier.

"I'm saying we should just go home."

Enough of late-night arguments. "Gentlemen, as your driver, I say we plow through both the lowcountry and the lurking evil until we find this House of Asbury."

Steve slumped back in his seat, muttering that I'd never but never drive him anywhere in the future.

"Dude," said Ransom, "you won't be around in the future with that appetite for MoonPies clogging your veins and arteries."

"That's right," said Maurice, taking down his cross. "You should avoid the red meat, too. That stuff may not kill ya fast . . . but it'll kill ya slow, kill ya dead."

"Men," I said, revving the engine, "this is no time to discuss red meat, MoonPies, or killin' us dead. So tell me, do we turn around or do we keep going?"

We voted three to one to keep going, while Steve the Dissenter clutched his arms in mock disgust.

After another mile of dust, roots, and claustrophobia, we spotted a rotting post in the headlights, the letters *S M O A K* carved from top to bottom. I turned my Blazer onto the driveway, a long, sandy path lined with six enormous oak trees. The oaks looked much friendlier than the slasher grass, so I parked beneath the last one and aimed my headlights at the front steps.

Overgrown bushes spilled across the bricks. Two black shutters dangled awkwardly from the second floor. Mongrel weeds, four feet high and bending from their own weight, shadowed the porch.

"That preacher had better be here," said Steve.

"I don't see no lights," said Maurice.

"I don't think he has electricity," Ransom added.

"I don't believe this," said Steve.

We'd been stood up. At 12:30 A.M. By a preacher who pets sharks on the head.

This never happened in Dallas. In Dallas, the preachers were punctual.

Or so I'd heard.

We sat in the Blazer, beneath the oaks, eating junk food and raw carrots, sipping orange soda and Perrier water. Too tired to drive home, too sleepy to make decisions.

"When's Jamie due?" I asked.

"Late February," said Ransom, unwrapping his third beef jerky. "And what about you? Ever hear from Miss Missionary?"

"Sent one letter each, but that was two months ago."

He chewed his jerky and said, "Cool."

High-pitched howls echoed through the blackness; three howls and a bark.

"Lock the doors," said Maurice.

"Already locked," Steve answered.

I told them to go ahead and hide behind locked doors, but that I was going for a look around with my trusty Coleman flashlight. I shut my door, breathed the lowcountry, then turned to see Steve's face pressed against glass, his eyes wide, the window foggy.

Stepping out from the shadowy cover of oaks, I let my light beam span across the house, revealing tattered curtains and more broken shutters. Another howl. Five more steps—I was almost to the porch—and some-

197

thing grunted loudly from behind a bush. So I was back in the front seat and okay let's wait till sunrise.

"What was that?" asked Maurice, pointing at the house with a half-eaten bagel.

"I dunno. Maybe a warthog," I offered, trying to catch my breath.

"Warthogs don't howl, dude," mumbled Ransom, nearly asleep.

"I was talking 'bout the grunts."

"Howls, grunts, dilapidated house . . . this-here work project beginning to remind me of my old neighborhood," said Maurice.

"We ain't sleeping here, Jarvis," said Steve. And there was a pleading in his voice.

"Yes, we are. Right here in this Chevy," I replied, cracking my window.

"What are we doing here?" Ransom asked. "I thought we'd at least be in some sort of development. And who organized this, anyway? *This* is our work project, our service to the Lord?"

"I needed a break from dating."

"I sold my Clemson football tickets," Steve said.

"My wife has all four sisters in town," Maurice said, crunching raw carrots. "I woulda gone anywhere to escape that. So I appreciate the invite, gentlemens."

"G'night," said Ransom, and he leaned into the headrest.

Maurice took a swig of Perrier, made the cross again, and shut his eyes.

Half an hour passed.

One by one, they dozed off.

Through my window, a tenacious drone of crickets buffered the snoring and the snorting. My back complained of the posture, my head of the glass pillow.

"I can't sleep in here."

"Shh."

"Neither can I," said Ransom. "This is even worse than white semi-glossed mosquitoes."

"Wanna tell ghost stories?" I inquired.

"No, we do not wanna tell ghost stories," said Steve, still miffed at our accommodations.

"Might as well," said Maurice, pulling a towel from behind his head. "Go ahead, Ransom, give us your best shot."

Moonlight poured through the windshield, highlighting Ransom's frown as he considered the request. "I got a beautiful wife—we're gonna be parents in five months—and here I am at 2:00 A.M. in the lowcountry, about to tell a ghost story to the church janitor? . . . Well, it's not really a ghost story, but if you dudes insist . . ."

"Yeah, the dudes insist!" said Maurice.

"But only if I can tell it fast."

"You cannot tell no ghost story fast," said Maurice. "You must pause for effect at appropriate moments."

"Oh, brother," said Steve.

Ransom cleared his throat. "I was twelve years old, still living with my dad in California. His house was only a mile from Newport Beach. My four friends and I had taught each other how to surf. Two of them, Carlos and Benny, were my best friends; the other two were twins, Perry and Peter. We learned mostly by watching the older dudes. We loved it so much we practically lived on the beach that summer. At night we'd sit on the sand and talk about surfing, then fall asleep and dream of the perfect wave . . . until a late Friday night in July when Carlos saw the white floating head."

"Aww, man . . ." said Steve.

"Hush," said Maurice. He had shouldered up against Ransom's seat to listen in.

"We'd paddled out at midnight, all five of us. It was one of those nights when the Pacific seems without motion, just slow rolling, as if the water was sloshing back and forth between L.A. and Melbourne. We were laying on our stomachs, feet dangling off the sides of our boards, talking of waves and girls and music. I was one month away from my thirteenth birthday. A mile down the beach, the lights from the amusement park went black, and only a quarter moon lit the ocean. We'd been out there for an hour, five junior high kids on a summer night. The ocean breeze had dried our mouths, so Benny wanted to paddle back in for a drink. Just then, Carlos said, 'Don't play footsie with me, Ransom.' I said, 'Wasn't me, Carlos-dude; my feet are on my board.' He turned to look behind him, and that's when he saw the head bobbing under the surface."

"Do we gotta listen to this?" asked Steve.

"Let the man tell his story," said Maurice.

"So I turned to look for the head, but it was gone. Carlos swore he wasn't crazy. He said, 'Yeah, Ransom, the head was white and I felt it bump my foot, and a floating head is weird, but a whole lot better than you playing footsie.' Benny wondered if Carlos had been sneaking in his momma's rum cabinet again, but Carlos swore he never touched the stuff.

"The twins who were with us—Perry and Peter—they said it must've been a jellyfish, but Carlos said it couldn't have been a jellyfish because it wasn't as soft, and besides, it didn't sting; it felt like firm Jell-O, only warmer. So we stayed out there, just floating on our boards, hoping to see the white head again while the twins insisted it was a jellyfish.

"Benny-dude said maybe Carlos had sipped something else besides rum, but Carlos said no, he wasn't under any influence and someone must've dumped a body in the ocean to hide the evidence, and surely the crabs and sharks ate everything but the head. Then we forgot about the head and went back to talking about girls and waves.

"Perry and Peter were arguing over who was gonna ask out Carisa, this girl surfer who was pretty good—actually, pretty and good—and I sorta wanted to ask her out myself, but before I could speak up, the head bumped my foot, and I said, 'Carlos, turn slowly; I think it's behind us again.'

"Carlos yelled, then panicked, then started paddling like crazy, so we all yelled and panicked, even though Benny still hadn't seen the head and the twins weren't allowed to cuss. We paddled to knee-deep, jumped off, and stood there holding our surfboards, looking in the dark to see if the head would bob up. But it didn't.

"Benny said it must really be a floating head—a head left over from the crabs and the sharks—and that two witnesses to a floating head were proof enough for him.

"Perry and Peter said they were through for the evening. Said they were going home to call Carisa and tell her all about the head, even though they hadn't actually seen it but trusted the opinions of me and Carlos, especially since Carlos wasn't on the rum. As the twins left, Benny yelled, 'You guys are just scared,' and Carlos whispered that Carisa didn't like either one of 'em.

"Benny-dude had two quarters, so the three of us walked down the beach to the closed amusement park. We found a Coke machine. Carlos wanted 7 Up, but I wanted orange soda. Benny bought a root beer instead. We drank it while walking back up the beach, speculating whose head it was bobbing out in the Pacific. 'It didn't have any hair,' said Carlos. So we figured it had to be a bald guy's head.

"I said, 'Dudes, wouldn't it be a surprise if it was some famous Hollywood star involved in a money-laundering scheme, so the mobsters must've kept his hairpiece and fed his body to the sharks and the crabs.' Benny finished off the root beer and started talking all sophisticated, like an adult, saying no Hollywood star would be so stupid as to get involved with the mob. Carlos said it must've been a fisherman who fell off his boat and had taken days to float in; that's why the head turned white, and can you guys imagine what it was like for that guy with no funeral and no organ music, and I'll bet the sharks started with the legs.

"I said that sharks would probably start with the arms, but Benny agreed it might well have been the legs.

"Well, we sat on the empty beach next to our surfboards, not talking, just thinking about that floating head. It was after three in the morning when we decided to wade back into the ocean for one last look.

"Benny saw it first. The light from the quarter moon angled across the breakers as the head floated through moonlight, bobbed twice, and disappeared. We moved to where the moon would highlight the head again. Carlos yelled, 'There it is!' and there it was, bobbing thirty feet away. Benny grabbed a piece of driftwood off the beach. He waded out slow and cautious, saying he was going to turn the head in to the police for evidence.

"Me and Carlos said, 'Wait, Benny-dude, we'll help you,' so now we all had chunks of driftwood. We waded out to neck deep. Carlos was the first to get near it. He said, 'Let's poke the head back to shore.' But when he poked it the first time, we didn't see any eyes or nose or face, and then the tentacle hit Benny in the leg.

"A dead octopus. A huge one. We dragged and poked it with the driftwood until we got it to shore. Carlos got his surfboard and laid it on the wet sand to get a measurement. When we stretched out the tentacles, they reached past the ends of his board, but even that may not have shown the true length—all but two-and-a-half tentacles had been eaten off.

"Benny said it didn't surprise him that the head was floating around uneaten, because he'd heard that eating an old, dead octopus head would be too gross even for the crabs.

"So the next afternoon on the beach, I told that surfer girl, Carisa, that Perry and Peter had lied and that it was just an octopus, not someone's head. So she got mad at the twins for lying and started hanging out with me instead.

"It was a month later, at my birthday party on that same beach, when Carisa introduced me to her best friend, Jamie, who eight years later became my wife.

"So you see, dudes, God does work in ways of mystery . . . even for a dumb little teenage surfer."

24

I woke to sweat on my brow, blackbirds in the driveway, and no sign of Asbury Smoak. Morning sunlight angled between the oaks, and Steve said he needed to be excused a moment, though he'd be avoiding the bushes.

"Me too," said Maurice, lifting the lock.

We all lifted our locks.

My first impression of the lowcountry on a hot September morning was one of stagnation, heavy air, and a near-total lack of motion. Breezes seemed nonexistent. Even the flies appeared lazy, and why shouldn't they have been, since no wind bothered to blow and help push 'em along.

On the hood of the Blazer, I unfolded a state map. Maurice yawned with disinterest, said he was going to take a look around, and off he went to trek through the backyard. I studied the map, which showed us being four miles inland from a wide expanse of inlets and salt marsh.

"Same part of the coast where Hurricane Hugo ripped through," said Steve, tracing the storm's path with his finger.

"Great waves that week," said Ransom, stretching his back. "Just awesome."

"You surfed in a hurricane?"

"Until I fell and my board washed through the window of a beach house. I figured it was time to leave, then."

The six oaks lining the driveway cast splotchy patterns of shade at midmorning. The driveway itself consisted of two sandy tracks split by a ragged patch of grass, as though man and nature had combined to carve a long green mohawk into the earth.

The sand was gray, the texture of flour. Below the oaks I sifted some through my fingers. It felt old, and I imagined the grains being squashed by one of Henry Ford's motorcars, or maybe the boots of a Confederate soldier all downtrodden and weary from losing the battle, spittin' in the sand and cursing Grant.

I tossed a rock at the blackbirds. They scattered en masse.

"Maybe the blackbirds kidnapped Asbury," said Steve, watching them flee.

"I think he was just too embarrassed to show up," said Ransom.

The house itself was just plain pitiful. The roof all raggedy. Shingles loose along the bottom. Shingles missing from the top. One hole large enough for men to crawl through.

The porch not only sagged but positively drooped, wrapping around from front to sides, where the sagging grew in proportion to the distance from the brick steps. Two old rockers occupied each end of the porch, their faded white paint cracking at the armrests, their rocking boards fixed in wooden grins as if inviting you to sit and grow old with them.

"We'll never repair this thing," said Ransom, surveying the scene while straddling the grassy mohawk. "Not in thirty weekends."

"Not a good fixer-upper," I offered.

"A good blower-upper," said Steve, unloading a box of nails.

Maurice returned via the weeds, and paused to brush tiny green pods from his pant leg. "Guess what?" he said. "There's a river way back behind the house."

"Then I'm jumping in," said Ransom, rejuvenated at the news.

In an instant, all thoughts of home repair vanished like the blackbirds.

The new plan involved jumping in the river, washing off the sweat, and driving the 250 miles back to Greenville. Steve slid the box of nails back in the Blazer and exchanged his sneakers for sandals. "Preacher Smoak should be disbarred from whatever association old preachers belong to," he professed. "Because even if a preacher has good reason not to show up at his own house, he could at least mow the yard and leave a note."

"Amen," said Maurice, reaching in the backseat for a towel and a shot of Perrier.

Around the back of the house, we separated weeds chest-high, the smell of wild onions rising sharp and distinct. After five minutes of trudging, we reached water's edge, where a sandy bank played host to fiddler crabs in full retreat and a pier in worse shape than the house. Edging in, I expected a river bottom of mud, but my feet whispered sand.

"Called brackish water," said Maurice, wading in the shallows beneath a water oak. "Has both freshwater and saltwater fish in here."

"Even a few piranhas," said Ransom, already waist deep.

Steve heard that and sloshed toward shore, mumbling that it was a bad weekend, what with having to sleep next to the exorcist before bathing with piranhas, and that we should've stayed home in Greenville to listen to the second sermon from Tyrus, who was now America's expert on vagueness and the Universal Force.

Across the river, against a thick fringe of marsh grass, a blue heron stalked lunch as if its method and mechanics were being carefully graded by a panel of judges. Everything about the lanky bird seemed timid and intermittent, from its movement to its feathered sheen, which appeared more grayish than any class of blue.

For a long while I watched it pose, slowly counting off seconds in my head to see if it would take a step or crane its neck or make any kind of gesture before I reached sixty. At ninety-seven I gave up and, curious as to the taste of brackish water, scooped a handful and readied my tongue.

It tasted awful—like a mixture of cold coffee and Alka-Seltzer. I spit it out as a horn blared from the driveway. The heron checked its footing and took off in a low, lumbering flight.

"That had better be the preacher," said Steve, draping a towel around his neck.

Through high weeds we dripped and trudged onward, led by Maurice, who said this looked like something out of Vietnam.

"So were you in Vietnam?" asked Ransom, right on his heels.

"Negatory," said Maurice. "Although it's certain the Vietnamese are healthier than Steve."

"Why, Maurice?" Steve asked, bringing up the rear and taking the bait.

"Because they eat their vegetables and resist the MoonPie."

Steve stumbled in the weeds over that answer and told Maurice he could not believe a Presbyterian church would hire such an opinionated janitor. Maurice said to be careful or he'd give his opinion of the blonde he saw Steve sneaking around with last month.

Asbury Smoak was leaning against the front of a white Ford pickup that had a fine beige dust covering its hood and windshield. He wore cutoff jeans, his red baseball cap, and a Pawleys Island T-shirt. His physique was still pudgy; his legs one shade south of pale.

"Enjoy the swim?" he asked, looking past us at his ramshackle house.

"I prefer the ocean," said Ransom, wiping dirt from his feet.

"My apologies to you men," said the preacher. "Couldn't phone."

"So what happened?" I asked, wanting to give him the benefit of the doubt.

Preacher Smoak checked his watch before answering. "The Lord smiled on me yesterday. Least it seemed like a smile. This property has three hundred feet of frontage on that river, ocean access and all. Some old Charleston money wants the place. We spent last night negotiating. And then, on the way here, I got a flat tire at 1:00 A.M. on that dusty back road. Lots of evil in the lowcountry, so I waited till this morning to change it."

"You slept in your pickup?" asked Maurice.

"Three miles down the road," said Asbury. "And your crew?"

"Ditto," Ransom said, stretching his neck.

"So you've sold the house?" asked Steve, who seemed delighted at the prospect.

The preacher propped one foot on his truck bumper and said, "No, not yet. And it's the land he wants; the house would get bulldozed. Strange part is that he's offering only partial money. He's also offering me a boat. He owns two offshore fishing boats at the city marina in downtown Charleston."

"You seen the boat?" I asked, enduring the soggy feel of river-soaked shorts.

"No, but the gentleman offered a short test drive today. Might let me take it to the Gulf Stream tomorrow."

I introduced everyone to Preacher Smoak, and Maurice asked if we were all invited for the test drive, because there was no way we could fix that wretched house with our two saws, duct tape, and a box of tenpenny nails.

So we changed into fresh shorts and T-shirts, and piled into the bed of Asbury's pickup.

The slasher grass mocked our exit until we reached the familiar pavement of Highway 17. The wind dried our hair, the sun warmed our necks, and Maurice gabbed to the preacher from the passenger seat.

While cresting the Cooper River Bridge, we looked out between steel rails and across the river to the shipyards and the waterfront, at houses tall, aged, and squished together. Even the social strata looked squished. In what seemed like only a mile of downtown, we passed slums, pseudo-slums, the middle class, upper-middle, and were rapidly entering don't-even-ask. I suggested we stop and ask.

"Show a little restraint, Jarvis," said Steve, perched on a spare tire.

We passed the historic and the renovated, then paralleled a seawall. Soon the preacher slowed, pointed right, and Charleston's battery of whitewashed porches glowed beneath September's sun. I'd now seen all of South Carolina's major cities, and this one just did not seem to fit in with the others, appearing instead to have been imported from another time, another place. There was some sorta cultural thing going on here; I could sense it, smell it, feel it ruffle my blond hair as we circled downtown.

My first visual impression came from the manicured yard of an antebellum bed-and-breakfast, from a lady in a powder blue hat, her brim trimmed in white lace, dress to match. She seemed surreal, like a first sighting of something rare, a sophisticated Southern plumage strutting about so that all might observe her in her habitat.

To provide audio commentary, Steve used his fist for a microphone. "Here she is . . . stepping onto the porch in historic Charleston . . . nodding politely to strangers . . . to see and be seen . . . to distinguish herself from those shameless Yankees and—"

."And her daughters will marry money or won't marry at all," Ransom said, his brown mop of hair flapping in the wind.

Yep, there was a cultural thing going on here.

We arrived at the marina in time to see boat owners lounging against teakwood, perfecting the pose and savoring the mint julep. The marina had few vacancies, just row after row of sailboats, yachts, and top-dollar fishing boats, the type where the captain could sit high on the fourth level to spot fish swimming under the surface and women sunning themselves atop the yachts.

Boat names crack me up. I strolled down the dock with Maurice, nodding at julep sippers and reading off the names. Charter boats called *The Jefferson Davis* and *Buddy Went West*. A forty-foot sailboat named *Play Lotto*.

"Look," said Maurice, nodding at a huge catamaran, "they named that one *Pre-Nup*."

"Our boat is this way," said Asbury, pointing two rows over.

Mr. Clayton Beaufaine was my first up-close glimpse of old Charleston money. At least six-foot-two and very tan, he sported a full head of gray hair and two cigars in the pocket of his red golf shirt. He had deep lines around his eyes and the shifty look of a Clint Eastwood gunslinger.

He raised one foot to the dock, left the other on his boat as Asbury made introductions. Beaufaine only nodded. No handshakes.

"This baby is a jewel," he said, sweeping his hand across it like he was guest-hosting QVC. "Thirty-six feet, sleeps five, plus a full kitchen."

Maurice grasped his own chin between thumb and forefinger, furrowed his brow, and to our collective surprise began interrogating Gentleman Beaufaine. "Tell us about the engine," he said. "Number of hours, horse-power . . . the routine maintenance."

"Engines are twin 3208 diesels," said Beaufaine, unwrapping a cigar. "Not certain on the horsepower, probably in the seven hundred range. I had the whole thing rebuilt this past spring, so she's got less than a hundred hours on her."

"I see," said Maurice, still rubbing his chin. "And how about radio communications?"

"New radio, GPS system, too."

"Ah yes," said Maurice. "GPS, that's good."

Clayton Beaufaine said he had to go register with the dock attendant before taking us for a test drive. He paused on the metal steps, then pulled a lighter from his white pants and lit his cigar. Puffs of smoke rose slowly over his left shoulder, the steps clanging to his departure, the dock boards vibrating beneath our feet.

Asbury looked stunned. He turned and asked, "How did you know to ask all those good questions about boats, Maurice?"

Maurice said he didn't know a thing about boats, but that when you're a poor sexton and the Presbyterians are stingy on the raises, then you have to learn to negotiate, and how else could he have found his son a '91 Plymouth for a mere four hundred bucks?

"We Baptists give better raises," said Asbury, taking a seat on a dock bench.

"How big's your church?" asked Maurice.

"Fifty-two members."

"That ain't a church," countered Maurice. "That's not even a good choir."

"I am the choir. The sexton, too."

"Nah! . . . You do floors?"

"Every Monday."

"I do mine on Tuesday."

Asbury paused a moment, mulling over their newfound chemistry. "Pine Sol?"

"Among the janitorial community, I am considered a connoisseur of Pine Sol."

"Regular or lemon scent?"

"Lemon is my congregation's preferred aroma. I took a poll."

Steve asked if we could please stop discussing floor cleaner while among the elite of Charleston's boating society, and man oh man, would you guys look at the size of those fishing reels mounted to the back of Beaufaine's boat.

I nudged Asbury. "Did you get the fishing gear included in the deal?"

Asbury hesitated, then said he hadn't thought about it yet, but come to think of it, those gold-plated Penn International reels went for six hundred bucks each and there was four of 'em, so how much would that be?

"Twenty-four hundred," I said, "not including the poles."

Asbury gently chewed his lip. "Then somebody help me get that stuff included in the deal."

"I've done my part," said Maurice.

"I don't know squat about fishing," Ransom added.

Beaufaine came clanging back down the dock but stopped to relight his cigar. When he arrived, I was ready to negotiate gold-plated fishing reels. "Mr. Beaufaine, did you know that Preacher Smoak here has only fifty-two members in his church?"

"Didn't know that, son." He puffed hard and looked off at the water.

"He has only three people in his church who tithe, and he hasn't given himself a raise in five years."

"That so?" muttered Beaufaine, blowing nasty smoke my way.

"Yessir, that's so . . . and the expense of rigging this boat with new reels and poles would be an awful burden on the poor preacher."

"Son, you ain't gonna get no sympathy from me, but if it's the reels you're wanting, I was including them in the deal anyway. I don't fish. I sit up on the top level and use this boat to chase the ladies, not tuna. Y'all can have those reels."

"Oh."

"Much obliged," said Asbury, smiling big.

"That's mighty nice of you, sir," said Steve.

Clayton Beaufaine leaned close and told me I'd never catch a good deal on a boat using my poor sympathetic negotiation skills; then I told him he'd never catch any women what with that cigar smoke fouling his old Charleston breath.

"That's right," said Maurice. "That smoke will kill ya dead. So will red meat and—"

"We know, Maurice," said Ransom, wiping his surfer shades.

Steve and I untied the ropes as Asbury and Maurice climbed aboard. They walked to the rear of the boat, then leaned over the stern to examine the name.

Shoulders slumped, Asbury shook his head and stared out to sea.

The boat was called *4th Marriage*. Asbury sat in the co-captain's chair and told Beaufaine that a Baptist preacher could not be seen in a boat called *4th Marriage*.

Beaufaine snickered and started the engine. "Preacher, after we agree to the deal, you can call her anything you like . . . and I'll even buy a quart of red paint for you to do the renaming."

"Thank you, sir," said Asbury. And he turned and winked at us.

"You'll have to get your own stencils, though," cautioned Beaufaine.

"We can afford stencils," said Maurice, inspecting the fishing reels.

On the bow of the *4th Marriage*, I sat between Steve and Ransom as we left the dock, waving at ladies twice our age. They sat on the backs of huge sailboats, sipping fruity drinks with tiny umbrellas and looking, quite honestly, a bit bored.

The sun slid west of noon. Preacher Smoak had the controls, steering us through Charleston Harbor like a teenager with his first car. Restless, I climbed around the side to check out the interior. Maurice crowded in between the preacher and Beaufaine and said to check out this GPS stuff, it'll let you steer by numbers.

I whispered to Maurice, "What does GPS stand for?"

"Haven't got a clue," he whispered back.

"Global Positioning System," said Beaufaine. He said the words slow and careful, as if tomorrow there'd be a quiz.

We passed a similar-sized boat—*The Blooky*—as it motored back to port, its sunburnt crew waving back as if we were now accepted members of the boating establishment.

"What's that little flag they're flying?" I asked, squinting into the glare.

"Called a catch-flag," said Beaufaine. "That one is for a sailfish. There's a different flag for each desirable species. They'll raise it so other boats can tell what's been caught."

Maurice tapped Beaufaine's shoulder. "So then, you would raise a different flag for blondes, brunettes, and redheads?"

Beaufaine puffed on his cigar, flicked ashes over the side. "You people ain't from around here, are ya?"

Rhythmic splashes soaked the bow, the spray salty and cool against our faces. We approached Fort Sumter, where I pictured Beaufaine's ancestors fighting with the Confederacy while puffing on nineteenth-century cigars—for surely a man with a French name like Beaufaine would've been blackballed from the Union, although Sherman just may have used a cigar to start the big fire in Atlanta.

Steve said he thought Sherman used a torch, but Ransom agreed it might well have been a cigar.

"That ol' Civil War," said Maurice, one hand on the rail, "what bickering it do stir in our state."

"Amen," said Asbury, his eyes on the depth finder.

Their comments were met with silent acceptance, and nothing else was said of it. Maurice just requested that he be allowed to steer before we returned, that he'd never driven such a fine vessel, and that he thought a thirty-six-foot boat with all the fishing gear included plus undisclosed cash was a great swap for Asbury's valuable land and historic house.

"The land, yeah," said Beaufaine, flicking ashes into the wind. "But that house ain't historical, it's a piece of . . . um, sorry, Preach."

"Watch your language around clergy," warned Maurice.

"Quite all right," said Asbury. "I'm sure it would've been an appropriate description."

Maurice took the helm, grabbed a navy captain's hat off a peg, and put it on his head. In a wide, liquid orbit, he circled Fort Sumter, our wake lapping against history.

We neared the marina, and Asbury had the wheel again, Beaufaine talking him through a very precise method of docking the *4th Marriage*. Asbury slowed the boat to a wakeless drift, then backed us into the slip on his first try. No bumps, starboard or port.

Ransom peeked over the railing and said, "Not bad."

"Not bad at all," said Beaufaine, who looked relieved that his boat was dent free.

We had docked between two yachts, a triple-decked white one named the *Lenny Dru* and a dazzling blue-and-silver vessel called *Dana's Darling*.

Asbury was first off the boat.

"What's the matter, Preacher?" asked Beaufaine.

"Gotta think up a new name," said Asbury, hands on hips, staring at the rear end of the *4th Marriage*.

Maurice climbed from the boat to join him, and they rubbed their chins to help summon the proper moniker.

Beaufaine watched them for a moment, then flicked the stub of his cigar in the water. "So, Preach, do we have a deal?"

25

We left Beaufaine squirming overnight. Dusk lowered over the slasher grass as we returned via McClellanville, the twisty dirt road, and the preacher's gray powdered driveway. After parking next to his dilapidation, Asbury grabbed a pair of pruning shears from underneath the seat. Ransom had slept most of the way home with a towel folded up for a pillow, and we left him sprawled out in the pickup bed along with our take-out dinner. We'd eat soon enough—after a bit of home maintenance.

Preacher Smoak snipped high weeds and low weeds, then attacked the bushes spilling over his porch. "I've sorta let it go lately," he admitted, pruning away. "But I'll have it livable momentarily."

"Can we help?" asked Steve, his head cocked to one side, watching in amusement at this hasty form of Baptist hospitality.

"Nah, almost done."

"Got a door key?" I asked, not certain that I wanted to go inside.

"Don't need a key," said Asbury. "She's open."

The hinges not only squeaked, they were downright ornery. Maurice tiptoed in behind me, his hand on my back, his breath on my neck.

"Mercy . . ." he whispered.

Cobwebs drooped from the wall corners, thick and dry like old shrimp net, pulled from the depths to come haunting. The floors were thick with grit, the air musty as old luggage, and from the roof hole, angular streams of light pierced the kitchen.

"Think the Addams family lived here?" asked Maurice.

"It certainly wasn't Jed, Granny, or Ellie Mae," I replied, toeing my initials in the dust. On the far wall we found a light switch. Nothing.

"Told ya," said Maurice.

Heavy footsteps pounded across the porch. Boards creaked. In rapid succession, the snip of pruning shears came fast and harsh. We rushed out of the house for a look, and coming around the corner was the preacher with a black snake between the blades.

One more snip and the head fell off. Snake blood stained the shears.

"Moccasin," announced Asbury, using his shears to fling the body in the woods. "Third one I've killed this year."

"Y'all wanna go get a hotel room back in Charleston?" asked Steve, ever hopeful.

We nixed that idea but decided not to explore the house any further. I sat in a faded white rocker and said, "Let's ask Maurice if snake meat is worse than red meat."

"Do not pick on the janitor," said Maurice, taking the seat beside me. "He might put something in your pipes."

Ransom woke hospitable, distributing dinner from two sacks of burgers and fries, plus orange drinks for all. He had insisted we try the orange. Preacher Smoak asked a blessing, both for the meal and his ongoing negotiations. He prayed with reverence, and I could not help but note his calm, unhurried pace.

We sat on the porch in the fading light, rocking in rhythm and eating a cheap supper in celebration of Asbury trading the house of dilapidation for a fourth marriage. "Whatever happened to that girl you brought to my church?" he asked, washing down his last bite.

"Actually, she brought me. But she's in South America now. Full-time missionary."

"Missionaries are only gonna be interested in other missionaries," muttered Steve.

"Well, Mr. Cole," said Maurice, lifting his drink from the floor, "I say a man who can't tell a can of Krylon from a can of bug spray ought not be giving relational advice."

Steve just shook his head.

Asbury laughed and said, "You been to see her, Jay? Go drifting again?"

"Haven't been invited. Plus, I've accepted a new job in Manhattan."

"No! You moving to the City?"

"Six weeks away."

Darkness descended over the lowcountry, the night unfolding through the narrow rectangle of our porch view, a sliver of night now alive with bugs and the ghosts of dead snakes. A manly silence had ensued, interrupted only by the occasional slurp of orange, the wadding of wrapper.

"I heard they don't even serve sweet tea up in New Yawk," said Maurice, munching his cheeseburger.

"No sweet tea, what a shame," said Ransom. "And you're eating red meat, Maurice."

"Don't tell my wife."

After dinner and a burp, Ransom prompted us for entertainment. "Dudes, we need another story."

"Steve might have some stories," I said.

Steve chewed his straw and said, "No, I don't."

"Go ahead, Maurice," said Ransom, egging him on.

"Naw, naw, y'all don't wanna hear no poor janitor's story." Maurice rocked in the twilight, paying Ransom scant attention.

"Yes, we do," said Steve. "Just leave out the floating heads."

Maurice took one last sip of orange soda. "Don't have no ghost story; no floatin' head tale, either. But y'all wanna hear about the worst whuppin' I ever got?"

"Tell it," said Asbury.

Maurice set his drink under the rocker, then looked at each of us before he began, making sure—now that he was on stage—that our full attention was his.

"We lived in the nicer half of town, the half with the dirt road and running water. Had a dirt field beside the house where my two older brothers and me played stickball. Every day. They would saw off an old mop handle for a bat and roll up some maskin' tape for a ball. They were nine and ten. I was six. We were forever having arguments after a good hit, 'cause the paper bases would blow away—we could never tell where we were supposed to run. The fielder would say out but the runner would scream safe. Momma would say not to yell, to behave, or we'd end up a foul-mouthed drifter like our daddy and someday abandon our kids like he did.

"I wanted to do something to please Momma, to stop all that arguing between me and my brothers. One afternoon I beat them home from school, and while sittin' in the dirt, I thought of it, how I could make everybody get along.

"I knew the good baseball fields had stripes running from home plate to first, and more stripes from third base to home. We just needed ourselves some stripes. First I found some sand in a ditch. But there weren't enough, plus the sand was too brown. Then I had myself a revelation—Momma had a new sack of flour in her cupboard. The sack was big. I was little.

"But I was determined. So I wrestled that sack out the house and onto our dirt field. Then I poked a hole in the sack with a stick and lined the bases straight as I could. I even lined between first and second and between second and third. It was like Wrigley Field . . . without the ivy and the bleachers, of course.

"When I got done, there was still some flour left in the sack, so I made us a batter's box, too. One on each side, since my oldest brother was left-handed. After that I stood and admired the field, proud of my work. Soon my brothers came up the dirt road and saw the field and yelled, 'Maurice, you lined them bases!' They were so happy that they dropped their schoolbooks in the yard, and one grabbed the mop handle to start a game. I was about to throw the first pitch when my oldest brother saw the empty flour sack. He laughed and slapped his hands together; then my middle brother stuck his finger in the flour for a sample lick, then laughed so hard he couldn't swing the bat.

"Five minutes later Momma got home from the neighbor's house. She didn't laugh.

"First she screamed, then she hollered and did something with her hair net, then somehow she had my shirt collar, dragging me to the house while my two brothers insisted they had nothing to do with it. She stopped on the stairs and beat my behind with the empty flour sack, then used her hand 'cause the sack didn't hurt enough. Then she switched hands, showed the family she was ambidextrous. Then after ten minutes of beating me for my own good, she beat me for my brother's good, my sister's good, my uncle Otis's good, and for the benefit of all our descendants.

"I said, 'No more, Momma, please Momma, ooh, ooowee Momma, not there, no, not there, Momma, oh please.'

"But she wouldn't listen. Said it was humiliating for her to have to borrow again from neighbors. Said she lost a whole quart of her dignity that day, never mind those fifty pounds of flour. Momma musta loved her dignity, 'cause my fanny didn't heal for a week."

Maurice grimaced at the remembrance, scrunching his eyes and mouthing, "Ooowee."

Asbury rose from his rocking chair, kicked a loose board off the porch, and pushed open his ornery front door. "Gettin' beat for Otis's good . . . mercy sakes. It's bedtime, gentlemen. We're going out deep tomorrow."

26

The preacher and Maurice had already left when we woke at midmorning. On weathered porch stairs we stretched our backs and tried to gauge the quality of sleep—blankets on dusty hardwood floors being a poor excuse for a bed, although blanketed floors were slightly better than black inner tubes, but slightly worse than sandy beaches with embarrassed missionaries, so who was I to complain.

En route to Charleston, we sipped take-out coffee and headed for the Cooper River Bridge. Enormous cranes were visible across the water, setting foundations in place for Cooper's replacement. Apparently the citizens had nearly worn out the current two bridges, one section for the small and agile, then a wider, more spacious section for the risk-averse. I took the agile route as Ransom yawned and said he was glad Clayton Beaufaine and his foul cigars were staying in port today.

"What's the preacher gonna name his boat?" asked Steve. He had sprawled across my backseat, munching clusters of cold fries for breakfast.

"Couldn't decide," said Ransom, finding his shades in the glove compartment.

"Something like *Jonah's Big Revenge*," I offered.

"Or *My Walk on the Water*," said Ransom

"Too long a name," said Steve.

"No, it ain't," I said.

"It's too long."

"Why are you suddenly the expert on boat names?"

"Yeah, dude," said Ransom, "why are you suddenly the expert on boat names?"

"Boat names are rarely more than two words," said Steve. "Never more than three."

Charleston's boating elite raised tomato-juice drinks in greeting as we strolled past their yachts and sailboats, the salt air diluted with faint whiffs of diesel fuel. Skies were clear, and a flock of optimistic gulls flew circles around the boat masts.

A dozen boats ahead, Asbury and Maurice squatted at the stern of the *4th Marriage,* stencils scattered at their feet.

"Any last guesses?" I asked, our view blocked.

"Haven't a clue," said Ransom. The two artisans rose and turned at our arrival. Then they stepped aside and asked us what we thought. The new letters were only half the size of the old ones. But in an upside-down triangle, in bright red, they had renamed the boat:

> *The Asbury Raspberry*
> *Strawberry Lemon*
> *'n Lime*

Steve stared at it for a moment and said, "That's not a name, it's a paragraph."

"Maurice thought of it," said Asbury, pleased with their fruited verse.

"You're quite the poet, Maurice," said Ransom.

"Rather be quite the poet than quite the janitor," Maurice replied, wiping his hands on a rag. He checked the paint and pronounced it dry.

I helped Asbury gather his stencils, and he accidentally kicked the *L* and the *A* into the water. The beige letters landed beside each other, and we watched them drift from the dock. "They served their purpose," said Asbury. "And besides, we used the whole quart o' paint."

"Too long a name," said Steve. "Although I kinda like the lime part."

Maurice disagreed, said it was pure poetry, a nautical haiku, then told Steve he'd never qualify as a boat namer, what with his short little nouns and fear of piranhas.

Preacher Smoak went aboard and checked the fuel level. "How far y'all wanna go out?"

"Faaarrr," said Maurice. He untied the starboard ropes; I handled port.

"Just remember the flare gun," said Ransom. And he took a seat on the bow.

"I'll rig the other two poles," said Steve, waving me off. Brother Cole was perched on a large cooler and seemed to possess a talent for rigging, tying complicated knots from line to leader.

I reckoned his life was chock-full of complicated knots.

Thick, rolling waves slammed the port side, splashing Ransom on the bow. I studied the gauges, our depth increasing from 90 to 120 feet, Charleston and its old money a mere speck on the horizon. Preacher Smoak seemed a natural at skippering boats. With a steady eye on the GPS screen, he sipped coffee with one hand, turned the chrome wheel with the other.

"Maurice," said the preacher, "what exactly is a nautical haiku?"

Maurice sat beside him in the co-captain's seat and said, "An ancient writing form, among the most disciplined types of verse."

Asbury increased our speed. "And how long has it been around?"

"Ever since late last night when I was struggling to think up a name."

Nine miles out, our bright teaser-baits speckling behind us, the ocean was a deeper blue, clean and unspoiled. I felt small.

We passed another boat—its sailfish flag waving—and ten minutes later another. Asbury said that one had the flag for tuna. Their crew waved; Steve and Ransom saluted.

Soon we came upon a small nation of anglers, like a secret club congregated upon familiar water, all making slow, trolling paths through blue seas in a quiet, measured game of waiting.

But not for long.

"Fish breaking water at 2:00," yelled Maurice, peering across the bow.

"Fish on starboard side!" said Asbury.

"There's another one!" yelled Ransom, standing, excited now.

Asbury cut the wheel as three long V-shapes burrowed just under the surface, trying to eat the yellow teaser. Steve whipped open a tackle box, tied on a humongous gold lure, and reared back to cast.

"Turn us to the left, Preach," he said, leaning over the side.

"Somebody get the outriggers extended!" yelled Asbury.

"I'm a little old to climb up there," Maurice protested.

"I don't know squat about fishing," said Ransom. "But I'm willing to learn."

"I'll get it," I said, climbing up the outside of the cabin.

A slow, magnified sway tilted me left, then right, then left again. The view was fantastic. Fifty yards away, strapped into the fishing seat of another boat, a woman battled who-knows-what as if the fish had hold of her only child. She leaned back and pulled on the rod, leaned forward and reeled the slack.

"Look at the muscles in that woman's arms," said Steve, pointing with his rod tip.

"I wanna catch me a fish, dudes," said Ransom.

"Looks like we found 'em, boys," said Asbury, steering us through the frenzy.

Maurice put his hand on the gaff. "Come to Poppa."

Steve's gold lure skipped across the water, tailed by three long shadows dark-finned and piercing the ocean. I hurried to reach the outrigger, and from my elevated perch I saw the V-shapes rise and break the surface. I had no idea what species they were, but they were long and dark and so very hungry.

I stretched to extend an outrigger, and the boat lurched.

27

I woke in room 521. A nurse and a doctor stood over my bed, talking in hushed voices.

My eyes struggled to focus. Doc left the room in a smudgy cloud of white. Then he was back, handing something to the nurse.

They were talking again, but it was a murky, medicinal dialogue.

My skull throbbed. I mumbled something about a recap. Doc and nurse glanced at each other.

They said I'd fallen over the side and hit my head, but I did not remember.

They said Steve had jumped in the Atlantic without a life preserver and kept me from drowning while Maurice hooked the gaff through my shorts and dragged me in, but I had no recollection.

They said Ransom, who didn't know squat about fishing, apparently did know how to stop a head wound from bleeding, but my memory had left with my blood.

They said Preacher Smoak had nearly burned out the engine getting us back to the marina, and that Clayton Beaufaine had been waiting on the dock and sped us in his Mercedes to the Charleston Medical Center, but it was all a blank.

They told me it was Tuesday, that eventually I would be fine, and that a transfer had been completed to Greenville Memorial Hospital—which was news to me 'cause I could've sworn my room had a rudder and I was circling Fort Sumter; but my head hurt and I no longer trusted my brain waves or sense of geography, the crisp smell of ocean now replaced with a sanitized whiteness that depressed me to no end.

Jamie Delaney, wife-with-child and role model for all things female, baked me a loaf of cinnamon bread. Ransom brought it to my room, but Doc said no snacking till Thursday. I spent Wednesday staring at it over on the table, thinking maybe this was reverse gear in the five-speed of life's momentum, and that, once again, I had landed in my very own Tarshish.

My very own nurse was named Sonya. She had the confident demeanor of a veteran, her light red hair and soft features combining in a package I would normally describe as pretty, although in my current state, judgments of appearance were cloudy at best.

She pulled back my covers, saying it was time to attempt a few steps. The tile floor felt cold when my feet touched down. She gripped my shoulder. I tried one step, but half my cranium was made of lead and the other half cotton candy; I teetered like a drunk, the walls bent, and down on the bed I plopped.

"Equilibrium still off?" she asked, still holding my arm.

"Just a bit. Back of my head throbs."

"The cut is stitched tight," she said, examining my skull. "And fortunately it's on the back of your head, so the hair will grow over the scar in no time."

"Pitiful . . . can grow hair but can't walk."

"Let's try one more time," she said, a firm grip at my elbow. "If you can make it to the window, there's a gorgeous view of our parking lot."

I was on my feet, teetering. "You smell nice, Nurse Sonya."

"I smell like antiseptic. One more try?"

I felt slobbering drunk. Needed to lie down. "What if . . ."

"Hold on to my arm."

"Thems really fine shoos."

"Will you stop it and take a step?"

"That was a poor excuse for a step, wasn't it?"

"We'll try again later. Lie back down. Can I get you anything?"

"No, thanks."

She was nearly out the door when she stopped, turned to face me. "Can't wait to hear the rest of the story, Jay."

"And what story might that be?" I asked, thoroughly confused.

"Well, when they brought you in last night, you were mumbling something about an octopus surfing on waves of flour at Wrigley Field. The attending doctor couldn't even finish the examination . . . had tears in his eyes."

Okay, now I was embarrassed.

Pride and independence aren't worth much when you're laying unconscious in seawater, bleeding from the head nine miles out in the Atlantic. For the second time in four months, the ocean had tried to swallow me. I was now fearful of the ocean, cautious of deep water, and a bit concerned that I did not know what would've become of me had I died.

Death, like dry oil wells, was always an unpopular topic in Texas.

But very popular that Thursday morning as I considered my surroundings: people suffering, bodies wearing out, and several floors below me, death lingering in that cool, quiet room with sheet-covered bodies, white tags hung from gray toes.

A new thought, death. A new reality for hospitalized Jay, mired in the sanitized muck of room 521.

Maurice brought me the captain's hat on Thursday. He was decked out in a purple golf shirt with the North Hills logo embroidered on the pocket. He looked like a member of the Senior PGA Tour. I placed the hat on my oblong head. Oblong, that's what I'd nicknamed myself. Because of my injury, I couldn't wear the hat in a normal fashion; the back rode high and loose, the brim tilted low over my eyes.

"Oblong?" said Maurice, taking the guest chair. "Yeah, I've heard worse names. My old neighborhood had a guy we called Mr. Pink. Wore lots of fur."

"I feel much better now."

Maurice handed me two get-well cards, the first one signed by the pastor, the assistant pastor, and the music minister, in that order; the second one signed by him and his wife.

*We pray for your swift recovery and trust God to heal you. Grateful
for our friendship. Blessings to you, Maurice and Roberta Evans.*

P.S. Sorry I scratched your fanny with the gaff.

We dined on Jamie's cinnamon bread while discussing offshore boats,
old Charleston, and why the wealthy spent more time in the marina docks
than sailing the high seas. Soon he rose and pulled a second slice from the
loaf, then returned to his chair. "I don't understand it either, Jay. With a
boat like that, I'd sail it till I ran out of places to stop."

"Me too, Maurice."

"I'd be in the Caribbean and the Azores and the Metaranium."

"The Mediterranean?"

"There too."

Refilling my juice glass, Maurice informed me that Preacher Smoak had
sent an open invitation for more deep-sea adventures. And Beaufaine was
bulldozing the house.

I set my glass on the bedside table. "I need to ask you a question,
Maurice."

He played with the TV remote and said, "Uh-huh?"

"How do you know for sure . . . you know, if ya die?"

He looked at me like I had just professed to be a martian. "Don't tell
me that," he said, his voice rising. "Don't go and tell me after you done
fell off a boat in the middle of the Atlantic and near bled to death, now
you're about to up and move to New York City without your salvation.
Please tell me you ain't gonna tell me that."

He put his hands on his knees and glared at me.

"Okay, I won't. But how would I know?"

He glanced at the half-eaten loaf for a moment, then contorted his face
in a whimsical half-frown. "You know what? . . . I ain't gonna tell ya."

"You're not?"

"Nope."

"Why not?"

"Because."

"Because you're selfish? You sound selfish."

"Not selfish. I just got a better plan, what I think you deserve. I'm gonna let you get an earful from a man who can teach it, preach it, even make it stand up and do a pirouette."

"A pirouette?"

"It's a ballet thing. My wife likes it. Anyway, I gotta find a pay phone. You—you relax. Just lay back there with your lump-headed, unsaved self."

At 5:00 P.M. the Reverend Tyrus Williams walked into my room, looking much larger than when I'd seen him in church from pew twenty-three. He wore Clemson-orange sweats and white sneakers. Perspiration covered his forehead.

"Just left the gym, so please excuse my appearance," he said, taking the guest chair under the television. I had no idea where Maurice had gone. Maybe he'd gone home.

"No problem, Tyrus." Then I told him all about falling from the third level of an offshore fishing boat and whacking my head on the starboard side and I could've drowned except for Maurice gaffed me in the pants and scratched my fanny then dragged me in with an assist from Steve and Ransom, and for the first time in my life I realized I could die in an instant, although pardon me, Tyrus, but simply saying I have faith sounded awful trite.

But I could've died. And at twenty-seven, that's a scary thought.

"God gets our attention in many ways, Jay," Tyrus said, allowing himself a plastic cup of juice. He seemed very at ease about the whole thing.

"So how'd he get your attention, Tyrus? Surely you weren't born pounding on podiums. Ya know you really do mistreat a podium."

He smiled, took a breath, then talked to the window as if in remembrance. "I am one of only three boys from a gang of twelve who are still alive."

"You? In a gang?"

"A gang of stealers, not murderers," said Tyrus. "But sin is sin."

"And now you guest-preach in clubby white churches?"

"God can do immeasurably more than all we can ask or imagine, son."

227

I pondered this thought a moment, then applied it elsewhere. "What about Maurice? How'd God get his attention?"

"Aww, who knows. Maurice hasn't changed since he was eight years old. He still plays cops and robbers in the church hallway."

I told Tyrus I wanted to get right with God, but he said getting right with God sounded a bit like the vagueness he preached against.

"You mean I'm vague like the Universal Force?"

"Well, not quite that vague," said Tyrus, "but still vague."

"So, I'm not a true waffle. I'm a circular grid of battered substance?"

Tyrus cleared his throat and continued. "Jay, the chasm is wide between God and man, and only if Jesus were fully man could he die, and only if fully God could he die perfectly to close the chasm; and for all these centuries of digging and searching, no one ever found his bones."

"I've always wondered about those bones . . ."

"Lemme finish, son," said Tyrus, wiping his forehead. "Now you done gone and ruined my rhythm."

"Sorry."

He breathed deep and regained his rhythm. With volume. "The reason no one found his bones is because the tomb was empty. The tomb was empty because he conquered death. You're searching for peace, right? Peace comes through faith, young man, and faith comes through hearing, and if you think you are looking for God then think again because it's actually God who came looking for you. There is one mediator between God and man and that is Christ and those aren't my words they're his words and the living words and the eternal words and those are the only words you're gonna need."

Maybe it was just my head wound, but I had visions of an orderly shouting amen, he and Nurse Sonya doing a charismatic dance, arms shaking in spiritual conniption.

"No one ever explained it like that, Tyrus. Or that loud."

"The explaining of it is one thing, Jay. But are you ready to accept it?"

I thought of myself floating in the Atlantic, unconscious, with blood pouring from my skull.

I was Custer again, surrounded by myself.

It was time to surrender.

For the territory was nothing man could conquer on his own, though the journey had been scenic. I was suddenly back on the sandy south end of Pawleys Island, seated next to Allie with our feet in the current, me about to be date-stamped like that gallon of milk in her poem.

How much better that my stamp read "eternal."

The dull, throbbing pain at the back of my head did not diminish with my repentance, but something did feel different. A bit vague—like a slow-rising air bubble of a thought—but I felt like no matter how many times I plunged unconscious into a roiling blue ocean, I'd never truly drown.

Maybe this was that peace-in-the-present-tense thing I'd been trying to figure out.

Hard to comprehend that all of my twelve million, nine hundred and four sins were washed away, forgiven in an instant. Seemed too good, too undeserved. Seemed like there should be a longer process, like writing on a chalkboard for each indiscretion until the sum total was recounted and confessed. But recounting twelve million sins would require a great memory, not to mention a great supply of chalk.

Like most Americans, I had heard the phony-sounding soliloquies of people who had come to faith and claimed that all their problems had vanished, all their desires purified.

I now concluded that to be so much southern-fried hogwash.

Because my head still hurt, my thoughts still ran the gamut, and I still wanted to trade my old Blazer for a Jag. But the overriding reality of what lay ahead, of moving to New York with my salvation, was that I didn't have to earn it.

Tyrus returned from the men's room, sat again, and began probing into my vocation.

"I've been a broker for six years, Tyrus."

He crossed one leg, nodded knowingly, as if he'd done this before. "You ever use your talents to benefit the community? I mean, like explaining money and investing to people outside the loop?"

"Outside the loop?" I parroted, placing the captain's hat back on my head. *Ouch.*

"You know . . . people from the other side of the tracks, and I'm not just talking about poor black people, though we have many on the west side. Financial ignorance knows no color."

"True, but is all that use-your-talent stuff a requirement for the newly converted?"

He rubbed his calf and said, "No, no you won't get any points for it; it's just figuring out how to give back, how you can be of use."

Yet another new thought, this giving back. I wasn't even finished with my first new thought, the one on death. Seemed my life was just going to be spilling over with new thoughts; I hoped I'd still remember to call my mom in Fort Worth.

Tyrus tugged on his sweatshirt sleeve, checked his watch, rose to leave. With his index finger, he thumped me on the ankle. "I got a wedding rehearsal in less than an hour, Jay, but think about what I said. God can and will use you. You just got to be willing." He shook my hand and turned for the door.

"Tyrus?"

"Yes?" His back was still to me.

"Do you know if Jesus would drink a brew on the beach?"

With one hand on the knob, he stared into the door inches from his nose, then turned to face me. "Mercy, son. Let's tackle that one when you start maturing in the faith. For now, you do the drinking. Drink of the living water."

"That would be the Lord, right?"

"My, you're a quick one."

Tyrus left me then, and as he walked the hall, I could hear him whistling.

28

Nurse Sonya hinted I would go home soon if I could take five steps without help.

I took ten. Even with that, they wanted to observe me for one more night.

But this night felt different than the previous two. Alone in room 521, I considered what Tyrus had said about God desiring to know me. Somehow I didn't think God wanted me to die in the Atlantic Ocean. And now I felt myself wanting to know God.

Instead of communing with the Almighty, however, I got a visit from Steve Cole.

At 9:00 P.M. he strolled into my room, bearing gifts of chocolate drink and MoonPies. "Cubs are playing," he said, grabbing the remote and finding the game.

I finished off the cinnamon bread; Steve ate his gift.

"Appreciate your diving in the ocean to get me."

"Don't mention it, bro," he said, adjusting the volume.

I wiped cinnamon from my chin. "You coulda died."

"Never thought about it. Just reacted. Say, are these the *monthly* rents in New York?" He had reached over and pulled a stack of papers off the dresser.

"Yeah, the office sent those printouts over to condition me. Shocking, eh?"

"Unbelievable," he said, shuffling them in his lap.

"They said those apartments are the most reasonable. Can you believe $2,200 is considered reasonable?"

Steve didn't hear me. Instead, he was staring at the book on my bed. "Jay Jarvis reads verses?" he asked.

"A few. . . . You ever get twinges of peace?"

"Used to. Not lately, though."

At that point we stopped talking to watch the game. It is a sin of the worse variety for guys to talk when a game is on.

But after only one inning, I felt groggy and began to nod off. Steve said he'd better go, then asked if he should leave the game on. I told him yeah, it was the top of the fourth and Sosa would be coming up to bat so maybe I could stay awake.

I could not stay awake.

The announcer shouted, "What a Herculean blast by the great Sosa!" But Sosa was already rounding third base, and I was disappointed—not for missing the home run itself, but for missing the announcer's animated descriptions, like "Getouttahere!", "Kissthatbabygoodbye!", and my all-time favorite, "Ladies and gentleman, Elvis has left the stadium!"

I hate dozing off and missing home runs.

The Cardinals were changing pitchers, bringing in a lanky lefthander, when someone knocked loudly on my hospital room door. I asked who it was, but there was no response. Then a second knock, this one softer. I figured it was the night nurse.

"Come in," I said, muting the game.

The door opened, and beneath the brim of my captain's hat, all I could see were long legs, khaki shorts, and a lime-studded ankle bracelet.

I removed my hat. "Hey, stranger."

"You still awake?" asked Darcy, looking elegant on this September night, even in a Carolina sweatshirt. Her blonde mane was fresh washed and combed pencil straight.

"Just barely, but thanks for stopping by."

"Smells so sanitized in here," she said, scanning the room.

"Lovely, eh?"

"How's the head?"

"Better. It'll be oblong for another week. Steve just left ten minutes ago."

"Sorry I missed him. I brought your mail." And she handed me a thick, banded clump of envelopes.

"Thanks. Wasn't sure you got my message." A quick shuffle through the stack revealed nothing any hospitalized person would care to receive. No more get-well cards. No letters, either. Only junk.

"I would've weeded that out," she said, glancing up at the television, "but wasn't sure if you were a coupon clipper."

"Never used a coupon in my life."

"Me either," she said, taking my unwanted mail and tossing it in the trash.

Darcy wanted to examine the back of my head, and I agreed to let her. She stood beside me, and soon I felt long fingers tracing through my hair.

"Careful, I'm fragile."

"They shaved a nice square. You don't remember falling?" she asked.

"Last thing I saw was a dark fin chasing a gold lure, and then it's all a blank."

"I don't like fishing," she said, dismissing the subject as she stopped her examination to dig in her purse. "But I did bring you some pepper-mints."

"Cool. Get any more speeding tickets?"

She returned to the guest chair and said, "Nope. I'm trying to repent."

I stuffed a second pillow behind my back. "So, bring me up to date on Lydia."

Darcy crossed her legs. "Lydia needs to keep her private stuff private, so she won't have to explain so much. There's public stuff, and then there's private stuff. Public stuff is cars and clothes and fashion and weather. Private stuff is, well, private. But I feel for Lydia; she'll have to learn to trust again . . . the crux of being single and female."

"That goes for the male gender, too."

She stroked her hair and said, "Pales in comparison."

"Does not."

"Does too."

"We're just more guarded with our emotions, Darcy."

"Emotions? Y'all compartmentalize us like a box of corn flakes."

"I have never compared a woman to a breakfast cereal in all my life."

Her eyes widened. "Jay, are you sure you want to defend the male gender from a hospital bed?"

Defending the male gender from a hospital bed sounded ominous, so I unwrapped a peppermint and changed subjects. "Okay, you win. Now tell me how you became best friends with Allie."

She eased her long frame back in the chair. "College. We had adjoining dorm rooms at Appalachian State my first semester, but I couldn't stand the place."

"But she told me it was great there."

Darcy frowned. "Too many tree-huggers and granola types. All that back-to-nature stuff and no good shopping malls. That's why I transferred to Carolina. But she and I stayed in touch through graduation. Every summer she tried to get me to come work at a camp near Grandfather Mountain. But I said no way, not living in a wood shack with five other girls and no air conditioning and her flinging food across the campfire. No wonder she ended up in the jungles of Ecuador."

"Seems to be called to mission work, that's for sure."

"I'm just glad God chose her for that and lets me write checks of support, 'cause I could never be a missionary." She glanced at her watch, rose from the chair.

"Wanna swap vehicles one weekend?" I asked, hoping she'd stay and chat.

"I'll think about it, Jay. . . . I really need to get going."

"But I love convertibles. I'll fill it up with gas."

"We'll see."

"Will wash and wax it, too."

"Sleep well," she whispered, patting my foot. "And congrats on the job in New York."

The door closed, and I knew only one person could've told her my job news. My feet touched down again on cold tiles, and I took three wobbly steps to the window. Four floors below, against the curb, Lime Sherbet sat empty beneath a streetlight.

I waited a couple minutes, and there they came down the sidewalk, hand in hand.

A quick peck from her to him. Then another, from him to her.

She even let him drive.

29

Friday noon, from the doorway of room 521, Nurse Sonya watched me walk the hall. She conferred with a doctor, then said I could go home. While I gathered my things, she issued one last warning, complete with wagging index finger. "Doc wants you to promise to work only half days next week."

"I promise."

Steve had his orange Jeep parked at the hospital's entrance, radio blaring, top down. Whoever heard of getting driven home from the hospital with the top down? Twenty minutes of sunshine, laced with exhaust fumes, and we reached my suburban cul-de-sac. I figured now was a great time to press him with regard to his incognito Presbyterian romance.

"Wanna stay and make tacos with me, Steve?"

"Nah," he said, stepping around his Jeep. "Got lunch plans."

"And with whom do we haveth plans?" I asked, reaching for my dirty clothes.

He shut the passenger door. "Just plans, bro. I'll grab your mail for ya."

So much for pressing. Walking to my front door, I felt a little weak, a little weird, trying to reorient. Six newspapers had faded to yellow on the sidewalk, and my Chevy Blazer somehow had returned to the driveway.

"Maurice brought your truck over," said Steve, returning from the mailbox. "Keys on the front tire."

"How original. Any letters?"

"Phone bill and power bill," he said, handing off the parcels.

"No letters?"

"Sorry, bro."

Rumbling out of my cul-de-sac, he seemed a most ambiguous sneak. Steve could save me from drowning, could even drive me home from the hospital, but after all was said and done, he was still a sneak.

Darcy Yeager?

Now there's a total mystery. Draped in lime.

> Jarvis, weren't you advised to visit a
>   Pentecostal church?
> Because as far as we know, they're not
>   predestined to fall off boats and whack
>   their skulls
> Your concerned boss, Tate

Within the blunt world of brokerage, such notes found on your computer monitor are considered warm and compassionate.

It was Monday, my first half day back at the office. Mr. Brophy and my fellow brokers stopped by between the buying and selling to ask, "How's the head?" though they seemed more interested in what types of fish were tailing Steve's gold lure.

In groups of threes and fours, they crowded around my desk, ignoring the market and egging me on. I began my story a fifth time but stopped in midsentence as Line One glowed red.

"*Mr. Franklin Gruber on the phone, sir.*"

"Thank you, Glenda. Put him on, please. . . . No sir, Mr. Gruber, I have not quit the brokerage business to go sit under a palm tree. I fell and hit my head. Yessir, the financial news is accurate, Toys 'R' Us is up 40 percent from where you sold."

Click.

Soon as Mr. Gruber hung up on me, I began telling the other brokers about Maurice and the gaff. They kept interrupting, asking me to tell it again, tell it again. Phones went unanswered as our oldest broker, Marty, even asked to see the evidence. I refused.

"Beatrice Dean on Line One, sir."

"Thanks, Glenda."

I ushered them from the office and grabbed my headset, holding it to my ear because of the stitches. "Hello, Beatrice."

"We're all packed, dear. And they fixed my hearing aid!"

"So, you're really gonna go see Europe?"

"We leave tomorrow. Have you been ill? I called thrice last week."

"Been in the hospital. Nurse Sonya sent me home Friday."

"Seeing a nurse, too? My, my, Mr. Jarvis, we do get around, don't we?"

"I meant . . . oh, never mind. But it's good to hear from you."

"Did you like the gingerbread cookies?"

"Delicious. But the eyeballs fell out."

"I'll mail you the recipe. So tell me, dear, is it time to buy stock again?"

"But Beatrice, you just sold. You're not becoming a trader, are you?"

"Just teasing, Jay. Actually, I've been shopping for fashions to wear in Europe. And you?"

"I'm being promoted, Beatrice. To New York City."

"Oh, heavens, you won't last a week. Besides, haven't you heard the news?"

"What news?"

"It's all concrete, dear. Nobody can grow a garden, unless, of course, they live on the roof, and then they gotta deal with all those pigeons tainting the tomatoes. It's just no good there."

"When were you in New York?"

"Oh, I've never actually been. Just read about it. But I have visited Hendersonville, North Carolina. We went square dancing. Back in the fifties, I think . . . or maybe it was the forties. I forget."

"Did you buy the traveler's checks like I recommended?"

"Have all the cash in my purse, dear."

"You're carrying cash? In your purse?"

"Thirty-six thousand. Spent the other four on clothes. And we're not coming back till Thanksgiving! I got our entire garden club to go. It'll be eleven of us women, plus Trevor the handyman."

"Do any of you ladies speak a foreign language?"

"We thought about lessons, but there's just no time. Too much else to learn. I've been teaching the ladies how to flirt. It's all in the eyes, you know."

"So I've heard. And you're paying for the trip?"

"We must live, dear. While we have the chance."

"I'm slowly learning about that."

"Yes, yes, we all have much to learn, don't we? Well, I just called to chat. I must go water my lilies; they're famished. And I'm sending over a fresh batch of flowers for that drab space you people call a lobby."

"Drab is right. You have a wonderful trip, Beatrice."

"Yes, dear. Now, if both the nurse and the one behind the aqua door turn cold, you give me a call."

And with that, my six-year brokerage relationship with Beatrice Dean came to an end.

Closure. . . . That word has always irked me.

Tyrus Williams was serious about my giving back. So serious that he left me four phone messages that Monday afternoon. I'd been summoned by clergy. Tyrus said the adults he had in mind for free financial advice could not meet that week. So Brother Tyrus—being a resourceful man of the cloth—took advantage of my time off and found an alternative Wednesday afternoon audience: a third grade class.

I was not aware that Greenville, S.C., extended so far to the west. After miles of empty strip malls, mill housing, and netless basketball courts, I arrived at the school, Thurmond Elementary. Their yellow buses stood at ease, idling in single file. Down a hallway of crayon-marred walls, I located room 9C, knocked once, and opened the door.

Tyrus stood near the back, talking with the youngsters.

"Come in," said the teacher, a Mrs. Dawson. She peered over bifocals and hushed the class. I scanned the room. Twenty blank faces stared back.

Mrs. Dawson allowed me fifteen minutes, but it was the last fifteen minutes of the day and the kids were bouncing in their desks, awaiting the bell. She was introducing me when a flat-topped boy in the front row raised his hand. I pointed at the boy, who had on an orange NASCAR T-shirt, and raised my eyebrows. "Yes?"

"What you do to your head?" he asked, noticing the square white patch taped to the rear of my skull.

"I fell off a boat."

"You was drinkin'?"

"No. I was fishin'."

"We think you drinkin'." Flat-top turned to face his classmates, and every one of them nodded their agreement. Mrs. Dawson shushed him, shook her head in disgust, and said she was going to the ladies room.

Composure gathered, I leaned against the front of her desk, returned three goofy grins, and asked the kids if they knew the word *finance*.

"We can finance stuff with a credit card . . . if it ain't full up," said a pigtailed girl. Again, all heads affirmed the speaker.

"And what happens if it gets full up?"

"Momma orders a new one."

"Yeah," they echoed, "Momma orders a new one."

Tyrus coughed loudly and made a throat-cutting motion with his index finger. I quickly changed direction, using the next ten minutes to explain the importance of saving and investing to these west-side kids, ending my talk with the pros and cons of buying stock. "Okay, boys and girls, we've covered a lot of ground quickly; now tell me and Mr. Tyrus what you learned about stock."

"There's livestock on my daddy's farm," said Flat-top. "And lots of poopy, too."

Three kids fell out of their desks.

"Mrs. Dawson wouldn't like that," I scolded.

"Mrs. Dawson raise chickens."

Seated behind the class clown, an attentive boy named Richie waved his hand over his head. "I know about stock," he said. "It rhymes with clock."

"And rock," said Pigtail.

Like dominoes, they fed off each other.

"And lock."

"And sock," said Flat-top.

A brief pause. Then a skinny kid in the back row piped up. "Momma's smock," he said.

"And what about block?" asked his back-row buddy.

Little thumbs twiddled. "And tick tock."

"And Doctor Spock," I offered, sensing a pause in the momentum.

"Who's Doctor Spock?" asked Flat-top.

"Never mind."

Soon the two in the back started again. "Chicken pox!"

"And fishin' docks!"

"And football teams!"

Flat-top turned and glared. "Man, football team don't rhyme with stock."

"I meant Carolina Gamecocks."

Sensing a frenzy, I held up my hands to calm them. "Okay, time out. I think you are all gonna be poets instead of financiers. So how about if I give your class one share of stock, a share of Wal-Mart, which Mrs. Dawson can sell for about fifty bucks, and you guys and girls can spend it all on candy. . . . Wouldn't that be great?"

Tyrus had his hand over his eyes. The kids whooped and slapped high fives.

Flat-top even called me "the Gov-nuh."

On the drive home, I was unsure if that experience qualified as using my talents.

But it was definitely outside the loop.

30

Doc pulled out my stitches on Thursday. Fourteen pricks and I reached back to feel the sprouting of thick blond stubble. Back home I lay on my carpet with a pillow under my head and, just for entertainment, found a TV evangelist on cable.

Amusing, those verbose tangents of the faith.

Especially with the volume turned up.

That day he had donned the sport coat of a former era but seemed not to concern himself with fashion, concentrating instead on rhythm and money and souls. In that order. Then he changed the order to money, souls, and more money, so I suppose rhythm, like Elvis, had left the stadium.

I felt for my stubble once more, and it covered my scar, though not nearly as well as Jesus had covered my sin, and now Mr. TV Evangelist was striving for the rhythm again but he had gotten the awfulest case of white-man's disease. His pounding and gestures and voice inflection were all out of whack, so bad that he would never have the rhythm like Tyrus, except for the sweat.

Sweat must be the reason why he had donned the sport coat of a former era. He had ruined his modern duds by sweating for God and begging for dollars, all without the benefit of rhythm.

I muted the sound and began practicing to myself how Tyrus made it stand up and do the pirouette: "If you think you are looking for God then think again because it's actually God who came looking for you. There is one mediator between God and man and that is Christ and those aren't my words they're his words and the living words and the eternal words and those are the only words you're gonna need."

I said it over and over, convinced that I could do a better job than Mr. TV Evangelist and that when the money rolled in I could multiply it faster because surely I was a better stock picker as well.

Next I thought of the bum in New York City with his blue-tinted water jug and the coins fluttering quietly to the bottom. When I moved up there I could buy him thirty jugs and teach him the proper flow and rhythm of Tyrus's great gospel presentation. Then the bum could line his jugs up and down 46th Avenue, prop himself against a skyscraper, and spend the day collecting soft-falling coinage from repentant New Yorkers. Each day after work I could go by and help him fish money from the jugs, and we'd distribute half to the less fortunate. Then we could buy shares of stock with the other half so the bum with thirty jugs could be God's entrepreneur, helping to save the souls of Yankees, plus a nice little nest egg for himself.

I did not know if these thoughts signified a maturing in the faith; it was just how my mind was working ever since the accident.

After the show ended, I logged on to the Internet, wanting to check my e-mail. The only new message I had was from someone named "Surferdude." It said to look up a personal ad.

I would do no such thing.

Instead, I speed-dialed Ransom's house. Jamie picked up. I asked her about the baby in her belly, and she said, "Oh, I'm getting fat and we think it's a boy and you won't believe the name we've picked out." But before I could even ask, she had Ransom on the phone.

"Duuude," he said, sounding half awake.

"So tell me the name."

"What name?" he asked.

"Of your yet-to-be-born baby, of course."

"I think we're going with Wally Kahuna."

"Wally Kahuna Delaney?"

"The third."

"Wally Kahuna Delaney the third?"

"Yeah. There isn't a first or second, but it sounds cool. Whaddaya think?"

"I think you should rediscuss it with your wife."

"Hey, I've been reading here about the cost of diapers. Unbelievable how many you gotta buy. Think if we feed it only twice a day, it'll only mess half as much?"

"Can we change the subject?"

"The key word, Jaybird, is *superabsorbent*. Man, I have never changed a diaper in my life."

"Me either, but can we please change the subject?"

"To what?"

"To this personal ad you forwarded to me."

"So did you figure it out? Another *A* girl?"

"I haven't even looked at it. And I'm not planning to."

"You'll be sorry, dude."

"No way, Ransom. No more Presbyterian girls whose names start with *A*."

"Just look it up."

"No! You got me to go out with crazy Alexis. But that is it. I am not so desperate that I need to resort to personal ads."

"You'll be sorry if you don't look it up."

"Not doing it. I am maturing in the faith and do not need to use the Net to meet a girl."

"Just look it up. Although, yeah, it could be a joke. Debated Jamie on that last night. She says it's real. I can't decide. Might be fake."

"A fake personal ad from a third girl whose name starts with *A*? Oh, man, I am not your friend anymore."

"Darcy thinks it's real."

"So now you're telling me lime-lovin' Darcy knows the third girl whose name starts with *A*?"

"I dunno," he said, laughing now, "but she passed the ad to Jamie, who passed it to me, and now I'm passing it on to you. But again, it may be a joke .... planted by Steve or someone bored outta their skull. Anyway, I need to go, dude. My night to cook."

"Ransom?"

"Yeah?"

I cleared my throat. "There is one mediator between God and man and that is Christ and those aren't my words they're his words and the living words and the eternal words and those are the only words you're gonna need."

"You musta really whacked your head hard."

"Thanks for stopping the bleeding."

"Just look up the ad."

Right before bedtime, with a load of whites churning in suds, I could stand it no longer. Barefooted and curious, I logged on, fully aware that deceit usually lurks behind anonymity.

No, I cannot do it. I will not do it.

Why couldn't I do it?

Because I was flustered.

So much so that I rose from my desk, strode into the kitchen, and poured myself a heaping bowl of cereal.

I stood there, barefoot atop ceramic tiles, trying to crunch perspective from each spoonful. No, I told myself, this net stuff could be habit-forming. I am maturing in the faith and should just log off, remove this hint of waywardness from my house. Ransom is a deceiver. He has a malfunctioning surf brain. Too much salt. He is stressed over his approaching daddyhood and is now trying to set up his single male friends with Internet kooks posing as Presbyterian girls whose names start with *A*: Presbyterian Amy, Presbyterian Amanda, Presbyterian Ashley, and Presbyterian Aretha. There will be no end to it. Soon he will have me scroll to the Baptists, and waiting there will be Baptist Amy, Baptist Amanda, Baptist Ashley, and Baptist Aretha until finally I'll be right back where I started—watching multidenominational Alexis rearrange the spoons while slurping in a posh French restaurant. Jarvis, you should just wait until New York, and maybe try to meet some nice Hispanic girl of the faith, whose name begins with a more exotic letter like *V*, *X*, or *Q*.

Cereal gone, I convinced myself that this was just one little personal ad.

Couldn't hurt. No life-changing consequences involved. With the glow of my flat-panel monitor giving urgency to desire, I shut off the living-room lights, went to my desk again, and placed my hand on the mouse.

After scrolling past the deceptive and the twisted, the liars and the just plain lonely, I found ad #74522.

```
My car is an old Beetle.
My sign is Presbyterian.
My fetish is foreign travel—with extended
stays.
I prefer real space to cyberspace, and real
jungles to concrete ones.


I survived puberty, but would go back if I
could because I find most adults boring.
And I'll probably spend my life poor
because I don't like rich guys—and I'm not
for sale because I've already been bought.
If you own a white horse and consider your-
self a knight, you likely smell and have
blisters from rubbing against all that shiny
armor, so don't bother.
But if you can figure out what I do, please
respond.
AK77
```

I read it three more times.

Then a fifth, each time mulling the risks of response.

But it was late by then, and words seemed distant and hieroglyphic, hovering just out of reach, eluding me in the murky manner of language.

I would have to think on this one.

It took me six days and five boxes of cereal to think up a reply. First I was timid; then less so; then I thought I'd simply type the word *hello* and see if anything happened. I even considered posing as a Brit and typing an uppity response in the King's English.

But late Thursday night—armed with a brand-new anonymous e-mail address and with my corn flakes piled high but unmilked in a pasta bowl—I decided that, whether or not the personal ad was for real, whether or not she was who I thought she was, and whether or not she had anything going with Thomas the Peruvian evangelist, it deserved my best shot. Just in case.

I logged on, found the ad again, and hit reply.

```
Dear AK77
I have never considered myself a knight in
shining armor, although a shiny armoire does
sit next to my nightstand with the empty
picture frame—the silver one waiting to be
filled with a damsel who lacks distress,
or a missionary in a black dress, she could
even be one and the same.
The moat around my castle was filled in
and planted with perennials; my lance was
swapped for golf clubs; my shield is now a
large sundial on the patio. My brave white
horse was traded for a blue Chevy Blazer,
but there is less mess in the yard now. The
castle itself has been repainted (the ser-
vants being partial to khaki).
In addition, I have rid the forest of the
evil band of robbers, replacing their wicked
```

```
traps and nets with a handmade rope hammock.
Would go into more detail, but the neighbor-
hood bulldog, Spartacus, scratches at the
castle door.
  Sincerely,
  Oblong
```

That was my absolute best shot, so I clicked send. Time to trust God and cyberspace.

31

The second batch of yellow dahlias had wilted all over our office lobby, failing in their attempt to ward off a premature autumn.

"Mr. Franklin Gruber on the phone again, sir."

With coffee sloshing over the rim of my UT mug, I hurried to my speakerphone, sat down, and propped my feet on the desk. "Thank you, Glenda. Put him on."

But this time, she did not put Mr. Gruber on. Instead, Glenda, our mild-mannered secretary with great nails, lowered her voice. *"He's been a difficult client, hasn't he, Jay?"*

"Yes, Glenda, he sure has."

"He's made me some good money, though."

But how was that possible? "How is that possible?"

She whispered into the phone. *"Well, the very minute he sold the Toys 'R' Us, I bought. I always do the exact opposite of Mr. Gruber. It's how I supplement my secretary salary."*

"You're my hero, Glenda."

"We're gonna miss you, Jay."

I had almost forgotten about closure with Glenda. So between sips of coffee, I wrote myself a note to buy more dark chocolates.

Near day's end, Vince Galbraith called me from his trading desk in Manhattan. Said he had sent me a book titled *Running Money: Secrets of Institutional Block Trading*.

Block trading is large blocks of stock—ten, twenty, fifty thousand shares at a time—sometimes bought and sold on the floor of the exchange and sometimes pedaled to other big-shot Wall Street firms. When too many of these blocks line up on the sell side all at once, it's called, in layman's terms, a market crash.

It's all numbers, said Vince. Just add two or three zeroes to the transactions I've done with individual clients, and there's nothing to it. Just make the numbers. Mirror the performance of the S&P 500 during good weeks, outperform during bad weeks, and I would make the numbers and a low-six-figure bonus. He guaranteed it. Just make the numbers.

The firm must've really wanted me to make the numbers, because with only two weeks left to my move date, they told me to take Wednesdays and Fridays off, to stay home in my renovated house on the cul-de-sac and study *Secrets of Institutional Block Trading*.

Follow along on the Internet, they said. Sign up for free real-time quotes and watch big blocks of stock as they trade. Try to gauge the flow, the movement; feel the momentum of the market. Pretend a million dollars rides on your next trading decision.

Above all, they stressed, prepare strenuously to make the performance numbers.

Friday morning I was home at my computer desk, deep into the book, studying how to scale out of large, million-share stock positions.

Thing is, I already knew how: feed the shares to the market like a duck waddling up a bank.

I logged on to real-time, streaming quotes to watch the trades execute. Since my specialty would be oil and gas companies, I concentrated first on refiners like Exxon, Phillips Petroleum, and Amerada Hess; then the oil drillers like Transocean and Nabors Industries. Tens of thousands of shares processed every few minutes, and I was feeling the momentum on the drillers but was at a complete loss on the refiners. The big trades seemed to cancel each other out, and I was worried that this would be harder than

I'd thought, nothing at all like trading Toys 'R' Us with Mr. Gruber. But maybe I could get Mr. Gruber to buy and sell the stock of oil companies and I could just do the exact opposite with big blocks of stock, thus setting the all-time performance record for a rookie Wall Street trader.

Just before noon I was into my third cup of coffee, savoring such prideful thoughts, when an Instant Message appeared on my screen, asking if I would like to chat on-line. I had only cyberchatted once in my life, so I typed *Okay, let us commence to chat.*

```
AK77: hello oblong, whoever you are.
Oblong: Howdy.
AK77: do you remember me?
Oblong: You placed the ad . . . and dislike
  royalty with blisters?
AK77: //d oops
AK77: silly computer . . . sometimes I miss
  the middle ages when missives were deliv-
  ered via horseback.
Oblong: Agree, but to Instant Message back
  then required a really fast horse.
AK77: ha!!!! your response to my ad was the
  best ever.
Oblong: Thanks. What did you like about it?
AK77: mostly that it made me smile the whole
  time i was reading it. i really placed the
  ad as a big joke, didn't really expect to
  get replies . . . gets lonely where I live
  . . . where are you, oblong?
Oblong: Somewhere in North America. And you?
AK77: somewhere in south america . . . i'll
  let you guess which country.
Oblong: Brazil?
AK77: nope.
Oblong: Chile?
AK77: farther north. think birds and rain-
  forest.
Oblong: Consulting my globe. Just a second
  . . . Ecuador?
```

AK77: bingo. i have a question for you.

Oblong: Go ahead.

AK77: how did you know I was a missionary?

Oblong: The parts about extended stays, jungles, and Presbyterian gave you away.

AK77: you're the first to figure that out. had 2 other replies, one from an old man in connecticut who thought I was on a journey down the nile.

Oblong: And the other reply?

AK77: a fourteen-year-old kid in miami who wanted to buy my beetle for two hundred bucks cause he said I wouldn't be needing it if I lived in a jungle . . . have you ever been out of the country?

Oblong: To Europe once, Caribbean twice. My passport has been in the drawer for a while, though.

AK77: ever been to australia?

Oblong: No. You?

AK77: no i almost went two years ago but my best friend darcy who is the worst driver in history she went 92 mph on a beach trip this summer and she wanted to go visit the outback but I'm afraid she'd wreck and i fear for the lives of all those kangaroos.

Oblong: They don't teach punctuation in Ecuador, do they?

AK77: sorry . . . it's one of my two quirks.

Oblong: And the other?

AK77: it's left over from childhood . . . involves food and baseball.

Oblong: Okay, so how long are you going to stay in the Ecuadorian jungle?

AK77: maybe all my life . . . but that's enuff questions from you . . . my turn . . . what do you do? r u a writer?

Oblong: I'm a financial consultant.

AK77: sounds impressive. i met a guy on the beach trip who did that . . . so why is a

252

finance guy in north america responding to
personal ads from missionaries?

Oblong: A friend found the ad and I liked
the freshness of it. So how can a missionary in the jungle get access to the Internet?

AK77: i rode into coca this morning with
some women from our village . . . they buy
supplies every friday.

Oblong: And you're playing on the Internet,
eh?

AK77: yeah but i'm in the back of the supply
store and i think this is the only computer
in town so I had to bribe the store owner
. . . with hershey's dark chocolates.

Oblong: Coca is a funny name.

AK77: there's actually a much longer name, but
that's what everyone calls it. coca is not a
pretty place; roads are very bad . . . basi-
cally a gateway to the rainforest.

Oblong: Do you have beaches? I mean, how far
away?

AK77: yes, pretty beaches (they're 11 hours
away and across the andes mountains) but
they're not as pretty as the ones in my
home state . . . sc.

Oblong: I've been to SC, which beach you
like best?

AK77: one called north litchfield. hey
you're asking questions again. i went there
on a singles retreat with my church back in
may.

Oblong: A singles retreat in May—sounds like
an adventure.

AK77: it was . . . met this guy, a strange
mixture . . . crazy, with manners, i call
him.

Oblong: Has he come to visit you in Ecuador?

AK77: no . . . we wrote each other once but
then i'm not sure on his motives since i

think he was at my church for the wrong
reason but if he straightened that up with
God then maybe.

Oblong: God is important 2 U?

AK77: well duh! . . . i'm a missionary.

Oblong: Just kidding. He's important to me,
too.

AK77: i'm glad.

Oblong: You could invite him down for a
visit . . .

AK77: who, God?

Oblong: No, not God, the guy from the beach
trip.

AK77: nah, missionaries tend not to make the
first move.

Oblong: Maybe he'll wise up.

AK77: maybe . . . but i'm not waiting
around.

Oblong: Are you coming back to visit the
states any time soon?

AK77: goodness, the perpetual questions of
mr. oblong . . . but no, not any plans to
. . . will be years.

Oblong: Maybe you should find a local man to
date.

AK77: i tried. the guy was in peru, but we
had no chemistry. plus he just took a new
mission in uganda, so I gave him a handshake and a wave.

Oblong: His loss i guess.

AK77: yeah, oh well . . . the store owner
wants his computer back now . . . he's
standing behind me!

Oblong: The owner wouldn't be named Miguel,
would he?

AK77: how did you KNOW THAT????

Oblong: Allie, it's me . . . Jay.

AK77: !!!!! you, you, YOU SCHEMER!!!!

Oblong: I thought the personal ad was a
fake.

AK77: SHOCKED IN ECUADOR!! . . . no idea
it was you. and who helped you write that
ad response because i know stockbrokers
aren't that creative.
Oblong: No one helped, but I hit my head and
went to the hospital, then this animated
preacher named Tyrus made the gospel do a
pirouette. So now me and that lobster are
headed in opposite directions.
AK77: that is great news! (though you'll
have to explain sometime about the pirouette).
Oblong: And I'm moving up in the world of
brokerage—going to Manhattan to work on
Wall Street.
AK77: wow, double-wow and congrats! . . .
make some big bucks, then fly down to visit
me next spring.
Oblong: Or you get on a plastic float and
come visit me. No wait, please don't do
that.
AK77: ah, memories . . . you would love it
here, jay, with the tropical weather and
the kids are great and God continually
gives me opportunity to witness . . . uh
oh, now miguel is REALLY frowning at me so
i really really need to go . . . sorry.
Oblong: But I didn't get to tell you about
Maurice and the gaff . . .
AK77: sorry . . . gotta go.
Oblong: Bye, Allie.
AK77: thx 4 dark chocolates will write again
soon bye.

I had spilled coffee all over *Secrets of Institutional Block Trading*, and the Friday cram session for Wall Street would have to wait. After scrolling to the top of our Instant Message, I realized how fast we'd been typing, and I simply wanted to reread the entire dialogue.

Transcontinental cyberchats . . . much preferable to hieroglyphics.

32

There were no spooky costumes spooking the room during the Circle of Nine's late October meeting. Even though the meeting took place on Halloween, not a man dressed up, save for Ransom and his plastic pumpkin hat. He had it tilted down over his left eye so that he had to raise his head up to see. Around him were the eight other men, circled chairs, eighteen feet crowding the edge of Steve's lime-tinged rug.

Stanley sat two chairs away from me, a quarter way round the circle. And he had worn his too-small religious T-shirt again.

"Men," said Ransom, "if it were up to me, we'd spend this night doling out candy to some poor little dudes and dudettes. But we need a unanimous vote to do that."

He got seven votes, plus his own.

Only Stanley dissented. "You won't get my vote, Delaney. Theologically, Halloween is a demonic convergence of universal proportion, and our participation would only de-edify the maturity which we've already attained."

"Is de-edify a word?" asked Steve, leaning back in his chair.

"If spongedom can be a word, then so can de-edify."

Ransom nudged his pumpkin hat up an inch and said, "I don't think it's a word."

"Me either," I offered. "But spongedom is."

Young Barry squirmed, raised his hand. "Instead of arguing over Webster, why don't you guys show some charity, toss out a little cash. It's been a long eight weeks."

He had already removed his navy blue Nike cap when the doorbell rang. And rang.

Steve had developed a knack for gadgetry and had installed a new doorbell for himself—when pressed, it played the first line of "Take Me Out to the Ball Game."

"I'll get it," said Steve. Barry plopped back in his chair and frowned.

"No, let me get it," said Stanley, jumping in front of Steve.

Steve stuck out his chest. "It's my house."

"But I'm good with kids," countered Stanley, reaching for the doorknob. "And someone needs to explain to them this evil holiday."

Steve shrugged and told him to be his guest.

The baseball tune rang out a fourth time as Stanley opened the door. Our circle turned to spectate, and all we saw were three paper grocery sacks held high, jiggling. They stayed that way for a good ten seconds, but when nothing rattled the insides, the bags lowered, revealing, in order, Casper the Ghost, the Lone Ranger, and Pocahontas, who could not stop grinning.

They shook their bags and repeated a second time, "Trick or TREEEEAT!"

Stanley looked back at our circle and raised his index finger, as if to say he needed a moment. He stepped outside, between Casper and Pocahontas, and shut the door behind him.

We were out of our chairs in a flash. Eight right ears quickly pressed against the inside of Steve's door and his living-room wall.

Stanley stayed out there forever, but we could barely hear the sermon. He preached so long that Ransom whispered we should just go ahead and call it a full service, do a hymn, and take up an offering.

So curly-haired Barry got his wish, each man turning from the wall to pull out a wallet, the navy blue Nike cap filling fast with dollar bills while Steve hummed a pitiful version of "Have Thine Own Way."

Our one-eared snoop resumed, and we heard young voices utter phrases like "You crazy, man" and "Stingy ol' preacher." Then we heard feet pattering down the sidewalk, bags shaking as they ran.

We hurried back to our chairs, and for camouflage I began the impure-thought confessional, raising my arm as Barry counted cash. We had nearly completed a right-hand revolution—seven of nine members in sinful agreement—when, in a quest for symmetry, Steve raised both his left and his right, a proxied vote for Stanley.

Just then, Stanley walked back in, rejoined our circle, and smiled big.

"Dudes," said Ransom, "this is getting monotonous. None of us ever goes a whole week without an impure thought."

"Let me think on that," said Stanley.

"You know you did," said Barry. "Steve voted you in."

"Well, maybe once."

"What if we met hourly instead of weekly?" asked Steve.

"That still wouldn't work," said Ransom.

Stanley turned in his chair and wiped something from the back of his religious T-shirt. A blue, sticky substance clung to his fingertips. "Silly kids," he mumbled.

"What happened, dude?" asked Ransom.

"The Lone Ranger is a pagan child," said Stanley. "If I ever have kids, I'm home-schooling 'em."

We tried our best to keep straight faces, but it was of no use. Stanley went to get a paper towel from Steve's kitchen. Upon his return, we saw him standing behind our circle, coughing loud, calling us to attention. "I have a big announcement for you guys."

"What?" Ransom asked.

"I'm engaged."

While the Circle of Nine peppered Stanley with questions and congrats, Ransom motioned for me to meet him in the kitchen. As soon as we were alone, he grabbed me by both shoulders. "Did you reply to the ad? Please tell me you replied to the ad."

"It was her."

"You sure?" He had surfer breath.

"She Instant-Messaged me Friday morning."

"From South America?"

"I didn't know you could do that either . . . gotta love AOL."

He released his grip, took a step back. "So, what're you gonna do?"

"She wants me to visit next spring."

"Then go visit next spring. Or better yet, fly her to New York City."

"She hates concrete jungles."

"Nah, dude, all girls love that sorta thing."

I wasn't sure whether to trust the advice of a man who could name his firstborn Wally Kahuna. But maybe he was just trying to make amends for setting me up with crazy Alexis.

I could not decide.

33

On Wednesday night, November 5th, a cold front slid down from the Appalachians. The smell of duct tape and cardboard mingled with the gas heat as I packed boxes in my living room, four and a half days before I would leave the South.

It was time to move on.

I had spent a week saying good-bye to Greenville. Performed closure with eighty-seven clients. Turned in my office key to Mr. Brophy. Mailed one share of Wal-Mart to Mrs. Dawson and her wacko, rhyming third-graders. Took one last call from Mr. Gruber, who wanted to buy a thousand shares of Gillette because he thought global warming would cause men the world over to shave their beards.

I gave no rebuttal, just bought him the stock.

And I said congrats to Stanley and Number Eight, oops, Rona, over their engagement.

After that last meeting, I had made my peace with ol' Stanley, and he with me. Two young men agreeing, between syllables, that there are many rooms in the Father's house, and although we shared eternal life, most likely we'd never share bunk beds.

While packing, I thought of that long Instant Message, Allie's uncluttered thoughts, her quiet beauty and commitment to God. Then I remembered the last stanza of her poem, the one she had scrawled in wet sand, and wondered if my own roots would grow through polished concrete.

By midnight I had cleared my closet, except for a black turtleneck and one maturing pair of black wool pants. New York fashion. Travel attire.

There was only one thing left to do.

My umbrella had not moved from that hall rack in four months; every Sunday I would leave without it.

Maurice was sweeping autumn from the sidewalk as I parked in the empty church lot. It was late afternoon, and the leaves had scattered their color across the manicured lawn of North Hills Presbyterian. He waved, set his broom against the brick sanctuary, and wiped his forehead with the sleeve of his jumpsuit. I paused at my back bumper to retie my sneakers.

"Well, well," said Maurice, twirling his keys on a chrome ring. "Mr. Oblong Head 'bout to leave for New Yawk without his umbrella. How is the head?"

Sneakers tied, I walked over and shook his hand. "Much better. But this time, do not let me get distracted."

He grabbed his broom, and through a side door we entered a church hallway laced with the fresh, lemony scent of Pine Sol.

"Your umbrella is still there," he said, pulling an envelope from his pocket, "but the church asked me to give you this." He handed me an official church envelope, addressed to Jay Jarvis.

"This can't be good," I said, removing the contents.

"They want you to preach?"

"We'll know in a second." I began reading. Maurice, he just tapped his broom handle on the floor in a kind of nervous, janitorial anticipation.

Dear Mr. Jarvis,

It has come to the attention of the elders of North Hills Presbyterian Church that you recently led a team of four on a short-term mission trip, a weekend of service to a fellow minister of the gospel down along the Carolina coast. Such selfless service can set a long-lasting example for our congregation. We are most interested in the details of your experience. Your injury and subsequent recovery would also be of encouragement to the church body.

We, the elders, would like to invite you to speak (just ten minutes or so) at our missions conference to be held at the church in early December. The content of your talk would be up to you, of course, although a short briefing with church leadership is standard procedure to ensure an appropriate message. You may confirm with the church secretary, Elaine, at your convenience.

Grace and peace, Robert Kyle, elder

I stuffed the letter in my jeans pocket. "Maurice, you wanna speak to the church mission conference in December? 'Cause I'm due in New York in three days."

Maurice propped his broom in a maintenance closet. "No way, Jay Jarvis. I'm a sexton and I'm a poet . . . but I ain't preachin' to no Presbyterians. Tyrus said this church has no emotion."

Maurice then told me to hurry up and fetch my belongings and that he'd lock up and walk out with me. I jogged the length of the hall to reclaim my umbrella.

He met me in dim light. For a moment, he admired the blue-and-white design. "Ya know, Jay, I almost took that one home. My sister got a birthday coming up next week."

Down the hall we strolled, a pair of unlikely comrades. And one more thing was certain—I was going to miss Maurice Evans.

We turned the corner, past the pecking order of church offices, past the New Members board. He nudged me to stop and look. I did not want to. But he nudged me again. This time there was one new family and two new single girls. However, a small spreadsheet was pinned to the bottom of the corkboard, and in red ink, a note was scribbled across it.

Your church has now dropped to 19th in city rankings

Better shape up and recruit some young men

I shook my head. "Won't even ask who did that, Maurice."

"Wasn't me," he said, palms raised in innocence.

"I know, Maurice."

He snatched the paper in one hand and held it up, tapping it as he spoke. "I've been thinking about this note all day. What are they talking 'bout with that nineteenth stuff? My cleaning skills?"

"No, Maurice."

He looked offended by the note. "Can't nobody say I don't keep a clean church. I know I'd be in the top five. I know it, Jay. I got twenty-four years experience."

"It's talking about the quality of single men, Maurice."

"The what?"

I leaned against the wall. "It's the latest fad. It's killing the nightclub business. The official term is *denominational hopscotch*. Lydia knows all about this stuff. Thinks God is very mad about it. That it shows a certain lack of faith."

Maurice held the spreadsheet aloft and quickly made for the exit. "Gomorrah comin'," he said, shaking the paper overhead. "She's on the way. We in a downward spiral now."

Umbrella in tow, I tried to keep up, but Maurice could not be caught. He was nearing the side door when suddenly he stopped, turned to face me. "You know what, Jay . . . I just might know who did it. I think I seen her."

"I'm all ears."

"Don't know her name," he said, fumbling for his keys, "but I saw this girl rush in at lunch hour and leave real quick. Real quick. Had black hair . . . and one of those shiny rings in her eyebrow."

I pushed open the side door to the parking lot. "It's a crazy world, Maurice."

"Yessir," he said, gazing out at the autumn sky. "Crazy world, indeed."

Act III

God . . . He is the great iconoclast.

—C. S. Lewis

34

I woke to the first beep of my alarm clock. One last shave, one last shower before lugging my duffel bag onto the front steps.

And onto the front steps we went, me 'n duffel bag. Then I opened my door again and peered back across my empty living room, my empty foyer, my khaki walls only six months dry. A chapter closed.

Strange to look out across your own dew-covered grass and see a FOR SALE sign impaled on a stake, a capitalistic dagger letting the world know a life is about to change, and that the change comes with a price tag, two and a half baths, and a vaulted ceiling.

I felt like I should take a picture or that someone should be in the doorway waving bye. I felt like chipping golf balls on the lawn one last time before leaving the South. And, to my relief, I felt like I would make my flight since my ride was on time, approaching the cul-de-sac with top up. Her Limeness, tailgated by an orange Jeep.

She backed Sherbet into my driveway. Steve left his Jeep on the street.

"All black? You look very New Yorkish," said Darcy, popping her trunk.

"Conformity," I said. "Appreciate you guys taking me to the airport."

"Don't mention it," said Steve, loading my carry-on. "Just save us some subway tokens."

"And opera tickets, too," said Darcy. She slid behind the wheel of her Caddy, its big V-8 rumbling with impatience.

From Sherbet's front seat, I stared into the chrome side mirror, watching my slice of suburbia fade away. Darcy made a left, and suburbia disappeared.

We ramped onto I-85 North, toward the Greenville-Spartanburg airport, and Darcy immediately blew by three minivans, an eighteen-wheeler, and a muscle car.

"I thought you repented . . ."

"Sorry," she said. "It's like you men and your silly fetish with baseball."

"You have a sports fetish, Steve?" I asked, turning toward the backseat.

"Not me," he said. "Well, maybe the Cubs qualify as a fetish."

At the US Air drop-off, I shouldered my carry-on bag. Darcy closed the trunk. In front of us, a yellow cab pulled to the curb. A businesswoman exited the cab, briefcase in one hand, purse in the other. She glanced at my black wardrobe, smiled briefly, then turned and walked quickly between sliding glass doors.

"You'll be seeing plenty of cabs, bro," said Steve, reaching for my duffel. "I'll carry this one in for ya."

"Nah, I can handle it."

"You sure?"

"Yeah, let's get all the good-byes over with."

"We'll miss you," said Darcy, hugging my neck. *Nice perfume, Darce.*

"Get us some Yankee tickets," said Steve with a shake and a bear hug.

I liked Steve Cole, regardless of his secrets. Darcy too. And I would use this moment to give them one last chance for confessional, one fleeting opportunity to come clean. "Before I leave the South, I wanted to ask you two a question."

Steve's face went blank. "Sure, what's up?"

"You two ever thought about, you know, being a couple? Y'all seem to get along pretty well."

"Naaah . . . us? We're just buds," said Steve.

"Yeah, just good buddies," said Darcy, stroking her shiny blonde hair. "We'll miss you, Jay."

I picked up my duffel and backpedaled toward the entrance.

Steve waved and said, "Send an e-mail when you get settled."

"Will do."

Inside the glass doors, I turned to watch Lime Sherbet, the car that had lent such color and adventure to my seven months in South Carolina, ramble away.

My window seat was over the wing, which would've really stunk had I not been changing planes again in Charlotte. While skimming through an article about the plight of spotted owls, I felt the plane bank left, saw urban sprawl extend over the wing, and figured the owls would have to fend for themselves.

In the lobby of Charlotte International, hordes of businesspeople crowded the restaurant bar at 9:20 A.M., watching a big-screen TV, where live from the floor of the New York Stock Exchange an attractive young woman smiled into the camera, telling us that stocks looked strong in premarket trading.

The smiling young woman was mistaken; the premarket is for fools.

I ordered an English muffin, link sausage, and orange juice, then sat in a booth and listened to the businesspeople chat about our new national pastime: Are stocks overvalued? Will the Fed lower rates again? Do you get real-time quotes at the office? Do valuations still matter in this new millennium?

The answers, people, are yes, no, yes, and yes.

While I finished breakfast, the young woman's TV smile morphed into a frown as she reported that stocks had reversed course in the opening minutes of trading and were now falling precipitously. Crowded below the television, the businesspeople mumbled curses and sipped their juice.

Then, with thirty minutes left till departure, I made a preflight visit to the men's room.

Not that I had to *go*, mind you.

No, this was larger in scope. This was premeditated. This, at long last, was the season. There are seasons for everything under the sun, and this day, November the 10th, was the season in which to turn the tables on Steve Cole and Darcy Yeager.

In the harsh light of a Charlotte men's room, I reached into my carry-on bag and pulled out an awful green-and-purple Hawaiian shirt, a pair of khaki shorts, my passport, and my well-worn beach sandals. My black wool pants and black turtleneck hung over a stall, like the remnants of a raptured New Yorker. In fact, I didn't even like those black clothes, so I just decided to leave them there.

I left the rest room in full stride, trekking past the businesspeople, the television, and the restaurant bar, my sandals flip-flopping as I made my way down the long and busy corridor, the corridor leading to the international boarding gates.

35

This time my window seat was in the rear of the plane, view unobstructed. At takeoff I watched Charlotte fade to miniature, until we were too high above the clouds to watch anything but the brighter side of cumulus. I may have been mentally ill, but I knew my cumulus.

We leveled off, and soon a flight attendant made her way down the aisle, smiling left and right while distributing peanuts. "And how about you two?" she asked, her brass name tag identifying her as Marlena.

"Yes, please," said the lady seated next to me. My seatmate looked fiftyish, heavyset and happy, like a youthful grandmother. She wore an orange bow in her hair, and I guessed she was Hispanic.

"I'll take one, too," I said, reaching to accept my freebie.

The lady opened her packet, then asked what I could see out the window. But there were only clouds out the window, so I really couldn't tell. We finished our snacks in silence. The clouds disappeared.

Marlena returned, took our trash, and offered us bottled water. We accepted, and the grandmotherly lady turned to admire my shirt.

"Like it?" I asked.

"Love it," she replied. "All those purple-and-green leaves . . . so colorful."

"It's my jungle shirt."

She unscrewed her bottle top, took a sip. "You could've hemmed those shorts, though."

"Just cut 'em off last night," I said, still nervous about my visit but glad to have a talkative seatmate.

She kept staring at my shirt, like it might bite. "It'll be hot when we land," she said. "Where in South America are you headed?"

I looked out the window and muttered, "Somewhere east of Coca, Ecuador."

"That's pretty remote," she said, adjusting her lap tray. "Very remote. Don't tell me you have family there?"

I chewed and swallowed three peanuts. "No, ma'am . . . she's, well, she's someone I met this past summer."

"Ah, visiting a young lady."

"She's supposed to meet me at the airport . . . if she can get use of a pickup truck. I figured it was easier for me to fly there than her fly to New York City."

She turned for a closer look at me. "You're from the big city?"

"No, ma'am, but I was supposed to move there today to begin training for a job on Wall Street. I delayed the training for a week."

"That's nice."

"Yeah, and this morning my friends Darcy and Steve, who try to hide their romance—even while I was in the hospital with an oblong head, can you believe that?—they dropped me off at the airport thinking I was flying to New York with all my black clothes, but I left those black clothes in the men's room back in Charlotte."

She looked confused and pulled a magazine from the seat rack. "Well," she said, "I think what you're doing is sweet. I met my husband while I was vacationing in Florida. Eventually, one of us had to move."

"I'm not moving to South America, ma'am. Just going for a visit."

The lady smiled, decided against the magazine, and looked through my window. She started to say something, then leaned her head back against the seat and shut her eyes.

We passed over the coast of South Carolina, and our Latino pilot said it was sunny in Charleston. I wondered if Preacher Smoak was down there steering his boat, his crew flying a marlin flag.

By noon we were over Key West; and by early afternoon, Costa Rica. The steady hum of jet engines lulled me off as I tried to pronounce odd

272

words. The pages of my Spanish/English dictionary were already wearing at the corners from rapid flipping, and I felt wholly unprepared for a visit to a new land. In her second surprise Instant Message, a quick one on my last Friday in Greenville, Allie had said some of the adults spoke English, though none spoke it well. Then she had typed *why don't you come visit NOW, before wall street totally consumeth?*

The Hispanic lady slept, her orange bow mushed against her seat. Nervous and wide-eyed, I watched our descent. Dark mountains rose through cloud cover, and I thought there just could not be room for a runway in this terrain.

Three pings and the pilot spoke.

I could only make out the word *Quito*.

"What did he say?" I asked the lady.

She rubbed her eyes. "He said we are thirty kilometers northeast of Quito and will be on the ground in six minutes." Then the pilot said it again, in English.

Approaching Quito, Ecuador, the pilot quickly dropped altitude; we had passed over a boundless chain of peaks, the Andes. Below the horizon, between slivers of gray cloud, the green canopy of rainforest draped the earth in a tangle of treetops.

I saw the blinking lights of a runway surrounded by mountains, us in near free fall, a tingly, sinky feeling caroming back and forth between my stomach and lower back, now sweaty palms, steep descent, and wow, this wasn't Dallas, this wasn't even close, this was my comeuppance, my omega—and a logical time to summon the good doctor.

With muscles tensed, eyes scrunched, I began a hasty composition.

> Will you die in mountains green?
> Would your body e'er be seen?
> Will this jet to Earth go blam?
> I am dust. Dust Jay I am!

"It's like landing in a salad bowl," the lady next to me said, wide awake and gripping the armrests.

273

Two bumps, a brief skid, and we were on the ground. Applause burst forth. The lady made the sign of the cross and exhaled, the jet engines whirring themselves into a low, metallic drone.

"That was better than Disney World," I said in genuine relief.

"Hope Mickey likes bananas." And she rose from her seat to open the overhead.

Squished together in the aisle and having survived the nauseous descent, the passengers tended toward chattiness, with scant similarity to the hushed reserve of American flights.

A stranger in a strange land am I. That was my thought as I looked around at the mass of people filling the aisles. I was one of maybe three with light-colored hair. I stood in the aisle parsing speech unfamiliar, with all tourists and South Americans moving slowly toward the cockpit.

An elderly gent was late in rising from his window seat, so I motioned for him to cut in. He squeezed into the aisle and mumbled something undecipherable, although his utterance seemed appreciative.

We reached the front, and sunlight pierced the exit, the old man, then me.

"Nice flight, Miss," I said to Marlena.

"Nice shirt, *señor*," she shot back, with the official flight-attendant's nod, which, come to think of it, was quite similar to the official preacher's nod.

They make you walk across the tarmac in Ecuador. No rolling tunnels or flexible hallways to ease the burdens of travel. Didn't matter—the afternoon was very warm, the chatter very Spanish.

Halfway down the jet's stairs, I took inventory of the glassed faces staring back from the lobby. Olive-skinned strangers, some young, some old, some small, actually they *all* looked a bit small . . . but there was no Allie.

I had that sinky, tingly feeling again.

On the stairs below me, the Peruvian lady looked up and blew a kiss toward a mustached man behind the glass. He sent back three.

I, too, wanted someone to send back three.

Instead, the elderly gent turned and sneezed at my leg, then a young boy bumped me from behind.

"*Perdón,*" said the youngster.

"*Perdón,*" I replied, trying to parrot his accent.

Two steps from the bottom, I glanced up a fourth time. Allie Kyle was standing at the end of the lobby, waving, and she was in that pale yellow sundress again.

Her hair was grown out past her shoulders. She was quite tan.

Suddenly it occurred to me that we really didn't know each other very well. There was a pounding in my chest.

I stepped onto the tarmac and waved back.

36

The old pickup had dents and rust spots covering the shell, a cracked mirror, and a brunette driver with an affinity for carving poems in sandbars. Her Spanish towel was laying across the seat, its loopy red words hiding torn upholstery. The air was thin, and she wore no makeup. Didn't need it.

"Only four more hours till we reach Coca," said Allie, steering the truck down and around a steep mountainside. We had just switched places.

Ecuadorian drivers love their horns; she'd passed three other vehicles, and each one signaled their displeasure like children who've discovered doorbells. All three passed us back, with volume, and she returned the greeting. We were sweaty and dusty inside the truck, but I barely noticed—the spiraling terrain and ridiculous views had all my attention.

"I'll drive again anytime," I offered. "Just say when . . ."

Allie wiped her forehead, pulled hair from her eyes. "Okay, but you rest first. We don't need any more close calls with mules."

"He was in the road."

"He was eating grass on the shoulder, Jay."

The capital city of Quito was nine thousand feet above sea level. But that was at 4:00 P.M.; at 5:30 and en route to the outskirts of the Amazon rainforest, we were only six thousand feet above and swiftly declining, circling and dropping, curving and descending to a never-ending, tire-wearing bout of counterclockwise rotation.

"I think I see Brazil in the distance."

"That would be Peru, Jay."

"I meant Peru."

The Andes are steep and treacherous for motorized passage; I couldn't fathom that people actually lived on them. Yet across the steepness and beyond the valley were countless fields in bold, patchwork patterns; rich farmland cut in huge, colorful squares of soft gold, reddish brown, olive green and umber, saffron and chestnut and bronze.

It looked as though someone had loaded the blades of a mower with dye and proceeded to color the mountainside in broad swaths of every earth tone that side of the equator. Even more striking was the angle of the patchwork; a farmer would need great balance to plow such acreage, and surely a dropped tomato would roll off the mountain and into the roiling river canyon.

In the distance, behind the patchwork, the top of a volcano jutted through cloud cover, the white tip frosted, as if dipped in coconut. "That one is over fifteen thousand feet at the peak," Allie said, honking thrice at a tourist bus.

"My camera is in my bag."

"Take pictures with your eyeballs," she replied, accelerating down and around the endless curve, this curve of dreams, one ceaseless spiral of downward momentum. Craggy rock jutted out from the overhang, and as we zoomed past I glimpsed the mother lode of moss clinging like barnacles to the mountain wall.

"Hold on," she said, and a thick splash of water wet our windshield.

My right arm was soaked. "You drove us through a waterfall?"

"That's a small one."

With one crank of the handle, I rolled my window all the way down for one long, curious sniff—and she was right, Latino air did tickle.

"What did Darcy think about you coming to see me?" Allie asked, honking her intention to a loitering Jeep.

A little voice whispered to fib, but I could not. "Well, Darcy doesn't really know about this."

She swerved left around the Jeep, then back right. "But I thought you said she and Steve drove you to the airport."

"Yeah, but I was wearing all black."

"I don't understand."

"When I left South Carolina, I was wearing—"

"Jay, you didn't."

"I did."

She shook her head and slapped the dash. "That's hysterical."

We continued our descent, passing a tourist bus, a rock quarry, and a kid on a single-speed bike who was ascending slowly in a determined effort at mountain biking. Beside him, on the outer shoulder, small white crosses protruded from the earth.

"No guardrails on these roads," said Allie, a firm grip on the wheel. "You go over, and you're a goner."

"No beach patrol, eh?"

"Yeah," she said, shifting gears. "No beach patrol."

On the inner half of the spiraling highway, a short, black-hatted man was pushing a cart filled with fruit. He had grapefruits and mangos and bananas and a scribbled sign I could not read. I asked Allie to pull over. She braked hard, gravel screeching at the rear tire. "All the men are short here, Jay . . . compared to Americans."

"What's with the hats?" I asked. "Everyone wears the same dusty hat."

"They're called derbies. Made of felt. Everyone from the highlands has one."

The cart man saw us looking and pulled his rickety cart around, guiding it downhill to meet us. He looked hopeful. Out of the truck now, I watched his lumbering approach but again felt unprepared. I stuck my head back in the window for an inquiry.

"Captain Kyle, is one U.S. dollar enough for a grapefruit and banana?"

"A whole dollar?" she replied, fiddling with the parking brake. "A whole dollar for two pieces of fruit and he might kiss you on the lips."

I stood on the graveled shoulder and looked past the river canyon and across steep farmland to a sky backlit and brilliant, fading to pastel in the distance, then to a gray-blue haze where the horizon exhausted my vision. The air was still thin but finding its appetite. I felt the intense rays from a sun that seemed to have lost its filter. There is no subtlety to an Ecuadorian sun.

"Hello . . . I mean, *hola, señor.*"

"*Hola,*" he said, stopping his cart at the front bumper. Thigh muscles bulged through his pants. With a crumpled dollar in my pocket, I reached first for a mango, then for an orphaned banana. I handed him the dollar.

Cart Man reached in his dusty pants for change, but I waved him off. He didn't smile, only muttered, "*Gracias.*"

Sensing opportunity, he held up a fat mango for Allie's inspection. "*Señorita?*"

She shook her head no.

My fruit smelled of rainforest, damp and earthy and humid. People will tell you a banana is just a banana, but until you've eaten one fresh from the picking, peeled one on the side of an Andes mountain with the sunlit fields of patchwork in the distance below a frosted volcano and the wind in your hair while a missionary girl does eighty around a curving highway with no guardrails . . . you haven't lived.

"How long can you really stay?" Allie asked, downshifting now, grinding the gears.

"Four days, maybe five. It was all I could squeeze out of my new boss-to-be in New York. He's a bit ornery."

She pointed a finger at me. "Those flashing numbers will wait. You should plan on two whole weeks. . . . You'll need it to experience the enormity of this place."

My banana peel slid to the floorboard. "I'll go without sleep then. Explore the jungle at midnight. And if you're nice, I might fly you up to Manhattan after the New Year."

She remained silent, ignoring my offer, as if totally uninterested in big cities.

"Okay, Allie, when's the last time you nailed Maurice with a Fig Newton?"

I couldn't tell if she was blushing or if it was simply the heat.

"About a month before you moved to South Carolina," she said, trying her best to steer and grin at the same time. "He made faces at me when I was in kindergarten; now, twenty years later, he can't stop. It's stimulus response."

Near the base of the Andes she pulled over to let me drive again. We stopped in tall grass, and she slid behind me on the bench seat, me at the wheel, she sitting neither close nor far but in the neutral zone; in the neutral zone she sat, this magnetic missionary, and as I pulled back onto the single-lane highway with the overlapping parachutes of rainforest now huge below the mountains, I silently thanked God that I'd met her, that she'd hit me with a roasted marshmallow and carved poems in sandbars and woke embarrassed but innocent on Litchfield Beach with her sandy, matted hair and the slightest hint of compromise, then shrugged it off because God knew nothing happened.

I was sure God knew nothing happened.

Don't you, God?

Before cranking the engine, I turned sideways in my seat to try and read her toweled verse.

"Figured out what it says yet?" she asked, removing the cap from a water bottle.

I was sitting on *Jehovah*, but loopy, red *cielo* stumped me. "One hint, please."

"Heaven, as in 'my help comes from God, who made the heavens and the earth.'"

And my Spanish lessons had commenced, courtesy of an Ecuadorian beach towel.

I felt like my lungs could hold twice the air now. I wanted to back us up and fly down the mountain again, do eighty one more time on that curve of dreams with its white crosses high above the river canyon. But the spiral did end, the descent did cease, and the patchwork fields were now a photograph on my eyelid.

The road became dirt, packed brown and potholed, though we were surrounded by endless vegetation and the wildest of flora; lush, limber plants rambling about as if preparing to swallow us whole.

"Welcome to the Amazon Basin," she said, gesturing like Vanna.

I was awestruck and did not notice the bright blue insect perched on my shirtsleeve—until it began crawling up my right shoulder. I raised my hand to slap it but hesitated.

"Ouch!"

Allie had crushed the critter with my banana peel, turning a bright blue insect into a very primitive, smeary blue goo.

"That happens a lot here, don't it?"

"Hourly," she said.

Deeper into jungle, I stopped the truck, grappling for words as I felt enveloped, caped in the greenery of this vast new world. Sunlight could not penetrate the cover, and from the ground, thick vines intersected each other like wooden noodles, weaving through tree limbs stiff and angular, a tented sanctuary to any bird, bug, or beast.

I had never smelled such abundance; never had my nostrils been such aliens to their duty. Warm scents of renegade moss, earth, and vegetation hovered over and around each other, a myriad of jungle aromas competing with an orchestra of birds to dominate my senses.

"It's lusher than lush."

And those were the only words I could muster.

We remained parked beneath the wildness, and time seemed to linger again. Allie was wearing a string of exotic-looking beads around her neck: round, wooden, and staggered in the earth tones of patchworked farmland.

Big, wooden jungle beads—not my first choice of souvenir. At least not for Manhattan.

After slipping them from her neck, she leaned over and draped me with the beads, then decided they looked awful with my shirt. I handed them back. She left them in her lap and pointed to a dense tangle of vines and limbs.

"See them yet?" she asked.

"See what?"

"Keep looking. They're small and hyper."

"I still don't see 'em. Wait, yeah, I see 'em."

"They're called howler monkeys."

I wouldn't have known a monkey from a chimp, though the little guys were howling and swinging, jumping and arguing, baring teeth and making outrageous leaps: leaps of abandon, leaps of faith, leaps that defied common sense, but then I had left common sense in the men's room back in Charlotte, so why should I have expected more from mere monkeys.

We watched them for several minutes, and as the sun set behind us, tinges of deep red glowed in strands of her hair. She knew I was staring. "Want the bad news?" she asked, looking up through the windshield.

"We got a flat?"

"Nope. We still have three hours to go."

"I want a pet monkey."

She rolled her eyes. "I'll steer us home from here, Jay. You're really not supposed to be driving."

"All yours, Captain." And she slid behind me on the seat again.

At nightfall we passed through the edge of Coca, a gritty little town that, according to my guide, served as a launch site for Ecuadorian jungle tours and river excursions. I dozed off once, then twice again, each time potholed from slumber.

We arrived shortly after 11:00 P.M.

In the headlights of the truck, I saw a well-kept village—dirt paths lined with rocks, and the main road also dirt but flanked by two torches rising from thick stalks of bamboo.

The bamboo was high, the flames low, and a row of tiny houses—more like wooden huts crafted by amateur carpenters—occupied each side of the road. They sat atop skinny stilts a few feet off the ground, and what looked like a pvc water line paralleled an outer wall. We parked next to a hut. She cut the headlights.

"Is there electricity?" I asked.

She smiled briefly and said, "Two generators. We use them sparingly."

"Running water?"

"Only the cold kind."

"Men on one side of the road, women on the other?"

"For the most part."

I opened my door, and a raucous symphony of bugs rung out at decibel levels that would put American bugs to shame. American bugs are wimps. These Amazon bugs should've been Pentecostal pastors; the sounds were piercing, and I detected alto bugs, bass bugs, soprano bugs, and one unmistakable tenor bug.

"Music to doze with, I assume?"

"Every night," she said, placing the keys under the mat.

"Appreciate the driving. If you sit still, I'll get your door for ya."

"I would," she said, releasing her seat belt, "but that's not a custom here. Thanks, anyway."

I grabbed my duffel from the rear of the truck, then reached back in the front seat to retrieve my mango. "What about the baritone bugs?"

She peeled her towel from the seat. "You're staying in that one," she said, pointing into darkness.

I clicked on my flashlight. "G'night."

"Keep the light to the ground. And we rise early." She turned and walked the opposite way. "Oh, and Jay . . ."

"Yes, Allie?" I could barely see her in the dark.

"We used to own a small water heater, for once-a-week hot showers. It sorta got broke."

"Well, is it sorta or is it permanent?"

"I ran over it with the truck."

With the light to the ground, I hauled my duffel up four stairs and into a plywood-walled, wooden-floored room. There were two single beds, split by a grass rug, and a male body lay sleeping in the one to my right. Screens covered the two windows but no glass.

I collapsed on the bed and watched a stream of moonlight grace the far wall.

I did not fight sleep. I ushered it in and served it drinks.

37

I woke in a narrow bed, unaccustomed to such balmy air at such an early hour. Greeted in broken English by my slender roommate, a young man named Juan, I was dazzled by the simplicity of our hut. No outlets. No pictures. Just the grass rug between us and a small stack of letters in Juan's windowsill. He sat on the edge of his bed in mismatched colors—brown shorts and red soccer jersey—then reached over, shook my hand, and said, "You duty of trash."

I figured out that he was the groundskeeper and coached soccer. He told me I could be the assistant groundskeeper and coach baseball.

He was not kidding.

"Pick up trash?" I asked, threading my leather belt through the last loop of my shorts.

"*Sí.* You duty of trash," he said, stretching his arms to touch our low ceiling.

Outside the hut, I took inventory of my jungled surroundings—thick trees moldy and damp, skinny vines random and green, and that filterless sensation of life at the equator.

I walked a few yards of the rock-lined path, then turned in a slow circle to view this remotest suburbia. Juan stood next to me a moment, then said, "No compare?"

"Yeah, Juan . . . no neon, no billboards."

He allowed ten more seconds before handing me the broom handle.

And at 7:20 A.M. on the second Wednesday of November, I found myself in a village of the Ecuadorian rainforest, a burlap sack flung over one shoulder, my hand gripping the sawed-off broom handle with its protruding nail—the official uniform of the assistant groundskeeper.

"Work both sides of the road?" I asked, glad that there was not much litter around.

"*Sí. Amigas,* then *amigos,*" he said, pointing at the two bamboo torches now smoldering against the sunrise.

A red macaw sat atop what I believed to be the village kitchen. Curious but guarded, it watched me like a feathered sentry, its beak half smile, half snarl.

If there was a fight, he would win.

Along the road, remnants of little visitors had peppered the dirt, the token tracks of animals small and rummaging. The tracks were bigger than a mouse but smaller than a deer. I followed them in a zigzag until they disappeared into the boundless undergrowth of Ecuador.

Behind the huts, a hodgepodge of vegetables grew over and around each other as if the seeds, like confetti, had been scattered at random. Tomatoes were having a good year; cucumbers were a bit scrawny. Long vines of thick red berries twisted grotesquely behind the huts, winding onward and upward, trying to grasp and strangle the skinny stilts.

While spearing bits of paper amid the dew, I spotted Allie strolling the road, past the torches, with over a dozen children in tow.

She leaned down to the children. "Say hello to Mr. Jarvis."

"*Hola, Señor Yarvees,*" they said, at once giggling and blushing. They all had straight, dark hair and grab-bag shorts and shirts, slightly soiled but tucked in and without wrinkles.

"We're on our way to breakfast," Allie said, holding little bronze hands in each of hers. "We'll save you some fruit."

"So, Miss Kyle . . . when do I get the private jungle tour?"

They walked on, and she spoke over her shoulder. "Patience, Americano."

And that was the extent of our morning visit.

285

Juan claimed twenty years of age, and with his lean, athletic build, he looked it. He had never heard of eBay or Yahoo, did not understand stock quotes or initial public offerings, but offered me everything I needed. Which wasn't much. I just needed some food.

We enjoyed a jungle muffin and two bananas each on the steps of our hut. Juan's grasp of English was shaky but no tougher to understand than some South Carolinians I'd met. Told me he'd almost made the national soccer team at age seventeen, though down here, "almost" seemed to come with less padding.

"You miss a trash," he said, pointing under the next hut.

"*Sí.*" And I speared the wayward scrap. He asked about jobs in America, then shook his head as I related the lifestyle of the middle class. I explained a currency conversion and found out that, converted to U.S. currency, Juan's paycheck was the equivalent of thirty dollars a month.

"Thirty?" he asked, still not sure of the comparison.

"Only thirty, Juany."

He rubbed his foot on a tree root, then looked up and grinned. "If employ, you make twenty a month." And there was satisfaction in his voice.

At noon, Juan asked me to please stop trying to feed an earthworm to the macaw. With no trash left to spear, I had spent a half hour tossing the worm underhanded up near the kitchen roof, only to have the bird constantly reject my offering. Juan motioned for me to come along, so I left my burlap and broom handle resting against a thick, yellow-green plant. The plant extended well over my head, and by the time we returned, I assumed it would have eaten my toolage.

We walked a quarter mile of dirt road, our view restricted to straight up or straight ahead. Side-to-side was impossible, so thick was the greenery.

"Tell me, Juan, is Allie always like that?"

He flicked something from his red jersey and said, "Like what?"

"So matter-of-fact."

"It is first day of her first North American visitor. Give her break."

Fair enough.

Onward we trekked, my thoughts now back to the critters and their vocal harmonics. I had figured the bugs to be nocturnal, but that was my

286

own myth—they never slept. In a loose blending of kingdoms, the insects and the birds formed a crude chorus of noontime accompaniment, the Amazon version of elevator music.

I tried to hum along, but theirs was a most peculiar ballad.

The more familiar sound of young voices signaled to me that we were nearing our destination. Rough and shabby, the makeshift soccer field had faded white lines marking the boundaries. There were no bleachers, only towering plants and banana trees looking on, bending over the field as green, leafy spectators.

Two dozen children ran their own zigs and zags across the field. Allie was sitting beside a goal, fingering her wooden beads. For shade, she had brought along a Panama hat, the sun giving a satin sheen to its burgundy band. The soccer goals were bent; their nets ripped.

"Nice hat, Teach," I said.

She nudged the cream-colored brim and said, "You'll roast here without one. That scrawny Cubs cap will . . . well, you'll see. You'll be burnt in no time."

Having remembered my sunblock, I turned my scrawny Cubs cap around backward, then challenged Juan to a one-on-one soccer match.

Mistake of my life, challenging Juan to a soccer match.

"Fewt-bohl," said the children, seated on the sideline and clapping their hands. "Fewwwht-bohl!"

"*Sí*, fewt-bohl," I responded, taking a position as goalie.

The ball went through my legs. No excuses; it just happened so fast. I tossed the ball back to Juan, and suddenly it curved around my legs and into the goal again. I fetched the ball and tossed it back, trying to keep my legs closer together. But the ball arched over my head, then off his own head, and into the goal.

We switched positions, and at the end of my three-second tap dance, I was not on offense anymore. Juan was slicker than a New York pickpocket.

The kids laughed and beat on the grass. Juan just shrugged and bounced the ball on his knees.

But I could whip him at surfing. Of that I was certain.

287

Allie stood, lined up the kids, and offered a challenge: all seventeen children versus the three adults. Two little boys fell on the grass in hysterics. "Only *tres*," they said, pointing at us. "Only *tres!*"

"Yes," said Allie. "Only *tres*."

After an hour of being outrun and outskilled and tripped more times than we could count, we had lost, *ocho* to *uno*.

From the net, I picked up the soccer ball and felt air seeping out. It was worn and squishy, like a bad orange. One kid tugged at my shorts like he wanted the ball back.

I bounced it off his head and told him no more tripping.

"The children like you," said Allie, smiling now, gathering the troops.

I leaned down to retie my sneakers. "Only the children?"

"I met you at the airport and drove you through the rainforest, didn't I?" And with that, she and the kids skipped and giggled their way back toward the village.

They were almost out of sight when she stopped, quieted the children, and yelled, "I really do have an afternoon surprise for you! Maybe today, maybe tomorrow."

I did not have a clue.

Like American kids, jungle kids occasionally get bored and succumb to an urge to smash things. With the burlap sack draped over my shoulder and not a scrap of paper anywhere, I discovered broken bottles against the side of the kitchen building. Rocks lay in the dirt beside the shards and shattered pieces: clear glass and brown glass, even some funky blue glass. What a mess, and for a moment I regretted not heading straight for Wall Street.

I had just emptied the sack into Juan's designated spot, a shallow hole at the edge of the jungle, when a bell rang from the kitchen hut.

At two in the afternoon, the village gathered around three outdoor tables—long, weathered, and carved upon. The tables were roofed by a covering of wood in a steep, A-frame pattern. The airy dinette sat just outside the kitchen, which was squeezed between the row of huts on the female side of the dirt road. Or the mostly female side. Who knew.

288

Children sat impatiently on their steps, watching Allie set out plates.

"How long is the workday around here?" I asked, wiping my hands on my shorts.

"Not long. We'll have a recreational event for you after lunch," she said, now pouring drinks from a wooden pitcher. Her white T-shirt magnified her tan, and that contentment, her childlike contentment, gave me guilt pangs for complaining about broken glass.

I walked closer, lowering my voice. "Over on the men's side, Allie, I heard a language . . . different from Spanish."

"Quechua," she said. "Some of these folks are native Indians. And they're curious about you."

"What did you tell them?"

"Not much. Can you go get the other pitcher? Lunch is our biggest meal."

Up the four stairs and into the humble kitchen, I spotted a second wooden pitcher—plus three women and two men cooking up an Ecuadorian feast. Their backs were to me, as were the fish heads and banana peels topping off the garbage barrel.

They hummed as they cooked, and their clothes were no better matched than Juan's. In fact, it looked as though the entire village had been given thirty seconds inside the summer section of a Goodwill and just grabbed whatever they could: pink over purple, turquoise over mauve, plaid over stripes.

The little woman in mauve was the most energetic, dipping into the iron pot with both hands on the ladle. Without being noticed, I took the pitcher from a side table.

"Smells good," I said.

There was no reply.

Back down the stairs, I made for the middle table, where Allie was arranging stacks of plastic cups between frequent swatting of flies. I began to pour.

"Okay, what did you tell them about me?"

She carried a stack to the far table and said, "Only a brief story. Fill them to the top, please. No ice out here."

"Which story?"

"The beach."

"You didn't."

There were two sizes of bowls on the table. She had placed the smaller bowls, for the children, in lines of three, interrupted by a larger, adult bowl.

"They already have a nickname for you, Jay," she said.

"Oh, great. You speak that Quechua language, too? Now we're two languages removed."

"I'm learning a few words. But most nicknames are in English."

"Okay, let's hear it."

"They call you 'El Marshmallow Head.'"

"Very cruel, especially for a missionary. I would think you'd get demerits."

"A few. Knock those insects off the cups, please."

The colorful, mismatched kitchen crew brought out the food, and I joined Juan in setting utensils. Like cafeteria spoons, they were so worn that no shine remained on the metal. The knives were dull and some were bent, but then I wasn't expecting to cut into steak. Nor was I expecting to be seated on the end, next to Plaid-over-Stripes, whose sense of small talk rivaled her sense of fashion.

"You prefer broiling or grilling?"

No response. She just rocked slowly on the bench.

"Corn flakes or Raisin Bran?"

Confused smile, more rocking.

"Democrat or Republican?"

Again, nothing.

"Ginger or Mary Ann?"

Finally she just reached over and patted my hand. Then she glanced at her comrades in cookery as if to ask "Can we please eat now?"

With no names on the huts and no way of knowing who was with whom in the village, I wanted to pull Juan aside and ask him about the men-and-women thing. But I figured there was plenty else to learn before delving into private lives.

Now Lydia, she'd probably know . . . if only by instinct.

Everyone stood, and a shaggy-haired boy asked a Spanish blessing. I peeked once—several of the adults had their eyes open and were just staring blankly at the ground, as if they either did not understand or did not care but simply were trying to be polite.

As heads rose, Juan grabbed a berry and flipped it underhanded atop the roof. I took a quick step back for a better view, and the red macaw snatched it clean. The bird wanted another berry, but everyone was seated now, and there would be no more charity.

Our lunch consisted of spicy soup, bites of fish, and boiled bananas. There was little talking during the meal, and when it was over, not a morsel was left on a plate. For dessert, Pink-over-Purple and the gregarious Plaid-over-Stripes served a fruit called *mora*. It tasted like a raspberry and, sprinkled with sugar, was quite good.

"More *mora?*" I asked.

"El Marshmallow *mucho mora!*" said Juan. The kids laughed and rose from their benches. No one left a tip, and everyone cleaned up.

"What was that afternoon surprise you mentioned, Miss Kyle?" I asked, helping Juan stack dirty bowls.

Allie wiped the chin of a toddler and said, "Patience, Americano."

Patience . . . a most elusive little fruit.

38

If authentic manhood precludes shell-hunting, then it most certainly precludes beading.

Beading. This was the recreational event of which she spoke—making funky strings of Amazon beads with five curious jungle orphans.

After lunch Allie and the women put the younger children down for naps. Then she came out in her Panama hat and escorted us to a structure she called the craft hut. It sat at the end of the village, below two towering kapok trees, its architecture even cruder than the dwelling in which I slept. No larger than eight by eight, the hut boasted front steps of cinder block, its bare wood walls interrupted only by three open-air windows, all of varying proportion and none fashioned with screens. Simple benches had been built into the four inner walls, and a weathered table stretched within a foot of the east and west ends. Atop the table, in dozens of shallow containers cut from brown gourds, wooden beads sat patient and diverse, many in earth tones, some fat, some raw, some coated with bright splashes of paint.

She and the children gathered around the table. I stood in the doorway, hands gripping the outer frame. "Maybe I should just go catch a fish or two and contribute to the evening meal."

"You will do no such thing," said Allie, setting out strings for necklaces. "Just have a seat and pay attention."

I sat in the far corner, glad my guy friends weren't around. "You know I can't do this and maintain my masculinity."

"No," she replied, "but you can help these kids learn a new skill."

When I grudgingly agreed to help, she sat the two boys on each side of me, the three girls surrounding her on the far side. My guess at ages produced a range of seven to twelve, though one could never be sure.

I turned a fat, wooden bead in my fingers, then dropped it back with its clan. "So the kids haven't done this, either?"

Allie arranged strands of string for each person at the table. "Those beads just arrived last week from Venezuela. A large Catholic church donated them. Pass me some of those cream-colored ones."

I reached for the container. "You didn't say please."

"Please and thank you."

After only a half hour, it became clear that we men were losing badly, both in terms of volume and pattern development. Pepe, the oldest boy, kept stringing thick, barrel-shaped bamboo beads one after another, a lone bright red one in the middle, until he had crafted something worthy of a Zulu warrior. His younger brother, Eduardo, employed the M&Ms' technique—whatever spilt out the bag would do; no order, just color.

Me, I just watched, masculinity still in my pocket, safely tucked between my comb and my worn leather wallet.

The ladies, however, led by young Isabel, had carefully laid out two distinct color schemes: cream with turquoise and dark wood, then natural wood with bone and deep red, alternating size, shape, and color. They strung two of one bead, then one of another, then two more of the first, until the string was fully covered, earth toned, and proportional. Then they switched to a three-one-three pattern, Allie tying off each necklace before draping it over a little bronze neck.

The first breeze of the day blew through the open-air windows, a brief but welcome zephyr to cool our humid hut. The two older girls had become like worker bees, silent and immersed in mass production, eight units each already complete, heaped on the table like colorful spaghetti.

293

Allie picked up one from the pile and inspected the design. "Good work, girls. We'll sell these in Coca's flea market. Buy you girls a new dress."

At that news the girls shifted into overdrive, beads bouncing off the wood floor like a rain of BBs.

"Y'all should make a necklace for Darcy," I suggested, watching Pepe tie a slipknot on his warrior beads. "Only takes one color."

Recognition widened Allie's eyes. "How thoughtless of us," she said. "Pass me those light green beads, Isabel."

Young Isabel reached for the container but stopped and said, "You not say please, Miss Allie."

"Please and thank you and you are so very pretty today."

Isabel beamed and handed her the beads. Allie winked at the little girl, then reached over and pulled the hair behind her ears. "You know what, Isabel? I just changed my mind. Darcy needs some variety in her life."

"What?" I asked. "You gonna send her something brown? Purple?"

"Nope. Since she graduated from South Carolina, we need us some good ol' garnet 'n black. In fact, Jay, we'll even let you string 'em up."

And on the eleventh day of November, I found myself in the craft hut of a remote Ecuadorian village, stringing a necklace of garnet and black beads for tall, blonde, lead-footed Darcy, who thought I was in New York City with all my black clothes.

The irony of it all.

Using a one-one pattern, I quickly crafted the thing and tied off the ends. No way was I autographing my work, but I did think it perfectly suited for Darcy to wear to fall football at Carolina. Though probably not with lime.

Pepe and Eduardo were picking out round red beads and firing them at a dragonfly on the hut's ceiling. I quieted them and said no more Zulu beads. Told them they needed to join the mass manufacturing movement and learn an ounce of capitalism.

Allie looked warily across the table at me. "Jay, promise me you won't teach them about stocks and Wall Street."

"I promise."

By late afternoon, the gourd containers were nearly empty, and before us lay enough units to drape each villager twice over—cream with turquoise and dark wood in one pile, natural wood with bone and deep red in another, the males' miscellaneous pile pushed to the side.

"How much do you think tourists would pay?" Allie asked, gathering inventory.

"I dunno . . . three bucks each?"

"I'll charge five."

Isabel left the craft hut in a giddy skip. She had the one string of Carolina beads slung around her neck, hanging nearly to her belly.

I glanced out a window and said, "So much for sending those to Darcy . . ."

Allie stood in the doorway and watched her go. "I'll swap 'em out after she falls asleep tonight."

The older girls cajoled Pepe and Eduardo to stack their necks with the day's production. The boys obliged, and soon the girls were heavily accessorized. Allie put her Panama hat back on and said, "Now, Mr. Jarvis, go ahead and admit to the children that this was far more entertaining than watching little stock numbers flash by on a computer screen."

I admitted to no such thing. I only asked her if she wanted to take a walk, just the two of us.

"I have to get the girls home," she said. "Clean 'em up and trim their hair. But tomorrow, Jay, you'll get a very different surprise."

From behind the hut, Pepe and Eduardo came bounding out with an old baseball bat and a pitiful gray softball trying to shed its stitching. They pointed across the jungle, back toward the makeshift soccer field, and motioned that I was the designated pitcher.

Masculinity had returned, and I hoped the youngsters could hit a knuckleball.

After a dinner of thin soup and rice and one piece of bread with cheese, I served the children a batch of sugar-sprinkled *mora*. With kids seated around her atop the table and the harsh Ecuadorian sun now low and tame, Allie read to them from a picture book, the Spanish version of Noah.

The kids were very curious as to how he got that many animals on one boat.

"Noah's boat was . . . *el grande,*" I said, standing behind them. Isabel, now wearing three strings of beads, looked up and frowned at my mixture of languages.

"*Sí, grande,*" said Allie, stretching her arms out for effect. Many questions followed, questions I could not decipher, although I figured from the gesturing that bathroom humor involving large animals was the obvious thrust of their dialogue.

Darkness soon descended over the outdoor tables, and on that night they let me light the two bamboo torches.

Very cool, being the bamboo torch lighter in a remote Amazon village.

The flames performed a slow dance, and everyone retired to their huts.

It was not yet 10:00.

I collapsed on my bed. By flashlight, I returned to Psalm 139, where I had unstuck the pages last spring in my initial search for Galatians. The psalm said how vast are the thoughts of God, and how, if I were to try and count them, they would outnumber the grains of sand.

I wondered what thoughts God had about my being here in this zany jungle, and what would be the take-away when I began life in Manhattan. I wondered what God thought about Manhattan, how it compared to this jungle so zany.

But sleep trumped wonder, so I left Manhattan and the counting of grains to him whose thoughts are vast. It was indeed an awesome thought . . . the counting of all those grains.

Maybe I was but a single grain.

Granular Jay, the repentant grain.

"G'night, Juan."

"Sleep you well, El Marshmallow."

39

The red macaw squawked at dawn, and I craved a shower.

But there was only the cold kind.

"Juan, wake up," I said, watching a tiny critter flee under the grass rug.

"*Cómo?*" he said, turning over, eyes still shut.

I reached down to look under the rug. "Would the village like hot water?"

He yawned and reminded me of currency conversions and his salary of thirty dollars a month.

I sat up on the bed, digging into my wallet. "I've brought American cash, Juan, and would like to purchase a hot-water heater for the village."

Two minutes later, Juan was behind the wheel of the old pickup, his hair suffering a bad case of bed-head. Honking and waving me into the passenger seat, he seemed fully awake now. I grabbed three pieces of fruit from the outdoor tables and hopped in.

Back through two hours of potholes, past the wild monkeys, and up the jungled road, we reached the town of Coca. My travel guide said the town had only a few hundred residents until 1969, when oil was discovered. Now the population numbered in the thousands. But it was not without cost. The dusty streets had a light coating of oil, as did the stray dogs, the sidewalks, even the car hoods. Juan said the trade-off was for roads cut through the rainforest in exchange for a school in Coca and a medical facility.

He searched for a parking spot and told me he was okay with the trade. "But some native Indian say *nada* to oil company. Are angry . . . throw rocks."

"At Texaco?" I asked.

"*Sí*, throw big rock."

"At Shell?"

"Hmmm . . . little rocks."

"At Hess?"

He hesitated a moment. "Not so bad. Build school."

"But overall you approve of the trade?"

"Is fair deal."

I felt a twinge of guilt for having traded shares of oil companies for profit, but capitalism confers a shifty set of values, and I was no exception.

In dusty, downtown Coca, Juan parked at a busy sidewalk, waved off two street peddlers, and pointed me toward the general store—just past a whole-roasted pig hanging for sale beneath the awning. That pig looked in serious pain.

One lonely water heater sat for sale in the disorganized depot that served as hardware store, auto-parts outlet, and grocery market. Juan located the owner. I knelt to inspect the water heater. Not that I knew a thing about them, but I found it had been manufactured in St. Louis and had no rust and only one dent, so I figured it would do.

There was a brief Spanish discussion over price, which Juan seemed to be losing badly—the mustached owner had the edge in both finger pointing and tone of voice.

"*Quatro!*" said the owner.

Juan pointed to the water heater, then to a shelf of candy, but the store owner gestured madly with his arms and pointed at my shirt.

I had worn a company T-shirt, with INVE$TMENT$ TO RETIRE ON embroidered across the front.

Too late.

Juan called me over. He was trying to convert the currency in his head but looked confused. With little hope now for negotiation, I pulled a wad of twenties from my pocket and handed half of them to the store owner. Suddenly he ran to the front door, pulled down the "Closed" sign, and grabbed the bottom of the water heater.

I lifted the opposite end, and together we shuffled out the door and onto the sidewalk, awkwardly loading the contraption into the pickup.

He shook my hand hard and said, "Have good day."

He did not sound sincere.

The owner then locked his door behind Juan, who, surprisingly, had his own armful. Juan set three full boxes of candy on the floorboard, then handed me a new soccer ball and a section of radiator hose.

"How did you buy all this?" I asked, eyeing his bounty.

"Was included in deal," he said, grinning.

Somehow, I sensed there would be more requests for shopping trips before I left Ecuador.

Juan cranked the engine, but I reached over and killed the ignition.

"*Por qué?*" asked Juan.

"One second," I said, holding up a finger.

After jumping out of the pickup and running back through the fruit peddlers and past the whole-roasted pork, I rapped on the front door. "*Por favor!*"

The store owner looked through the glass, frowned, and unlocked his door. He opened it six inches and peered out.

"Your name wouldn't be Miguel, would it?" I asked.

"*Sí* . . . Miguel."

"I need to use your computer. You know . . . Internet. Don't lie. I know you have one. You take dark chocolates for bribes."

He pursed his lips, then turned and looked at his clock. "Four minute," he said, pulling a shade over the window. "Only four minute. Then I close for day."

He led me to a back room cluttered with papers, canned foods, and miscellaneous auto parts. I sat down at the computer, logged on, and accessed my e-mail account.

I typed quickly, sensing Miguel looking over my shoulder.

Dear Steve,

*It has been a very hectic and busy first three days. New York City
is much different than you'd expect. There are vast, coconut-frosted
volcanoes in the distance and wild monkeys making outrageous swings
from the Empire State Building. The insects on the subway are incredibly big, and a giant red macaw lives on the roof of my apartment.
Food is cheaper than I thought, the menus less varied. And the Yankees
aren't nearly as popular as the local soccer teams.*

*Last night I saw a play on Broadway; it starred a lovely actress who
played a missionary, and the cast looked very much like Spanish-
speaking Indian kids from some remote region of South America. They
all wore funky jungle beads. The job training is going well. Mostly
currency conversions and easy stuff like that. Great views here, and
warmer than expected.*

Black clothes going out of fashion. Sak's and Macy's both overrated.

Say hello to Her Limeness,

Brother Jay

I hit the send button. Miguel snickered, then asked about Broadway
and if I had ever seen Gloria Estefan in concert.

"No, Miguel, I have not. But I have seen the light."

"De light?"

I logged off, rose to face him. "Miguel, there is one mediator between
God and man and that is Christ and those aren't my words they're his
words and the living words and the eternal words and those are the only
words you're gonna need."

He pointed at the door. "Your four minute are up."

Back in the village, Juan and two of the older men wrestled the water
heater into place at the rear of the largest and most updated hut, a long

wooden dwelling that housed many of the young girls and, I suspect, Allie and the other women.

I still didn't know where she slept.

After a trimming of gaskets and a brief argument between two of the men, the water heater slid into place. I held the tools. There was a twisting of knobs, a tightening of screws, and handshakes all around.

But the cold was hot, and the hot, cold.

There was finger-pointing and the inaccurate hurling of three dirt clods. The older man pointed at me and said something in Quechua.

"What did he say?" I asked.

Juan stepped close to whisper. "Next thing we know, white man want cable."

40

My very different surprise began at 4:30.

We walked that steamy afternoon—just the two of us—out past the banana trees and down the dirt road and past where the elephant ears shade the jungle grass. We heard a distant orchestra of birds, and every few minutes we stopped to splatter a neon insect.

With the village no longer in view, I heard drumming, deep, persistent drumming.

"Bongos?" I asked.

"You won't believe it," said Allie, pausing in the road to listen.

"Try me."

"Well, we get donations like boxes of clothes and tools and stuff sent in from churches who support this ministry, and it's always a big time for us digging through it all and last month we got a huge box from a high school boy in Atlanta who'd donated an old bass drum like they wear in marching bands."

"Commas, Allie. Commas."

"Sorry. We gave the drum to Raul. He's a sixteen-year-old orphan with the mind of a five-year-old but a talent for music. He mostly keeps to himself. Carries that bass drum out into the jungle every afternoon. Don't walk, just listen."

I cupped one ear for clarity, since the engulfing vegetation was well over our heads. His rhythm pulsated around us, the beat resonating through rainforest, surround sound for the jungle.

"Can't we go and watch him?" I asked.

"No. He'll leave if he sees us. C'mon, I have something to show you."

We walked another twenty minutes. The drumming faded. Soon, she pointed between a dense tangle of vines to a path better suited for rabbits. The path led deep beneath the cover of jungle, and after another ten minutes of hiking, we reached a set of moldy stairs, endless stairs, a staggered equivalent to the curve of dreams. The stairs rose into oblivion at a steady pace, wrapped in wildness and supported by an ever increasing scaffold of wooden poles.

"This your tree fort?" I asked, amazed to find such structure in the midst of such remote locale.

"It's an observation tower," she said, looking skyward from the base. "It goes way above the treetops . . . a South American crow's nest, if you will."

Penlights of sun hit the stair rail just over her head. Birds screeched and warbled from above, from origins deep in the greenery; muffled sounds, sounds of jungle, sounds of life—primal, sightless, and random.

"Who built this thing?" I asked, testing it with one foot.

"The scientists and the bird watchers. You know . . . those opno . . . orlamologists?

"Yeah, starts with an O."

"Yeah, anyway, 237 steps. I counted 'em last month."

I motioned her to the stairway. "Shall we?"

"We shall."

The bird people had numbered every twenty-fifth step, so I had doubts about her math skills. At step fifty I stopped to admire the huge trunks of ancient trees, all wrapped in a creeping undergrowth.

"C'mon, slowpoke," she said, ten steps ahead.

At step ninety-nine, darker now beneath the canopy, she stopped and pointed to a thick, curvaceous limb. "Saw a snake there last time I was up here."

"What kind of snake?"

"Just a snake," she said, shrugging her shoulders and resuming her climb. "But it had a red stripe on its back and hung from the limb in circles, like four bracelets. I call it the Barbie snake."

At step 150, countless streams of sunlight sparkled and expanded, filtered in their passage through the moist, layered mesh. Wet leaves brushed our faces. My legs ached. At step 200, the muffled noises unmuffled, then we bolted past 225, and I inhaled the blue sky. The air had a minty flavor.

"Surprise," said Allie, panting. "We made it."

And I turned to see our molded stairs poking through leaves in a crude, angular sprout, as if man had tried his hand at creation but ended up a mere observer.

"How many times you been up here?" I asked, gripping the railing.

"Four. Even spent the night once."

Above the canopy of rainforest, I breathed deep from lofty layers of air. And again the volcanoes rose in the distance, full and frosted against the overarching parachute of treetops; and once again, the horizon, the inexhaustible horizon, was a dreamlike periphery, unbounded, unsolved.

For several minutes, neither of us spoke. Just absorbed.

Then, the earth moved.

"This thing'll sway a bit if we do this," said Allie, shifting her weight to and fro.

"Then let's do this." A tiny roof extended over the middle portion of the floor, like a hat too small for one's head. We centered ourselves under the roof, stood side-by-side, and commenced to rock the birdhouse. A right, a left; a right and a left.

The wooden tower, rounded off and bordered with abundant railing, moved little at first, but soon we had it in a slow, lethargic sway.

"I heard a squeak."

"Squeaks are bad," she said, now pounding from one foot to the other.

"That squeak was louder."

"Okay, let's stop."

That's what I'd missed when she left Carolina—the spontaneity. I wanted to kiss her, right there, in that moment, in full view of God and whoever else was out there watching, hidden in the canopy.

But instead, I chickened out and pointed north. "So that would be Peru over there."

"No, that would be Colombia," she said, resting her elbows on the railing.

"Of course, Colombia."

Two hundred and thirty-seven steps from the floor of the rainforest, there were no pelicans swooping low in quiet glides of unity, but rather a diverse and noisy collection of brightly colored birds, their size varied, their feathers a broad spectrum of grays and golds, reds and yellows, greens and violets and blues.

"That gray one is flirting with the yellow one," she said, leaning over the rail.

Beside her again, I followed the flight patterns. "No, the yellow one stole food from the gray one."

"Did not."

"Did too. I saw it."

We watched the two birds weave and glide for another ten minutes, until our pride demanded resolution.

"Definitely flirting."

"Definitely stealing."

With elbows on the rail, she propped her head in her hands. "You're just a visitor."

I mimicked her posture. "What's the name of that river?"

"Rio Napo."

"It's huge. Can we swim in it?"

"Not if you value your limbs."

"How about blind drifting in a dugout canoe?"

She glanced at me sideways. "Now there's a thought." She looked away. "Can you see the parrots?"

A putty-colored clay bank rose high and steep across the river, the pastel backdrop peppered with barely visible birds. I squinted hard. "How can you tell they're parrots?"

"They eat the clay. Good for their stomachs."

"Sick. I'd as soon eat beach sand."

305

With daylight depleting, Allie continued my bird education with a monologue about various species, occasionally pointing at some distant fowl and proclaiming it a lance bill, a white tip, a scarlet tanager. She had schooled herself in the nuances of her flightful friends, and a gentle confidence crept into her lecture. Only when she got to the largest birds of prey did she get animated.

"I haven't told you yet about the harpy eagle."

I turned and leaned my back against the railing. "Oh, lemme guess. National bird? Like our bald one?"

"Hardly. It's the largest, most aggressive eagle in Ecuador, in all of South America, really. Has thick, powerful legs. Giant claws too. And for food it snatches little monkeys out of trees. Can you believe that, Jay? It snatches little monkeys out of trees! Those poor monkeys."

"Yeah, poor little monkeys."

This monkey-snatching was obviously a sore spot with her. She stared out over the rainforest and said, "I've only seen one harpy my whole time in Ecuador. But next time I see him, I'm gonna throw something. Hard!"

"Poor little monkeys and eagles." And I scooted closer.

'Tis a regal feeling to look down at bird flight, the top colors of wide-spread wings sharp and distinct against the green floral canvas. The birds appeared to be in slow motion, the glide-happy birds, cruising around and below us in flights of leisure, flights of thievery, and okay, maybe even a few flights of flirtation.

"You understand my poem now?" she asked, gazing out across her boundless, very lush backyard.

"I thought I did, before it vanished in seawater."

"Which lines do you remember?"

"About your roots . . ."

"That's all?"

Think, Jarvis. "Across your azaleas, prosperity winked?"

"Well, holy Elizabeth Barrett Browning . . . the boy has a memory."

As light faded, I edged even closer. Our arm hairs flirted.

We stood on our Amazonian veranda through sunset, using the circular platform to observe and absorb, to behold all that gives life to such a far-flung panorama.

For it was surely panoramic, and most definitely far-flung. As far-flung as my being there, given where I had been six months ago. Suddenly I was back on that sandbar, our flimsy floats anchored on the bank, her with a stick of driftwood, bent over and oblivious to me, the ocean, and everything else. She was carving words in the sand.

"I get it now, Allie . . . your poem."

She leaned into the rail again. "I thought you would."

It was nearly dark as we descended the 237 stairs, darker still when we reached the base, and on our way back through the jungle, she reached for my hand.

The hand of a missionary—graceful, magnetic. I felt like reversing course, climbing the tower again, and asking her to dance. Just us, quietly twirling above the rainforest as moonlight soothed the leaves of a thousand Amazon treetops. Maybe someday.

We hardly talked, just strolled back toward the village in the twilight.

She squeezed my fingers.

I squeezed back.

A quarter mile ahead, the two torches were burning. We had missed dinner, and when we arrived, she let go of my hand and we departed into our respective huts.

41

It was Thursday, day four of my five-day visit to the rainforest. After assisting Juan in replacing the radiator hose, we were allowed two-minute hot showers while the children had their English lesson.

People will say a shower is just a shower, but until you've gone without a hot one for four days and have the grit of the rainforest between your toes and fingers, not to mention the blue goo of squished insects . . . you haven't showered, you've merely rinsed.

"*Nada!*" said Juan, stepping out of reach as I showed him the fine art of towel popping.

He was mildly amused, but apparently towel popping was not a custom in the rainforest, either.

Juan joined me for the 2:00 lunch of soup, cheese, bread, and fruit. We ate on the steps of our hut, because the kids were cutting and pasting on the lunch tables.

Allie had them cutting letters from dark paper, then gluing them on white. I walked over to watch, and the kids were spelling *hello* and *good-bye*. Pepe and Eduardo were seated on the end, spelling *potty*.

"Did you teach them that?"

"The kids want to know what American children call it," said Allie, "so I do my best." After all letters were arranged and glued, she led the small children away for naps but let the older ones go for a ride in the truck with Turquoise Over Mauve.

ₗI waited for her at the lunch table, nervous about feeling the need to have "a talk." She took her time inside with the children, then carefully closed the door. She tiptoed down the four steps, her olive shorts just visible below her untucked T-shirt, the yellow one with the toucan embroidered on the left sleeve, the one she'd worn at the beach.

Having washed and dried my jungle shirt, I felt clean again. "Is now a good time to take a walk?" I asked.

"Okay, but just a short one."

In silence, we strolled past the dining area, then out of the village and past the banana trees. Minutes passed with no hint of conversation. Finally I just blurted it out.

"Do we need to talk about the holding hands thing?"

She hesitated a moment. "It gets lonely here, Jay. There's so little social life with other single people. It's good to feel a warm hand. Hope you didn't mind."

"Not at all . . . it was quite nice. Really."

"Really?"

"Even better than poetry."

"Whose poetry?"

"Um . . . Elizabeth Whatsername."

"That's what I thought you meant."

We passed the soccer field, watching dark clouds loom against the mountains, with a band of lower clouds visible where the road split the jungle.

I nudged her arm. "That wasn't quite good enough."

"What?"

"Your answer. There's more to it than you just having the occasional bout of loneliness."

"You don't know that. How could you know that?"

"So how many times have you held Juan's hand?"

Not willing to give in, she stopped right in the middle of the dirt road and fingered her beads. "I am female, and your logic is different than mine."

309

We resumed our walk. I nudged her again. "You could just say it was nice to hold my hand."

"It was nice to hold your hand."

The first heavy drops peppered the road. In front of us, brown dust rose with each drop, then the drops rained down faster and the road swiftly turned to mud. We ran for leafy cover. There was no shortage of leafy cover.

"Pull the leaves down," she said, already half soaked.

Underneath the elephant ears, we watched the drops bounce and roll, then wobble and drip off the ends. Damp scents of earth rose in reply.

"Those drops are huge."

"Wild, isn't it?" she said. "When the river floods, our village takes in the refugees from tribes downstream. Our huts got pretty crowded last spring. Smelly too."

We made a tent by pulling four enormous leaves together. Dark green shadows dimmed the day. "I thought you said November started your dry season."

"It does . . . except for when it rains."

"I think the tenor bugs just drowned."

We were shoulder-to-shoulder now beneath our makeshift tent. She nudged my arm. "What I never told you, Jay, is that there was a time when I was much different, when I never desired to be a missionary or live overseas. My first high school poem sorta sums it all up."

"Am I going to have to drift off to some Amazonian sandbar to read it?"

"No, it's a short one. I brought it with me. Care to give your opinion?" She pulled a tattered 3 x 5 card from her shirt pocket.

"You keep them all on cards?"

"Yep."

"Filed alphabetically, I assume."

"No way. That's just more male logic. I file them by emotion . . . sad ones in the front."

She handed me the card. The blue ink had faded with the years, and a raindrop had smeared the first line.

But suddenly she took the card back, just snatched what looked like iambic pentameter right from my fingertips. "No," she said, tucking it back in her shirt pocket. "I don't think you'll get it."

"Get what?"

"The irony."

"How can I get the irony if you won't let me read it?"

"I was very young when I wrote it."

"You're still young."

"Maybe I'll show it to you later."

I adjusted our leafy tent and said, "Well, can you at least tell me what heading you filed that one under?"

She paused a moment. "Reflections."

Big sloppy drops splattered off the leaves just above our faces. She said it was like Jesus deflecting sin.

With her hair now moist and matted, she turned to face me. Her brown eyes, sharp and probing, met mine. "Thank you for coming to see me, Jay."

"I'm gonna hate to leave this."

The rain continued to rata-tata-rata-tata off the elephant ears, although I no longer saw it as rain; it seemed a kind of baptism.

I clumsily let the edge of our tent tilt. Water ran down our backs. She squealed and returned the favor.

"Can't you stay a few extra days?" she asked.

"You have no idea how much I'd like to . . ."

"I wanted us to paddle the river. And we could hike out to the tower, take lunch and watch the birds again."

"I'll never forget that."

She turned away. "Let's not say these things."

"What things? That I'm going to miss you? Of course I am."

She turned back, her eyes misty. Then she blinked rapidly for a moment and slowly let her head drop. "Okay. I can't believe I'm saying this. Same here."

The rain lightened, only a soft patter now, trickling off the leaves.

311

I lay in my hut at midnight—wide awake. Juan slept soundly in his narrow bed.

I'd kept a journal of my visit, scribbles of scenery and birds, conversations and misinterpreted language, monkey leaps and leaf-cutter ants, unmanly beads and bamboo torches, ridiculous views from the sides of mountains and the incredible contrasts of the rainforest to the only world I'd ever known.

My picture frame—the silver one—sat in the window. It now had an occupant. Great smile.

By flashlight, I began to write.

The entry was dated November 12th–13th. I detailed the activities with the kids, the afternoon on the observation tower, my struggle with the language, and what we'd said under the elephant ears. Then I realized what she meant, not only to me, but to the village.

I formed the letters carefully.

God means for her to be here. She is, for this corner of the globe, his chosen one. She is the consummate servant, storing up a treasure, a wealth for others, with little earthly benefit to herself. The village sees her as I do. She is the humor and the holiness, the laughter and the spontaneity.

Below that, I wrote, *Springtime, fly her to New York. First class.*

That was all that made it on the page, though I considered writing more. What I did not write was the following: for my tomorrow is a concrete jungle in a numbers-driven world, and hers remains a ministry to a lush little village. Thus time will pass and letters will be sent, and letters will arrive and letters will be sent, and one day I'll be seated at a noisy Manhattan trading desk, oblivious to markets in motion, and will wonder once again how God got me into a Presbyterian church, to a particular beach with a particular girl on a certain weekend in May, and gave me wacky new friends and a new fresh perspective, the living words and the eternal words and the words of a black man who gives rhythm to the gospel, and once again it will occur to me that all this just cannot be happenstance . . . no, surely not happenstance, nothing Presbyterian is ever happenstance. But what you didn't tell me, Asbury, is how much of life derives simply from *choice*.

None of those words made it on the page. I figured that if I reread them in later years, they would only make me sad.

I placed the journal under my bed.

Moonlight, as if on call, poured through the screen to grace the wall again.

I held the picture frame up to the light. My plane was leaving at 4:00.

I could not sleep.

42

In addition to my black clothes and my common sense, the men's room at Charlotte International could now claim my career. My best guess was that the career had languished and expired, like a high-priced deodorizer, somewhere between the porcelain and the paper-towel holder.

Still four thousand miles from amber waves of grain, I'd become accustomed to life in the jungle. I'd lost my farmer's tan, half my southern accent, and my six-figure job on Wall Street. I was pleased with the tan and the accent, could've cared less about the job.

No, I had not eloped with anyone. But I kept the village clean, taught Pepe the curveball, recovered from a swollen calf after a soprano bug had me for an appetizer, and convinced my roommate, Juan, that our bare-walled hut needed a new color scheme. There had been much debate over this, but he finally conceded after I explained my reasoning. By mail, we special ordered one gallon of interior latex, to be air-shipped from the Home Depot in Greenville, South Carolina. The color? Sea green, of course.

After my visit had reached eleven days, I figured it was time to drive the old pickup back through the potholes and into Coca to use a pay phone. I called Vince Galbraith to discuss matters; I called him at his trading desk in Manhattan; I called him collect.

He had been buying an oil stock and remarked—with unmistakable Yankee disdain—that I had missed a crucial training week with the managing director of stock analysis. I told him I was learning to be the assistant director of trash pickup in the outskirts of the Amazon Basin and, except for a few insects, I kinda liked it in Ecuador.

Vince had offered a curse, then a second and a third, saying he'd seen the "God thing" ruin many a great stock trader.

I'd asked him to define the "God thing."

He'd mumbled something about Jesus not knowing anything about the markets and then hung up on me.

On the fourteenth day of my visit, I'd spent hours alone in my hut, mulling over America's obsession with net worth, the comparative glances, the corporate hierarchy, the purgatory of numbers that is modern-day Wall Street: numbers measuring performance, numbers stroking egos, numbers converted to percentage and compared to other numbers, numbers up, numbers down, numbers flashing, numbers stagnant, numbers bragged on, cheered on, pouted over and prognosticated.

Sickened of numbers, I'd poured myself a glass of jungle juice and read ten pages of a Jane Austen novel that Allie had loaned me.

Then I read a psalm.

Number forty. That one seemed more musical than numeric.

Then I'd spent another hour contemplating my becoming yet another corporate lemming, clinging to a yuppie existence instead of service and adventure, clinging to subsistence rather than real experience, clinging to it all with a death grip when death was gonna come anyway. But then, death had been conquered, so what was I worried about?

It was on that night that I wrote my official resignation letter to Vince, resigning from a job at which I never arrived.

I was about to become employed in the hot, humid outskirts of a South American jungle.

I would pay myself twenty-five dollars a month.

43

Life without cable, VCRs, and paved roads required adjustment, but the pace invigorated the soul. I had always pictured myself living on the face of a huge clock, running just ahead of the second hand that would slam me in the butt every time I tried to slow down. But in Ecuador I felt like I was being pulled along by the minute hand, slow and steady, with enough leisure to enjoy circumference, the arc of a day.

Now, finally, I understood the difference between tick and tock. Tick flips from the end of the tongue like something fast and hurried, as something instant, surfacy, and shallow. Tock comes from a deeper place; it's a bass note, or at least a tenor. Tocks moves more slowly. If there were a tocking time bomb, I would not run out of the building, but rather stroll through the lobby, order a cafe mocha, check the sports page for standings in the American League East, then hold the door open as a good Southerner should.

My house in South Carolina sold the Wednesday after Thanksgiving. 'Twas about time. After paying off the mortgage, I had $28,000. I put two-thirds of it away to live off, then gave the other third as an anonymous donation to a certain mission agency that sponsored a certain young lady who could certainly throw better than any Baptist I ever met.

The time had arrived—the time to rejuggle the pertinent priorities in the life of this twenty-something.

Tock . . . tick. Tock . . . tick.

There was a Quechua pregnancy in the village: Pink-over-Purple was married to Plaid-over-Stripes.

Figured that out myself.

What I still hadn't figured out, though, was how Raul found the stamina to keep beating that bass drum every day, noon to dusk.

On a Friday afternoon, in the strange eighty-five-degree heat of December, I was down the dirt road, emptying the burlap sack into Juan's designated spot for dumpage, when across the elephant ears and through the banana trees came the mongo bongo Ecuadorian backbeat of Raul's steady thumping. In throbbing waves of jungle percussion, it simply continued to continue.

I had met Raul during my second week and found out that he actually worked two hours per day. Every morning he wove a thick collage of thread into bookmarkers, varying the patterns and sending them off to Miguel in colorful lots of fifty. I purchased two for myself—one for novels, and one for, um, quiet times.

Miguel sold the bookmarkers to American tourists for a quarter each, with a small commission for himself, of course. Raul may have had the mind of a five-year-old, but even amid the shady markets of the rainforest, he had found a way to buy low and sell high.

My kinda guy.

In the distance, coming toward me from the village with two dozen giggly children, she wore jungle casual: khaki shorts, an untucked burgundy top, and her ever present wooden beads.

"*Hola*," I said, waving to Allie as she trekked the dirt road, ushering her troops along.

"*Hola*, Mr. Ex-broker person," she said, closer now. "How's the new career going?"

I glanced at my mop handle. "Corporate ladder is very short. Only one rung, I think."

317

"A toast to short ladders. Follow us to the soccer field. I got a letter from Darcy."

I draped the burlap sack over a tall yellow plant, leaned my broom handle against a kapok tree, and fell in line behind the kids. Two of them tried walking backward, both of them grinning and losing their balance.

"What'd she say in the letter?"

"Haven't read it yet," she said, helping a child out of the undergrowth. "Okay niños, split into two groups . . . and be sure and kick the ball, not each other."

Led by Pepe and Eduardo, twenty children sprinted to the shabby soccer field. Isabel and the rest began searching for bugs, hunched over, stalking.

I could already sense the effect of her work with the children. They were cumulative, those kids, each new day a small addition to their development, like papier mâché for the soul.

On a thick cushion of jungle grass, we sat face-to-face. Tiny beads of perspiration glistened on her cheeks. Anxious, she pulled three pages from the lime green envelope and began reading to herself.

I gave her ten seconds. It was all I could stand. "What?"

"Shh, just a sec."

"You're killing me."

Her eyes skimmed the page. "Darcy broke up with Steve!"

"Doesn't surprise me."

"Well, it absolutely shocks me. . . . I didn't even know they were dating."

"I sorta had a clue."

"And she's my best friend!"

Excited, she glanced once at the kids, then quickly devoured page one.

A bright blue insect landed on page two. She swatted it away.

I nibbled on straw, my curiosity running wild. "So what else is happening at good ol' North Hills?"

"She said Ransom and Jamie are sure it's a boy. Wonder what they'll name it?"

"You don't wanna know."

"And she saw Steve at lunch with some pierced girl named Alexis. Do you know her?"

"We met."

318

She gripped the stationery with both hands, her necklace swinging slow and wooden at the lower margin. "Darcy says she wants to find herself an attorney who loves God."

I considered this for a moment, then pronounced it reasonable. "Sounds like a plan."

Page two landed atop page one. Allie sighed. "Poor Lydia, she's still in the dumps."

"Baseball players," I offered, "such primates."

"Yeah, such primates . . . oh no, not Maurice!" Her eyes darted again.

I sat up. "Is he sick?"

"He's left the church."

"Oh, I thought you were gonna say . . . but why?"

"Here, you read it."

And I thumped a tiny grasshopper from page three.

In addition to the bad news (or new news) concerning Steve and me, the church is sad to be losing our old friend Maurice. Our church newsletter said he stuck a "For Sale" sign in his yard, packed his wife and luggage in the car, and moved to Pawleys Island. He is now the co-captain of an offshore charter fishing boat (and you know, Allie, how I loathe fishing . . . ekh!) along with some old preacher guy named Asbury. Do you know of him? The boat is named something crazy like Asbury with Raspberries and Lemons 'n Lime, and business has been slow because the customers think they are fruit importers instead of fishermen. I miss Maurice, although I kinda like the boat name (but I always thought boat names were two words). And I miss YOU, Allie Kyle! Thanks for the Carolina beads! I'm wearing 'em to a bowl game. When can you fly back home and go on another beach trip with me and Lydia? Lots of new guys showing up on Sundays. I'll even let you drive Sherbet again! All blessings to my bestest friend.

Darcy

P.S. Do you ever hear from Jay? Steve said he got an e-mail that said Jay was really enjoying New York City.

Across the dirt road, the jungle absorbed the cackling of unseen birds. She picked up page one again, fingering beads of dark red, bone, and natural wood as she reread what was rare on the mission field—the hand-written letter.

"Allie, that letter reminds me of some questions I have about the beach trip . . ."

"Ask 'em," she said, not looking up.

"You remember all those readers in their beach chairs?"

"The ones you numbered? Most of 'em were friends of mine."

"What was Number Eleven's real name?"

"Anne."

"And Number Twelve?"

"Sheri," she whispered, still reading, squirming to get comfortable.

We shifted to where we sat back-to-back, for support.

"Much better," she said.

Kids zigzagged across the field, giggling and snatching at bugs. The soccer game was now chaos. Minutes passed before we spoke again. Finally she stuffed her letter in the envelope, set it on the grass beside me.

"Thought any more about your plans?" she asked.

"Spanish lessons, certainly."

"The mission agency sends everyone to a school for that. There's one in Quito and another in Costa Rica. It's an intense four months, believe you me."

"Can't be more intense than my former profession."

"And eventually you'll have to raise support. Quite a pain these days finding folks with money."

"Then I'll start with the elderly."

"What elderly?"

"Former clients, old ladies with great market timing."

I felt Allie's weight firm against my back, like she was napping.

In silence now, I contemplated the fruit, pausing at each piece to gauge the relative ripeness. After a few minutes she tilted her head back until it gently knocked against mine.

"Whatcha thinking about, Mr. Jarvis?"

"The fruit."

"Which piece?"

"Patience."

"So give me a definition of patience."

"Okay. Patience: Across the arc of a life lived in faith, it allows the Almighty to *be* all-mighty."

"Goodness, Mr. Oblong learns fast. Remind me to write that one down."

Earthy whiffs of fruit and flower glided by in the breeze, and as I pondered what I'd given up and what I'd now gained, I compared the scents quite favorably to the hot, acrid exhaust of yellow taxicabs.

Still sitting back-to-back, I felt her lean into me. "Jay, if you do go through the program, God could send you somewhere else besides our wacky little village . . . although we can definitely use you."

"Would you like it if he did that?"

"Sent you somewhere else?"

"That's what I'm asking . . ."

"No, I wouldn't like it. But you'll need to listen, regardless of my feelings."

I didn't answer immediately, just stared out at the green canopy, losing myself in thought. "Okay, Allie, I'll listen. But I need to ask you something."

She elbowed my rib. "Ask it."

"Today, doing stuff like this, just hanging out, are these dates?"

"We don't call it dating out here, remember? We don't call it anything."

Jungle grass clung to our legs and ankles. I nearly tumbled backward when, for a third time, she turned to pick up the letter. Face-to-face again, I watched as she pulled a pen from her pocket and began writing furiously on the back of Darcy's lime green envelope.

"Sudden inspiration?" I asked.

"Take a look at this," she said, still writing, not looking up. "I've been trying to chronicle the experiences of my life . . . to write a story about walking with God, the known and the unknown. I may use these words as the beginning."

And she handed me the envelope.

321

There are potholes on the road less traveled. Some deep, some not so deep, some you dig yourself. Most are filled with mud. Many contain rocks. Once in a while, however, you'll be walking along and step in one a bit more accommodating . . . shabby, green, and pulsing with life.

It'll tickle your feet, like clover.

I read the words twice, pausing to compare them to my own journey, a journey I no longer cared to control. "Good stuff, Allie."

With mock pride, she tilted her head back. "Yeah, I think that's a keeper."

"Final draft?"

"Final draft," she said, taking back the envelope.

"Would you mind at some point if I borrowed those first two lines?"

Gently, she bit her lip, considering my request. I didn't think she was going to answer at all until, finally, she tucked the envelope in her shirt pocket. "I think not, Jay. Considering what you carved in that sandbar, you have very little talent for verse."

"But what about my ad response, the shiny armoire, my brave white horse?"

She rose from the grass to check on the children. "I still think someone helped you with that."

I reached up and took her hand. "So, Allie, if we don't call it dating out here, how would two people get past where we are?"

She pulled away slowly—palm, fingers, fingertips. Then she leaned down to pluck a weed, turned and tossed it, spearlike, at my head. Another bull's-eye. "They'd let the Almighty *be* all-mighty."

Angling down from behind her—across the elephant ears and a jungle in mid-yawn—a glaring Ecuadorian sun backlit the brunette hair just below her shoulder.

With a wave and a whistle, Allie had the children in single file. Little bronze hands brushed dark hair from glistening foreheads. They had begun the long walk back to the village when she stopped and turned into the sun to face me. "There's still one more surprise waiting for you, Jay . . . after sundown."

"I won't even guess."

Squinting now, she quieted the children. "Once every quarter our entire village has a kind of battle. Twenty dozen bananas per team. We peel 'em and squish 'em into balls."

Somehow this seemed not the least bit shocking, but twenty dozen? "Twenty dozen?"

"We call it Gettysburg for Latinos. Juan and the others are picking ammo as we speak."

I sat up, shooed a fly. "And just how long has this been tradition?"

She reached out to hold Isabel's hand. "Ever since I started serving here."

"And y'all do this in the dark?"

"We border the soccer field with bamboo torches and have at it. It's one awesome night of conflict, kids red-faced and delirious; might be your first look at Amazonian conniption. Wanna captain a team?"

That sure beat beading. "How many teams will the village have?"

"Just two. So do you wanna be a captain? Plaid-over-Stripes usually leads the second team, but as you know, she's pregnant."

"And you lead the opposition?"

"Of course. You wanna be Ulysses S. Grant or Robert E. Lee?"

I didn't hesitate. "I'll be Lee."

"Then you'll probably lose."

She regathered the kids, and they strolled away, slow, like beachcombers. Meanwhile, I was trying to figure out what Robert E. Lee would do if ammo were limited to bananas.

I'd figure it out . . . and I would make the South proud.

No white flags. No Appomattox.

But again she quieted the children and turned to face me, her face sunlit, her voice raised. "How about an early dinner in the bird tower again? Just the two of us."

My stomach growled, reminding me—even though I was with Plan A—not to call this a date. "It is Friday, isn't it? You cooking?"

"I cooked last week."

"Okay, I'll cook."

She and the kids marched onward up the dirt road, dust hovering behind them. I leaned back on my elbows. I'd catch up shortly.

Summer was stretching across the grass when I looked up and saw Allie in a familiar posture. She had a stick in her hand, and with the kids behind her, she was sideways in the road, leaning over and carving words in the dirt, writing east-west in a road that also ran east-west. They moved backward together, forty-eight little feet backpedaling from one side of the road to the other as Allie and her stick began each new line. I watched this earthy composition from a distance, then she stood and waved me over, and I got up and jogged toward them.

I arrived panting.

She and the kids were all facing me, though I was separated from them by seven lines of poetry that must have covered twenty feet.

"What?" I inquired, all sweaty from my jog. "More inspiration?"

She flung her stick into the jungle, smiled, and said, "Nope, that there is my first high school poem."

I stood at the seventh line and read the thing. Twice. "Allie Kyle, that sounds nothing at all like the words of a missionary."

"But you like it?" She had that half-child, half-woman look again.

"It's not as complex as your sandy, antimaterialistic verse, but not bad. Not bad at all."

I walked between the fourth and fifth lines, then the whole group of us continued on toward the village, Allie holding Isabel's hand, me with my arm around Eduardo and his Zulu beads.

She spoke over her shoulder. "I only carved that one, Jay, to show you that God often has very different plans than what our earthly brains think is best for us."

I was about to agree with her when the drum sounded.

He was way back behind us, just coming out of the jungle and onto the dirt road, his bass drum strapped to his neck and back and wobbling left and right in front of him.

Raul was no fashion god either; his daily garb was a green-and-yellow rugby shirt with the sleeves cut out, plus a baggy pair of brown army fatigues that were much too big for his slender frame. I didn't know if he had suddenly lost his shyness or just felt like joining in, but he was hurrying toward us with that oversized drum. Then he saw the poem. He stopped in his tracks.

This opportunity was not going to get away from me. I quickly motioned for Eduardo to continue on with the others. "Allie, I've just got to have me a turn at that drum."

She turned and waved left-handed at Raul. "You can ask, Jay. But he's pretty attached to it."

So I jogged back down the road, wiping sweat from my forehead every few seconds before stopping again between lines four and five.

Raul was standing over the poem with his head cocked to the side, looking around his drum at the dirt. I was pretty sure he couldn't read.

"You like it, Raul?" I asked.

He didn't answer, just kept staring at the strange words hogging the center of his roadway. I motioned to him that I would very much like to beat his drum. He glanced at me briefly, stuffed his drum sticks in his army pants, then stared at the words again.

I repeated my wish, and after a moment of hesitation he kneeled and pulled the straps over his head. I also kneeled, and when I stood up, I was a bass drummer.

Lighter now, Raul pulled a mango from his baggy back pocket, peeled a layer, and took a bite. Then he pointed at the poem with his fruit.

Allie's first high school poem read thusly:

The South melts into its seasons
Refusing to let one go before its time.
Likewise I melt, a youthful candle, into adulthood.
And into adulthood I'll simmer above a volatile Southern flame.
Let my soul grow old and ripe in the South
Where warmth may still be found, even in the midst of
   bitter cold.
May my heart grow old in this place.

The irony was pure and immediate—anticipating one's adulthood in the South but ending up content in the jungles of Ecuador.

But with the drum blocking my vision, I walked right through the fifth line, end to front, then turned to see that my feet had smudged *South, ripe, old, soul,* and *Let.*

Raul walked beside me toward the village, peeling away, mango juice covering his chin. Allie and the kids were now a hundred yards ahead, the whole lot of them trying to do cartwheels in the road.

As the newest member of the circus, I beat that drum for all I was worth, using deep strokes of percussion to signal to the jungle that I was sticking around, that I'd be the white man among its greenery, the stranger in its bird tower.

I considered stopping just so I could ask Raul if he wanted his soul to grow old and ripe in the South. But I was certain he would not answer. He was slow of mind and short of speech, a young man content to be an odd spice in a village stew that nourished everyone regardless of pedigree— slow, fast, plaid, striped, mismatched, or North American.

So I just kept pounding away, trying to find some semblance of melody. Raul walked along, eating his fruit, occasionally glancing over at the drum when I lost the rhythm. It was my guess that Raul never gave a second thought to where his soul might grow old.

Me? Why, I did not know if my soul would grow old somewhere south of Colombia, South America, or Columbia, South Carolina. Like that drum, I really just wanted to stay tight—tight to the south of God, right there in his shadow. Because outside of God's shadow I was just a gaudy plastic float filled with stubborn air, drifting off like a blind Jonah in search of Plan B, manipulating circumstances and wondering why I kept waking up in my very own Tarshish. But in God's shadow I had been dazzled by the detour, amazed at the fraternity, and flabbergasted by the depth that comes from simplicity, from serving in a village that was shabby, green, and pulsing with life.

Raul had finished his snack when we got within a stone's throw of the village. Everyone else had already gone inside their huts. I gave the drum back to Raul, and after he stopped grinning he launched into a beat worthy of a collegiate halftime show.

It was right then that the urge to carve overwhelmed me. I stepped off the road and into the rainforest to find a stick. I carved quickly, limiting myself to two lines because it was my turn to cook. And though it was plagiarism, what I wrote was to affirm to Allie in writing what I had signaled to the jungle with drumming—that I would be sticking around. I knew that in one hour we would walk right by my verse on our way to the bird tower, and it just seemed like something a missionary poet might appreciate.

What I wrote in the dirt road I wrote in big, beach-sized letters.

Jay's roots grow like kudzu
Thru God's luscious jungle.

Then I went and picked three mangos and used them to dot the *i*'s and the *j*.

Acknowledgments

This book could not have been written without a day-long journey with Dan Osterhus, a Mission Aviation Fellowship pilot stationed in Shell, Ecuador. Dan flew me and a buddy, Tal Groce, over and into the jungle, including a visit to the awe-inspiring site where Jim Elliott and four other missionaries were martyred by Waodani Indians in 1956. We landed on a grass strip and were met by the natives, who paddled our MRPC mission team to that sandbar in a dugout canoe. To Dan the Man I dedicate the last chapters of this book. He and two other men died September 14, 1997, while attempting a rescue mission in the mountainous Banos Pass, in Ecuador. He left behind a young wife and an eight-month-old daughter. All blessings to his family.

Also, much appreciation to the Principe de Pas orphanage in Guayaquil, Ecuador. The kids there had few of the advantages we enjoy in America, but, shockingly, seemed to be happier . . . go figure. And they could really play soccer! Our hosts were Ron and Lizanne Johnson.

Attending the Urbana Missions Conference, put on tri-annually by IVCF, fostered my friendship with three missionary girls. Each one is a model of humor, faith, and compassion, and their examples of servant-hood make for the presiding spirit of this book. Their names are Mary, Terri, and Rachel. Their last names and locations are confidential.

Next, a tip of the hat to the Metro singles group and the Focus Class, for all the memories and adventures. Who *were* those rebels who stayed out on the beach all night?

The scenic South Carolina coast was made available to us by Sloan Smith and her hospitable gang at James W. Smith Real Estate (www.jw smithrealestate.com) in Pawleys Island, S.C. And yes, they do rent a few beach houses with crow's nests.

Special thanks to Holly Branyon Grant, a Greenville, S.C., poet and French teacher who read and critiqued chapter after chapter. Her input was invaluable. Holly also loaned Allie her poem of the South, "Unseasonable Warmth," in May of 2002. *Merci*, HG!

Jeanette Thomason and Kristin Kornoelje from Baker Book House walked me carefully through the editing process. Their input was thorough, sensitive, and crucial to the book's final shape.

My dad, Charles, built me a way-cool writing table one spring Saturday in Carolina. (And confirmed on that same day that God had gifted me for words, not power tools.) Many prayers were offered on my behalf by Brian and Debi Ponder, Roger Throckmorton, Ken Harris, Sandy "Stokes" Covington, and Stan and Connie Beasley, among others. Appalachian State info came courtesy of two gregarious ASU roommates, Laura Jarrard and Marla Mclean. Flower info came courtesy of an enthusiastic Master Gardener, Phoebe, who happens to be my mom. Bird info came courtesy of an eleven-year-old ornithologist wannabe named Jonathan, who happens to be my nephew.

The original, shorter version of Maurice's "flour story" was told by fellow South Carolinian Pokey Reese, the fleet-footed second baseman of the Pittsburgh Pirates. Go Pokey!

Nancy Koesy Parker, a talented freelance editor in Greenville, helped me with first chapter motivation.

Jim "3-Green" Hamlett flew our writers group to a conference in a sleek, twin-engine Barron.

Roger Throckmorton and his magic graphic arts machine developed the original lime green Caddy convertible. If this book sells, I am planning to get me a real one.

The jungle beads worn by Allie and the kids are available through *ddp designs*: www.ddpdesigns.com.

The beach music on the drive home with Plan B was from "Summertime's Calling Me" by The Catalinas.

Stock market lingo courtesy of the hedge fund managers at Real money.com.

Offshore boat knowledge courtesy of Bruce Braynard at Georgetown Landing and Marina.

The bum and his blue-tinted water jug were last seen on Michigan Avenue, downtown Chicago, during January of 2002. I am not kidding.

Joey Schooler and family are dear friends. Thanks, Bobby C, for Cooper River Bridge info!

Sidney at the Laurens Rd. Post Office rushed my manuscripts out the door.

Kwame Dawes at the University of South Carolina Graduate School offered advice on book contracts.

Ditto for real-estate attorney Brian Ponder. (Hey, I take what I can get.)

A preacher/friend loves the Waffle House, but he's still learning to give rhythm to the gospel.

Frequenting North Litchfield Beach with Jay, Steve, and Ransom have been the following people.

In the guys house: Mike Bell, Scott Teague, my brother, Ted, Mike Armor, George Champlin, Walter Moore, Danny from Trinidad, plus the guy who came in at midnight through the screened window.

In the overcrowded womens house with Darcy, Allie, and Lydia: Becky Brandon King, Marie Gardner, Karen Hartney, Cheryl Hutcheson, Amy Bell, Sheri Forehand, Ann Vaughn, Nell Kennedy, Ruth Ann Kennedy, Jane Brice, Melanie Champlin, Beth Blackston, and my groovy sister, Dana. Plus a few stragglers who just showed up at the last minute.

Many late-night revisions occurred at Coffee Underground. Thanks, Donna, for the refills!

Going to a U2 concert with missionaries was a real hoot!

And to my friends and small group at Grace Church . . . your prayers fuel my writing.

Singing to the lobsters happens frequently on Friday nights in Murrells Inlet, South Carolina.

Armed with the knowledge that his second grade teacher always liked his stories and poems, **Ray Blackston** of Greenville, South Carolina, departed the field of finance. He simply walked away from the corporate cubicle, bought a laptop, said a prayer, and began typing the first words of *Flabbergasted*.

He does not recommend this method for the faint of heart.

You can read more of the background of *Flabbergasted* at Ray's website: www.rayblackston.com. For instance, Ray's grandfather, the late Reverend A. F. Smoak, was pastor of Pawleys Island Baptist Church.

THE GHOST ON SATURDAY NIGHT

Sid Fleischman

THE GHOST ON SATURDAY NIGHT

**Illustrated by
Laura Cornell**

**GREENWILLOW BOOKS
NEW YORK**

Library of Congress Cataloging-in-Publication Data

Fleischman, Sid, (date)
The ghost on Saturday night / by Sid Fleischman ; pictures by Laura Cornell.
p.   cm.
Summary: When Professor Pepper gives Opie tickets to a ghost-raising
instead of a nickel in payment for being guided through the dense
fog, Opie manages to make money anyway by helping
to thwart a bank robbery.
ISBN 0-688-14919-7 (trade).   ISBN 0-688-14920-0 (pbk.)
[1. Ghosts—Fiction. 2. West (U.S.)—Fiction.
3. Robbers and outlaws—Fiction.] I. Cornell, Laura, ill. II. Title.
PZ7.F5992Gk 1997 [Fic]—dc20 96-43551 CIP AC

In memory of
Bill Grote

CONTENTS

1

FOG

There's nothing bashful about a tule fog. It'll creep inside your clothes. It'll seep through the window cracks and get right into bed with you.

When I got home from the schoolhouse on Tuesday, there wasn't a wisp of fog. I lived with my great-aunt Etta and she was waiting for me.

"Opie," she said. "How would you like chicken for supper?"

"Yes, *ma'am*!" I said.

"Splendid. I've got the chicken. You go out back and pluck it."

I gave a groan. She gave me the chicken. She had a way of foxing me into doing pesky chores like that.

I sat myself on the chopping stump and began to pull feathers. I passed the time thinking up names for my horse. I already had a list a mile-and-a-half long.

I didn't own a horse—yet.

But I had one promised. Aunt Etta had struck a bargain with me. When I earned enough money to buy a good saddle, she'd buy a good horse to fit under it.

The trouble was I was only ten and kind of runty in size. The older, bigger boys seemed to get all the after-school jobs around town.

"Wild Charlie," I said aloud. I liked the sound of that. A horse ought to have the exact right name. I mean, you wouldn't name a fine horse Hubert. He'd die of shame.

I could see myself galloping across the meadow on Wild Charlie. But when I looked up I couldn't see the meadow. Or the trees. Or the barn. And before long I couldn't even see the chicken in my hands.

A tule fog had sprung up.

My heart gave a mighty leap. There was saddle money to be made in a good thick fog! I had already saved $2.11. But I needed

heaps and heaps of money—$17.59 exactly.

I began plucking the rest of those feathers so fast you'd think that hen was in a rooster fight. The fog around me was dripping wet. All you needed to wash your ears was a bar of soap. Not that I had a mind to.

I guess there's nothing thicker and wetter than a ground-hugging California tule fog. Aunt Etta was always saying not to stand in one too long. You'd grow webbed feet.

I felt my way back to the house and handed the bird to Aunt Etta.

"I'll be back for supper," I said.

"Don't you got lost," she said. "That tule is so thick you'll need a compass to cross the road."

"Yes, ma'am."

"And don't stay out too long. You'll grow webbed feet."

2
THE GHOST IS COMING!

I lifted my feet for town. I guess I was the only boy in Golden Hill who'd gone into the fog business. I'd gotten the idea from Aunt Etta herself.

Even in the thickest tule she was sure-footed as a mountain goat. She knew every brick, every post, and every building by heart. So did I. I could streak through town with my eyes shut.

I passed one end of the old Horseshoe Mine tunnel. I couldn't see it, but I knew it

was there because of the dip in the road. Before long I reached the hotel hitching rack. I crossed the dirt street and counted forty-seven strides. That brought me to Muldoon's General Store.

"Any special errands you want run, Mr. Muldoon?" I asked. He was one of my best tule customers.

"Opie," he said, "if that fog gets any thicker you could drive a nail in it and hang your coat. Think you can find the barbershop?"

"Yes, sir."

He filled a can with lamp oil and I set out to deliver it. I turned the corner and kept going until I reached the livery stable—I knew it by the smell. Then I crossed the street. When I sniffed hair tonic I knew I was at Ed Russell's barbershop.

It turned out there was a stranger in

town. Mr. Russell had just finished cutting his hair.

"Opie," he said, "you could do this gentleman a service if you scouted him back to the hotel."

"Be pleased to," I said.

That stranger was a big man and uglier than homemade soap. He clasped my shoulder

with one hand as I led him out along the wooden sidewalk. That hand of his was cold. It felt like ice melting on my shoulder.

He followed along behind me without saying a word.

I didn't say much either. He was kind of scary. But when we passed the bank I said, "You ever hear of anyone buying a horse with a penny?"

He didn't answer.

"Well, sir, that's what my great-aunt Etta is going to do," I added.

He wasn't interested—that was clear. So I didn't tell him it wasn't a common, ordinary Indian-head cent you might find in your pocket. It was an 1877 Indian-head penny. Rare as a hen's tooth, that date. And mighty valuable. She had Mr. Whitman, the banker, keep it in his safe. She was always worried that she'd spend it by mistake.

"Here we are, sir," I said. We reached the hotel porch. He lifted that freezing claw of his off my shoulder. I was glad to be rid of him. But I hoped I would be a nickel closer to my saddle.

He dug in his vest pocket. He handed me a card. And he disappeared through the door.

I was sorely disappointed. He was not only big and ugly; he was stingy, too. What did I want his card for?

It was kind of hard to read in the fog. The sun was giving off about as much light as an orange cat. But as I held it closer I saw that it wasn't a calling card. It was a ticket of some sort.

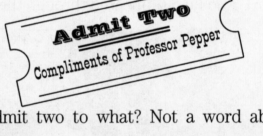

Admit two to what? Not a word about that. I might have thrown it away if I weren't so puzzled. I jammed it into my back pocket and went about my fog business.

By the time I reached home I had the jingle of thirty-five cents in my pocket. I hoped the tule fog would hang on for weeks.

But it lifted around noon the next day.

And all over town signs had been tacked up.

THE GHOST IS COMING!

See the ghost of Crookneck John!

Famous Outlaw
Murderer
Bank Robber
Thief & Scoundrel

☥☥☥ Hung three times before he croaked!

THE GENUINE GHOST

Brought back by Professor Pepper, the famous ghost-raiser. Don't miss this event. Startling! Educational! Ladies welcome. No children under twelve allowed.

Saturday Night   **Miners' Union Hall**
8 p. m. sharp   **50 cents Admission**

3

SATURDAY NIGHT

Professor Pepper! I could still feel the chilly clasp of his hand on my shoulder.

I ran home and showed my ticket to Aunt Etta.

"He gave it to me himself!" I said.

"Who did?"

"Professor Pepper. He's a famous ghost-raiser!"

She looked at me over the tops of her glasses. "What on earth is a ghost-raiser?"

"Haven't you seen the signs? He's going to raise the ghost of Crookneck John on Saturday night. Right here in Miners' Union Hall."

"Poppycock," Aunt Etta said.

"The signs say so. The genuine ghost, too."

"I'll believe that when I see it," she snorted.

"Ladies are welcome," I said. And then I added with disappointment, "But they won't let me in."

"Why not?"

"I'm not old enough."

Aunt Etta stared at me. I didn't have to tell her how much I wanted to have a peek at the ghost of Crookneck John. She could see that for herself.

"Well, I'm old enough for both of us," she said. "We'll go."

"But Aunt Etta—"

"You don't think I'd visit a spook show *alone,* Opie. Why, I might faint. We'll see it together. That's that. Leave it to me."

I thought Saturday would never come.

Everyone at school was talking about the ghost of Crookneck John. Talking about sneaking in, mostly. The trouble was there was no way to sneak into the Miners' Union Hall. It stood over the bank. The only way to get up there was by climbing a stairway along the side of the building.

I didn't want to tell anyone that I might be seeing Professor Pepper do his ghost-raising. Aunt Etta wouldn't try to pass me off for twelve years of age—that would be dishonest. I could see myself climbing those stairs with her and being turned away at the door.

Thursday and Friday passed and I didn't think up one new name for my horse. I didn't even look at the Sears, Roebuck catalog. It had a picture of the $17.59 Winfield Special stock saddle. That's the one I was saving up for.

Saturday morning arrived at last.

Then it was Saturday afternoon.

Then it was Saturday night.

Aunt Etta put on her hat and we set out for the Miners' Union Hall.

4
TICKETS FOR TWO

We climbed the wooden stairs to the hall. A toad-faced man stood at the door. He was taking folks' money and tossing it into a cigar box.

When he saw me he shook his head. "That boy ain't old enough to be twelve," he said.

"Correct," Aunt Etta said.

"Then he can't go in."

"Nonsense," she said.

"Ma'am, that ghost will scare him skinny."

"He's already skinny."

"Then his hair will turn white," the man said.

"Horsefeathers, sir." She handed him my ticket from Professor Pepper himself. "Will you kindly read that."

"It says admit two."

Aunt Etta straightened to her full height. "Exactly. I'm *one* and he's *two*. And the ticket orders you to *admit* us. Step aside, sir, before I call the sheriff."

That man turned white as an oyster at the mention of the sheriff.

"Come along, Opie," Aunt Etta said.

We breezed right through the door. Oh, she was clever as forty crickets, my great-aunt Etta.

The hall was long and shadowy. Two oil lamps burned and smoked in front of the curtain. That's all the light there was.

We took chairs near the front and waited. Before long all the chairs were taken. And folks were standing along the walls.

"It's past eight o'clock," Aunt Etta announced.

We could hear noises behind the curtain. There were creaking sounds. And sawing sounds. And hammering sounds

"Maybe it's the ghost," I said.

Aunt Etta shook her head. "Crookneck John was an outlaw—not a carpenter."

We waited. And waited some more.

At ten minutes to nine Professor Pepper stepped through the curtains.

5
Professor Pepper

"I will ask the ladies not to scream out," he announced in a deep voice.

"Moonshine," Aunt Etta whispered.

Professor Pepper took a grip on the lapel of his black frock coat. "What you will see tonight is stranger than strange. Odder than odd. Aye, a man deader than dead will walk among you. A cutthroat, he was. Bank robber. The most feared outlaw of the century!"

I began to scrunch down in my chair. I couldn't help it.

"Hung once, he was," Professor Pepper went on. "Hung twice, he was. Hung three times before the meanness was jerked out of him! Aye, that's how he came to be known as Crookneck John."

"I don't wonder," Aunt Etta muttered. "Opie, sit up straight."

Professor Pepper lowered his heavy brows. "I would advise the fainthearted to leave before the ghost-raising begins."

He paused. Everyone seemed to look at everyone else. I saw the Widow Sellers rise and hurry for the door, fanning her face with a handkerchief.

"Now, then, I must have absolute silence!" Professor Pepper said. He clapped his hands sharply.

The curtains parted.

A pine coffin was stretched across two sawhorses. It looked old and rotted, as if it had been dug out of the ground.

"Aye, the very box holding the bones of Crookneck John," the professor declared. "The coffin is six feet long. Crookneck John was almost seven feet. Buried with his knees bent up, he was. Most uncomfortable even for a ghost."

Then Professor Pepper clapped his hands again. His assistant, the toad-faced man, appeared and blew out the two oil lamps.

Pitch darkness closed in on the hall.

For a moment, I don't think anyone took a breath.

Professor Pepper's voice came rolling through the blackness.

"Crookneck John," he called. "I have your bones. Is the spirit willing to come forth, eh? Give a sign."

Silence. All I could hear was my own heart beating. Then there came a hollow rap-rap-rapping from the pine box.

"Aye, I hear the knock of your big knuckles, Mr. Crookneck John. Now rise up. Rise up your bloody bones and stretch your legs, sir."

My eyes strained to see through the darkness.

A minute went by. Maybe two or three. When Professor Pepper spoke again he was getting impatient.

"Rise up, you scoundrel! Ashamed to show your crooked neck to these honest folks, eh? This is Professor Pepper himself speaking. Aye, and I won't be made a fool of, sir!"

Black seconds ticked away. Then a minute or two. Professor Pepper became as short-tempered as a teased snake.

"Rise up, I say!" he commanded. "I've a hanging rope in my hand! Aye, and I'll string you up a *fourth* time!"

Silence.

And then there came a creaking of wood. And a groaning of nails. My neck went cold and prickly. *The lid of that pine coffin was lifting!*

"That's better, you murdering scum!" snarled Professor Pepper.

It was scary to hear him talk that way to a dangerous outlaw about to rise from his coffin.

"I can't make out a thing," Aunt Etta said.

I stared hard, wanting to see that seven-foot ghost stretch his legs.

But suddenly the snarl went out of Professor Pepper's voice. "No! No!" he gasped. "Down! Back, sir! Not the rope!" Gurgling sounds escaped from his throat. "Help! Help! The lamps! Light the la—!"

I was sitting so straight by then I must have shot up six inches taller. The toad-faced man struck a match to the nearest lamp.

The air lit up. And there, against the curtain, staggered Professor Pepper. A hangman's noose was pulled tight around his neck.

The lid of the coffin stood open.

Professor Pepper clawed at the rope around his throat and caught a breath. "Save yourselves!" he croaked. "Run for your lives! Lock your doors! Shut your windows! Stay off the streets! The Crookneck Ghost is loose!"

6

THE COFFIN OF
CROOKNECK JOHN

I don't know how many ladies screamed.
But three fainted and had to be carried out.

"Come on, Aunt Etta!" I said.

She was calm as an owl at midnight. "Sit
where you are."

The hall emptied in a whirlwind hurry.
Even the toad-faced man was gone.

There was no one left but Professor Pepper and us.

"Madam," he said. He'd freed himself of
the hangman's rope and was hammering
the lid back on the coffin. "Your lives are in
terrible danger!"

"Pish-posh," she answered. "I'll expect you to refund everyone's money, sir."

At that, he banged his thumb with the hammer. "What!"

"Other folks paid at the door to *see* a ghost. They have been flimflammed."

"Really, madam!"

"*I* didn't see a ghost. *Opie* didn't see a ghost. No one *saw* that ghost of yours."

He stopped shaking the pain out of his thumb. "Unfortunately, madam, my assistant appears to have flown for his life. And with the cigar box full of money. Why, it wouldn't surprise me if we find him with his neck broke and robbed by that thieving ghost."

"Pay up, sir," was all Aunt Etta would say. "Come along, Opie."

"Hold on," Professor Pepper said with sudden politeness. "I've been near strangled. Aye, short of breath I am. Perhaps that fine lad will help me carry the pine box downstairs."

I wasn't anxious to get *that* close to either Professor Pepper or the coffin.

"What on earth for?" Aunt Etta said.

"Why, Crookneck John must return to his

dry bones before the crow of dawn, madam. That's the way of ghosts, you know. I'll have the burying box moved to the jailhouse. He'll wake up behind bars, the scoundrel! Aye, with the cigar box, if he has it."

Then he turned an eye on me. "I'll reward you for your trouble, lad. Cash money."

It wouldn't be much if I knew him, but cash money was saddle money.

"Yes, sir," I answered.

Aunt Etta could read my thoughts. "I've seen enough playacting for one night," she said. "It's past my bedtime. I'm going home, Opie."

"I won't be long," I said.

That pine box was heavy. I didn't think dry old bones could weigh so much. Then I reminded myself that Crookneck John had been seven feet tall.

The moon was rising and full.

When we struggled down to the foot of the stairs Professor Pepper's breath gave out.

"This'll do, lad," he said. "Oh, I should have known better than to raise the Crookneck Ghost on a full moon night. Turns him wild."

Then he dug in his coat pocket and handed me a coin. A mighty small one.

"Run home fast as you can, hear? Make sure that fine lady of yours is safe. I'll manage for myself."

"Much obliged for the cash money," I said politely. But I could tell from the feel it was only a cent piece.

I didn't run home. I wasn't worried about Aunt Etta. She'd said it was all playacting. Professor Pepper *himself* could have done the rap-rap-rapping on the coffin. And he could have tied the noose around his *own* neck.

I wasn't even past the hotel when the moon faded out of the sky. The tule fog was creeping back.

I gave the cent piece a flip in the air and caught it. I put it in my pocket and then took it out again. Awfully clean and shiny, I thought, as if it had never been in use. Like

Aunt Etta's rare Indian-head penny in the bank safe.

There was just enough moonlight left to make out the date.

My breath caught. It was an 1877 Indian-head cent.

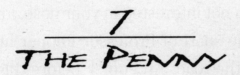

7
THE PENNY

The tule fog came seeping up around me. It appeared to be Aunt Etta's very own penny, I thought. The penny that was going to buy a horse to fit under my saddle!

But how had it come to be in Professor Pepper's coat pocket?

Just then I heard the snort of a horse and the creaking of wagon wheels.

"Bah! This fog's so thick I couldn't find my nose with both hands and a lantern."

I knew that voice. It belonged to Professor Pepper's assistant.

"I'm not interested in your nose, idiot!" It was the snarl of Professor Pepper himself. "Find the road. And quick before this town has the law on us."

The law? Suddenly I knew the only way Aunt Etta's rare cent could have gotten into the professor's pocket.

He'd robbed the bank!

"Give me those fool reins," he growled.

I had to do something. I felt my way along the hotel hitching post until I could make out the faint glow of their wagon lamp.

"Stop, sir!" I called out. "You're heading straight into a tree. Need help?"

"Help indeed!" said Professor Pepper. "Where's the road out of town, eh?"

Then he paused.

"Don't I know that voice?"

I was having a time to keep my teeth from clacking now. "Yes, sir," I said. "I'm Opie. I scouted you from the barbershop to the hotel in a thicker fog than this."

"Well, take that nag by the nose and lead us out of here. When Crookneck John wakes up in the jailhouse he'll be after my blood."

More playacting, I thought! Oh, he was full of tricks. He'd scared folks into staying off the streets while he got away. But he hadn't counted on the tule fog.

Or me. An idea had already sprung into my head.

I led the horse and wagon step by step along the road toward home. When I came to the dip, I stopped. We were at one end of the old Horseshoe Mine.

"There's a big tunnel on the left, sir. About

two miles long. It's kind of a shortcut through the fog."

"Aye, a shortcut would please me!" the professor laughed.

A moment later they went clattering into the mine tunnel.

I was in such a hurry to reach Mr. Whitman's house that I must have barked my shins six times and run into a wall at least once.

Mr. Whitman owned the bank. I showed him Aunt Etta's 1877 one-cent piece. I told him I thought Professor Pepper had robbed the safe. And we went for the sheriff.

Sure enough, the bank safe was empty.

"But the walls of the bank are solid stone," Mr. Whitman said. "How did he get in?"

I had already noticed bits of sawdust. I looked up. The sheriff looked up.

"Yup," he said. "Professor Pepper cut through the floor of the Miners' Union Hall upstairs. Probably let himself down with the hangman's rope and up again. Then hammered the wood back in place."

I remembered hearing hammer sounds behind the curtain during the long wait for the show to start.

"And he must have hoped we'd believe it was the Crookneck Ghost who'd robbed the bank," the sheriff said. "Well, Professor Pepper can't have got far in this fog."

"Not far at all," I said. "He's in the Horseshoe Mine."

"The Horseshoe Mine!" the sheriff said.

"Yes, sir."

"Doesn't he know it makes a perfect horseshoe and comes out about forty feet from the jailhouse?"

"No, sir," I said. "I didn't tell him that."

8
CAPTURED!

The end of the tunnel was dark as a sack of black cats. The sheriff waited. His three deputies waited. And I waited, too.

Before long we could hear the echo of horse's hooves. My heart began to beat a little faster. The glow of a lantern appeared like a firefly deep in the tunnel.

The sheriff lifted his shotgun and nodded to his deputies. "Get ready, boys. The rest of you stay back."

The wagon lantern grew larger and brighter. Then I could see Professor Pepper himself—chuckling and singing.

But when he saw the law waiting for him he gave a gasp and a groan.

"Great jumping hop-toads!" he cried out. He grabbed the reins and tried to turn the wagon around. But the mine shaft wasn't wide enough. He kept snapping the whip, but all the horse could do was snort and whinny.

The sheriff charged forward and caught the horse by the halter.

"That will do, gents," he said. "Welcome back to Golden Hill. Easy, now, or you'll end up buckshot ghosts."

"Thunder and lightning," the professor snarled. "We've been out-foxed!"

His helper was still clutching the cigar box full of flimflam money. The deputies led him away, together with Professor Pepper.

The sheriff climbed on the wagon and called to me.

"Opie. Did you say this coffin was un-common heavy?"

"Yes, sir."

"Hold the lantern."

As I held the lantern he pried off the lid. There were no bones in that pine box at all.

It was full of money. The stolen bank money.

9

THE REWARD

The sheriff looked through his reward posters.

"Sorry, Opie," he said finally. "There's no reward offered for Professor Pepper. You do deserve one."

"That's all right," I said. "I got Aunt Etta's penny back for her. Rare as a hen's tooth, that penny. She's going to buy me a horse with it someday."

Mr. Whitman was sitting nearby counting

the stolen money. He looked up. "A horse," he said. "Well, a horse has got to have something on it."

When I got home from school on Monday a saddle was waiting for me in the parlor. The whole room smelled of fresh leather.

"Aunt Etta," I said. "That's the finest looking saddle I *ever* saw!"

"Not much use without a horse under it," she said. "I've already plucked a chicken for supper. If you've got nothing better to do we could go looking for your horse."

"Yes, ma'am!"

"You might start thinking up a name."

"Aunt Etta," I said, "I've got a list a mile-and-a-half long."